Legend

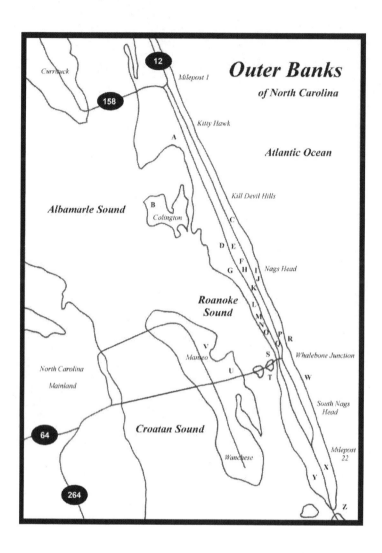

Outer Banks of North Carolina

A.   Holy Redeemer by the Sea Catholic Parish

B.   Colington Harbour

C.   Port O' Call Restaurant

D.   Kelly's Restaurant and Tavern

E.   Secret Spot Surf Shop

F.   Jockey's Ridge Crossing/Kitty Hawk Kites

G.   Jockey's Ridge State Park

H.   Mulligan's Raw Bar & Grille

I.   Surfside Plaza/Harley-Davidson

J.   Cavalier Surf Shop

K.   Animal Hospital of Nags Head

L.   The Village at Nags Head/Golf Links/Outer Banks Mall

M.   Harvey Sound Access

N.   Miller's Waterfront Restaurant

O.   Kitty Hawk Water Sports

P.   Cahoon's Market & Cottages

Q.   Sam & Omie's Restaurant/Dune Burger

R.   Jennette's Pier in Nags Head

S.   Sugar Creek Seafood Restaurant

T.   Tale of the Whale Restaurant

U.   Blue Water Grill & Raw Bar/Pirate's Cove Marina & Condominiums

V.   Manteo Waterfront Marina

W.   Outer Banks Fishing Pier/Fish Heads Bar & Grill

X.   Coquina Beach/Wreck of the *Laura Barnes*

Y.   Bodie Island Lighthouse

Z.   Oregon Inlet

Also by Joseph K. Waltenbaugh

The Elephants' Graveyard

A Guide for Getting and Keeping Your Welfare Entitlements

TheElephantsGraveyard.net

Legend

An OBX Novel

Joseph K. Waltenbaugh

WALTENBAUGH.NET

WALTENBAUGH.NET

Most of the locations and settings used in this novel are real as are several of the individuals described on these pages; however, like the shifting sands of the Outer Banks themselves, people come and go, businesses open and close, and the landscape changes with the passage of time. The reader, therefore, may encounter several irregularities where the people and places identified in the story are no longer present in this land of enchantment, beauty, and history—colorful characters and idyllic locations recognized only as myths and legends in the recollections of those with physical and emotional ties to the Outer Banks of North Carolina.

CONTENTS

CHAPTER 1   1

CHAPTER 2   18

CHAPTER 3   50

CHAPTER 4   74

CHAPTER 5   103

CHAPTER 6   113

CHAPTER 7   143

CHAPTER 8   176

CHAPTER 9   183

CHAPTER 10   234

CHAPTER 11   237

CHAPTER 12   276

CHAPTER 13   308

CHAPTER 14   361

ACKNOWLEDGMENTS   370

Though in many of its aspects this visible world seems formed in love, the invisible spheres were formed in fright.

— Herman Melville, *Moby Dick*

CHAPTER 1

Plop!

"Shhh! Turn out the light!" In response to the half-whispered command, a tiny hand reached for the lantern, hastily pressing a switch that plunged the tent into total darkness. The unpleasant stickiness of the August night made the absence of light even more unnerving to the three boys who remained perfectly still, straining their ears to hear things that were not there. Amid the chirping of crickets off in the distance, the children allowed their imaginations to soar as they endeavored to identify the nocturnal sounds echoing around them. The boy who had given the order knelt on both knees, groping for something in the darkness but unable to find it due to some lingering night blindness from the extinguished lantern. The other two boys sat quietly in the darkened tent while awaiting further orders from the older child, who continued looking for something on the floor. Older is a relative term in childhood, for, in fact, the boy on his knees was no more than six months older than one of the other boys sitting on the far side of the tent, his friend Jay. The third child present that night was Jay's younger brother Jeffrey.

"Here it is," the older boy muttered while grabbing something off the floor. He then turned back toward the door with the item in hand. The dome-shaped tent sheltering the three boys had a D-shaped door flap on the front and a single mesh window in the back, neither of which provided much ventilation. Although it was a hot, muggy night, the boys had zipped closed the door flap despite the need for fresh air.

"Tim, what if—"

"Quiet, Jeffrey," Tim ordered softly but sternly while silently unzipping the nylon flap and cautiously sticking his head into the humid night air. With his tee shirt removed and his shorts hanging low on his hips, he knelt bare-chested on the floor, the smooth skin of youth tugging tightly across his ribs.

At two o'clock in the morning, it was an entirely different world outside the tent, a world to which he was unaccustomed. As his eyes adjusted to the darkness, he glanced left where he saw the dim outline of his friend's house silhouetted against a colorless sky set aglow by a nearly full moon, its haunting rays glistening off a layer of dew coating everything in the Michigan neighborhood that night. Not far away, he could discern the contour of his bicycle as well as the hump of an abandoned football lying in the yard; however, when he peered beyond that, he found things less distinct, especially the trees that melded into a single shaded mass, their long, menacing shadows spreading across the earth beneath the syncopated flashes of fireflies.

Feeling confident that nothing in that direction posed a threat, he shifted his attention toward the back of his own house where the windows appeared dark and gloomy, indicating that everyone in his family had gone to bed. The only exception was an attic window that gleamed like the beacon of a lighthouse in the night, its reflective glass mirroring the glowing orb of an ominous moon hovering overhead. Tim and the brothers had erected their tent at the juncture of their backyards, exactly half-way between their respective homes, a prime location from which they could detect the approach of any unwanted visitors or prowling monsters.

All seemed safe and normal, but Tim was reluctant to take any chances because he did not know what constituted normal for that time of night. Maintaining a wary posture with his head outside the tent, he partially exposed the item he had retrieved from the floor, inching it closer to his face with each breath he took. Pausing a moment with the tip of it positioned just below his chin, he then thrust out his arm, fully revealing the barrel and body of a CO_2 pistol that he waved back and forth like a blazoned sword, a warning sign to any malevolent intruder wishing to do them harm. With his index finger on the trigger and his thumb resting on the hammer, he brandished the Western-style pellet gun as if he had some familiarity with its use.

Thud.

The sound came from his right, so he quickly turned and pointed the gun in that direction only to hear the stillness broken by another *thud*, this one directly in front of him just a few feet away. Rather than challenge it with the barrel of the gun, he merely stared off into the darkness where he detected some movement on the ground the moment another *thud* echoed in his ears. Relaxing his grip on the gun, he slowly tilted his head upward, directing his eyes overhead toward the branches of an old oak tree under which they had erected their tent.

"Acorns," he said quietly as he receded back through the door flap, leaving it unzipped to allow for air circulation. Turning to the two other boys, he said, "All safe. Just some acorns."

Jeffrey immediately switched on the lantern and placed it on the floor where he sat cross-legged in front of it as if he were sitting before a campfire. The glowing bulb cast ominous shadows across the roof and sides of the tent, dark specters that danced and swirled whenever the boys moved around inside the small enclosure. The light also illuminated Jeffrey's face along with his soiled tee shirt and shorts that had become grass stained from wrestling in the yard earlier that evening. It also revealed green smudges on his brother's shirt and shorts, stains that would undoubtedly precipitate a scolding from their mother the next day.

At seven years old, Jeffrey was the youngest of the three. He was there that night only because his father had insisted he be included when Jay had asked permission to camp out in his new tent. Although Jay and Tim were three years older than Jeffrey, they never objected to his inclusion in their activities because he was a pleasant, likable kid. He had a round face and straight blonde hair that hung down in bangs, and he talked with a slight lisp due to a speech impediment for which he had received therapy. A little short for his age, he was the only one who could stand erect in the tent.

Jay, on the other hand, was large for his age, solid and strong. He also had blond hair, which he kept very short on the sides and a little longer on the top, much like a military haircut. Although bigger and more powerfully built than his friend Tim, Jay always deferred to Tim, as did most of the other boys, because of Tim's more outgoing, take-charge personality. A thin and gangly youth, Tim had sharp, angular features and hair the color of rust that was extremely thick, a little long, and always unkempt.

With the interior of the tent again brightly lit, Tim leaned out through the open doorway to scan the terrain one last time, looking around the neighborhood for signs of trouble. Confident that all was well, he ducked back inside the tent and spun around on his knees toward the other two boys, pointing the gun away from himself but straight at Jeffrey and Jay. At the sight of the barrel aimed in their direction, Jay shoved his brother aside and dove for safety against the opposite wall. "Don't point that at us!" he cried.

Initially, Tim seemed startled by Jay's reaction until he realized what had freaked him out. "It's just a pellet gun," he said with a grin while glancing down at it.

"I don't care. It will hurt! Is it loaded?"

"Of course, it's loaded!"

"Can I see it?" Jeffrey asked enthusiastically.

"No way!" Jay barked at his brother.

"I'll tell Daddy that you guys have a gun," Jeffrey countered with a devilish grin that appeared even more mischievous because of the heavy shadows created by the lantern on the floor.

The two older boys looked at each other in silence before Jay cocked his arm as if threatening to smack his brother against the side of his head. Refusing to flinch, Jeffrey growled at his older sibling, "Asshole!"

Although he tried to sound vulgar and tough, Jeffrey had neither the temperament nor the personality for it, and his attempts at cursing always came across as ludicrous. Not only did his insult trigger raucous laughter in the other boys, but it amused him as well, immediately bringing a smile to his face. He could not easily conceal his good nature, and it was one of the reasons the older boys allowed him to hang around with them.

Jay smiled and said to Tim, "Take the pellets out and let him see it."

Tim unloaded the gun and offered it to the younger boy stock-first, but each time Jeffrey reached for the gun, he would pull it back. "C'mon, stop it," Jeffrey playfully moaned while trying his best not to laugh until Tim finally relented and let him have the gun.

He said to Jeffrey, "You have to cock it with your thumb each time you want to fire it. It's just like a Colt .45 from the Old West." Reaching over the top of the pistol, Tim pulled back the hammer for his friend's brother until he heard a distinctive click telling him that the hammer had locked in place. Jeffrey smiled and immediately pulled the trigger to discharge a whiff of gas through the empty chamber.

"Don't point it at anyone," Jay admonished him.

"But it's not loaded," Jeffrey said dismissively without looking at his brother.

Jay glared at his younger brother and rebuked him once again,

"You don't know that—not for sure."

Click-whiff. Jeffrey fired it again in a safe direction. *Click-whiff. Click-whiff. Click-whiff.*

"Jeff, stop it, or you'll use up all the CO_2," Tim scolded him.

At the sound of the older boy's admonition, Jeffrey stopped firing the pistol and placed it on his lap, stroking the dull metal finish with his right hand, smiling because he liked the feel of it. "Does your dad know you have this?" he asked the older boy.

"Are you kidding?" Tim said with a crooked smile. All three of them then burst out laughing.

Just then, a new noise resonated from outside the tent, one much different from the dropping of acorns. Something about the sound had a human quality to it that disturbed the boys, so they went silent and listened for it again, straining their ears to hear over the chirping of crickets and the barking of a dog far off in the distance. Tim reached over and doused the light before creeping across the tent floor to peek out the door. "Oh, no," he groaned.

"What is it?" Jay asked.

"Come here and look."

Climbing past his younger brother, Jay pulled open the flap and looked outside. "Oh, no," he said.

The validation of Tim's fear seemed to disturb Jeffrey, causing him to tighten his grip on the stock of the gun. "What is it?" he whispered to his brother.

"Mummy and Daddy are up."

"Oh, no," he moaned, crawling over to peer through the door as the other boys moved out of his way. Across the lawn, he could see his family's two-story home appearing large and foreboding in the night, murky and dark except for a light burning his parents' bedroom window. His father had warned them against making any noise if they wanted to stay out there all night. Having broken that rule, the only thing they could do now was to remain quiet and hope for the best.

While Jeffrey was watching the house, the bedroom light flicked off. "It's out," he whispered to the others who then pushed him aside so they could stick their heads out to confirm his report. When they retreated back inside the tent, Jay said, "We're going to have to be quiet." Jabbing his brother in the ribs, he continued, "And no more lights."

"And no more shooting," Tim said as he took the gun away from Jeffrey.

Part of the deal they struck for being allowed to spend the night in the tent was their surrender of all electronics—no games, no phones, no nothing. That was the joint decree of their parents, who told them that they must rough it if they wanted to camp out overnight. Now the boys faced the challenge of finding something to occupy their time. They did not want to go to sleep, but their options seemed limited. "What do we do now?" Jeffrey asked.

Tim thought for a moment and said, "My dad told me that he and his friends used to tell ghost stories whenever they camped out."

"Ghost stories, all right!" Jeffrey was never one to hide his enthusiasm.

Tim then took out a Mini Maglite flashlight and switched it on. Unscrewing the lens cover, he exposed the tiny glowing bulb. He then slipped the flared cover onto the opposite end that created a foundation for it to stand upright in candle mode. Reassembled as such, it gave off just enough light to brighten their faces but not enough to alert their parents that they were still awake. "There," he said.

"Cool!" Jeffrey exclaimed in a low voice.

"I've never seen that done before," Jay added.

Tim smiled. "Pretty neat, isn't it? My dad taught me that."

Jeffrey was impatient. "What about the ghost stories?"

"Well," Tim began, "it's not exactly a ghost story, but it's close. I heard it yesterday from Brian."

Jay turned to Tim with a curious look. "You saw Brian yesterday?"

"Yeah, he and Steve came by on their bikes, and we shot some hoops at Ziggy's. We stopped by your house, but you weren't home." Suddenly, he remembered something he wanted to tell Jay. "Oh yeah, they asked if we wanted to go to the creek on Thursday. Steve has his dad's fishing boots, and he said we could use them to wade into the caves down by the railroad tracks. Do you want to go?"

"Sure!" Jay said. He seemed genuinely thrilled at the idea of exploring the three limestone caves. There were many legends about what lay inside of them, but their entrances were always flooded, preventing the boys from getting any further than the cave openings.

"What about the ghosts?" Jeffrey pleaded.

"Okay, okay," Tim said while glancing sideways at Jay, who had moved his hand behind his little brother's back. "But first," he said, speaking in a tone barely above a whisper, one that drew Jeffrey closer to him as the younger boy leaned in to hear every word. Speaking distinctly and purposefully, he slowed his delivery to increase the level of suspense. "First," he continued, "you need to understand something about ghosts."

"What's that?" Jeffrey asked, the volume of his voice reduced to a muted tone.

"Sometimes, just sometimes … they sneak up on you!" The moment Tim delivered his warning, Jay clawed his little brother's back, causing Jeffrey to shriek involuntarily. The cry echoed throughout the tent, its sheer volume causing Tim and Jay to start laughing hysterically to which Jeffrey frowned and called them "assholes" again, this time with a more pronounced lisp. The sound of his insult only served to increase their amusement, embarrassing and infuriating Jeffrey even more until he jumped on the two older boys and began wildly swinging his fists at them, pummeling them with punches that mostly missed their marks. Tim and Jay did not retaliate against his attacks but merely protected themselves from his blows while howling with laughter.

Amid the laughter and their tossing about inside the tent, Tim leaned back and glanced out the door flap. "Hush," he said with a motion of his hand. Once again, he saw light spilling from the bedroom window. "Quiet, quiet, quiet," he continued before reaching over and dousing the small flashlight. A profound stillness then fell over the three of them as they sat quietly in the dark, listening to the nocturnal songs of the night creatures while wondering if this marked the end of their camping adventure. After a few tense moments, however, the bedroom light was extinguished, and they were granted one final reprieve.

"Okay," Tim spoke in a low voice as he restored order and returned to his storytelling. "Like I said, it's not actually a ghost story, but it's close. It's a new Dave Rasputin story."

"Dave Rasputin, all right!" Jeffrey said approvingly, forgetting his prior anger at the mention of his beloved hero. He enjoyed listening to the stories told by the older boys about the legendary local figure, someone of questionable character who drove a hearse and was purported to have inflicted unspeakable atrocities on his brothers and sisters. Jeffrey had memorized all the Dave Rasputin tales, and he already had begun spreading them among his own friends. Now he would have a new one to tell.

"Well," Tim began. "Brian said that it had happened years ago when Dave was about Jeff's age. It was during the summer when school was out. His parents worked during the day, and Dave's older sister would watch him while they were away. He and his sister were supposed to go bowling one afternoon, but she got mad at him and refused to take him. Instead, she went out into the yard and fell asleep under a giant oak tree, kind of like the one we're under now." Tim elevated his eyes toward the roof of the tent as he made the remark, noticing that both Jeffrey and Jay did the same.

The two brothers listened intently and hung on every word uttered by Tim as he related the tale, their passion and interest piquing when Tim paused and again switched on the small Maglite, placing it on the ground in candle mode. There, at that moment in the lives of all three boys, the only thing that mattered to them was the recounting of another episode in the ever-continuing saga of Dave Rasputin. As the two brothers hovered like moths around the light, their friend continued his discourse, acting as a chronicler of culture and entertainment, of no less importance among his peers than a Dickens or a Homer. With the storyline building to its climax, all three paused to absorb the full impact of its deep and mysterious meaning, the significance of which they could not discern but which surely must be present due to the excitement and emotion it aroused in them.

Tim continued in a slightly subdued tone that added an air of suspense to the listening experience of his audience. "So," he said, "Dave decided to get even with her. He snuck out into the yard with a bowling ball and managed to climb the tree with it. Because his sister was asleep, she didn't see or hear him. Then, when he was on the branch directly over her, he let the bowling ball drop right onto her stomach. Strike!" he said with a snap of his fingers. "Killed her just like that!"

"All right!" Jeffrey exclaimed with a grin, excitedly looking around at the other two boys.

"You know," Jay said in a softer tone. "I saw a big black hearse coming down the street the other day and felt sure it was Dave Rasputin. However, when it got closer, I didn't see a hangman's noose dangling from the inside mirror, so it couldn't have been him. What do you think? Is Dave Rasputin real?"

In response to such an open and honest admission of doubt, all three boys became despondent. It was almost sacrilegious to express any skepticism whatsoever about their hero, but, being a common suspicion shared by most others, it never seemed to evoke a rebuke whenever acknowledged. The only reaction it stirred among the true believers was a disheartening sadness or melancholy sparked by the realization that their faith and boyish admiration was directed at someone who probably did not exist.

Jeffrey then perked up and broke the silence with a reassuring thought, a lifeline tossed to his forlorn companions faced with the prospect of having to declare Dave Rasputin a fraud. "Hey, doesn't

Wolfgang live on the same street as Grandma?" he asked his brother.

"That's right, Jeff!" The older boy instantly sensed the point his brother was trying to make. "As a matter of fact, I saw him drive by the house last time I was at Grandma's—and Mummy even said she went to school with Wolfgang's big sister."

"So?" Tim asked.

"So," Jay continued, "everyone knows that Wolfgang and Dave Rasputin used to run around together. Therefore, if Wolfgang is a real person, then Dave Rasputin must be real too."

"Yeah!" Jeffrey said enthusiastically, voicing confidence in his brother's opinion.

With that glimmer of hope, the boys felt their spirits lifted and their faith renewed in someone they had never seen and probably would never meet. It also helped restore a measure of peace and tranquility to that warm summer night until a nervous hush fell over the campers the moment a twig snapped outside the tent door, reigniting their imaginations and furthering their belief in people and things purported to exist only in myths and legends.

A black 1965 Cadillac hearse with Florida license plates sat in the parking lot at the southern end of the Herbert C. Bonner Bridge over the Oregon Inlet, a channel separating Bodie Island from the Pea Island National Wildlife Refuge at the northernmost tip of Hatteras Island. Dredged to maintain a water depth of fourteen feet, the channel represented one of the few navigable routes into Pamlico Sound from the Atlantic Ocean beneath the arch at the southern end of the bridge. Like many other inlets of the Outer Banks, it was in constant motion, its sands displaced by strong tides and powerful ocean storms.

Standing barefoot on the giant boulders of a breakwater along the inlet's southern shoreline was a handsome young man in a relaxed pose reminiscent of Michelangelo's *David*, his lean body undisturbed by the falling rain as he gazed thoughtfully at the surging tide flowing into the sound from the sea. Like the Oregon Inlet itself, he too was subject to the vagaries of shift, flux, and drift, rarely staying in one place more than six months at a time. However, the only migration on his mind at that moment involved the itinerant sands beneath the water near a small beach next to the parking lot. Alone on the rocks, he listened impassively to the cries of the gulls and terns as he mentally performed a calculated study of the deserted beach and its environs.

Focusing his eyes, he tried to identify the shoals beneath the surface of the water, but the dark clouds hindered his ability to do so. Additionally, his rain-streaked sunglasses impaired his vision, so he removed them and hung them on the neck of his tee shirt, squinting and straining his eyes but still unable to detect any variation in water color. On a bright sunny day, it would have been an easy matter for him to discern the shallows of the inlet, but on that day, under those conditions, the task was nearly impossible; he would need to stop back on another day when the sun was out.

If there was one thing about which Dave Rasputin was knowledgeable and passionate, it was the sea. Moreover, he was an aficionado of water sports, namely: surfing, windsurfing, and kiteboarding. In matters related to any of those activities, the man was the sport, and the sport was the man. His reason for stopping along the highway that day had been to scout a new location from where he could launch his sailboard. Having never before sailed the Oregon Inlet, he wondered what it would be like to windsurf from the ocean into Pamlico Sound and back out again. Earlier in the day, he had driven down to Hatteras Island to pick up some replacement parts for his kiteboard and to look for a new windsurfing sail, stopping first at Ocean Air Sports in Avon and then Fox Watersports in Buxton. It was on his return trip home to his cottage in Nags Head that he had pulled off the highway to investigate the beach at the Oregon Inlet as a potential windsurfing launch area. He was in no hurry to get back north because the wet weather had already washed out his scheduled surfing lesson for the day.

The rain striking his body as he stood on the rocks was not the torrential downpour of earlier that morning, but it still fell steadily, although it did not seem to bother him. He found it far less vexing than the malicious flies he had encountered on the path between the parking lot and the beach, nasty insects that had attacked him savagely, biting him on the neck and refusing to surrender even in death. It was only after he had scaled the large rocks of the breakwater that they had suspended their assault, and it was for that reason that he was reluctant to come down despite the rain.

Dave Rasputin cut an impressive figure in or out of the rain with a youthful appearance that made him look ten years younger than his actual age, something he used to his advantage whenever it served his purpose. His haunting, enigmatic look created an aura about him, one that naturally attracted people to him, especially those intrigued by his facial features, most notably his high cheekbones and somber expression that made him resemble James Dean when viewed in a particular light. It was especially noticeable whenever he squinted, so he usually wore a pair of Wayfarer sunglasses—both indoors and outdoors—to shield his eyes and avoid the embarrassing comparison to the deceased movie star. While he did not attempt it, he personified the film star in much of his bearing as well as his mannerisms and appearance with his slow, halting speech pattern and his dark, wavy hair swept up in typical Dean fashion.

The long, smooth lines of his extremely tanned body made him resemble a distance swimmer without the sharp angular cuts of an athlete, although he was incredibly athletic with a well-defined musculature that even his weathered tee shirt and baggy cargo shorts could not conceal. Having spent the better part of two decades tossing around heavy sails full of wind and carving out radical turns in large ocean waves, he had sculpted for himself a slim body of high tensile strength and phenomenal flexibility that did whatever he commanded it to do. He exuded confidence, poise, and grace while always appearing lean and hungry. His emotional state, however, was not that easily defined. It was complicated.

It is a common belief that most myths and legends have their origins in truth, something he would not dispute, although he made a determined effort to avoid such reflections if only to prevent the onset of melancholy. Sadly, however, thoughts of that nature often crept into his mind, usually at odd moments, almost always in the rain. Standing in the late morning drizzle while perched atop the rocks, he experienced one such moment.

Turning his gaze from the water to the shoreline, he directed his eyes toward an old lifesaving station in the distance, and he thought about the station's watchtower, especially the way it aided rescuers in helping those in peril. The sight of it made him reflect on his past and how life might have turned out differently had there been more lifesaving stations placed strategically along the way. The sad thing about his past is that many of the tales told about him in his hometown were true, at least partially true, with the reality of that truth gnawing at him both emotionally and spiritually. He had heard all the Dave Rasputin stories recounted by people, mostly strangers, and he knew the events from which they had sprung, tragedies from his past that had shaped his present and threatened to govern his future unless something happened to alter that trajectory, unless something—or someone—stepped in to fill the emotional void within him.

The disturbing tales told of him claimed that he had thirteen brothers and sisters, all of whom had died as a result of his actions, murders in which he had employed unconventional means to snuff out their lives. The sordid details of the executions constituted the essence of the Dave Rasputin legends, but, like most myths and legends, they misrepresented the truth.

The truth told a different story, a heart-wrenching story, one more tragic than even the worst of the fabricated fictions. It told of a young boy who had seven, not thirteen, brothers and sisters, all of whom had suffered extremely violent deaths of an accidental nature. It also told of that same boy who had been present at all of the accident scenes but who had survived totally unscathed. Additionally, it spoke of the stigma attached to the boy by the community because of his unfortunate presence at all of the grisly scenes. The fact that he was not responsible for any of the tragic events became an insignificant and forgotten detail as the legends emerged and spread throughout the town.

The truth also told of a young man who had run away from those memories to pursue a wandering, unconventional lifestyle, one viewed as reckless and foolish by many, leaving behind everything in his troubled past—even his name—becoming known only as Buddy to his friends and to those with whom he made contact. Now, after years of running, he approached the end of his third decade of life and found himself standing alone on a stone breakwater in the rain, staring at a lifesaving station while asking the question, "Where were you when I needed you—when they needed you?"

In order to banish the thoughts of his past and dispel the melancholy, he tried to concentrate on the image before him, focusing on the physical appearance of the lifesaving station—the gabled roof, the dormers, the porch, the watchtower—and how the shapes and colors came together aesthetically to create a design pleasing to the eye. It looked as if someone had rebuilt or restored the building, and he did not know if it remained a lifesaving station or if it had become a museum or something else. For all he knew, it could have been empty or abandoned. He briefly considered trudging back there to see it up close, but he quickly dismissed the idea because of the biting flies along the path. He then stood quietly on the rocks, staring at the lifesaving station in the distance, reflecting on it as a concept, on what it meant spiritually. He also pondered the dedicated men who had devoted their lives to upholding its noble ideals, especially long ago when manning the station had been a much more dangerous occupation.

He wondered what kind of man does something like that, risk his own life to save others, total strangers he has never met, and he questioned whether or not he was such a man; if he possessed that kind of courage, that kind of integrity, that kind of love. The question was one he dared not answer, so he jumped down from the rocks and ran toward the parking lot, wildly swinging his arms over his head to ward off the flies.

Upon arriving at the hearse, he glanced through the half-open window to see his partner sleeping soundly in the passenger's seat. The weather that day had scared away the fishermen and beachgoers, so there was no one around to disturb his friend's napping until Dave arrived and opened the door, at which time his slumbering associate stirred with a tremor and began looking around with unfocused eyes.

"Forget this place," Dave said to his sleepy partner while grabbing a towel from the front seat to brush the sand off his feet. Carelessly tossing the towel into the back of the hearse, he slipped on an old pair of deck shoes and climbed into the driver's seat. Again addressing his droopy-eyed friend, he said, "Too many biting flies out there, Grave. They may not be bad on a sunny day, but they're terrible in this heat and rain." Grave did not respond but simply stared blankly at him for a few moments before easing back on the seat to continue his nap.

Before starting the engine, Dave glanced back over his shoulder to where he had thrown the towel, wincing at the muddled collection of surfing, windsurfing, and kiteboarding equipment crammed into the rear compartment of the hearse. The clutter and chaos disturbed him, so he made a promise to himself to carve out time that week to clean it out and put everything in an orderly fashion. The fact that his entire life was a mess did not mean his sole legacy had to reflect it.

The hearse had once belonged to his father who had been a collector of vintage automobiles in his spare time. He would purchase vehicles to restore and customize with the intention of reselling them. Although the activity never earned him much money, he never complained about it and labored hard at the endeavor until the day he died simply because he liked restoring old cars. The hearse was a joint project he had undertaken with his son, a project he never finished because of his untimely death. Dave then completed the work himself, seeing it as the perfect vehicle for hauling around his watersports equipment. Additionally, it provided him shelter whenever he needed a place to sleep.

If anything, Dave Rasputin was a pragmatist. Once he found

something he liked, he stuck with it, rarely questioning his choice after making his initial determination. As a result, he displayed an intense loyalty toward the people and things he valued in life, caring little for style or the opinions of others, and his physical appearance and sailing equipment reflected that attitude. He owned two sailboards, an original Windsurfer recreational board and a custom fiberglass race board, along with about five windsurfing sails and an assortment of booms. One of his most prized possessions was a set of antique wooden booms from a vintage Windsurfer of the 1960s. They had long since become obsolete, replaced by aluminum production booms, but he relished the look and feel of the teak wood, and he liked to show them off to other sailboarders. He had two surfboards, a short board and a long board, and he owned one kiteboard and two kites, a performance kite and a trainer kite for instructing beginners. Additionally, he had a few sectional masts and a variety of windsurfing and kiteboarding accessories. He likened his hearse to an old Woody station wagon, the kind favored by surfers in the 1950s and 1960s, which he found comfortable as well as practical, doing whatever was necessary to keep it in good running condition. All of his personal possessions fit rather nicely, albeit chaotically, into its long, spacious back compartment.

When not in one of his melancholy moods, he felt comfortable with his chosen lifestyle along with his selection of vehicle and watersports equipment as well as the people with whom he chose to associate. That, in effect, summed up his entire philosophy of life: a feeling of comfort. By comfort, he did not mean a hedonistic or material comfort but, rather, a spiritual comfort—a sense of oneness with the object, the product, the person, the universe. In certain respects, he tended toward the spiritual because he saw it as the pathway to a deeper understanding of life, something he had yet to discover fully within himself. When not in a swimsuit on the water, he wore baggy, wrinkled cargo shorts because he found them comfortable and because they suited his spiritual lifestyle. He also possessed a large selection of logo-bearing tee shirts from all the surf shops, restaurants, and bars he had visited while traveling with his partner, Grave, whom he had picked up on Interstate 95 in Georgia a few years earlier. They had been together ever since because they felt comfortable with each other and because they shared a common spirit.

While he had been outside on the rocks of the breakwater, the air had been perfectly still without even a breath of wind to deflect the raindrops from their vertical plunge. Now, however, a nearly imperceptible breeze had developed, wafting in through the open window of the hearse to brush lightly against the side of his face. To anyone else, this slight change in the wind would have passed unnoticed, but Dave sensed it immediately, prompting him to lean his head out the window where he observed the clouds thinning and moving eastward. It was only a few seconds later that the rain stopped entirely. Besides being an expert on wind and water, Dave had an intimate working knowledge of the weather. By merely glancing at the clouds, he could predict improving conditions based on his meteorological expertise as well as his emotional reaction, the level of *comfort* he felt about what he was seeing.

Jamming his hand into the side pocket of his dirty cargo shorts, he pulled out his cell phone and clicked the Windfinder application to check the speed and direction of the wind. What he saw pleased him, so he started the engine and turned on the radio, tuning it to 1610 AM to hear to the National Weather Service forecast, a recorded message joined in progress: ... *the tropical forecast. A tropical depression has formed in the mid-Atlantic region off the coast of Africa with a high probability of developing into a tropical storm and possibly a hurricane—*

Unwilling to wait for the weather recording to recycle to the local forecast, he reached up and silenced the radio, opting instead to study the satellite images on his smartphone. "It's going to get nice, Grave—and windy," he quipped while putting down the phone and grabbing the shift lever on the side of the steering column. Pausing a moment, he glanced over the top of some reeds of *Phragmites australis* growing wild along the side of the parking lot, directing his eyes toward the tower of the lifesaving station rising in the distance. The sight of it once again stirred in him an emotional response similar to the one he had experienced while standing on the rocks of the breakwater, but he stopped his emotional plunge by jamming the hearse into gear and swinging the long vehicle into a half-turn while grabbing the sunglasses from his shirt and slipping them onto his face. Driving toward the entrance of the parking lot, he spotted no cars approaching from the south, so he turned onto the northbound lane of the highway without stopping or slowing down.

As the hearse proceeded onto the bridge and started across the Oregon Inlet, he listened to the sound of his tires pounding rhythmically against the sectional slabs of concrete, and he glanced through the open window at the ocean waves rushing over the sandy shoals, the same shoals he had tried to identify while standing on the rocks near the beach. The higher elevation made it easier for him to discern the shallow water below, but he was traveling too fast to take note of anything; therefore, he turned his attention back to the highway and again switched on the radio, punching a preset button for The Shark 102.5, a local station on which was playing an old Tommy James and the Shondells' song.

Ah, I don't hardly know her,
But I think I could love her,
Crimson and clover ...

The words and music of the familiar oldie filled the interior space of the vehicle, and Dave reached out to change the channel but hesitated a moment and then lowered his hand. Smiling at his friend, he said, "Wouldn't be right to cut off a hometown boy like that, would it, Grave?" His partner, having stirred and awakened, chose not to respond and instead stared directly at the road ahead. Not expecting a reply, Dave continued, "Did I ever tell you that Tommy James is from Niles, Michigan, my hometown up north? Actually, his family didn't move there until he was ten or eleven, but that was long before your time—and mine too." Again, Grave did not answer but merely yawned and looked out the window.

The song continued playing as they traveled north across the bridge with the thumping of the tires and the rocking of the vehicle augmenting the rhythm of the music while a refreshing breeze blew in through the open windows of the hearse. Grave seemed to enjoy both the melody and the feel of the wind on his face.

Crimson and clover,
Over and over.
Crimson and clover,
Over and over ...

The hearse ascended the high arch of the bridge to the very summit from where Dave had a panoramic view of the flat terrain extending north toward the towns of Nags Head, Kill Devil Hills, and Kitty Hawk. Looking up the coastline beyond the curve at the end of the archway, he spotted the black and white horizontal stripes of the Bodie Island Lighthouse, its tall, recognizable shape springing from the earth like a symbol of hope and strength to anyone in need of guidance and assurance. The clouds directly above it had opened up, and, for a brief second, a single shaft of sunlight descended from the heavens to illuminate the clean white stripes of the lighthouse, causing them to glisten brightly against the backdrop of the gray, gloomy sky father north where the rain continued falling.

Staring intently at the shimmering beacon, he experienced an inner stirring—almost an awakening—when the light of the tower pierced his consciousness, its powerful ray illuminating a darkened cavern in his soul, a void he endeavored to keep hidden from everyone, most especially himself. Whereas his past life had been one of running from something, the image of the lighthouse seemed to nudge him onward, forward, toward something—toward the promise of a brighter future that he longed to discover. Grave, on the other hand, experienced no such awakening as he sat placidly on the front seat, his mind vacant and his emotions numb, entirely content to sit and listen to the music while gazing hypnotically at the swaying motion of a macramé noose dangling from the rearview mirror.

Chapter 2

The region identified as the Outer Banks—or "OBX" as it is commonly known—is a narrow band of barrier islands running two hundred miles along the eastern seaboard principally off the coast of North Carolina. Unlike other barrier islands, the landmasses of the Outer Banks migrate and shift under the eroding forces of nature. In fact, some people maintain that the islands are marching steadily toward the mainland as they lose beach on the Atlantic side and acquire it along the shores of the sound, the body of water separating the Outer Banks from the mainland. Because of their direct exposure to the Atlantic Ocean, the islands are vulnerable to powerful ocean storms and destructive hurricanes that continually reshape the region, giving rise to treacherous seas that have led to many a shipwreck, over five hundred of them, resulting in the Outer Banks being labeled "The Graveyard of the Atlantic" with all the legends and ghost stories that accompany such a distinctive designation.

In addition to its unique topography and climate, the Outer Banks has a rich historical past. It is the birthplace of Virginia Dare, the first English child born in the New World, who, with her fellow colonists, vanished without a trace from Roanoke Island in 1587. Another historical figure, Blackbeard the Pirate, left his mark on the area, plundering the coastline and fighting his final battle aboard the *Adventurer* in the waters off Ocracoke Island. Although most noted for its treacherous seas and ghost fleet of sunken ships along the Atlantic floor, the Outer Banks is also recognized for its consistent and prevailing winds, explaining why the Wright Brothers chose Kitty Hawk as their initial flight location. Founded as a village in the 1830s, the Town of Nags Head was one of the first tourist spots of North Carolina, attracting people of means who sought relief from the summer heat by crossing Roanoke Sound to enjoy the cooler breezes of the region. However, before the influx of tourists, the locals—known as "Bankers"—had called the Outer Banks their home since the eighteenth century.

Many of the original cedar-shake cottages and stilted summer residences with their wraparound porches, pitched roofs, and extended dormers, built mainly in the 1850s, are still present today in a region known as the "Unpainted Aristocracy" or "Cottage Row," but they now share the region with more modern beach houses, bars, restaurants, and shops. The Outer Banks has become the ideal tourist destination, but it has done so with more restraint than a Myrtle Beach, South Carolina, or an Ocean City, Maryland. Wishing to avoid the sprawl of high-rise resort complexes that only detract from the natural beauty and relaxed atmosphere of the region, the communities of the Outer Banks still promote the "Nags Head style" or "coastal style" of building and construction. This respect for architectural preservation, along with the ambiance of the region, has enabled the Outer Banks to retain its character along with a sense of Southern charm, an enduring quality imbued by the native Bankers and residents of the Unpainted Aristocracy.

The Town of Nags Head is home to the tallest natural sand dune in the eastern United States at Jockey's Ridge State Park. Several legends recount how Nags Head received its name with one story describing how the local inhabitants would tie lanterns to the manes of wild ponies and walk them along the top of the dune so that ships at sea, spotting the lanterns, would mistake them for boats rocking on their moorings, causing the ship captains to steer too close to the darkened shoreline where they would run aground. In the morning light, land pirates would scavenge along the beach for whatever treasure washed ashore or row out to the shipwrecks in small boats to pillage and plunder the cargo.

The approach to the Outer Banks from the north is down U.S. Route 158, known as the Caratoke Highway, across the Wright Memorial Bridge over Currituck Sound. In the summer tourist season, the traffic often backs up along the bridge as travelers stream into the Outer Banks and departing guests leave at the end of their vacations. The traffic congestion is particularly heavy on

Saturdays and Sundays, the days of the week when rental properties typically change hands.

The Wright Memorial Bridge connects the mainland to the Outer Banks at the first milepost marker from which travelers can continue north or south. North Carolina Route 12, known as the "beach road" by locals and seasoned visitors, extends north along the shoreline into Southern Shores, Duck, and Corolla. It also stretches southward where it becomes the North Virginia Dare Trail through the communities of Kitty Hawk, Kill Devil Hills, and Nags Head. Another road, U.S. Route 158, known as "the bypass," also runs southward as a five-lane highway that parallels the beach road. Its fifty-mile-per-hour speed limit allows for faster transit than the thirty-five-mile-per-hour speed limit of the two-lane beach road.

Both roads converge at Whalebone Junction where the bypass becomes the Nags Head/Manteo Causeway—or just the "causeway"—crossing over the sound to Roanoke Island where the towns of Manteo and Wanchese are located. The beach road then veers inland at Whalebone Junction where it enters the Cape Hatteras National Seashore to proceed over seventy miles south across the Oregon Inlet to Rodanthe, Avon, Hatteras, and eventually to Ocracoke and Cedar Islands via ferry service. At the Whalebone Junction convergence of the beach road and the bypass, an ancillary beach road, known as South Old Oregon Inlet Road or the "beach road extension," branches off to follow the coastline an additional four miles through the district of South Nags Head before merging with North Carolina Route 12 near the twenty-second milepost.

People in the upper regions of the Outer Banks speak a distinctive numeric language not heard anywhere else in the world. It is especially true of tourists and visitors who focus primarily on two numbers: one being the number of vacation days they have remaining and the other one the milepost marker where something is located. Almost any place in the northern portion of the Outer Banks can be pinpointed using milepost markers, a numbering system that, for practical purposes, begins at the first milepost near the southern end of the Wright Memorial Bridge and ends at the twenty-second milepost slightly north of Coquina Beach and the Bodie Island Lighthouse.

Numbers were something he understood. Mark Allen sat at the

bar, mentally tallying the strokes on a scorecard from the Nags Head Golf Links while brushing his hand across the top of his head, allowing the short stubble of his flat-top to spring up in the spaces between his fingers. Touching a thinning patch on the crown of his head, he ignored the disturbing discovery and continued adding the golf scores without the aid of a calculator. He liked to boast that he was accurate out to two decimal places whenever performing complex mathematical calculations in his head, so he easily handled the addition needed to tally the golf strokes. Dropping the scorecard between his drink and an expensive calfskin portfolio, he glanced up and down the bar in search of something, appearing slightly miffed that he could not find it. Afterward, he looked inside his leather folder but found only a pen clipped to a legal pad.

The bar at Miller's Waterfront Restaurant had enough seats to accommodate about six people, but Mark sat alone on a stiff wooden chair dressed neatly in a white polo shirt and tan shorts, looking as if he had just stepped off the pages of a golf apparel magazine. Climbing off his chair, he strode to the end of the bar where a glass door led to the outside deck overlooking Roanoke Sound, but he stopped at a server station before reaching the door. Protruding from a pile of guest checks next to a computer, he found what he was looking for—a pencil—which he used to tap on the backs of the vacant chairs as he walked back to his seat. He liked the fact that he was alone in the barroom without even a bartender present because he was not much of a "people person" despite his occupation as a certified financial planner.

Most of the customers in the restaurant were sitting outside on the deck or in the gazebo over the water, but there were also patrons in the dining room next to the bar beyond a six-foot dividing wall. At a towering height of six feet, eight inches tall, Mark easily saw over the partial wall into the dining room where the muffled conversations of the dinner guests made it sound far more crowded than it was. He had not yet requested a table because was waiting for his golfing partner—a potential client—to show up.

Confident of getting a prime seat with a good view of the sunset, Mark returned to his drink and scorecard at the bar. He was not much of a drinker, but he always enjoyed a gin and tonic after a round of golf, especially on a hot summer day. Shifting his attention back to the scorecard, he added several strokes to his score on seven of the eighteen holes, increasing his final score to nine over par, a significant reduction in his margin of victory. Mark was a two handicap, but he had been a scratch golfer in his college days when was golfing for the university team.

Setting down the pencil, he began rubbing his eyes, rolling his fingers around the sockets to relieve the fatigue and strain from all the squinting he had done on the fairway. It had been a bright, sunny day in August without a cloud in the sky, but he had inadvertently left his sunglasses at home. The slow massage of his powerful fingers helped ease the pressure and thwart what threatened to become a headache. Stretching out his free hand for his gin and tonic, he saw the glass virtually disappeared into the hollow of his massive grip. The flicker of the tendons on the back of his hand and the rippling of the muscles across his massive forearm left no doubt that he could have crushed the glass with minimal effort had he chosen to do so, but he instead took a tiny swallow and gently lowered the glass to the bar. These days, he was not into public displays of strength; however, that had not always been the case.

Mark's physical prowess on the golf links was nothing compared to his past performance on the football field. He currently weighed two hundred and eighty pounds, but he had been heavier in his college days when he was an All-American running back in the Big Ten. It was his height and weight along with his speed and agility that had made him such a formidable force coming through the line. Despite receiving several offers upon graduation, he had not pursued a professional career because he was not an inherently violent person and felt he lacked the temperament to make it in the pros. He had played football in college only to fund his education so he could work with the things he truly loved; namely, numbers. Coming from two generations of barbers, he had been the first one in his family to attend college, relying entirely on football scholarships to pay his tuition because his father, who worked in a small barbershop in Nebraska, lacked the financial resources to help with his college expenses.

Back in school, he had secretly had used steroids to increase his size and strength, and he continued taking them for a while after college. Although he no longer played football, he still maintained his weight training, exercising in his garage, which he had converted into a fully stocked weight room, a home modification that left him nowhere to park his car except in the driveway. Religiously, he scheduled time each day to pump iron, compulsively refusing to miss even a day no matter what the reason. As such, he was able to maintain his muscular physique without the need for steroids; however, it was Nikki who had ultimately convinced him to stop using them.

The thought of his girlfriend caused him to forget the weariness of his eyes and the building pressure in his head. His expression then relaxed as he stared blankly across the bar, lifting his eyes toward a flat-screen television tuned to a cable news show. No sound came from the television, but a crawl ran across the bottom of the screen that read: ... *Tropical Storm Kim, having formed in the lower Atlantic region, is making its way toward the Windward Islands. Kim is expected to hit portions of the Lesser Antilles, U.S. Virgin Islands, Dominican Republic, Haiti, and Cuba early next week ...*

Just then, the door at the end of the bar burst open, and a server walked in carrying a clattering tray of dirty dishes on her shoulder. Her entrance ushered into the room a whoosh of air that brought with it the voices and laughter of the crowd on the deck, shattering the subtle resonances of the dinner conversations emanating from the other side of the dividing wall. Turning with a jerk toward the noisy commotion, Mark noticed the outside flags flapping wildly in a stiff breeze, signaling a significant uptick in wind velocity over what he had experienced on the golf course that day. Such a change in weather systems, however, was quite typical for that region in the summer months, especially in the late afternoon and early evening hours.

Once the door closed, everything grew quiet again until another server charged through the barroom carrying several plates filled with burgers and fries. When she opened the door, another blast of wind surged into the restaurant, this time bringing with it the sound of a barking dog. The lingering smell of food from her tray triggered Mark's appetite, and he wondered what was keeping Bill.

Pulling out his cell phone, he checked the time, wincing slightly when he saw that it was already five o'clock. It was getting late, and he still needed to return home to clean up before driving to Norfolk with Nikki later that evening. Their travel plans involved staying at a hotel near the airport in advance of catching an early flight to Hawaii tomorrow morning. The trip was an incentive award for the premium business he had generated through annuity sales. He and Nikki had never traveled together before, and it surprised him greatly when she had agreed to go with him. He often wondered why she even dated him at all because he was not the kind of man most women found exciting. If it had been anyone else other than Nikki, he might have thought the attraction was purely physical.

Besides being tall and incredibly strong, Mark was a ruggedly handsome man with a large square head and a strong jaw to match his physique. His teeth were brilliantly white and remarkably straight, and they would shimmer and sparkle whenever he chose to smile, something he did sparingly except when trying to close a deal or generate sales. He had a well-defined cranial ridge above his eyes and a conspicuous scar on the right side of his forehead, one caused by a deep laceration he had sustained during a college bowl game. His short, sandy-colored hair stood straight up like an inverted hairbrush, making him resemble a football player from the Vince Lombardi era. Lately, he had noticed his hairline receding at the temples, but, having reached the age of thirty-five, he expected it based on his family's history. Women like to be seen with him, which is how he got most of his dates. However, his past relationships had never lasted long because he was rather dull. He knew that Nikki's friends disliked him, but that knowledge did not seem to bother him. Nikki liked him and, as far as he was concerned, nothing else mattered. Other than Nikki and his business associates, he had no actual friends.

He and Nikki had been seeing each other steadily for two years, and, to propel their relationship to the next level, he had asked her to accompany him on his vacation to Hawaii. To his shock, she had said yes, but not without spelling out a long list of demands regarding the accommodations and such. Being a Catholic girl of strong faith and high moral standards, she viewed dating as a path to a permanent, meaningful relationship leading to marriage, so she required special assurances from him before acceding to his request, assurances he was more than willing to give. He knew what a profoundly spiritual soul she was, and he was ready to promise her anything to get her to accept his invitation. He also knew that he must be on his best behavior and adhere to his pledge if he hoped to achieve his real goal in making the trip with her. Concluding that their courtship had satisfied the requisite number of days, months, and years, he had quietly concocted a plan where he would propose marriage to her in Hawaii, preferably on a sunset beach somewhere on Oahu, although he had no idea how to go about making the request.

Before putting the phone back in his pocket, he switched it to silent mode so it would not disrupt his dinner with his now overdue golfing partner. Drinking down the last of his gin and tonic, he smacked the empty glass on the bar top before getting up to go to the men's room. Having touched something sticky on the pencil, he wanted to wash his hands.

The men's room at Miller's was a clean, well-maintained restroom with cyan-colored walls and light tile flooring. It contained two bathroom stalls along with a baby changing station where a urinal had once stood. Directly opposite the door was a double sink over which hung a huge mirror reflecting the hulking image of Mark the moment he stepped through the door. The sight of his reflection triggered an instant surge of anxiety that made him want to turn and flee; however, he stood his ground and peered into the mirror, unable to break eye contact with the familiar image staring back at him. There had been several episodes over the past few weeks that he could not explain, frightening encounters he did not wish to ponder because they made him wonder if he might be losing his mind. Fear was not an emotion common to him, but he found himself encountering it more and more recently, especially whenever he looked into the reflective surface of a mirror.

Prying his eyes from the glass by physically shoving himself away from the counter, he swung his body violently to the left in an attempt to avoid his reflection only to encounter it again on another mirror attached to the side of the bathroom stall, a smaller one designated as a handicapped mirror for customers in wheelchairs. With his eyes fixed on the disturbing image and his body as rigid as steel, he could feel the veins in his neck bulging like overheated radiator hoses primed and ready for bursting. There—he thought—it happened again! Experiencing a sickening dryness his mouth, he tried to escape the unfounded fear by spinning back toward the sink counter where he again saw his own likeness staring back at him in the glass, displaying the same frightened and dismayed look he bore on his face.

This must be what they call a panic attack, he told himself while questioning why he would he be experiencing one. Trying to remain calm, he placed both hands on the sink counter and leaned closer to the glass, not stopping until his nose was but a hair's breadth away from the polished surface. With his brow furrowed and his face set like flint, he looked primitive and angry as he peered deeply into his own green eyes, refusing to flinch or vacillate despite the terror seizing his soul. He then slowly and methodically withdrew from the mirror while purposefully turning his head to rest his eyes on the handicapped mirror of the bathroom stall. This time, however, the sight of it elicited no reaction in him because everything appeared normal.

These types of episodes had plagued him over the past several weeks, instances where he would see something in a mirror or any reflective surface that was not an accurate replication of reality. It typically was a small thing like a hand wrongly positioned or his head tilted in an odd fashion, and it always corrected itself by the time he focused his full attention on the anomaly. It also only occurred when he made sudden movements or when he happened to catch a glimpse of his reflection out of the corner of his eye. Initially, he had experienced the phenomenon only in reflective surfaces other than mirrors, in things like polished steel poles or glass windows, which he explained away as imperfections in the materials themselves or just odd refractions of light. However, when the frequency of the episodes increased and they began occurring in mirrors, he started to worry. On a few occasions, he swore that he had seen his reflection facing the opposite direction, one time even staring straight at him while he stood sideways to the mirror, but he could not be sure because everything was always back in place once he did a double take of whatever it was he thought he was seeing.

He blamed the occurrences on his overtaxed mind and intemperate imagination, but he never told anyone about these episodes, not even Nikki, fearing that people would question his sanity if they knew about them. The scheduling of his Hawaiian getaway was how he had chosen to deal with the anxiety caused by the hallucinations, counting on the rejuvenating effect of the vacation in concert with the love and support of Nikki to cure him of this minor psychological disorder. Despite his doubts about his sanity, he was sane enough to realize that he had been under a lot of stress.

Mark never did wash his hands but, instead, backed slowly away from the sink while casting alternating glances between the two mirrors, his twin reflections watching him as he shuffled backward toward the door. Gradually sliding his hand behind his back to grasp the door handle, he yanked it open forcefully and charged out of the restroom only to collide with his golfing partner who had been walking down the hallway toward the bar. The force of the collision almost knocked Bill off his feet, but he quickly recovered and immediately noticed the distraught look on Mark's face.

"Mark, what happened?" he asked. "You look as if you've seen a ghost."

"Eh ..." Mark was a slightly bewildered himself and unsure how to respond. "Ah, yeah—well ... What took you so long?"

"Sorry. I had someone ahead of me at the bank who took forever. I should have stopped there before we played golf, but I needed to talk to them before this weekend. We're heading home on Sunday."

Bill did not know Mark that well—or even that long—but he liked him. He enjoyed being around him because Mark had the appearance of a real man, and he thought it boosted his own masculine standing being seen in the company of someone that large and athletic. A local realtor had put them in touch with each other because Mark had made the realtor a bunch of money through stock investments. It was Bill's hope that Mark could do the same for him.

Bill's recent visit to the area constituted a vacation, but he had plans to turn it into more than that. He had been coming to the Outer Banks for years with a goal of retiring in Nags Head and living out the remainder of his days in a house on the beach. In three years, he would be old enough to collect his pension, so he had already begun talking to realtors about buying a home now, which he would use as a rental property until his retirement date. The only thing holding him back at this point was money. He needed to earn some additional capital before signing the purchase agreement, and he hoped that Mark with all his financial planning experience would have some ideas.

After a few seconds, Mark had fully regained his composure, so he smiled at Bill and said, "I've already finished my drink in the bar. Let's get a table, and have a drink there before dinner. Go see the hostess while I'll grab my folder off the bar?"

Nodding his agreement, Bill said, "Okay, see you in the dining room." He then turned and started toward the front of the restaurant to find the hostess.

"Oh, yeah," Mark called to the receding figure of Bill. "Get a table by the window."

Without turning around, Bill raised his arm in acknowledgment of the seating preference while continuing to the hostess station to request a table with a view. A man in his early sixties, Bill had the soft face of a middle management executive with narrow eyes and dark eyebrows that flared wildly at the ends, a sharp contrast to his pure white hair that was well-groomed but thinning on top. He wore a blue monogrammed golf shirt and white shorts that were a little too roomy around the waist but cinched tightly with a black belt beneath his protruding belly. He had not bothered to change his shoes and was still wearing his rubber golf spikes.

Meanwhile, Mark returned to his empty glass and portfolio to find a young man behind the bar washing and stacking glasses. Paying the bartender for his drink, he picked up his leather folder and glanced over the wall divider to see Bill taking a seat by one of the many picture windows stretching the entire length of the west wall. Each large window was comprised of smaller panes arranged in a gridiron pattern similar to the structural divisions of the dining room itself with partial and half-walls partitioning the room into corral-like sections with columns rising to the ceiling. Trimmed and molded to create a frame-like impression, the columns and walls carried the window theme throughout the dining area, keeping everything open and airy in a way that permitted unobstructed sunset views from every table in the dining room. The clean lines of the design along with the classic dark cherry finish of the tables and chairs added to the pure aesthetics of the place.

Walking into the dining room, Mark took a seat at the table while Bill sat ordering a drink from a young waitress. Placing his portfolio on an empty chair beside him, Mark asked the girl to bring him another gin and tonic and then waited for her to leave before handing the scorecard to Bill while saying, "You did pretty well, especially on those last two holes."

Bill studied the card with a satisfied grin before looking up. "If you consider our handicaps, you only beat me by one stroke," he said proudly before returning his attention to the scorecard.

While Bill reviewed and compared their golf scores, Mark began his sales pitch. "We talked quite a bit on the course, but I didn't want to delve into this too deeply while we were playing. Maybe we can do that now before we eat. I know you're leaving on Sunday, and I'm also getting out of town tonight."

Bill glanced up. "Oh, yeah. Where're you going?"

"Hawaii"

"Hawaii? I've always wanted to go there,"

"Yeah, so have I," he said. "It's an award trip from one of the companies I represent. You know, you generate so much business, and they give you a reward of some sort ... kind of like Pavlov's dog." In punctuation of his remark, he flashed a contrived smile, a sales tool he had learned to use effectively.

Bill found many aspects of Mark physique fascinating, but, at that moment, he could not stop staring at the clean, razor-straight lines of the financial planner's front teeth. As Mark spoke, Bill found himself unconsciously using his tongue to probe the flaws and irregularities of his own teeth. Dropping the scorecard onto the table, he then forced himself to ignore Mark's dental work and focus on his financial presentation instead.

"Many guys in my profession will try to sell you only the proprietary products pushed by their companies in order to qualify for these kinds of rewards, but I don't work that way. I only promote what's best for my clients. If it earns me a bonus or an award, so be it. If it doesn't, that's okay too. I honestly don't like putting pressure on people to win these trips. My view is if it happens, it happens.

"We have a term for it—commission breath. The guy is so

anxious and desperate to make a sale that you can smell it on him. That type of salesman will tell you anything to get you to sign on the dotted line."

The waitress then returned with their drinks and placed them on the table. Handing menus to the two men, she said, "I'll stop back in few minutes to take your order."

"Could you make it about fifteen minutes?" Mark asked. "We're finishing up some business." The girl acknowledged his request with a nod and left them to their conversation while Bill took a large gulp of his beer and Mark set his menu on the table. Picking up where he had left off, Mark continued, "I never liked operating like that. I've found that the more you push clients, the less likely you are to make the sale."

Pausing a moment in his sales pitch to take a small sip of his gin and tonic, Mark then grabbed his portfolio off the chair and placed it on the table. "I already know one of your questions," he said. "What's my fee?" He again flashed his rehearsed smile. "Well, there are a number of ways for me to get paid, but I'm not going to go through all of them here. You've already made it clear that you're only interested in stocks and bonds. Therefore, I would get a percentage of assets under management on an annual basis. I take one percent annually paid on a quarterly basis—that's one-quarter percent per quarter—and I don't take that fee until the *end* of the quarter. That gives you several months to see if you like what I'm doing for you. If you don't like what I've done and decide to bolt before the end of the quarter, I get nothing. If you stick around for the first quarter and decided to leave before the end of the second quarter, I only receive a fee for the first quarter. But I don't think you'll leave me once you see what I can do for you. So, my approach is kind of like *try before you buy*. Investing with anyone else, you'll lose more money if you walk away because you pay the fee upfront. Also, I have an incentive to make you money because I only earn more if *you* earn more."

Bill liked what he was hearing; he liked Mark. He watched him open the portfolio and remove some pre-printed investment plans, but what really caught his attention was the size of Mark's bicep when he held up one of the charts. The way the elastic band of the golf shirt stretched and strained to accommodate the sheer size of Mark's upper arm intrigued him, making him recall to his own youth when he too had the ability to build and maintain muscle mass.

Despite his best efforts to focus on Mark's presentation, he found himself too mesmerized by the sheer size and stature of his new friend to listen attentively to what Mark was saying. He seemed more interested in judging Mark's professional expertise based on his physique and grooming rather than his resume or any of his proposed investment strategies. What he found most remarkable was that, after eighteen holes in temperatures of over eighty-five degrees, Mark looked as fresh and crisp as when they had met to play golf that morning. Even the deck shoes Mark was wearing looked as if they had come right out of the box, just like the golf shoes he had worn on the course that day. Bill decided that anyone that meticulous about his appearance was someone with whom he could entrust his money.

"So, I'll tell you what," Mark concluded. "If you like what you've heard, I'll put together a package with all the forms we need to get started. But I won't be back from Hawaii for ten days, so you'll have time to think about it."

Bill nodded his approval and was about to speak when the faint baying of a hound caught his attention. The sound was loud enough to penetrate the glass, so he knew it must be close, although he could not locate the dog when he turned and looked through the window. On one side of the restaurant was Kitty Hawk Water Sports, a place for renting wave runners, stand-up paddleboards, and other water sports equipment. On the opposite side was the Harvey Sound Access area, a public area managed by the Town of Nags Head and the Dare County Tourism Board for the launching of watercraft into Roanoke Sound. Despite the proximity of the dog's barking, Bill could not discern from which direction it came.

"Where I live," he said, "that kind of barking denotes a hound dog on the scent of a rabbit, but it doesn't look like rabbit country out there, just a lot of water and marsh." As he spoke, a windsurfer came soaring into view, racing past the windows at a high rate of speed while skimming across the water like a skipping stone. "Will you look at that?" he said. "Looks like fun, doesn't it?"

Mark watched the agile young man on the sailboard effectively stop his forward progress by carving a tight turn in front of the restaurant, his swift, smooth motion launching a plume of sea spray into the air when the edge of his board cut deeply into the choppy surface of the water. With the acrobatic flair of a trained athlete, the rider then spun the sail completely around the board and grabbed the wind on the other side to catapult himself forward in a new direction, moving away from the restaurant faster than he had approached it. "Not really," Mark responded, almost to himself.

"No?" Bill seemed genuinely surprised.

Mark looked at him a little sheepishly. "You see," he said,

pausing a moment, "I can't swim."

"You can't swim?" A curious smirk spread across Bill's face. At last, he thought, something this guy can't do.

Mark grinned as he spread his arms and looked down at his body. "This frame sinks like a stone. My dad used to say that my bones were made of solid steel. I've tried several times to learn to swim, but I always go straight to the bottom. No buoyancy. That's why I make it a point to stay on dry land."

They both chuckled and remained silent for a few moments while watching the receding figure of the windsurfer skim across the water toward Roanoke Island. Looking farther into the distance, Mark could see the Washington Baum Bridge stretching over Roanoke Sound to end at Pirate's Cove Marina and Condominiums, the complex where Nikki lived. He already had given Nikki her airline boarding pass; he just needed to pick her up later—around nine o'clock—and then drive to Norfolk. However, he first had to return home to finish packing and get his own boarding pass. Because of the weekend tourist traffic entering and leaving the Outer Banks, they had decided to drive at night, thereby avoiding the daytime congestion on the road heading north.

The sun had begun its descent in the sky, and it shone directly into the restaurant where it illuminated all parts of the room except for the shadows created by the low wall dividers of the dining bays. Softened by the tinted glass, the muted sunrays gently irradiated Mark's face as he stared across Roanoke Sound and affectionately thought of Nikki until his eyes detected the ghostly reflection of his face floating like a disembodied head in the tinted glass. Finding the sight unnerving, he tore his eyes from the window and forced his attention back to the table in a desperate attempt to prevent another surge of panic similar to the one he had experienced in the restroom. Just then, the waitress returned to their table, and her reappearance swept away the uncomfortable feeling before it spoiled his mood. Smiling at Bill, he picked up his menu and placed his dinner order.

When Mark walked out of the restaurant, it was almost seven-thirty with the sun hovered just above the horizon. By eight o'clock, it would be down. Bill had decided to order another drink and watch the sunset from the back deck, so they said their goodbyes and parted company with the agreement to talk again in two weeks.

As Mark walked toward his gray Infiniti Q70 sedan parked near some colorful flags snapping briskly in the rich, warm air, he used his key fob to unlock the doors but then paused briefly to view the sky set aflame in brilliant oranges and yellows. Moving slightly to his right, he peeked around the corner of the building to get a better view the fiery sunset, but he found his vision blocked by the slatted railing of the service ramp, an obstruction that also prevented him from seeing the black hearse parked in the Harvey Sound Access area beside the restaurant. Realizing that he had wasted too much time already, he abandoned the sunset and instead jumped into his car, telling himself that there would be plenty of time for majestic sunsets and other breathtaking vistas once he got to Hawaii.

Motoring out of the parking lot along the driveway shared by the restaurant and the recreational area, Mark pulled up to the bypass and stopped his car. An inherently cautious person, he never took unnecessary risks, so he waited patiently for a chance to turn into the heavy traffic. The opportunity presented itself when a gap opened up between two vehicles, so he bolted quickly onto the highway, joining the mad rush of other drivers heading north from Whalebone Junction. Fortunately, he did not have to endure the traffic congestion long because his house was only about a mile up the road near the fifteenth milepost.

Mark lived in a residential development called The Village at Nags Head where he owned a charming cottage-style home, a pale blue house with white trim overlooking the twelfth green and fairway of the Nags Head Golf Links. Built as a split-level dwelling over a single car garage, its construction was such that the living room, dining room, and kitchen were all located on the upper floor of the right side directly above the spare bedrooms on the ground level. The left side of the house was but a single story high, situated between the floors of the opposing side. Its rooms included a master bedroom, bathroom, and a small office. It was out of this modest office that Mark ran his investment business.

Although the interior of the home was accessible through the garage, the main entranceway was located at the top of a wooden staircase off a tiny porch large enough to accommodate only two or three people. Next to the porch, hanging on an outside wall, was a circular Aztec calendar stone about four feet in diameter, which Mark had purchased while in Mexico. The center of the stone contained a depiction of the feared sun god Tonatiuh to whom the Aztec people had offered human sacrifices to satisfy his need for blood. With eyes cold and dead, Tonatiuh held a human heart in each hand while extending a tongue shaped like a ceremonial blade used in ritual human sacrifices. Although Mark liked the design of the stone, he never truly understood why he had bought it or why he had gone to all the trouble to have it shipped home from Mexico. For some mysterious reason, the urge had been too powerful to resist. Upon its arrival, he determined that it was too large to put anywhere else, so he hung it on the outside of his house.

Another prominent feature of Mark's home was the number of decks incorporated into its design. Although the front of the house had but one deck placed high off the ground outside the dining area, the back of the house contained more, all constructed of white decking material with spindled railings. The rear upper deck sat outside the living room with another one positioned directly below it, functioning almost like a back porch. A third deck, located on the opposite side of the house, stood midway between the other two decks, connected to them by staircases. On this deck sat a Jacuzzi.

It took Mark only about a minute driving up the bypass to reach the traffic signal at the intersection of the Outer Banks Mall and West Seachase Drive, the only road traversing the entire residential community along a winding course that snaked past the golf course clubhouse to reemerge on the bypass farther south. Both routes led to his house, but he chose to turn on West Seachase near the strip mall because it was more convenient than driving through the entire development. Traveling a short distance down the road, he then turned left onto his street and pulled into his driveway.

Remaining a few moments in his car, Mark quietly observed the stark shadows cutting across the façade of his house as well as the glow of the white trim tinged by the final rays of the setting sun. Although it was not yet dark, his neighbor had switched on his two floodlights, powerful luminaries directed at the space between their houses as well as their backyards. Although the neighbor relished the radiance provided by the lights, Mark found it annoying, mainly because of the intensity of the mercury-vapor lamps and the way they illuminated the side of his house, flooding the upstairs with a blinding white light. Even with the blinds drawn, narrow bands of light would leak through the window coverings to pierce the darkness like laser beams, offensively striking his eyes whenever he sat in the living room watching television.

Fortunately, the light did not disturb his sleep because his bedroom sat on the opposite side of the house. His houseguests were also spared the annoyance by the high shrubbery growing outside the windows of the lower bedrooms. However, in the upstairs living area, there was no escaping the maddening light. The only reprieve came on nights when the neighbor did not turn on the floodlights, which were not many. Mark always meant to discuss the matter with him but repeatedly forgot to mention it whenever he saw him. Staring at the intense flood lamps spewing out their unwelcome light, he did not feel the usual acrimony that night because he knew he would leave soon to pick up Nikki and head north to Norfolk.

Grabbing his leather portfolio, he got out of the car and removed his golf clubs and shoes from the trunk to make room for the luggage they would be taking on vacation. Struggling with the awkward load, he then trudged up the porch steps and let himself into the house, tossing his car keys into a brass dish sitting on a small table in the foyer. The entranceway shimmered softly in the final rays of sunlight refracting through the cut-glass panels of the doorframe, so he did not bother switching on the light, turning instead and setting the golf clubs in the corner by the door. Bending down, he then placed his golf shoes at the base of the bag before stepping back and smiling at the illusion they created, the bizarre impression that the golf bag was standing erect on two feet.

Along the left wall of the foyer past the table with the brass dish was an open doorway leading into the largest of the bathrooms. Next to it was another door, slightly ajar, that led to the master bedroom—Mark's room—and beyond it, straight ahead, was another smaller room that served as his office. Off to Mark's right up a staircase of five steps was the living space that included the living room, dining area, kitchen, and half-bathroom. The staircase also extended down to the lower bedrooms with a simple wooden handrail running the entire length from the living area down to the guest bedrooms.

The radiance of the red and orange sunbeams refracting through the glass of the doorframe created an atmosphere of quiet, restful slumber as Mark stood in the foyer and glanced upstairs at the last rays of sunlight spilling onto the cathedral ceiling, tinting it with a warm pink glow. He decided that nothing up there needed his immediate attention, so he proceeded straight ahead into his office where he tossed his cell phone and leather portfolio onto the desk after flicking on the overhead light as well as a banker's lamp sitting on the corner of the desktop.

The small office had an undersized oak desk positioned precisely in the center of the room with two chairs facing it, each one constructed of high-grade hardwood with upholstered seats of a matching floral pattern. Behind the desk sat a sturdy executive chair crafted to fit someone of Mark's enormous size. Covered with supple, high-quality leather, it projected a sense of comfort and durability. Only three other pieces of furniture graced the room: a filing cabinet also made of oak and two matching wooden tables, one holding a combination printer and fax machine and the other a large potted fern. The whole interior of the office was dust-free and immaculately clean.

Sitting down at the desk, Mark turned his attention to his leather portfolio, a tri-folding design with pocketed side flaps that collapsed inward over a center notepad. He opened one of the hinged flaps and let it fall flat against the desktop. Removing some printed investment charts from the pocket, he then attempted to flip open the other flap but discovered that a framed picture of Nikki prevented it from fully extending. Instead of repositioning the portfolio, he simply turned the picture frame face down, which allowed the flap to open flush against the desk, covering Nikki's picture along with the cell phone lying beside it. Withdrawing the written notes he had recorded at the restaurant, he then sat and studied them in a relaxed manner.

It only took him a few minutes to digest the recorded notes, after which he turned to his computer keyboard and began entering Bill's contact information along with some investment strategies and comments. Additionally, he recorded the day's expenses and filed the business receipts in a side drawer of the desk. Satisfied that he had completed all his required tasks, he shut down his computer and flicked off the desk lamp with an exaggerated flair that marked an end to his workday and the start of his vacation, an escape he hoped would lead to a new life, one filled with unlimited possibilities shared with the woman he loved. He did not immediately rise from his chair but, instead, sat serenely in the twilight, letting his mind go blank while enjoying the pervading stillness of the approaching nightfall until the ticking of a large wooden clock on the wall caught his attention. What it announced caused him to rise quickly and leave the office.

After having played eighteen holes of golf in the blazing sun, Mark knew he needed to shower and shave before picking up Nikki, but he first walked up to the living area to get something before heading to the bathroom. Climbing the stairs out of the foyer, he stepped onto the polished floor of the upper level and mechanically flipped on the light switch at the top of the stairs, flooding the room with recessed lighting from the ceiling fixtures.

For the most part, the upper level of Mark's house was a large open area except for an enclosed kitchen and a half-bathroom occupying one corner of the room. The door to the bathroom stood next to the light switch at the top of the stairs with a full-length mirror set in an antique frame hanging on the wall beside it, its highly polished surface reflecting the totality of the living room on the opposite side of the house. The wall on which the mirror hung extended halfway across the room, ending at the dining area and entranceway to the kitchen.

Directly to Mark's left was another wall, one containing shelving with an assortment of knickknacks, mostly items of a nautical nature that included a brass compass, anchor paperweight, and miniature carved sailboat. One shelf held some artifacts from a barbershop once owned by his grandfather, an old straight razor and a ceramic shaving mug inscribed with the barbershop's name as well as his grandfather's initials. Mark had bought the house fully furnished, and the purchase price had included the small decorative appointments found throughout the home. His grandfather's barber tools had been his only contribution to the décor.

Mark realized that he lacked the artistic talent to decorate a home himself, so he was happy to have found a house fully furnished and adorned regardless of the theme. Although not a boating person, he appreciated the tasteful maritime décor and the various nautical items spread throughout the house, such as the Marconi-rigged sailboat sitting on the mantle opposite the stairs and the seascape photographs hanging on the walls. There was, however, one feature of his home that he truly relished, that being the gas fireplace on the wall beneath the mantle. He enjoyed nothing more during the winter months than relaxing with Nikki in front of a blazing fire. Aware of his fondness for the fireplace, Nikki had given him a decorative set of antique fireplace tools that he kept beside the hearth. The set included a poker, broom, shovel, and tongs.

In keeping with his bland nature, Mark also liked the white and off-white coloring of the walls, a design scheme reflected in the furniture as well. A tall white television cabinet stood between the fireplace and the far corner of the house with a cream-colored loveseat sitting in the center of the room angled toward the sliding glass doors leading to the rear deck. There was also a matching leather recliner near the knickknack shelving at the top of the stairs and a larger leather sofa along the wall. In front of the sofa sat an oval shaped glass coffee table holding an impressive replica of a three-masted clipper ship. Everything in the living room, as well as the entire house, was spotlessly clean and impeccably neat. Mark may not have had an artistic bone in his body, but he was fastidious in the way he looked and the way he lived.

Pausing at the top of the stairs, he stood quietly at the corner of the room, struggling to remember where he was going and why he was going there. Reluctant to take another step forward until he first determined his destination, he racked his brain, trying to recall why he had gone upstairs. Back in the office, the reason had been clear and immediate, but now his mind was entirely blank. "Must be getting old," he said as he switched off the light and trudged back down the stairs toward his bedroom.

The afterglows of the dying sun were still painting the foyer in soft colors, but the house next door was preventing the subtle light from penetrating the side windows, making it quite dim when Mark stepped into the bedroom. Flipping on the overhead light, he first glanced at his bed on which sat his satchel that was neatly packed but unzipped. On top of it was his pre-printed boarding pass that he had placed there earlier as a reminder not to leave without it. Lying on the bedspread beside the packed bag was a change of clothing for that evening, traveling clothes that he had laid out for himself before going to play golf that morning. Mark may not have been an exciting individual, but he was incredibly well organized.

There was a separate entrance to the bathroom from the bedroom, but Mark did not immediately head to the shower. He, instead, wandered across the room and peered out the glass doors leading to the rear deck on which sat the Jacuzzi. The twelfth green was directly behind the house beyond his small yard, and he was curious to see if any golfers were out there hurrying to finish a late round before the onset of darkness. If they were, he thought to himself, they had already lost the battle. He should know; he had lost more battles with the setting sun than he could count. Not seeing anyone on the green, he closed the curtains and proceeded into the bathroom where he turned on the light before returning to the bedroom, peeling off his shirt as he walked toward the bed.

The light from the ceiling fully exposed what his shirt had only partially concealed, the astonishing sight of his immense, bulging pectoral muscles. They appeared as hard as steel yet pliable enough to expand and contract with each breath he took. Distending from his chest, they shaded his stomach from the overhead light but failed to obscure the spectacle of his impressive lower abdominal muscles, perfectly cut and defined from years of sculpting exercises. As he bent down to loosen the laces of his deck shoes, only three razor-thin folds of skin formed at his waistline, indicating a complete absence of fat anywhere on his body. Mark then removed his shoes and stripped off the rest of his clothes before proceeding naked into the bathroom.

With his mind untroubled and his spirits elevated by a mild vacation high, he directed his eyes toward the wall above the sink counter where he glimpsed his reflection in the mirror. The sight of it triggered a rush of anxiety that swept across his emotional state like a herd of stampeding elephants, trampling his confidence and obliterating his sense of wellbeing. Hoping to avoid a complete emotional collapse, he averted his eyes and jumped into the shower, seeking refuge inside the protective glass walls of the shower stall. Hearing the click of the metal doorframe, he again felt safe and breathed a sigh of relief, unaware that he had been holding his breath until he felt a surge of air escaping from his lungs.

The shower stall occupied the entire far corner of the room, its frosted glass walls obscuring his view of the mirror. Although relieved at having taken shelter inside the enclosed compartment, he was all too aware of an indistinct danger circling him like a predator in the night, its menacing presence lying in wait, watching for the perfect opportunity to strike. He could not explain it, but something did not feel right.

Refusing to dwell on the undefined threat, he forced aside the disturbing thought and turned his back to the door panel to begin washing his hair, enjoying the relaxing massage of his powerful hands and the refreshing fragrance of the shampoo, familiar sensations that soothed his troubled mind and quieted his unsettled emotions. The spray of the warm water felt good on his body, and the comforting caress of the soap provided a much-needed sedation despite the lingering tension buried just beneath the surface of his freshly bathed skin. Increasing the water temperature to produce more steam, he wished he could stay in there forever but knew that he must abandon his water sanctuary because it was getting late. Upon emerging from the shower, he was relieved to find the mirror clouded by a film of moisture.

Reaching for a bath towel, Mark smiled when he recalled what Nikki had said upon noticing the standard size towels he used to own. She said she could not imagine him drying himself with one of those "postage stamps," so she bought him a set of oversized towels that matched his dimensions, finding them in a catalog for big and tall men. Wiping himself down with one of her giant towels, he chuckled as he removed a can of shaving cream and his safety razor from a drawer under the sink.

The moment of truth had arrived, he thought to himself while slowly lifting his head to confront the steamed mirror, unable to escape the trepidation starting to supplant his confidence and determination. Hesitating in front of the clouded glass, he felt a gnawing sense of doubt percolating up from within him as he struggled against an irrational desire to flee. The former All-American running back had become a prisoner of an unexplained neurosis that he could not shove aside like some would-be tackler. Try as he might, he could not block the resurgent anxiety swelling inside his brain, bringing with it a familiar yet unwelcome guest—fear. The shower had only masked the fear; it had not dispatched it, and he found himself questioning what he feared the most, the mirror or his own questionable mental state. As his respiration increased, he struggled to control the pounding of his heart that echoed throughout his body, especially in the recesses of his mind where the internal thumping drowned out all sensations and sounds. Although acutely aware of his current state of alarm, he could not explain why he felt the way he did.

In an extraordinary display of self-discipline, he struggled to calm his mind by forcing himself to think soundly and rationally, telling himself that he was sane and that he needed to start acting that way, that his phobia about mirrors was simply juvenile and foolish. After all, he thought, mirrors were nothing more than polished glass. How could one possibly harm him? Mark then resolved to purge the fear from his mind and, in a sudden and singular act of courage, he reached up and gallantly swept his hand across the steamed mirror, clearing a broad swath that revealed his familiar visage, the same one he had observed throughout his life. Despite his assurances to himself that his fears were unfounded and silly, he still found himself expelling a sigh of relief when nothing appeared abnormal in the mirror. Convinced that everything was all right, he reached for the can of shaving cream and spread the lather across his jaw and upper lip.

Mark's only complaint about his house related to the cheap hardware of the bathroom fixtures, especially the set screws of the faucet handles that often came loose, making it difficult to start the flow of water and nearly impossible to stop it whenever it happened. Reaching down to rinse his razor, he attempted to turn on hot water only to discover the handle spinning freely in his hand, and he remembered encountering the same problem earlier that morning. Additionally, he recalled his plan to tighten the setscrew before leaving to play golf that day, something he had forgotten to do. Annoyed by the whole situation, Mark thrust his brawny hand down onto the faucet handle and applied enough downward pressure to get the hot water flowing. The other handle was tight, so he had no problem turning on the cold water to reduce the temperature a few degrees.

The calmness he had experience in the shower returned once he became involved in the familiar routine of shaving. Looking himself dead in the eye, he dragged the safety razor across his freshly washed face without flinching or exhibiting the least amount of agitation. His beard was quite heavy, and its shadow would often appear by late afternoon, giving him an un-groomed appearance that many in his generation sported but which he found unacceptable. He preferred the clean-shaven look and endeavored to maintain that image even if it meant shaving twice a day. For years, he had used his grandfather's straight razor, but the inevitable nicks had made him switch to his father's old safety razor that cut almost as close but without all the blood. He then relegated the straight razor to artifact status, consigning it to a shelf in the living room. As he pulled the safety blade one last time across his chin to complete his second grooming of the day, he jumped slightly when a plastic soap dish fell inside the shower stall, hitting the tile floor with a loud crack. The involuntary jerk of his head caused the corner of the razor to cut his chin.

"Damn," he muttered while peering at his face in the mirror. Using the back of his wrist, he wiped away the blood oozing from the small laceration before splashing several handfuls of water onto his face. The water managed to wash away all traces of blood and shaving cream, but the tiny nick started bleeding again within seconds. To stem the seepage of blood, he applied pressure to the wound with his index finger as he turned toward the towel rack on the wall behind him, an action he never completed because of the shocking anomaly he perceived out of the corner of his eye, something that stopped him dead in his tracks.

Frozen like a statue, he allowed his mind time to ponder the illusion before it disappeared entirely from view. Unlike his prior reactions to occurrences of this type, he felt neither distressed nor frightened, and he made no sudden movements, responding instead with a considerable amount of restraint and self-control. Motionless and naked, standing with his finger pressed tightly against his chin and one arm extended toward the towel rack, he attempted to process all the sensory data flooding his brain, uncertain what it meant but determined to find out. Hoping to confirm his suspicions once and for all, he then pivoted slowly back toward the mirror, gradually rotated his body while simultaneously sharpening his peripheral vision to detect any irregularities in the world just beyond his normal gaze.

Mark did not have to turn his body far to view more of the mirror from the corner of his eye. Capturing and holding the distorted image in his mind, he stopped his motion and turned no further for fear of alerting the apparition of his intentions. This time, however, he did not do an immediate double take of the anomaly in the glass, and his restraint seemed to be paying off because the nebulous specter at the edge of his acuity remained unchanged. Laboring to *see* without actually *looking*, he strained his vision and expanded his mind to construct a mental picture of what he thought he was witnessing. The result was something he knew to be outrageously impossible, an altered reality that left him dumbstruck and doubtful of everything he had ever learned in physics class. Despite the fact that he was leaning slightly forward and standing sideways to the bathroom counter, his reflection remained erect, facing him head-on in the mirror.

With measured composure and absolute certitude, he assured himself that his observations were not the hallucinations of a madman, and the manner in which he mentally and emotionally separated himself from the moment made him feel like a scientist. No—he thought—the lunatic explanation was totally out of the question. A crazy person was never that calm or dispassionate in studying the evidence. Despite having struggled through high school physics, Mark knew that the angle of the lights and the placement of the mirror had nothing to do with any of this, although he could proffer no theory to explain the phenomenon. Nevertheless, he was convinced that all of this was real and that he was a witness to it—a sane witness.

Aware that he could not sustain his awkward pose much longer, he decided to take action, an effort he knew must be quick and unflinching. Additionally, he understood that he must be prepared to accept mentally and emotionally whatever outcome resulted from his actions, so he paused briefly to weigh his options and devise a battle plan. Then, without a moment's hesitation, he channeled all his strength and courage into one bold assault by valiantly flinging his eyes, body, and mental awareness at the mirror, demonstrating his legendary fleetness and balance, the same speed and grace he had used to attain his All-American football status. He was once again that nimble running back floating unmolested through the line, moving like a cheetah or perhaps a cobra, striking in the wink of an eye, only to have his efforts confounded by his own congruent image moving in perfect synchronization, mimicking each of his bodily movements with mocking precision. Prepared for battle, he had cast himself wholeheartedly into the arena, but his opponent had refused the challenge, leaving him frustrated and alone at the sink counter staring blankly at his own pathetic face in the mirror.

"Damn, damn, damn!" he groaned while peering into the glass. Tilting his head to one side, he watched his reflection do the same. Baring his teeth and raising his eyebrows, he saw the face in the glass to do likewise. He then turned and took a step toward the bedroom before whirling back toward the mirror only to come face-to-face with his own pivoting twin. "Damn!" he cried out again.

While all this was going on, the water from the faucet continued pouring into the sink, so he reached down and tried to shut it off, succeeding only in stemming the cold water due to the loose set screw of the hot water handle. Frustrated with himself, the mirror, and the faucet handle, he abruptly turned and stormed into the foyer without bothering to dress or even cover himself with a towel.

Across the Outer Banks, the sun had finally set leaving the external world in a dusky orange hue from the last spurts of daylight burning softly on the western horizon. Inside the house, it was mostly dark except for the bathroom, bedroom, and office doorways pouring light into the foyer. The diffused lighting also migrated upstairs into the living area where the only other source of illumination came from the horizontal beams of floodlighting leaking through the narrow slats of the window blinds.

Mark stood completely nude in the foyer with a spray of light from the bathroom doorway painting one side of his naked body. He paused briefly and glanced upstairs where he hoped to find a screwdriver to tighten the faucet handle. Deep down inside, he knew he should not be wasting time on home repairs, but he also understood the need to escape the haunted bathroom mirror if for only a second or two. Fears of mental derangement had begun gnawing at him again, and he required a distraction to quell the disturbing thoughts. Climbing the few steps from the foyer to the living room, he proceeded toward the dining room and kitchen only to halt suddenly in front of the framed mirror hanging on the wall beside the half-bathroom. The shock of what he saw nearly knocked him over, and he once again found himself frozen in disbelief before a confounding glass surface.

In the weak illumination of the ambient light filtering up from the foyer, he was able to look into the mirror and see the reverse image of the entire living room behind him. Although murky and hard to define in the subdued lighting, it was all there—the recliner, the sofa, the loveseat, all of the lamps. He could even make out the shape of the model ship on the coffee table as well as the one on the fireplace mantel. The television cabinet in the corner and the glass doors leading to the deck were also clearly visible. Everything was there—all of it—with nothing out of place, nothing except for the most prominent object in the room. Despite the fact that he stood only four feet away from the mirror, his likeness appeared nowhere in the framed glass surface. The reflection that had haunted him for weeks was entirely absent—gone—and Mark's mind could not fully comprehend what he was seeing or, rather, what he was not seeing. Consequently, he did not know what to think or what to do.

With his body as stiff as steel, he allowed his lower jaw to drop as he stared blankly at the void in the center of the mirror. Naked, with blood trickling from his chin onto his chest, he stood paralyzed with his mouth agape and his mind frantically trying to piece together all the available information to construct a theory that would explain the impossible scene playing out before him. Unfortunately, his mental faculties were not up to the task, leaving him with nothing but unanswered questions until an opportunity for gathering additional information presented itself when he spotted something along the inner edge of the mirror. At first, he paid it little heed but then redirected his eyes back to it, wondering if it might hold the key to solving this disturbing mystery. Imagining himself a scientist on the threshold of an unknown discovery, he drew closer to the mirror driven by his need to know and his desire to understand.

Slowly approaching the polished glass with his head inclined forward, he felt no fear, only awe and wonder. He stopped within a foot of the reflective surface where he identified fully what had caught his attention, something that should have upended his world but which did not even prompt a startled reaction because he was still operating in scientist mode and dispassionately willing to accept the facts as they were revealed. Emotionally detached, he displayed no reaction other than pure amazement at what he saw, recognizing the rare phenomenon for what it was, a unique and astonishing sight rarely seen in the natural world or any world of which he was aware. Uncertain if he was even sane anymore but appearing not to care, he focused his eyes on the glass and peered questioningly at his own reflection standing sideways just beyond the inner edge of the mirror, hiding from view like a thief in the night. Despite the incongruity of all he observed, he remained steadfast without recoiling at the disturbing sight, fueled on by his need to understand along with a strong desire to confront the apparition once and for all. Defiant and undaunted, he drew even closer to the mirror.

After far too many games of cat-and-mouse played with his one-dimensional opponent, Mark finally achieved the outcome he had so desperately sought, a face-to-face encounter with the elusive specter in the mirror. The outcome, however, marked much more than just an end to his confusion and uncertainty; it also signified an end to his life as he had known it. Just one more step brought him to within an inch of the mirror's surface where he observed his likeness step out from its hiding place to oppose him from the parallel plane. This time, however, it did not mimic his movements or replicate his shocked expression; it simply stood straight and tall, projecting no emotion while moving of its own volition.

When the reality of the situation finally sank in, a chorus of alarm bells began sounding in Mark's head, shattering his confidence and spreading panic through his brain. Gone was the bravado as well as his warrior spirit. Fright and bewilderment now served as the motivating catalysts driving his thoughts, leading him to conclude that retreat was his only viable option. Backing up a few steps, he watched in absolute horror as the sinister apparition move forward to the plane of the mirror, pausing just briefly before stepping through the glass as if passing through a transparent, liquid barrier. The sight of his reflection standing before him in solid form only intensified his fear, causing him to shuffle backward even faster until he tripped over the edge of the recliner, his body hitting the floor hard with a resounding thud.

In contrast to Mark's panicked reaction, the specter appeared relaxed and in complete control as it peered through the living space with an expansive sweep of its eyes, stopping momentarily when it spied something on a shelf behind the recliner. Despite the pervading darkness, the menacing twin seemed to perceive everything in the room while focusing its attention on the man sprawled helplessly on the floor before it. With a deadly glare as cold as ice, one devoid of sympathy or emotion, it took a single step forward before falling suddenly onto its prey, dropping its knee violently onto Mark's solar plexus while simultaneously sweeping the straight razor off the shelf on the wall. The speed at which it moved and dexterity with which it seized the blade were incredible, leaving Mark no time to react or even understand what was happening. Caught entirely off-guard, he responded only with an embattled groan produced by the painful expelling of air from his lungs, something that prompted the first sign of emotion in his assailant, a partial smile that tugged at the sides of its mouth in response to the sensation of Mark's breath blowing forcefully against its naked body.

Drained of both strength and oxygen, Mark found it difficult to fight back with much resistance, although he gallantly attempted to thwart his attacker by defensively raising his arms. Sadly, his efforts proved futile as his body-double easily swatted away his hands in preparation for delivering the fatal blow. With all hope lost, Mark then employed the only defense strategy left open to him, an entreating look directed at the specter bearing his likeness but not his soul. It was a silent, final plea for mercy answered only by a flicker of light from the polished steel of the straight razor beginning its descent in a curved downward trajectory, one expertly controlled by the heartless assailant. The blade then sliced through Mark's exposed neck like butter, sending a spurt of blood flying several inches into the air. Neither deep nor gaping, the wound was just large enough to sever the carotid artery.

The doppelganger did not wait for Mark to bleed to death but, instead, thrust its mouth onto the open wound, gulping blood faster than the dying heart could deliver it. It took the murderous fiend only a few seconds to drain all the life-giving fluid from the traumatized body of Mark, after which it shoved aside the corpse and began slurping the spilled blood off the hardwood floor. When it had finished, the only trace of blood left anywhere on or around the body was that of the shaving cut on Mark's chin, which the nefarious twin licked off for dessert.

The new Mark Allen then rose calmly and triumphantly to greet his new life in a foreign yet somewhat familiar world. His first action was to study his new body, an examination that left him feeling astonished and gratified at his good fortune. This was too good to be true—he thought—more than he had anticipated, far more than he could ever have imagined. "Amazing, just amazing," he said excitedly with a voice that replicated that of his host in both tone and inflection. Despite the subdued lighting in the room, he saw everything clearly, especially the strong, well-developed features of his naked, blood-spattered physique. Tensing and relaxing the various muscle groups like a bodybuilder proudly flaunting the results of years of training, he relished the invigorating feeling of absolute power radiating through the tissues and tendons of his massive frame. This is going to be fun, he whimsically mused.

Upon completing the probe of his newly acquired body, he turned his attention to the mirror from which he had emerged, approaching it with a smug expression but seeing no visual echo bearing a similar smirk, his reflected likeness now lying dead on the floor behind him. If there had been a reflection in the mirror, the only perceived difference between the old Mark Allen and the new Mark Allen would have been the eyes. The old Mark Allen possessed emerald green eyes with a hint of turquoise, an alluring feature cherished by Nikki, one she considered his most attractive quality. She would not, however, have felt the same way about his successor's eyes, which were nothing more than lifeless voids lacking any pigment whatsoever due to their inoperative irises rendering them entirely transparent. The absence of light-controlling muscle fibers also left his pupils grossly dilated, causing them to float like giant black orbs in a sea of white, which gave him an unearthly appearance and, consequently, made him extremely sensitive to light, especially sunlight, a peculiarity that also gave him incredible night vision.

Fascinated by the mirror, he seemed unable to tear himself away from it, carefully studying it as a child encountering something for the first time. Stretching out his hand, he gently touched the glass with his middle finger and watched the hardened surfaced transform into a thick, transparent liquid with waves and ripples emanating out from the spot where his finger had broken the fluid surface. The mirror then undulated for a few seconds until he pulled back his hand, at which time the rippling ceased and the liquid coalesced around the void left by his fingertip. Instantly, the glass became as solid and brittle as before.

Turning away from the mirror, he noticed the straight razor lying on the floor where he had dropped while feasting on his host, so he picked it up and returned it to the shelf after carefully licking off the residual blood. Afterward, he stepped over the remains of his morbid meal and began exploring his new world, prowling through the living room with the night perception of a cat, careful to protect his sensitive eyes from the light rays leaking through the window blinds. Fascinated with his new surroundings, especially the household furnishings, he showed a particular interest in the ship models, which he examined for several minutes before proceeding into the dining room.

The dining area extended all the way to the front of the house where sliding glass doors opened onto a raised deck. A wooden table with six chairs sat close to the wall opposite a breakfast bar next to a doorway leading into a modest-sized kitchen with lots of counter space and plenty of cabinets above and below the countertops. Yellow cabinet doors offset the brilliant white walls and appliances, but the colors were indistinguishable in the darkness when Mark walked into the room.

The moment he entered the kitchen, he experienced an intuitive ping, a mental flash of awareness brought on by a free-floating fragment of an unfulfilled desire of the former Mark that involved the kitchen and an object. Closing his eyes, he thought for a second and then smiled when it dawned on him—a screwdriver. Yes, he thought, a screwdriver. But not just any screwdriver—a Phillips head screwdriver! With that in mind, he began searching the kitchen drawers for the tool, not knowing why he needed it but surmising that the reason would eventually make itself known.

Despite his superb night vision, he found it difficult seeing into the darkened drawers; however, he was reluctant to switch on a light due to his ocular sensitivity. Casting his eyes around the kitchen, he spotted a pair of Ray-Ban sunglasses lying on the breakfast bar, so he slipped them onto his face and then flicked on a small light above the sink, grinning upon discovering that the polarized lenses made the artificial light source bearable. "Good," he said as he continued searching for the screwdriver, ultimately finding it in a drawer next to the stove.

His journey back to the stairway was more direct and less halting than his first trek through the upstairs because he no longer had to evade the stinging rays of the outside floodlights. Still wearing the sunglasses, he resembled a naked movie star as he paraded casually down the stairs into the foyer. The avant-garde image he projected was not quite Marcel Duchamp's *Nude Descending a Staircase, No. 2*, but it was close, and the contrast of his outlandish appearance to the famous French painting amused him, leading him to chuckle as he muttered some obscure saying in French.

Having already confirmed his ability to tolerate artificial light sources while wearing the dark glasses, he walked boldly into the lighted office but did not stay long, making only a quick pass around the desk before flicking off the overhead light on his way out of the room. Sticking his head into the bedroom, he thought heard the sound of running water, the same faint sound he had heard while upstairs and in the foyer but which he had chosen to ignore. Now, drawn to the noise, he followed it into the bedroom where he noticed the packed satchel lying on the bed along with the airline document sitting on top of it. Picking up the boarding pass, he glanced casually at it and then tossed it into a wastebasket before proceeding into the bathroom, once again following the sound of running water.

Hot water continued gushing out of the open spigot as Mark reached down and turned the faucet handle several rotations, scowling at the faucet when he detected no change in the water stream. Determining the problem to be the setscrew, he glanced curiously at the screwdriver in his other hand and then smiled broadly upon ascertaining the purpose of the tool, becoming extremely satisfied with himself for having solved the mystery.

Firmly placing the tip of the screwdriver into the slots of the setscrew, he gave it a few tight turns to secure the faucet handle, a simple act that let him stem the flow of water and restore silence to the room.

Except for a small area directly above the sink basin, the wide bathroom mirror was clear of moisture, leading Mark to examine it with the same curiosity he had displayed while studying the upstairs mirror. Gazing into the polished glass, he saw only the reflection of the bathroom behind him along with a small portion of the bedroom visible through the open doorway. Once again, his likeness was absent from the reflected scene. As he had done with the other mirror, he tapped it lightly with his finger, softening the glass in a way that sent small wavelets racing across the liquid to the corners of the mirror.

Although his image did not appear anywhere in the glass, his face bore the look of fierce determination and lethal intent. Behind the sunglasses, the tiny muscles of his spectral eyes contracted while the ridge of his brow furrowed and the corners of his mouth drooped. He looked to be deep in thought as if formulating some kind of a grand scheme while standing sullenly with his fingertips resting on the bathroom counter, his eyes peering defiantly and resolutely into the glassy void before him. After a few moments of intense deliberation, his features softened and his body eased, giving the impression that he had reached some sort of resolution. Pulling back from the sink counter, he glanced briefly at his blood-spattered arms and then lifted his eyes once more toward the mirror, broadly smiling while patting the erect hairs of his flattop, creating the false impression that he could actually see himself in the mirror.

Having assumed a new demeanor, he acted like a man on a mission as he walked into the foyer and flipped on the wall switch, flooding the entire entranceway with light that also illuminated the corpse lying near the top of the stairs. He then charged up the steps and headed straight to the kitchen where he began noisily opening and closing cabinet doors before returning to the living area with four heavy-duty trash bags and a large butcher knife, which he deposited on the floor beside the body of his host. Standing above his vanquished foe, he glanced down at the remains, peering impassively at his own likeness for a few moments before bending down to begin his grisly chore.

Forty-five minutes later, a reanimated Mark Allen stepped from his bedroom, freshly washed and fully clothed. The time was nine-thirty. Still wearing his sunglasses, he adjusted the collar of his white Oxford shirt and then grabbed his car keys from the table in the foyer, jamming them into the pocket of his neatly pressed jeans as he opened the front door and stood pensively on the threshold of his newly-acquired albeit ill-gotten life. By then, nighttime had spread throughout the region, and he found himself acutely aware of the nocturnal sounds and smells surrounding him in the warm night air. Closing his eyes, he inhaled deeply with the eagerness of a newborn child greeting the world for the first time before he reached down and lifted four bulky trash bags, two in each hand, which he carried off into the night. His departure from the house marked the beginning of his long-awaited adventure, a journey requiring that he first lay to rest his deceased host in an undisclosed location, one that would forever remain a mystery to the inhabitants of this world.

CHAPTER 3

"He's such an ass. I don't know what you saw in him in the first place." The girl punctuated her sentence by jamming an oversized portion of seafood salad into her mouth.

"Maria, I think I know what she *saw* in him." The blonde girl giggled while sheepishly glancing in Nikki's direction.

"Yeah, yeah, yeah," Maria said between chews. "He may be built like an Olympic weightlifter, and he may be the only man on the beach taller than Nikki, but he's still an ass—and a boring ass at that!"

All three of Nikki's friends began laughing while she smiled politely at them from across the table. She knew that they meant well, and that is why she had agreed to dine with them at Mulligan's that Sunday evening. Two days had passed since Mark had stood her up, and she had no real reason for feeling lighthearted; however, she felt obliged to make her friends believe that their efforts to support her had not been undertaken in vain.

Two of the girls at the table, Maria and Patty, were former schoolmates of Nikki. They had followed her down from Norfolk shortly after she landed a job in Nags Head. Maria quickly found work as a dental hygienist, but Patty had difficulty finding a good paying job, bouncing around from temporary job to temporary job until Nikki found her a stable position as a receptionist in a doctor's office. Nikki always felt a little protective of Patty, knowing that she needed someone to look after her. Conversely, she did not feel the same way about Maria, who was quite capable of fending for herself.

With an alluring dark complexion and a sultry personality to match, Maria always made a conscious effort to emphasize her Latin heritage in the way she dressed and the manner in which she presented herself. Even at their casual get-together that night, she wore a bright red off-the-shoulder top with black eyelet shorts and black high heels. Patty, on the other hand, projected an innocent tomboy image at all times, that night wearing her usual beach attire: a white Dolman tee shirt with lemon printed cut-off boyfriend shorts and white sandals.

The third girl at the table was Jan, an attractive girl with long dark hair and a deep, raspy voice that men seemed to love. Like Maria, she looked a little overdressed for the evening in her strapless tie-dye dress, hoop earrings, and large sea-life necklace. Conscious of the coordinated overdress of Maria and Jan, Nikki suspected that they had more in store for her that evening than just consoling her at a sunset meal at Mulligan's.

Jan was the first person Nikki had met after moving to Nags Head. She worked as an executive assistant at the local bank where Nikki kept her financial accounts, and she took it upon herself to show Nikki around the Outer Banks upon her arrival, introducing her to some of her friends and ensuring that she felt at home in the area. After that, Maria and Patty arrived on the scene, and they immediately bonded with Jan. The three of them then formed a wild trio that frequented all the local nightspots, going wherever dance music was playing and alcohol was being served. The one stabilizing force in all of their lives was Nikki.

Nikki had never shown much interest in the party scene. Despite the prodding of her friends, she rarely joined them in their nightly escapades, but that never stopped them from asking. Her relationship with Mark had been the expressed reason she had given for declining their invitations; however, that relationship had now ended, and she knew she would have to come up with a new excuse.

Jan noticed Nikki's smile fading, so she chimed in. "Well, did you go over to his place and confront him?"

"Actually, I did." Nikki quickly answered, awaiting an opportunity to give a full accounting of what had happened. "When he hadn't shown up by ten o'clock, I started calling him on his cell phone, but he never answered. The call kept jumping to voicemail, so I left him messages—*many* messages. I also tried his landline, the one he keeps in his office, but I only reached a recorded announcement telling me to call back after he returns from vacation. The voicemail function was turned off, so I couldn't leave a message on that phone."

A waitress stopped by the table just long enough to drop off four more glasses of Pinot Grigio before disappearing into the crowd on the second-floor deck. The sun was setting over Jockey's Ridge State Park along the bypass, and almost everyone was outside on the Tiki Deck listening to the sounds of the guitar player and enjoying the vibrant colors of the sunset over the dunes. With several people blocking the girls' view of the retiring sun, they could only glimpse the magnificence of the sunset by observing the tinting of the clouds overhead. However, their seats along the railing afforded them an unobstructed view of the ocean and Cottage Row where the old-style beach homes stood ablaze in a spray of waning orange sunlight. Nikki reached down for her glass and took a sip of wine before continuing.

"By ten-fifteen, I was starting to worry, so I jumped in my car and drove over there. Since I have a key to his place, I went inside, but everything looked normal—spotlessly clean as usual."

"Yeah," Jan said while tugging up the front of her dress to prevent it from exposing more than she had intended, "We've heard all about Mr. Clean and his hygiene fetish."

That remark started Patty giggling, and she quickly glanced at Nikki to see if it was okay to laugh. Just then, a blast of wind swept across the deck, blowing napkins off the tables and causing the pink and yellow flags on the railing to snap briskly in the stiff breeze. While observing Patty brush away the blowing strands of hair from her face, Nikki smiled benignly at her, signaling that her giggling had not been offensive.

"In his bedroom," Nikki continued, "I found his duffle bag sitting on the bed, packed but not zipped shut. I looked through it, but nothing seemed odd or out of place. Nothing in the entire house seemed out of place except for one thing."

"What?" Maria asked.

"His airline boarding pass for our flight to Hawaii."

"What about it?"

"I found it in the wastebasket beside the bed. Why was it *there?*" Nikki asked with an air of incredulity.

"Because, Nikki," Maria said, "he's a chicken shit who decided at the last minute he didn't want to go to Hawaii with you, and he didn't have the balls to tell you to face-to-face or any other way for that matter. I don't care how much the guy can bench press, he's a coward and a wimp—and a freaking ass!"

Nikki did not say anything for several minutes. Rather than respond to Maria's assertion, she remained stone-faced and gazed across the deck at the guitar player in the corner. Meanwhile, her three friends stared at her, each one wondering who should say something next.

Despite all she had endured over the past few days and the emotional toll it had taken on her, Nikki remained in control, wholly in command of her life both present and future. Composed as always—and confident—she projected an image of assertive self-assuredness softened by the grace and poise of an inherent kindness. At five feet, eleven inches tall, she cut quite a figure for a woman. Tall, slender, and athletic, she attracted a lot of attention from the opposite sex; however, it was mostly restrained attention from men who found her too intimidating to pursue, remaining content to observe her from afar. Her hair was extremely blonde, almost to the point of appearing white, and she usually had it pulled back into a ponytail. Dressed far more conservatively than both Maria and Jan that night, she wore cropped linen lime-green pants with rolled cuffs and a cream-colored tunic top along with simple flat canvas shoes. Because of her stature, she rarely wore heels. No flashy or lavish jewelry adorned her appearance except for a pair of gold hoop earrings and a fine gold chain around her neck connected to something concealed beneath the neckline of her top.

When she turned back to her friends and saw them watching her, she continued her tale. "At that point, I wasn't sure what to do. I thought maybe something had happened to him, but I didn't know if I should call the police or check the hospital. I eventually left his place, and, while I was sitting at the traffic light by the Outer Banks Mall, I saw him drive by!"

"You what?" Jan asked.

"Yeah, I saw him drive by. It was him all right, driving his storm gray Infiniti, and he went right past me, heading south down the bypass. Even though it was dark, I could see into the passenger's side of his car, and there was no one there, just him."

Jan reached over and touched Nikki's arm. "What did you do then?"

"I tried to pull out before the light changed, but the traffic was too heavy. Eventually, I was able to make the turn, but not before a bunch of cars got between us. By then, he was too far away, and I couldn't see him anymore."

"Did you manage to catch him?" Patty asked in her usual squeaky voice.

Nikki shook her head. "No. By the time I got to Whalebone Junction, I didn't know which way he had gone, if he had headed down toward Hatteras or if he had crossed the causeway over to my place. I figured he must be going to see me, so I went back to Pirate's Cove, expecting to see him sitting outside my condo, but he wasn't there when I arrived. I asked Gene at the guardhouse if Mark had come through, but he said he hadn't seen him. At that point, I really didn't know what to do. I couldn't call the police to file a missing person's report because I had just seen him. He seemed all right when he passed me on the highway, driving his car as if nothing was wrong. What could I do?"

Taking a bite of her Asian chicken salad, Jan attempted to speak but realized that she had put too much in her mouth, so she raised her hand for the others to wait a second. Visually frustrated, Maria shot her a perturbed look and asked the question for her. "What did you do after that?"

"Nothing."

"Nothing?" Jan asked after swallowing her food.

"Yes, nothing. Well, I have to admit, by then I was starting to get angry."

"*Starting?*" Maria was beside herself. Wagging her head violently, she said amid the jingling of her gold medallion earrings, "Nikki, you're too nice. If it were me, I would have already hired a hit man to take him out. You were just *starting* to get angry?"

Her question made Nikki smile. "Yes, I understand," she said, "but you know." Shrugging her shoulders, she continued, "Anyway, I was really pissed off by then. Not just then but all Friday night— and Saturday too. I didn't call him the rest of that night or during the day yesterday, waiting to see if I'd hear from him, which I didn't. By nine o'clock last night, I was really fuming, so, once again, I jumped in my car and drove over there."

"All right," Patty chimed in. "That's my girl!" While she spoke, she bobbed and weaved like a shadow boxer, jabbing punches at the others sitting around the table.

"So get this," Nikki said. "Before going there, I stopped by Cahoon's Market because I needed to pick up something."

"A gun?" Maria asked with a wink in Jan's direction. "Oh, that's right. I forgot. You can't buy a gun at Cahoon's."

Jan laughed and added, "Yeah, you can buy everything else at Cahoon's but not a gun."

Nikki waited for them to finish clowning around before resuming her story. "I pulled up in front of the place and saw that there was an open spot right at the bottom of the steps by the entrance. I was so focused on getting that parking space that I didn't pay attention to the other cars parked around me, so it wasn't until I turned off the engine and prepared to open the door that I saw him."

"Who?" Patty blurted out.

"Mark … walking out of Cahoon's," Nikki answered, her face totally expressionless.

"You mean *The Asshole*." Maria quipped with a laugh and a snort.

"No, no," Patty said, trying to quiet Maria. "I want to hear this. What did he say?

"Nothing," Nikki said while raising both hands in a posture of defeat and disbelief. "He looked at me through the windshield and acted as if he hadn't seen me or, worse yet, as if he didn't know me."

"What?" Maria asked skeptically.

"Yes," Nikki said. "He looked straight at me—actually straight through me—sitting there in my Jeep Patriot before he turned and walked to his car. He was parked about four cars away, but I hadn't noticed his Infiniti when I first pulled in. And get this. He was wearing his sunglasses in the middle of the night. What's with that? Oh yes, it also looked like he was carrying a bottle of wine when he walked out of the store."

Patty seemed the most intrigued by what she had heard. "Nikki, what did you do? Did you go after him?"

"No, I was too dumbstruck—and paralyzed. I just sat there staring out the windshield until I finally glanced over in his direction, but, by then, he had already driven away. I don't even know which direction he went. He was just gone, and I continued sitting there like a fool." Nikki's mood immediately changed, and the girls got their first glimpse at the sorrow and grief she had been concealing.

At that point, Maria spoke up. "Let me see if I have this right," she said, "because I still can't believe that anyone, not even an asshole like Mark Allen, would have the balls to do this. He invites you to go to Hawaii with him for ten days despite your demand that he sign a chastity pledge, which probably included forced neutering before the trip."

Patty started giggling again when she heard Maria's comment about the neutering but stopped the moment she saw Nikki glance her way.

"Of course," Maria continued, "you then have to go out and buy all new clothes, which probably cost more than the vacation itself. Afterward, the jerk doesn't pick you up when he says he will or even call with an explanation, and you end up missing your flight, not to mention your entire vacation. He won't answer his phone or return any of your messages. And, to top it off, the next day he pretends not to see you or, rather, not to know you, and he simply drives away. Is that an accurate portrayal of this whole sordid affair?"

Nikki slowly shook her head as tears began pooling in the corners of her eyes.

Maria then leaned toward the middle of the table as if preparing to divulge a secret, which caused Jan and Patty to do the same in order to hear what she had to say. While poking the air a few times with her salad fork, she spoke sharply and distinctly, "Well, then I say, f—" Making eye contact with a five-year-old girl at the table next to them, she cut short her comment and paused briefly to rephrase her remark, delivering it in a more subdued tone but with added flair. "I say s-c-r-e-e-e-e-w him!" With an exaggerated wag of her head, she leaned back and punctuated her statement with a dramatic toss of her fork into her empty salad bowl.

All three girls, including Nikki, burst out laughing at her theatrical display. Even the young girl at the table next to them started giggling, causing Maria to hunch forward and wave at the little girl, who happily waved back at her. The levity of the moment seemed to dispel the tension and seriousness of the matter with the girls soon laughing, joking, and taking turns debasing the name of Mark Allen, now former boyfriend of Nikki, who had become the brunt of every joke and insult they could contrive. At one point, Jan said to Nikki, "What's he going to do? He has no friends other than you. It serves him right if he's forced to spend the rest of his life alone."

From the sound of the merriment coming from their table after that, it would have been hard to guess the disappointment, pain, and frustration Nikki felt at being rejected and abandoned by someone she had considered her soulmate. To forget and move on would require tremendous effort on her part along with the assistance of her three rowdy friends. They were a fun-loving crew, always capable of raising her spirits, but, most of all, they were friends in the true sense of the word. When they had heard of Nikki's misfortune, they immediately dropped everything and insisted that she join them at Mulligan's for dinner. Their primary mission had been to cheer her up, which they seem to have accomplished. Their secondary objective was to get her interested in someone else, another man much more deserving of her affections, someone who would treat her right and make her forget Mark

Allen, who by the end of the evening had been sardonically dubbed "The Asshole."

Mulligan's Raw Bar & Grille where the girls sat on the outside deck was a two-story building with yellow shingles and pink storm shutters. Located between the bypass and the beach road at Milepost Thirteen near Jockey's Ridge, it served food on both levels and drinks at all three of its bars: an outside Tiki Bar on its second-floor wraparound deck, an upstairs bar that zigzagged the entire length of the room, and an octagon-shaped tavern bar—also known as the Gazebo Bar—attached to the side of the building next to the downstairs dining room. The pale yellow of the lower dining room walls nicely complemented the conch-shell pink of second floor, giving the establishment a beachy, almost island-like charm and atmosphere. Known for its excellent food and a lively crowd, the upper bar and Tiki Deck would get jammed during the summer season, especially on Karaoke nights and whenever musicians performed on the outside deck, and that is exactly the way Dave found it upon climbing the stairs to the second-floor bar that Sunday evening.

"Commodore!" The man behind the bar became as rigid as steel with his hand glued to his forehead in a military-style salute the moment he spotted Dave at the top of the stairs. With a small nose out of proportion to the size of his head, the bartender appeared to be in his early thirties with a slight paunch around the middle and a perfectly round face that bore an affable expression at all times. His hair was short and sandy, and it stood straight up, giving him a fuzzy Kuala bear appearance.

Remaining at attention, the bartender held his salute while shuffling his feet in place, turning his body to follow his friend's progress toward the bar. Dave's usual seat was taken, as was every other chair and table in the place, so he sauntered to the end of the bar and stood by the waitress station near a glass door leading to the Tiki Deck. It was not until Dave had parked himself at the corner of the bar that the bartender relinquished his formal salute.

Dave did not say a word but instead glanced longingly at his usual seat currently occupied by someone else. The bartender immediately caught the inference and spoke up. "You know ... tourists," he said with a shrug and a grin before commenting, "What can you do?" Dave did not reply but continued gazing despondently at his favorite chair, to which the bartender said, "Oh, I suppose I'm now expected to anticipate your arrival and reserve that chair for you." He said it loudly and emphatically while glancing around to ensure that everyone at the bar was watching his performance.

Dave still did not respond and instead began searching the space on the bar top in front of him as if looking for something he had misplaced. Picking up a cardboard drink coaster, he peeked beneath it before directing a forlorn gaze at his friend behind the bar.

The bartender understood that inference as well. "Oh, pardon me!" he said. "How is it that I failed to have a brew waiting for you so that you might quench your parched lips? And, lest I forget, a bowl of clam chowder to replenish your strength while you unload your burdensome day upon the shoulders of this lowly bartender?" As he turned to fill another customer's drink order, he pointed his finger back at Dave and said rather good-naturedly, "Buddy, you've been hanging around the Mayor too long."

Grinning at his friend's antics, Dave finally engaged him. "Well, Travis," he said, "since I stop in here every day, sometimes multiple times a day, is it too much to ask that I receive stellar, immediate service?" He spoke the words to the retreating figure of his friend who pretended not to hear him. "Besides," he said a little louder, "I'm your best customer." Seeing that Travis intended to ignore him, he added, "And how about a little more respect from the hired help around here?" In response to that comment, the bartender glanced over his shoulder and flashed a broad grin before returning to his drink mixing.

Dave was right; he was their best customer. In fact, the inside of Mulligan's is where he had spent most of his time since his arrival in the Outer Banks three months earlier. He stopped in every afternoon, usually after an exhausting day of watersports, and he stayed until after dark. Most of his meals were consumed there, usually a large bowl of New England style clam chowder and several beers. Sometimes he would add a little variety by switching to the Coastal Carolina Crab Bisque or by adding a salad to his order, but his diet consisted mainly of clam chowder of which he was somewhat of a connoisseur, having sampled many versions of it up and down the eastern seaboard.

When Travis had finished with the other customers, he returned to his friend at the corner of the bar while signaling to a waitress on the floor to bring Dave his nightly order of soup and crackers. Taking notice of this, Dave called over to her, "Make it the crab bisque tonight. Okay, Susie?"

The girl nodded while Travis laughed and said to his friend, "So, we've decided to make some changes in our life, have we? What's next? Will you be getting a regular nine-to-five job?"

"Fat chance," Dave remarked with a smirk.

"So, Buddy, what are you drinking tonight? Maybe you want to make some changes in that area too. Scotch? Vodka? Ouzo ... maybe a blender drink with a paper umbrella? How about you get crushed with our Orange Crush signature drink?"

"Have you started carrying my beer yet? If not, I may have to start going somewhere else to get it."

Travis smirked at the mere suggestion that Dave would take his business elsewhere, and he said to him, "Do I look like I wield any power around here? You need to talk to Gus about your alcohol preferences. Until then, the beer selection remains the same." Glancing to his right, he noticed Sally joining him behind the bar at the far end of the room. "Ah, my executive assistant has arrived," he said with a hand gesture, one indicating that he had seen her. Signaling back, she noticed Dave standing there, so she waved to him also. Sally was a mousy-looking girl in her late twenties with curly brown hair and a terse expression suggesting a volatile personality. She worked chiefly as a table server but would occasionally fill in behind the bar whenever needed. Continually complaining about being cold, she always wore a Mulligan's sweatshirt even when working the outside deck on hot summer days.

"Well," Travis said to his surfer friend, "what's it going to be?"

Dave thought for a moment and then noticed a banner for Dos Equis hanging behind the bar. He said, "I'll have a Dos Equis—no, a Dos Equis Amber."

"Good choice," Travis said as he turned to fill the order.

It was extremely crowded in the upstairs bar that night with the indistinct garble of voices filling the room. Occasionally, the door to the deck would open as servers passed in and out, allowing the music of the outside guitarist to drift in and blend with the overlapping voices and laughter of the people in the barroom. While listening to the snippets of songs and partial conversations, Dave waited patiently for his beer and soup while watching the others eat and drink around him. Although he was inside, he still wore his sunglasses, not bothering to remove them because their photochromic lenses had lightened to where he could see indoors without straining his eyes. Glancing through the door, he was unable to see anything on the Tiki Deck because of the outside darkness, and it surprised him how quickly night had fallen. Just then, several overhead strings of clear incandescent bulbs flicked on, illuminating everything on the deck so that he could observe the many customers sitting at the wooden picnic tables as well as those standing along the railing. One customer, in particular, caught his attention.

It was almost impossible for him not to notice the blonde girl in the light green pants sitting with her friends at the table just outside the door. He did not want to stare, but he could not help himself. She was quite possibly the most attractive girl he had ever seen in his life, at least up close and in person, and the effect she had on him was most unsettling. It was not his normal reaction to women, especially girls he had never met before. Despite the physical distance that separated them, he felt disarmed and vulnerable in her presence.

From her outward appearance and demeanor, it was apparent that she was not the bar hopping type of girl he expected to find in the places he often frequented. No, there was something more to her—more substance, more culture, definitely more style. Even the clothes she wore complemented the smooth curved lines of her body, appearing as fresh and new as the image she projected. Glancing down at his own attire, his old green cargo shorts and his tee shirt printed with a faded advertisement reading *Surfboards by Dewey Weber*, he chuckled while turning back to the bar, saying under his breath, "Yeah, a woman like that would really be interested in someone like me."

Just then, Travis returned with Dave's beer. "Stay thirsty, my friend," he said as he placed the bottle on a coaster. Looking around, he asked, "Where's the hero?"

"Grave?

Travis nodded.

"He's back at the house. Tough night last night." Dave said with a grin, playfully excusing his friend's absence.

Despite his name, Grave had the ability to endear himself to people and to soften the hardest of hearts. Everyone who met him liked him, and that included Dave, who allowed him to tag along solely because of his good nature. They both shared a small cottage a short distance down the beach road from Mulligan's, a one-bedroom guesthouse sitting next to a larger beach house. Being quite old and rustic, Dave assumed that the structure had once been a fish-cleaning shack that someone had converted into a cottage. A local realty company owned the home, and the property managers allowed the duo to stay there in exchange for work performed by Dave on Saturdays and Sundays. The place was really too small to rent, plus it required too many renovations to bring it up to modern day standards; therefore, the arrangement benefited everyone involved. The company acquired some cheap labor, and Dave and Grave got to spend the summer season on the beach.

Dave's principal sources of income came from giving surfing, windsurfing, and kitesurfing lessons arranged through Kitty Hawk Water Sports and a few local surf shops, mainly when they needed an additional instructor. He also earned commissions selling watersports equipment on the side. The combination of lessons and commissions generated just enough money to support his beach-bum existence, an entirely unencumbered lifestyle that he was quick to defend at the first sign of reproach. With life expectations limited to the wind, waves, and hanging out on the beach, both he and Grave seemed to have found contentment and happiness doing exactly what suited them best, and, according to Dave, nothing else mattered. However, if money ever got tight, Dave knew he could go over to Wanchese and make a few bucks repairing and maintaining marine diesel engines, tasks at which he was reasonably proficient.

"Ah, that's too bad," Travis said upon learning that Grave would not be joining them that night. "I have something for him."

"Well, you know, you really can't expect him to come back here after the way he was treated the other night."

Travis raised his hands. "I had nothing to do with that."

"I'll have you know," Dave said with a smile, "he's considering a discrimination lawsuit. Pretty soon, he'll be a protected class like every other whack-job in this world. Hell, he may even end up owning this place!"

Travis pointed his finger at his friend. "If he does, tell him I need a raise." The bartender then changed the subject by asking, "Were you out on the water today? Nice wind. Looked like some pretty good waves too."

"No, it's Sunday. I was working."

"Working?" Travis looked confused but then remembered. "Oh yeah, I forgot about that realty company gig." Pointing to the surfboard logo on Dave's tee shirt, he asked, "Are you entering Mulligan's surfing contest on Wednesday?"

"No, my competition days are over." He took a long swig of beer after making the assertion.

"What competitions?"

Dave smiled, mostly to himself. "You'd be surprised."

"We'll, anyway," Travis said while folding his bar towel, "be sure to stop by Wednesday night for the party and celebration afterward."

Just then, Sally's voice beckoned from the other end of the bar. "Travis, am I working alone here?"

"Take it easy, babe. It's good training for you." He concluded his remark with a wink in Dave's direction. Before going to wait on other customers, he turned to his friend and told him, "Let me know when you're leaving, and I'll give you that stuff to take home to Grave."

"Okay," Dave replied reflexively while glancing over his shoulder, once again casting his eyes at the captivating blonde on the deck until the sound of a bar stool scuffing across the wooden floor caught his attention. Turning back toward the bar, he saw a man vacating his favorite chair, so he grabbed his beer and scrambled straight for the empty seat, plopping himself down on it before anyone else did. Once again, everything was right with the world as he sat imbibing a cold brew in his preferred spot, a prime location that afforded him an expansive view of the entire bar. Then, as an added bonus, a waitress arrived a few seconds later, delivering to him a steaming bowl of crab soup and some crackers. Life did not get any better than this, he told himself.

Travis suddenly remembered something he wanted to tell Dave, so he rushed back to the end of the bar but found no one standing there. "Where the hell did he go?" he said under his breath while pivoting around, scanning the length of the bar with his eyes. Locating Dave in his usual seat, he walked over and pointed his index finger at him saying, "Stop with the vanishing act. Who do you think you are, Virginia Dare?" Glancing down at the bar, he asked, "What is it with you and this seat anyway?"

"I like it here, "he said. "I can keep track of everyone's coming and going. Also, this small section has more character than the rest of the bar. It's made of real wood with ceramic tile inlays on the top." He ran his hand across the tiles and smiled as he did so. Pointing to the larger portion of the bar that ran nearly the length of the room, he said, "I'm not even sure what that is made of, some sort of blue-gray composite material or something."

Travis reached over and lightly tapped the composite bar top with his fingernails before swirling his palm over the top of it. "It's Formica," he said, "And it's really smooth, kind of like dolphin skin. Almost as smooth as the Mayor's head!" A mischievous smile crept across his face. "Speaking of the Mayor, have you seen him lately? You know, he won't come in here anymore."

"And why is that?" Dave asked, the two of them exchanging smiles that revealed a common understanding. "As a matter of fact, I had lunch with him at Sam & Omie's the other day."

"What?" Travis asked melodramatically. "You ate somewhere other than here?"

The smiled vanished from Dave's face as he feigned a sober demeanor. "I warned you what might happen if you refused to stock my beer."

Travis turned and yelled down the bar. "Hey, Sally, did you know that Buddy has been dining with the Mayor at one of our competitors?"

At the mere mention of the Mayor, Sally came running down behind the bar to where Travis was standing. She spoke in a scolding manner to both of them. "I think it's terrible the way you two talk about him, especially behind his back."

"We can't say it to his face," Travis interrupted. "He's mad at us—well, mad at me at least—and he won't come around anymore."

"Shut up!" she said, shooting Travis a reprimanding glare. "I'm not through."

Travis accepted her rebuke like a schoolboy, sheepishly covering his mouth to suppress his laughter. Hoping to escape her wrath, Dave quickly lowered his head and began eating his soup, pretending as if he was not part of their verbal exchange.

"This is meant for you too, Buddy, so don't try to hide in that bowl!"

At that, Travis burst out laughing but quickly contained it when Sally turned and glared at him.

"You know," she continued, leaning closer to the two instigators, the harshness dissipating from her voice. "You guys even have me doing it now. I never noticed bald men before, but now, all of a sudden, I see them everywhere. Yesterday, at the bank, I saw five of them lined at a teller's window, and I felt obligated to call Travis so that he could come down and see them too. Of course, I didn't do it."

"Ah!" Travis let out a groan. "Five of them at once, and you didn't call me? I don't think I've ever seen five chrome domes assembled in one place at the same time—and arranged in single file to boot! You should have at least taken a picture of them on your cell phone. *You know what I mean?* Buddy does." He nodded his head toward Dave while looking at Sally.

She shook her head and glanced sideways at Dave while rolling her eyes in disgust. Then, flaring up again, she pointed a finger at Travis and said, "It serves you right if you lose your hair after all the crap you've given poor old what's-his-name. I can't even think of his real name right now."

"The Mayor!" Dave finally chimed in.

"It's not the Mayor," she said with a grin, lightly slapped his arm. "You guys just call him that, and for the life of me I don't know why. He's no mayor."

Travis saw this as another opportunity to expound on his favorite subject, so he began. "Sure he is," he said authoritatively. "He's the Mayor. He's the man. He's in charge. He runs things around here. If you don't believe me, just ask him. He knows exactly how things should be done, and he's going to tell you how to do it whether you want to hear it or not. Not only that, he'll tell you all the things you're doing wrong and how to correct them because the Mayor's way is the only way—the *approved* way. Moreover, as an added bonus, he'll tell you his entire life's story while explaining why you don't know what the hell you're doing. You have to understand, though, when you have that kind of power and authority, you've got to expect some grief. What can I say? I'm that grief!"

"You're an ass!" Sally remarked before returning to her spot at the other end of the bar.

Travis ignored her insult and her subsequent departure, continuing on the same topic with Dave. "Buddy, you should have seen this afternoon. A guy was in here all *mayored-out*, not a hair on his head. I immediately anointed him the vice-mayor." He turned and shouted down the bar, "Hey Sally! I'm telling him about the vice-mayor who was in here today."

"That poor man!" Sally exclaimed, trudging back down the bar to stop right in front of Dave. "Do you know, Buddy, that Travis had me take a picture of the two of them together, and I was stupid enough to do it."

"Yeah," Travis said, "She took a picture of us on her phone. When she sends it to me, I'm going to have a print made and hang it downstairs in the Gazebo Bar. I've decided to have pictures taken with all the would-be mayors who come in. Then, later on, when we have a number of them, you can bring the real Mayor in to choose his successor. You know, Buddy, you're the only one who can get the Mayor in here. He likes you. He won't even speak to me. For some reason, he blames me for all this mayor crap."

"I wonder why?" Sally retorted.

Dave looked at both Travis and Sally with an odd glint in his eyes. He said, "You realize, don't you, that the Mayor is not totally bald."

"What do you mean?" Sally asked.

"He's not bald. He has hair on both sides of his head that he shaves off. You can't see it, but it's there. He has male-pattern baldness—a 'commode-head' as my grandfather liked to call guys like him."

Travis looked perplexed. "A *commode-head?*"

"Yeah, someone with hair only around the sides of his head like a toilet seat—a *commode* seat as my grandfather would say."

Both Sally and Travis started laughing.

"When we were young, he'd call us commode-head kids, but we had no idea what a commode was. We just thought it was a funny name he used, so we began calling each other commode-heads."

Travis could not contain his laughter, which quickly spread to the others sitting close to them at the bar. "I love it," he said, "but I don't care about the reason for his hair loss. He's still the Mayor and still a know-it-all chrome dome!"

Sally and Travis continued bickering with each other while Dave enjoyed the rest of his soup and the humor their playful confrontation provided. Ultimately, the two bartenders had to suspend their arguing and return to waiting on customers, leaving Dave alone to observe and study those around him that evening, especially the blonde girl and her friends sitting out on the deck.

"So it's settled," Jan proclaimed while raising her wine glass in the air. "All men are bastards, especially the one whose real name shall never be spoken, *The Asshole*!

"Hear, hear!" exclaimed Patty with a lift of her glass as Nikki and Maria followed suit, consummating the toast with a resounding clink.

By this time, Nikki was ready to concede that her friends were probably correct, that she had been foolish to become involved with Mark, a man somewhat lacking in charisma almost to the point of being totally dull as Maria liked to point out. Perhaps Maria was right, she thought. Perhaps all three of them were right. Perhaps it was not so great a loss after all.

At the sound of their glasses chiming in unison, she made an internal pact with herself not to let disappointment get the best of her. Her personality was too strong and her temperament too confident to be broken by—of all people—an investment counselor. Perhaps it was the liquor causing her sudden change in attitude, or maybe it was the influence of her three rowdy friends. Whatever it was, she knew that she could not rely on alcohol or her friends to sustain her over the long run. Ultimately, it would be her faith in herself and her trust in her own capabilities that would get her through this stormy period of her life, a promising life that had followed a prescribed and foreseeable course up until then.

Nikki was not your average woman. Even at her young age, she possessed the poise and strength most women never achieve in a lifetime. Her depth of character combined with her high intelligence quotient made her a threat to most men, and, for that reason, she had rarely dated prior to meeting Mark, finding the whole male-female relationship game unappealing. As she toasted the fact that most men are jerks, she truly meant it, as opposed to her three friends who were only clowning around.

Despite her ability to intimidate men and her dislike of dating rituals, she and Mark had somehow managed to forge a relationship that had lasted two years. He did not seem threatened by her, if only because he was too boring to be threatened by anything, and he did not engage in the silly relationship games she found so repugnant, being too preoccupied with his investments and numbers to even think in such terms. He was quite good at his profession. In fact, it was his expertise and sound investment advice that had enabled Nikki to purchase her condominium at Pirate's Cove using the money she had acquired in the stock market along with what she had earned working in a profession that she loved. She knew that she would miss Mark, but their breakup would give her more time to devote to her career. Although their relationship had ended—at least as far as she was concerned—she still wished to learn why he had done it, why after all this time he had decided to start playing games. As she drank the last sip of wine from her raised glass, she made a mental note to look into it if the opportunity ever presented itself.

To her, that swallow marked the end of the evening, so she glanced up at the string of incandescent bulbs suspended over her head and said, "Well, girls, the streetlights are on, and that means I must call it a night. Tomorrow's a work day."

"What do you mean?" asked Maria. "You're on vacation for ten days."

"I called and canceled it."

Patty reached over and touched her arm. "No, Nikki, you should still take some time off."

"Yeah," said Jan. "Go away somewhere. Fly down to the islands—St. Thomas, St. John, anywhere."

Nikki smiled. "I don't think so. I wouldn't have any fun. If I'm going to use my vacation days, I don't want to be in a funk while I'm doing it. Besides, there's a hurricane down in the Caribbean." She turned toward Jan. "You have to work tomorrow too." Glancing at the others, she added, "All three of you do."

Jan sipped her wine and looked sideways at Maria. "I never let my job interfere with my social life," she said with a devilish look on her face.

Nikki studied Jan and Maria suspiciously but said nothing at first. Knowing them well, she could interpret their eye contact and read their thoughts. "I knew you two were dressed a little too hot for our girl's get-together tonight. What are your plans?"

Jan and Maria continued looking at each other, waiting to see who would be the first to speak, when Patty started giggling and said, "We're heading down to the Port O' Call to hear the band—and to dance. You should come along." At that, Maria and Jan turned toward Nikki.

"Not on a Sunday night. Not on *this* Sunday night," Nikki said.

"What are you going to do instead?" Maria asked. "Go home and watch an old movie on TV, probably one of those ancient musicals you love so much?"

"What's wrong with musicals?" she asked. "They're wholesome ... and romantic."

"Yeah, look where romance got you," Maria added bluntly.

Using a smile to hide the pain reignited by Maria's comment, Nikki said, "You forget, Maria, that I danced in high school and college, and I also performed in a lot of musicals."

"Well, then," Jan added while gyrating her torso and waving her arms in the air, "dance the night away with us!"

Nikki turned and gave Jan a matronly stare that caused her to drop her arms.

"Okay, okay," Jan said. "Then, instead, come out with us to Kelly's on Saturday night. My brother's band is coming down from Norfolk. You can show me your dance moves then."

"That's a great idea," Patty chimed in while Jan and Maria stared silently at Nikki, all of them awaiting a response.

"Okay," she said a little reluctantly. "Saturday at Kelly's—unless the hurricane hits us."

"Wonderful!" Jan said with a beaming smile. "I also want you to meet my brother. He's a fantastic guy. I think you'd like him. Besides, you need a little excitement in your life. You need to set that dancer free, and my brother can help you do that. He is anything but boring, not like you-know-who."

"*The Asshole?*" Maria asked.

Jan did not answer but sipped her drink while smiling at Maria.

Maria turned to Nikki. "Now don't forget; you agreed to go out with us on Saturday night. We're holding you to it. And that's the only reason we're letting you go home tonight to dance with Fred Astaire on TV."

"Actually," Nikki said, "I prefer Gene Kelly."

Patty looked over at Maria and asked, "Is that the guy that owns Kelly's Restaurant?"

Seeing Maria's annoyed reaction to Patty's question, Jan began giggling while Nikki smiled. Nodding over toward Patty, Nikki said to Maria, "You look out for her tonight." Addressing them collectively, she then added, "And, remember, tomorrow is a workday."

"Yes, mother," Maria answered.

"And if you drink too much, take a cab or call me."

"Yes, mother," they all said in unison before starting to laugh.

Freeing herself from the clutches of her three friends, Nikki rose from the table and walked into the restaurant where something caught her attention, a comical sight that brought her to a standstill before reaching the staircase. It was a familiar scene she had seen played out many times in the past but never in real life, and she found herself intrinsically drawn to the back of a stranger sitting at the bar between two empty chairs. On either side of him, directly in front of the unattended chairs, were two old fashion glasses, each one holding a clear beverage. One glass had ice cubes in it along with a swizzle straw while the other one contained only the clear liquid with a slice of lime wedged onto its rim. Despite the overcrowded conditions in the room, no one had moved to claim the seats beside the young man, a vagabond-looking character dressed in baggy shorts and a surfing tee shirt, appearing as if he had just wandered in off the beach.

"Brigadoon!" It was a one-word observation she blurted out when directly behind the young man, her voice betraying an underlying excitement at having uncovered a ruse being perpetrated on the bar patrons that night. She felt certain she was in the company of a fellow traveler who would immediately recognize the code word she had uttered.

The unexpected force and volume of her voice startled Dave to where he almost knocked over his beer bottle. "Huh?" was all he could grunt as he spun around in his chair, becoming instantly dumbstruck at the sight of Nikki standing there. The girl from the deck—he thought—the one he had been staring at the entire evening. Her presence bewildered him, rattling his mind to where he could not recall the word she had uttered as he peered into her pale blue eyes, nervously trying to come up with something clever to say in reply.

"You know," she said with a grin, brushing away the hair from her eyes and smoothing it back behind her ear, "Van Johnson—the old movie actor in the 1954 production of Lerner & Loewe's musical *Brigadoon*."

"Miss, I don't know what you're talking about," he said honestly while silently praying for an understanding of what she was referencing so she would not turn and walk away.

Pointing down at the two glasses on either side of him, she smiled and said, "Sure you do."

With a quick glance at the drinks sitting in front of the two empty chairs, he said resolutely, "They aren't mine."

"Oh, really?" she replied with a skeptical look. "Well, then, let me refresh your memory. The scene takes place in an overly crowded barroom, such as this one." She then nodded her head toward the room, drawing his attention to the people all around them. "Van Johnson is at the bar, annoyed and bothered by the people crowding his space, especially the ones sitting on either side of him, so he comes up with a plan for when they vacate their seats. He immediately orders two glasses of water and lights two cigarettes, placing them in front of the empty chairs so it looks like the seats are occupied and just temporarily vacant. As a result, no one else sits down to bother him."

Pointing to the old fashion glasses on the bar, she continued, "Two glasses of water, just like in the movie. Of course, you can't have lighted cigarettes indoors anymore, but the straw, ice cubes, and lime garnish are a nice modern touch."

From the tone of her voice, he could tell that she was entirely pleased with herself. The smug expression on her face also made it apparent that she felt certain of her conclusions. Like a detective laying out evidence in a difficult case or a prosecutor making closing statements to the jury, she spoke with authority and conviction, unwavering in her belief that she had exposed a charade involving the two glasses.

Dave looked down at the bar, taking a few moments to study the scene before lifting his head to say with a grin, "You're absolutely right; there are two glasses on the bar. However, you're wrong about what they contain. That's definitely not water."

Nikki was an incredibly perceptive individual. Her profession required that she glean information solely through observation, making her highly attuned to visual markers. Her father liked to gamble, and he had taught her to play poker as a child. Having spent many hours playing penny ante poker with him, she had perfected the skill of knowing when he was bluffing, and she thought she saw it again on the face of this stranger.

Glancing down at one of the glasses while observing Dave do the same, she inched a little closer to the bar, moving her hand slowly toward the glass with the lime slice. Conscious of her arm movements, Dave removed his sunglasses to get a better view of what he sensed was about to happen. Nikki, for her part, studied his face, bronzed and tanned from the sun, before peering intently into the gunmetal gray of his eyes while internally struggling with a decision. Their gazes remained locked for several seconds with neither one daring to move or breathe until Dave noticed a subtle change in her demeanor, a sudden flash in her eyes that announced her decision to proceed along a course of action from which there was no return. She then reached down and removed lime garnish from the disputed drink before picking up the glass and downing the clear beverage in a single gulp.

Straight tequila passing through the esophagus on its journey to the stomach is a sensation not easily forgotten, especially when it is occurring for the first time. Such situations usually end badly with the distilled beverage exiting the stomach via the shortest possible route. Fortunately, however, Nikki was able to get her hand to her mouth in time to stop herself from vomiting all over Dave's shirt, but it meant that she then had to swallow the tequila a second time.

The hue of her face nearly matched the green of her pants as she stood gagging by the bar, fighting desperately to regain her composure. Dave also struggled, but his efforts were more to contain his laughter than anything else, something he tried to hide from her because he still considered her the most beautiful girl he had ever seen in his life despite her odd green complexion. At that very moment, the occupant of one of the chairs returned from the restroom to find his tequila gone and Nikki coughing violently beside his vacant seat, the empty glass still in her hand.

"I apologize, sir," Dave said, coming to her rescue. "You see, she started choking and picked up your glass thinking it was water. Well, you can guess the rest."

Glancing at Nikki, the man gave a snicker and then looked back at Dave with a smile. By then, Nikki had managed to stop coughing, and the greenish tint of her face had changed into the fire red of embarrassment.

"Let me get you another drink," Dave said to the man. "That was Tequila Silver, wasn't it?"

As both men turned toward the bar, Dave waved for service, but it took a few minutes to get anyone's attention because both Travis and Sally were at the far end of the room. When he leaned back to check on Nikki's condition, he found her gone, causing him to chuckle slightly as he looked down to see if humiliation had caused her to melt through the floorboards. He was still visualizing of the cool blueness of her eyes when he turned back to find Travis standing opposite him, his arms outstretched with both hands resting flat on the top of the bar. "Did you see that girl who was

70

just here?" Dave asked his friend.

"Yeah," Travis replied. "That's what I came over here, to find out who she is. I've been curious about her for a long time."

"You've seen her before?"

"On certain nights, maybe around six o'clock or so, she jogs past here. Comes down the bypass and cuts over to the beach road. I see her when I'm out on my cigarette break." He then smiled, "Actually, I plan my cigarette breaks around her appearance. What can I say? It's the highlight of my day if *you know what I mean*. Unlike the Mayor, I can still get it up. It's one of the reasons I still have my hair."

Travis then went to refill the tequila order, leaving Dave by himself to cultivate an interior quietness amid the noisy clamor of the barroom. In the serenity of the moment, he contemplated what had just occurred, and he acknowledged that he understood none of it; however, he hoped to find out someday or, at least, learn more about the pretty blonde who undoubtedly would have a lifelong aversion to tequila.

It was around ten o'clock when Dave finally left the bar and started on the short jaunt down the beach road toward his house. The location of the cottage made it convenient whenever he had to walk home after drinking too much, but that evening he was able to drive unimpaired. The night was warm and muggy with a stiff breeze blowing onshore that did little to lessen the oppressive heat. Even the wind felt hot as it surged through the open windows of the hearse. Since no one had rented the larger beach house next to him that week, he was free to park anywhere in the shared driveway before walking onto the porch where he looked through the window to see Grave lying on the couch, his face illuminated by the flickering light of the television tuned to The Weather Channel.

Dave was a daytime person, rarely staying out late so he could rise early the next morning to enjoy his favorite activities in the brilliant sunshine. He found nothing alluring about the darkness of night, viewing the long gloomy hours as nothing more than an annoyance, wishing the sun could shine continually so he could spend more time exploring the many delights daytime had to offer. However, since nighttime and his need for sleep were unalterable realities, he tried to optimize the time he spent in the sun by retiring early each evening, usually around ten o'clock, sometimes eleven. Grave, on the other hand, showed no preference for either daytime or nighttime activities, sleeping in spurts both day and night, falling asleep virtually anywhere.

When Dave walked into the house, his partner awoke with a

start, yawning dramatically before glancing at the television screen on which a meteorologist was talking about tropical storms formations in the Caribbean. "Sorry to awaken you, pal," he said to his sleepy friend, smiling as he watched the sluggish lump prop himself up on the edge of the couch in response to his greeting. The sight of Grave's yawning and stretching then sparked a memory, and Dave said, "Oh, I almost forgot. Travis sent something home for you." Turning around, he walked back out to the hearse, leaving open the door that failed to close because of a broken hinge spring. Grave then rose and followed him outside through the open door.

Dave was the first one back into the house, and he carried with him a white plastic bag holding something about the size and shape of a shoebox. "Sorry, Grave, but I have to hit the head," he yelled through the open doorway as he tossed the package at a small round table where it teetered on the edge before toppling onto the floor.

The beach house shared by Dave and Grave typified the old Nags Head style of home construction with cedar shakes covering the roof and exterior walls. It also had a tiny porch on the front of it and an outside shower located down the steps around the corner of the structure. The cottage was small, very small, sitting off the ground only about four feet, and it had only three rooms—a bedroom, a bathroom, and a single room serving as a living room, dining room, and kitchen all in one. The tiny kitchen area was equipped with a few appliances and a circular table with a single chair. The rest of the room served as living space and contained several pieces of dilapidated furniture that included a roughly hewed cedar couch and matching chair along with a heavy cedar coffee table that functioned mainly as a footstool. An antiquated nineteen-inch television set stood along an adjacent wall between two doorways, one door leading into the bedroom and the other the bathroom. On top of the television was a portable compact disc player.

The bedroom was equally Spartan, containing only a chest of drawers, a lampstand, and two uncomfortable looking twin beds arranged side by side in the center of the room. Cheap wood-grained paneling covered the cottage walls on which hung framed nautical prints more reminiscent of New England than the Outer Banks, and industrial grade linoleum served as the floor covering in all of the rooms. Rusted Venetian blinds covered the windows, and noisy, wobbly ceiling fans providing the only source of ventilation and cooling for the place.

When Dave emerged from the bathroom, he saw the white

plastic bag lying on the floor beside the table and Grave sitting next to it feasting on a rack of spareribs. The bag had concealed a Pigman's Bar-B-Que box containing the ribs. "Oh, Pigman's," he said when he saw the logo. "Travis didn't say anything about ribs."

Grave did not respond or even look up. He instead continued scarfing down the unsolicited meal. Watching his friend gnaw on the end of a rib bone, Dave said, "Next time I play delivery boy, I'll be sure to check the cargo."

For a brief second, Dave contemplated tearing off a few ribs at the end of the rack but banished the idea because he had future plans for his fingers. He knew that Grave was funny about things like that. Unwilling to endure the sight of his friend gorging himself, Dave closed the front door and switched off the television before heading to the bedroom to undress. Turning back to his friend, he said as a reminder, "Don't forget, you have that doctor's appointment tomorrow morning at nine." In response, Grave grunted rudely and continued eating without acknowledging the reminder. Unless it was slow roasted and smothered in spicy barbecue sauce, it did not rate a response.

While lying in bed, Dave thought about the crazy blonde at the bar and the strange word she had uttered at their meeting—something about a movie or a Broadway play. What was it? Brig-a-something. Brigadoon? Yeah, Brigadoon. That was it! "Hmm," he muttered aloud while pondering its meaning. Too bad she had disappeared. He would have asked her more about had she stuck around longer.

Sprawled atop his bedsheets, feeling the air from the ceiling fan lightly stroke his body, he thought more about the girl and realized that he could picture her in his mind as clearly as if she were lying there beside him. He was not usually that observant, and he found it strange how precisely he could recall the hue of her eyes and the tone of her skin. Had he been a painter or sculptor, he could have created an accurate depiction of her totally from memory. For that and other reasons, he hoped to see her again, to test his mental recollection against her unblemished countenance. If Travis were right about her jogging schedule, he might just get that opportunity. Nurturing that whimsical hope while entertaining other fanciful thoughts of Miss Brigadoon, he slowly and softly drifted off to sleep while Grave continued ingesting his late-night snack with an unrestrained abandon and gusto rarely seen in civilized societies.

CHAPTER 4

Monday morning arrived earlier expected, heralded by the disturbing blare of Dave's small but surprisingly loud alarm clock. Somewhat disoriented, he silenced the noisy beast and struggled to his feet, blinking his eyes erratically as he stumbled toward the bedroom door. He was never one to spring right out of bed to greet the day, and it usually took him a few moments to clear his head and adjust to his surroundings. Standing in the doorway, he had a clear view of the adjoining room where he noticed a piece of greasy aluminum foil lying on the floor near the kitchen table. Shaking off the lingering drowsiness, he broadened his vision to focus his eyes on the scale of the mess left by his roommate during his nocturnal eating binge.

"Pig!" he said as he leaned back into the room, grabbing a pillow off his bed and hurling it at Grave sleeping soundly on the other bed. The impact of the launched projectile caused only a slight jolt in his friend's body, causing Grave's well-defined muscles to tighten briefly before easing as he lay motionless beneath the pillow. An offensive belch was his only rejoinder to Dave's attack.

"Get up! You have your doctor's appointment this morning." Dave delivered the reminder curtly as he shuffled into the living room to clean up the mess from the previous night. Picking up the discarded foil and reaching under the table for the empty rib box, he heard snoring coming from the bedroom and realized that Grave was once again asleep. "Lazy bastard," he said with a shake of his head before walking into the bathroom to dress, putting on the same clothes he had worn the night before. Returning to the bedroom, he grabbed another pillow off his bed and tossed it at Grave with even greater force. "On your feet—now!" he commanded.

The second unwelcome assault jostled Grave just enough to get him moving, shoving his lazy bones to where inertia and gravity carried him off the bed amid a few grunts and groans. Landing unsteadily on his feet, he yawned and stretched but did not to go anywhere, choosing instead to stand perfectly still while staring at the wall. Dave might have been a slow riser, but Grave was ten times worse, welcoming the day even more gradually than his roommate. Turning toward the living room, he spied Dave standing by the front door, holding it open like a hotel doorman, so he lowered his head and marched silently onto the porch.

Since the clinic was nearby and the weather was so pleasant, Dave decided to walk. Crossing the driveway, he headed straight for the beach road with Grave following close behind. The temperature was surprisingly warm for that early hour, but it was still cooler than it would be later in the day once the sun reached its zenith. In the sky overhead, excited seagulls were enjoying the day as they cried loudly to one another, their playful songs awakening a joyful feeling in Dave as he walked along. He savored the physical sensation of being outside on such a beautiful morning with the salt air filling his lungs and the unfiltered sunshine warming his body.

The two strode briskly along the paved bicycle path of the beach road past the many houses and cottages filled with summer tourists and seasonal residents. Beach grass and sea oats grew alongside the walkway and beside partially buried snow fences erected to protect the small dunes from wind and rain erosion. Many of the cottages sat totally exposed to the elements while scraggly pines and heavy thicket encircled the other homes, insulating them from the weather and preventing a clear view of the ocean from the road. That morning was a trash pick-up day, so ninety-gallon garbage bins lined the pathway, forcing Dave and Grave to dodge them in addition to avoiding the joggers and bicyclists sharing the sidewalk with them. At times, Dave tried to hurry Grave along because it was obvious his companion was not eager to keep his scheduled medical appointment.

At East Dunn Street, directly across from the Holiday Inn Express, they crossed over to the bypass and began walking toward the clinic over the sandy soil near the edge of the road. Unlike the beach road, the bypass was bustling with cars and trucks zooming down the highway, generating hot blasts of air as they rushed past them. In the stillness of the morning, the displaced air of the vehicles was the closest thing to a breeze, and the heat of their air drafts along with the rapid rise in temperature had Dave looking forward to the air conditioning of the facility.

Seeing the white trim of the medical building a short distance away, he realized that he had misjudged the spot where he should have crossed over from the beach road. He knew that the clinic was located at the fourteenth milepost, but he had forgotten that the milepost markings on the bypass and the beach road were not always in alignment.

Like everyone living in Nags Head, as well as the many visitors to the region, it had not taken Dave long to start thinking and talking in terms of mileposts. When he had first arrived in the area, the numeric jargon of the locals and tourists seemed strange to him, everyone identifying the mileposts where they were staying while announcing how many vacation days they had left, but it did not take him long to appreciate the quaintness of the local custom and to adopt as his own. He truly enjoyed telling people that he had three hundred and sixty-five days remaining before he had to leave the Outer Banks, that is, if he chose to do so at all. Their reaction upon discovering that he was a genuine beach bum and not a vacationer made him savor his chosen lifestyle even more. Whatever it was in the real world that caused people to exhibit such envy was not something he wished to experience.

One day while sitting at the bar in Mulligan's, he found a copy of the Outer Banks Sentinel that someone had left behind, so he picked it up and began browsing the want ads. It was only out of curiosity that he opened the paper to the classifieds because he wondered what it would be like to hold down a full-time job. For the life of him, he could not imagine it or, rather, he chose not to imagine it. As he scanned the dull solicitations of mundane jobs, he finally understood the looks of envy on the faces of people when they learned what he did for a living.

His thoughtful expression while perusing the want ads must have startled Travis, who immediately came bounding down the bar, stopping directly in front of Dave where he stood grinning with a quirky look on his face. Nodding at the newspaper in Dave's hand, he smiled and said, "When I used to search the classified ads for work, the first place I'd look was under the M's for *millionaire* and *movie star*. But, I'll be damned, there never seemed to be any jobs listed." The last thing the bartender wanted was for his only living hero to grow up and get a job, so he used his offbeat humor to return Dave to reality and put an end to this want-ad foolishness.

As Dave entered the clinic, a blast of frigid air hit him square in the face, prompting him to issue a welcome sigh of relief. The outside temperature and humidity had increased dramatically during their short walk, and the air conditioning provided a welcome respite. Turning to say something to Grave, he stopped short when he found himself alone in the waiting room. "Coward," he said under his breath as he walked back outside, discovering Grave cringing near the corner of the building. "There is no use in hiding," he chided him. "C'mon, let's go!"

Realizing that escape was not an option, Grave grudgingly trudged in through the open door while Dave trailed close behind, fully prepared to thwart any attempted retreat. Grave's slow, faltering steps resembled a prisoner marching to his execution, a reaction that was totally understandable in light of his past encounters with doctors, unpleasant experiences that left him fearful and distrustful of the medical profession. The only reason he was willing to keep his appointment this day was that Dave had taken control of the situation and was forcing the issue; however, Grave's acquiescence to his friend's wishes did not mean he had to act amicably one he arrived at the clinic. Without speaking or looking around, he marched sullenly across the room and collapsed in the corner.

The waiting area was small and quiet with benches arranged around the perimeter of the room and a restroom situated at the far end. A counter stood just inside the entranceway where a receptionist in a flower-print medical smock sat updating an appointment log. Several computer keyboards and flat-screen monitors surrounded her workspace with rows of shelving positioned behind her, tall shelves filled with case files organized alphabetically and indexed with color-coded tags.

Despite Grave's proclivity for fierceness and his ability to inflict serious injury whenever threatened, he was one of the biggest wimps imaginable when it came to receiving medical care. He did not even attempt to hide his anxiety or the ridiculous image he projected by his nervous shivering and shaking while he sat huddled in the corner. Unable to register himself, he suspiciously eyed everything in the empty waiting room as Dave approached the receptionist on his behalf.

"Hi. My name is Dave Rasputin. I'm here for a nine o'clock appointment under the name—"

"Don't tell me," the receptionist interrupted. "Grave."

Dave nodded.

"That's spelled G-R-A-V-E?" she asked.

"Yeah," he said.

"And I suppose that's him over there?" She pointed to the quivering mass of Jell-O in the corner.

"The one and only," he said with a grin. Over the course of their time together, he had seen Grave face many difficult challenges, some quite dangerous by anyone's standards, situations that had required him to demonstrate a significant amount of fortitude and self-reliance just to survive. That is why Dave could not understand why Grave always fell to pieces when forced to interact with the medical profession. "What a hero," he said aloud, partially to himself and the receptionist but principally to his terrified comrade.

"Has he been here before?" she asked.

"No."

"Okay, then he—I mean you—will have to fill out these forms." She handed Dave a clipboard and a pencil and asked that he return the forms once they were completed.

Dave planted himself beside his trembling companion and looked over the two-page questionnaire. "Relax," he said. "They aren't going to hurt you. Besides, you'll feel better after you have this done." He then filled out the forms and returned them to the girl while Grave stared blankly at the wall. Afterward, they both sat and waited in silence.

"Grave ... Dave!" The call came from a young medical technician wearing navy blue hospital scrubs. She stood beside the receptionist counter holding a manila case folder in her hand. "Please come with me," she said in a cheery tone.

The two followed close behind, but Dave occasionally found it necessary to nudge his friend along when his steps began to falter. The girl motioned them toward an examination room, but she first weighed Grave on a scale in the hallway before allowing them to enter the room. Once inside, she pointed to two chairs sitting side by side. "You can have a seat over there," she said. "The doctor will be in shortly." After making some quick notations on Grave's chart, she turned and left the room.

As the door slowly closed behind her, Grave nervously eyed her exit like a condemned man watching the guards vacate the gas chamber prior to his execution. Dave, however, ignored her departure and strolled casually through the sterile room, examining the items on the counters and peering into the cabinets labeled with words he could not pronounce. Meanwhile, Grave positioned himself in a distant corner, determined to stay as far away from the examination table as possible.

Staring up at a poster extolling the benefits of some new arthritis medication, Dave had his back to the door when Nikki walked in. Upon entering, she instantly spotted Grave in the corner and exclaimed in a naturally joyful tone, "What a beautiful basset hound!"

Turning at once toward her cry, Dave did a quick double take and then grinned, astonished at seeing her again. His surprise was such that he failed to notice the dourness of her expression the moment she recognized him. "Well," he said, "if it isn't the girl who drinks her tequila straight from the bottle." His unrestrained smile became even broader once he delivered the wisecrack.

"I don't drink it straight from the bottle," she said tersely but professionally. Caught off-guard, she really did not know what to say. The embarrassment from the previous night was starting to creep in—she could feel it—but she managed to control it before it became too obvious.

"My apology," he said. "I forgot. You just drink it straight ... from large water glasses."

Dave found the whole situation ironic as well as amusing. Additionally, he experienced an overwhelming sense of joy at having found her again. He desperately wanted to confess that truth to her, but he did not think it the appropriate time or place to do, so he remained quiet instead and merely stared at her. With her blonde hair pulled back into a ponytail, she appeared exactly as he had remembered her, identical to the previous night with the exception of the white lab coat she now wore. He looked for a name tag, but she was not wearing one.

Enough time had passed for Nikki to regain her composure, enabling her to assume a more professional demeanor. In her best veterinarian voice, she said, "So, this is Grave, and you must be—" She looked down at a clipboard for his name, but Dave beat her to it.

"Van Johnson," he said. "But you already know that." The look in Nikki's eyes communicated her displeasure and told him that he better cut the humor because it was getting him nowhere.

"Please bring Grave over here," was her only response to his attempted joke.

From the tone of her voice, he knew that it would be all business from that point forward. He was on her turf now, and she had calmed down enough to regain command of the situation. Dragging Grave toward the mechanical examination table that she had lowered to the ground, Dave forced him onto it with a shove of his foot while Nikki hit the switch to raise it up again. Grave's exceptionally long toenails prevented him from gaining traction on the stainless steel table, so he stood frozen in place like a statue, totally immobile except for the uncontrolled quivering of his hind quarters. The shaking of his heavily muscled form also sent waves of motion through his incredibly long ears that hung down to the surface of the table; however, the trembling stopped and all tension faded from his body the moment Nikki placed her hand on his back.

Dave did not comment, but he noticed an immediate change in the dog. The tense, immovable rock he had dragged across the floor and forced onto the table had become a docile, furry lump. As Nikki ran her hands around the white ring of Grave's neck and plied the tan patches of his muscular shoulders, he relaxed even more and began panting in slow deep breaths. Watching all of this, Dave wished he could trade places with Grave on the examination table.

Nikki turned Grave's head so that he faced her directly, and she began feeling around his neck and under his ears, causing him to issue a long, over-dramatic yawn a few inches from her face. "Am I boring you?" she asked with a grin. Taking a stethoscope, she placed it against his ribcage to monitor his heartbeat and then moved it to his abdomen. When she encircled his body with her arm to listen on the other side, a pendant attached to a delicate gold chain slipped from beneath the open collar of her white blouse to rest against the black saddle of Grave's back. Dave took notice of the distinctive oval shape of the tiny golden medallion, but he could not clearly discern the relief image imprinted on it because it was too small. It appeared to be that of a woman with words inscribed around the edge of the medal, but he was not sure. When he tried to look closer, Nikki straightened up, and the pendant slipped back inside her shirt.

She completed her examination by checking Grave's eyes and ears before opening his mouth and inspecting his teeth. During all of this, Grave complied without any resistance or even the slightest hint of fear or distrust. Her final act was to stroke his body from his head to tail while he happily licked her face. Smiling at Grave, she said in Dave's direction, "I can see that you're not overfeeding him." A quick glance at Dave's lean body confirmed her suspicion that neither one of them ate too much. "Actually, that's a good thing," she continued. "A lot of people overfeed their basset hounds and allow them to get heavy, which leads to all sorts of issues. Their short legs make them ride too close to the ground, causing problems, especially in males due to their—"

Just then, the door to the examination room opened, and a vet technician entered, the same one that had led them back from the waiting room. "Sorry," she said. "They needed an extra hand next door." She walked over and put her arm around Grave to secure him, an action that prompted him to turn and lick her face as well.

Nikki asked Dave, "What was your main reason for bringing him here today?"

"His anal glands," he said. He's digging back there again."

Pushing on the sides of Grave's hindquarters near his tail, Nikki said, "Oh yes, they feel like they're full." She caressed his head and said, "You poor boy." Both she and her assistant then put on latex gloves and grabbed some paper towels while Nikki looked at Dave and warned, "This is going to smell."

Having been through this before, he knew what to expect, so he took a few steps back toward the wall. It was not just the threat of the odor that made him retreat; it was also an awareness of Grave's past reactions whenever others had tried to express his scent glands. He smiled inwardly as he waited to see how the two women would handle the volcano of resistance set to erupt the moment they touched his hindquarters, but, to his astonishment, there was no eruption, and everything was over in a matter of seconds without a fight. Grave's only reaction was to emit a sigh of relief in conjunction with the release of the internal pressure.

While wiping Grave's backside and winking at her assistant, Nikki looked at Dave and said with an amused twinkle in her eye, "We could teach you to do this yourself if you'd like."

"No, no, that's okay," he said without hesitation. "I'll bring him here whenever he needs it done."

In response to Dave's rejection of their offer, both Nikki and the technician smiled at each other. Nikki then began scratching Grave's ears and caressing his head. She asked, "How did you end up with such a finely-bred specimen like Grave? You don't seem like the show-dog type, and basset hounds like this are not cheap. Also, what's with his name?"

"Actually," he said. "I found him."

"*Found* him?"

"Yeah, it was along Interstate 95 in Georgia on Halloween a few years ago. I was heading to Florida for the winter, and I spotted a mother and three pups walking along the side of the highway. I pulled over to get them before a car hit them, but they all ran off, disappearing into a dense clump of bushes—all but one. I managed to catch him, and we've been together ever since. I tell people that I saved him from an early grave, hence his name."

Dave told his story casually without revealing how much he cared for Grave and how his affection had grown over the years. Before their meeting, Dave had not been a dog person. If anything, he had been dismissive of pet ownership. Even now, after their years together, he insisted that Grave was a free agent who could leave anytime he wished; however, Dave knew would search high and low if he ever lost him. So far, Grave had chosen to stay, and Dave's life was a little less lonely because of it.

Nikki looked at him, unsure if she should believe him; but, because of his admission that the dog had once been a stray, she grabbed a scanner and checked Grave for an identification microchip. The results were negative, so she examined the tags on his collar and asked, "Are you aware that he's due for his rabies vaccination?" She did not wait for an answer before telling the technician, "I'll need a dose of rabies' vaccine." The girl immediately dashed out the door, leaving Dave and Nikki alone together in the examination room where they stared at each other in silence.

Dave enjoyed their time together waiting for the return of the vet technician, and he studied Nikki in the bright, sterile light of the examination room. She was even prettier than he remembered. In the dim lighting of the bar at Mulligan's, he had not noticed the small dimples on the sides of her face that appeared only when she pursed her lips, which she was doing at that moment. He could sense the tension and stiffness in her body, and he attributed it to how they had met last night; however, he did not let her anxiety deter him from enjoying every moment spent in her presence. Similar to the previous night, a few strands of hair had broken free from her ponytail to dangle softly across her pale blue eyes. She made no effort to brush aside the fine threads while maintaining her unbroken gaze, staring at him through the golden filaments. He found himself standing unusually straight, unsure of his height in relation to hers but feeling confident that their eyes were meeting on a parallel plane. He then noticed for the first time the slight upturn of her nose a well as the soft hairs near her ear and jawline, delicately wisps that resembled peach fuzz. He wanted to reach up and caress them with the back of his fingers.

As delightful as Dave found their time alone together, Nikki's experience was the exact opposite, a living hell that seemed to drag on forever. This guy is dangerous, she thought, and yet she was unable to look away from him, finding herself drawn into his steel gray eyes and imprisoned by his piercing stare. The longer she looked at him, the harder it became for her to control her anxiety and its peculiar effect on her, that of pulling her closer to him rather than pushing her away. She was losing the battle—she could feel it—but she was unable to do anything about it. Where is that damn vet tech?—she silently asked herself.

At that very moment, her assistant returned carrying a hypodermic needle. Relieved, Nikki took the syringe and escaped back into the safety of her profession. Pinching some loose skin between her thumb and index finger, she stuck Grave with the needle and then discarded the syringe. Grave did not resist or even react to the shot, indicating that he had not even felt it. Looking down at his overgrown toenails, she said, "He needs those nails trimmed. The tech here will take care of that."

Nikki backed up as the vet technician grabbed a clipper from the counter and reached down for one of Grave's legs. The moment she touched his paw, he began bucking like a small Brahma bull, so Dave jumped in to help control him. As he did so, Nikki slipped out the door, leaving Dave and the technician alone to wrestle with the unsettled dog. When Dave looked around and saw that Nikki had again vanished from sight, he just shook his head and mumbled under his breath, "Her name must be Virginia Dare." Just then, Grave started getting the best of the girl, so he refocused his attention and double down on his efforts to restrain the dog.

The final moments at the Animal Hospital of Nags Head resembled a World Wrestling Federation cage match with Grave displaying none of the serenity he had exhibited while Nikki was in the room. It took all the strength and energy of both Dave and the vet technician to hold him down and complete the trimming of his nails. With each toenail, a new battle ensued, until they ultimately completed their task and restored tranquility to the small examination room. Soon afterward, Grave was running free around the Animal Hospital grounds, frolicking in and out of the shrubbery while Dave stood on the lawn and observed the lively antics of the dog. He could see that his friend had fully recovered from the trauma of the nail trimming and was now back to his normal self, reinvigorated after having had his scent glands expressed. Dave, likewise, sensed an uplifting of his own spirits, an elevation that came from seeing Nikki again and learning her name from the vet technician amid the flying fur and toenails.

Outside of the Animal Hospital, it was still hot and muggy, but it had become surprisingly breezy, a perfect windsurfing day in the Outer Banks. Feeling the air on his face, Dave estimated the wind speed to be about ten to twelve knots with a potential for increasing as the day wore on, and he smiled while observing Grave run around the yard, his long ears rising in the air, buoyed by the steady breeze. He then watched the playful basset hound charge straight at him and run three complete circles around his legs, stirring in Dave a similar passion for life in which he felt himself internally sprinting circles of joy and happiness with the same abandonment as his four-legged friend. Yes, he thought to himself, things were looking up. It was going to be a good day.

"Look at that arrogant little wimp. I could crush him with one hand."

"Mark, stop it! So what if he cut you off in the parking lot? There were plenty of other parking spaces."

"I don't care. He's still a wimp. Did you hear what he said to the hostess? And what's that he's drinking? I doubt he's even old enough to order that." Looking at the young girl sitting across the table from him, he flashed a bright smile that let her know he was just playing with her while he reached for his water glass and took a sip. Condensation rolled down the sides of the glass to dribble onto his tan slacks, but he did not seem to notice it. Despite the watermark on his pants, he still looked crisp and neat in his blue button-down Oxford shirt and unsoiled deck shoes.

"Oh, stop it," she said. "He looks old enough to drink."

Setting down the glass, he pushed back from the table in a feigned attempt to get up. "I could go over and find out if you'd like," he said.

"Stop it," she said again, slapping his large forearm. "I'm beginning to wonder why I even agreed to go out with you." She grinned at him and reached for her wine glass.

The petite young woman and Mark sat in the dining room of the Blue Water Grill & Raw Bar overlooking the marina at Pirate's Cove. The restaurant was on the second floor above the Ship's Store, and the couple sat in an enclosed porch area off the main dining room. Having secured a table by a window, they had an unobstructed view of the marina and the large, expensive fishing yachts occupying the slips.

The girl peeked flirtatiously at Mark over the top of her glass as she sipped the wine before returning it to the table. Unrolling a cloth napkin, she placed it on her lap saying, "I'm not sure what I want to eat. I can't decide between the crab cakes or the pan-seared scallops."

Glancing down at the menu lying open on the table, Mark said with a smile, "Why not both?"

Wrinkling her nose in a quirky fashion, she peered across the table at him and asked, "How can you read the menu with those dark glasses on? The sun went down hours ago. Don't you think it's time to take them off ... or are you hiding from someone?" Raising her eyebrows, she added, "I certainly hope you're not embarrassed being seen with me?"

He did not respond to her question but simply glanced at her with an expression that betrayed a note of seriousness. She immediately noticed the subtle change in his mood and became fearful that she might have offended him with her last remark. She had intended it as a joke, but his reaction indicated that he had not taken it that way. He watched her fidget nervously in her chair a few moments before speaking. "You are aware that I am blind, aren't you?" he asked in a manner that was very straightforward.

"What?" The candor of his admission startled her.

"Yes, I'm blind," he said, "in one eye. I used to wear a patch, but I got tired of looking like a pirate all the time." A deadening silence hung in the air for a few seconds until he shattered it with a hearty chuckle and a smile that slowly broadened across his face.

Realizing that he was not sensitive about his admitted handicap, the girl relaxed and made light of the moment. "Ah, but then I could call you Patch, or rather Patches. I used to have a dog name Patches. Here, Patches! Here, Patches!"

"You know," he said, raising one eyebrow over the top of his sunglasses, "the kids in school really put me through hell over my disability. That's why I'm not bothered by it now. You can't imagine the insults those deviant young minds could conjure up, their sole purpose to offend me and make my life miserable."

Sensing that he was being honest and not playing another one of his pranks, she said softly and sincerely, "You poor thing." Although they had just met the previous night at Kelly's Restaurant, it seemed like she had known him for years, and she felt totally at ease in his company. Surprised when he called to invite her to dinner, she had rushed out to purchase the colorful sarong she was wearing that evening because all she had with her at the beach were shorts and tee shirts. Her sisters always traveled with smart, stylish clothing that she could have borrowed, but they had left two days earlier with her parents. In fact, the whole family had gone home before her chance meeting with Mark, and she looked forward to calling them later that evening or early tomorrow to tell them about him.

"Yeah, the eye is pretty disgusting to look at," he said. "Do you want to see it?" He did not wait for her answer but leaned across the table and began sliding the glasses down the bridge of his nose.

Screening her face with her hands, she turned away, yelling back at him, "No, you stay there! I don't want to see it. I have a weak stomach and things like that bother me. Besides, I want to enjoy my dinner."

"That's funny," he said. "That's the same reaction I used to get from the girls at school. Well, okay. You don't have to look … at least not yet." With a devious grin on his face, he settled back into his chair.

Not trusting him, she first peeked out of the corner of her eye to see if he was still wearing his sunglasses. Finding him sitting in his chair with his glasses firmly in place, she shifted back toward the table and lightly brushed aside the bangs of her cropped black hair.

"You don't know what you're missing," he said, continuing on the same subject. "There are plenty of carnival goers out there who would pay good money to see this eye. It's really neat. Not only does it not work, but the eyeball tends to float freely in the socket as if it's unattached. One minute, it's searching the sky for UFOs, and the next moment it's scanning the ground for lost change or glancing sideways at a hot babe across the room. I'm told that it's very distracting if you try to talk to me with my glasses off. Are you sure you don't want to see it?" He feigned another movement of his hand toward his face that sent her spinning away.

Once again, peeking sheepishly at him, she concluded that it was safe to turn back, but, in doing so, she promptly raised her hand and pointed a finger at him. "Promise me," she said in a solemn tone. "Promise me that you will not remove those sunglasses tonight."

He thought silently for a moment and grinned, almost to himself, before offering her reassurance. "I promise," he said.

With a slight tilt of her head, she studied his expression until she was convinced he meant what he said. "Why didn't you ever get it fixed?" she asked.

Picking up the stemmed glass of expensive white wine, he gingerly levitated it before his shrouded eyes while gazing placidly at her altered image through the clear liquid. With and enchanting smile, he said, "Because it makes such light and lively dinner conversation." Lifting her own glass, she playfully touched it to his as they both giggled and took a sip.

When the waiter stopped by the table to take their orders, Mark convinced her to order both entrees instead of choosing between her two favorites. He also ordered several selections himself that he thought she might enjoy sampling in addition to appetizers, salads, and soups. He could tell from her expression that she had never received this kind of attention before, at least not on a first date, and he seemed to enjoy adding to her delight by satisfying all of her culinary desires. Ravenously, she ate or, at least, tasted all of the assorted delicacies placed before her while Mark ate sparingly. That, however, did not prevent him from ordering more side dishes and desserts for her to sample.

The cost of the extravagant meal seemed to be of no concern to him. Early on, she had commented about the exorbitant waste of money, but he had addressed her concerns with a mild rebuke. As a result, she shoved aside her guilt and continued grazing on the cuisine until their table looked like a veritable buffet of half-eaten food.

"Look at all of this," she said while leaning back in her chair and taking a gulp of wine. "I almost feel ashamed. It's so wasteful."

He spoke reassuringly, "Don't let it concern you. I've seen some scrawny-looking cats roaming the streets around here. Tonight, they'll be dining in style. Besides, the condemned woman is entitled to a last meal, and there's no reason it can't be a feast." He flashed another engaging smile. "Considering the danger you're in, it should be a feast."

Condemned? Danger? Intrigued by his words and the intonation of his voice, she decided to play along. It was not every day that a strange man in dark glasses invited her to dinner, spent a fortune on her, and then began talking of danger.

"Yes," he continued in a subdued tone as if divulging a great secret, "My intention is to sweep you off your feet, thereby making you totally and entirely mine. Say goodbye to your old life, and prepare to embark on a new one, one you cannot even begin to imagine."

The timbre of his voice had a hypnotic effect on her, as did all the talk of danger and intrigue. She found herself swept up in vignettes of sensual fantasies created by her subconscious mind until the sound of someone laughing in the adjoining barroom awakened her from her trance. Glancing into the interior of the restaurant, she noticed that the dining room was entirely empty. The candles in the mason jars that had once burned brightly on the tables were no longer glowing brilliantly, and the reduced lighting made her blink several times as she mentally strained to grasp its meaning. "I was so engrossed in my eating," she said in amazement, "that I failed to notice anything else. It looks like everyone has gone."

"Not everyone," he said, speaking in a lighthearted yet serious tone. "We're still here."

"You know what I mean," she replied with a grin.

"No, there are others here too." He craned his neck to see around a wave-shaped wall. "There are a few people in the bar."

"It must be late," she said, "and it's a Monday night. Don't you have to work tomorrow?"

He smiled at her question. "I make my own schedule, and right now you're on my schedule."

"But really," she said, "we probably should hurry up and go so they can clean up. They probably want to close." She was beginning to feel like they were imposing on the staff.

"There's no hurry," he asserted. "Believe me, the money we're spending here tonight, they don't want us to leave."

"Well, if you hadn't insisted on waiting until dark, we could have been here earlier and eaten at a decent hour like normal people." Her voice had a playful yet matronly sound to it.

"Normal people—who wants to be like them?" he asked. "They don't have any fun. They don't order twenty-five-course meals with fourteen side dishes. Besides, I like the view here at night."

She turned and gazed out the window, sharing his sentiments while staring quietly at the boats in the marina. She had never before seen so many similar looking yachts gathered in one place, mostly charter fishing boats rocking gently in the breeze, their whip-like antennas and outriggers waving at the sky. The polished fiberglass of their white hulls reflected the glow of the lampposts lining the boardwalk, splashes of light that also illuminated the planked walkway and finger docks. At the far end of the marina, she saw the headlights of several cars arching over the Washington Baum Bridge on their approach to Roanoke Island, their piercing beams melding with the lights in the marina to sparkle off the water like shimmering stars in the fabric of night. She likened the whole scene to a fairytale setting from a romance novel.

"It's beautiful," she remarked with a sigh, finding herself captivated by the view until her attention was drawn to a number of lights at the far end of the marina. "Those lights down there," she said, "they're from the condos, aren't they?"

Mark did not immediately answer but instead peered keenly at the windows of the condominiums, his expression one of uncertainty.

The girl continued admiring the nocturnal scene framed by the restaurant window. "Those condos are nice," she said. "This whole place is exquisite. Do you live around here?" Sliding her eyes in his direction, she noticed a strange expression on his face, a look of puzzlement as he stared solemnly across the marina, his mind challenged by a vague, stalking recollection he could not entirely comprehend. She watched him in silence for several seconds, unsure if he had even heard her question.

"No," he eventually answered without looking at her, "but I think I know someone who does." He seemed perplexed as he gently stroked the underside of his chin with the back of his knuckles.

"What do you mean you *think* you do?"

"I don't know," he said. "Forget it." He smiled shyly at her. "Did I tell you how delectable you look tonight?"

"No, but I think I remember hearing you say that to one of my crab cakes—or was it the scallops?"

"Well, you know," he said. "You, crab cakes, scallops, I could devour all of you."

"I could let you," she said without hesitation, recalling his prediction about sweeping her off her feet but disregarding his warning about the danger. "It's too bad we can't get on one of those boats and take a midnight sail ... alone." She spoke longingly as she returned her gaze to the boats in the marina.

"Those are fishing boats," he said. "They are not really suited for romance or moonlight sails unless, of course, you have a tuna fetish."

His remark made her laugh as she commented, "You never know. I might be a little kinky. Remember, you just met me." Pointing at the boats, she asked, "What are those long, skinny things sticking up in the air? Radio antennas?"

Glancing out the window, he answered, "No, they're outriggers used for trolling. Just think of them as large fishing poles. They're hinged to the boat so they can be lowered off the sides. The fishing lines pass through them and run to the rear deck. We'll take a walk on the dock when we leave, and I'll show you."

"Well," she said looking at their empty glasses, "the wine is gone, so perhaps we should go too. What mysterious things do you have planned for me after our stroll on the dock?"

He grinned and said, "I won't reveal that now, but we should stop and get some wine to take with us. That's the only clue I'll give you."

"Why don't we just buy it here and save time? I'm sure they'll sell us a bottle."

He looked at her approvingly. "I like the way you think."

"Good," she said while rising to her feet. "I need to stop in the ladies' room. Why don't you get the wine from the bartender, and I'll meet you by the door." Bending down, she kissed him on the cheek and then quickly scampering off to the restroom.

Mark smiled while watching her step briskly across the knotty pine floor of the dining room, but his expression turned grave the moment she passed out of sight. Rising and walking into the bar, he found the waiter along with a bartender and a lone customer watching a hurricane tracking report on a television screen high on the wall below two mounted blue marlins. The three men tried to involve Mark in their weather conversation, but he seemed uninterested, opting instead to pay for his dinner and purchase a bottle of wine before walking toward the front entrance to rendezvous with his date.

The girl dawdled several minutes in the restroom, preening herself in front of the mirror, but she eventually emerged to find Mark waiting patiently by the hostess station, tightly clutching a bottle of wine in his powerful hand. Gazing a little starry-eyed at him, she said, "I don't know if you noticed it or not, but I'm really impressed ... with everything."

"Really?" he said with a warm smile. "I hadn't noticed." Dipping his head down to her level, he added, almost a whisper, "Please understand that I've been trying hard all night to accomplish that goal—and the best is yet to come."

Reaching out with his long arm, he held open the door and motioned her through. She deliberately passed close enough for him to catch a whiff of her freshly applied cologne before taking his arm and walking down the stairs to the lower level. Once they reached the bottom of the staircase, she unexpectedly broke free and darted ahead, merrily running off the lighted walkway into the darkened parking lot. "C'mon," she said while twirling in the darkness, her arms extended like a helicopter. The intoxicating effect of the wine was starting to kick in, and she cheerfully surrendered to its liberating influence. When Mark reached her, she seized his strong arm and tugged him onto the docks past some honeysuckle bushes near the closed bar of Mimi's Tiki Hut.

A forty-five foot Viking Yacht sat moored at the spot where they emerged from the bushes. It was a sport fishing charter boat equipped with twin Detroit diesels and all the electronics needed for offshore navigation. Mark used the yacht to identify the outriggers he had previously referenced, and he noted, "As you can see, these charter boats aren't designed for taking leisurely moonlight cruises under stars while sipping wine and doing … well … you know what." He paused a second, just long enough to grin, before adding, "What we need is a sailboat with nice long lines and plenty of style and grace." Taking her by the hand, he began leading her down the dock.

"Yes," she said as they strolled along. "That would be nice, but where are we going to find one of those? These all seem to be fishing boats."

Halting abruptly under a lamppost, he did not release her hand but allowed her to continue walking ahead until the tug of his arm stopped her, at which point she turned around and stared curiously at him. He did not say a word but only gazed lightheartedly at her with a mischievous look on his face.

"No," she said in disbelief. "Don't tell me that—" She stopped herself before saying it. This was too good to be true, she thought. In addition to being the perfect physical specimen and wealthy to boot—at least he appeared to be wealthy by the way he tossed around money—he was now hinting that he owned a sailing yacht.

"Okay," he said. "I won't tell you, but I'll show you if you like."

"No … Yes … No … I mean, yes, show me … but, also, tell me."

"Well, truth be told, I took possession of a sailboat … yesterday."

"Yesterday?"

"Yep, sealed the deal yesterday, and what a deal it was. I met a Canadian who had decided to throw caution to the wind and head south to the Caribbean to live out his days in the sunshine. He had no kids, so he divorced his wife in Halifax and told her to keep the house, the car, the dog—everything—and he bought himself a boat on which he planned to sail down the east coast to St. Thomas. His goal was to get to there by winter, but he made a temporary stop here on Roanoke Island because of the hurricane down there right now. Unfortunately for him, this marked the end of his voyage because he died the other day, quite unexpectedly I might add. Fortunately for me, I was right there to take advantage of the situation and acquire the boat with everything in it. I haven't had to purchase a thing for it yet, except for this bottle of wine. Now, I'm considering following his lead. I've been seriously thinking about sailing to the St. Thomas myself when I grow tired of this place."

"That's unbelievable," she said, amazed at his good fortune.

"Yeah, it is pretty unbelievable, isn't it?" he replied with a nod of his head.

She looked up at him and asked, "Is there anything else I should know about you?"

"Yes," he answered seriously, "but that comes later."

She raised her eyebrows and widened her eyes in response to his intimation before eagerly looking around the docks. "Where's the boat? Is it here?"

"No, no," he said. "It's over in Manteo along the waterfront. Would you like to go see it?"

"Well, yeah," she quipped as she began tugging him back toward the parking lot, wondering how her sisters were going to react when she called and told them the about this.

Her family owned a beach house in Kill Devil Hills where they got together every summer for four weeks. Everyone had gone home on Friday, but she had remained behind to prepare for the upcoming school year. She was embarking on her last year as a graduate student, and she had decided to use the solitude of the empty beach house to finish parts of her dissertation, hoping to complete much of it before the start of the fall semester. She had even given orders to her family not to disturb her before the end of August. However, despite her pledge to focus solely on her graduate studies, she had ventured out last night, stopping at Kelly's Tavern to hear the band where she ended up meeting Mark. Now, she wondered if she would be able to adhere to her study schedule. Who knows?—she thought. She might even chuck it all and sail to St. Thomas with him—if he asked her.

It was a short drive from Pirate's Cove to the town of Manteo where Mark pulled into the parking lot beside The Tranquil House Inn along the boardwalk of the waterfront district. The car had barely come to a stop when his excited companion jumped out and began sprinting toward the marina. "Race you!" she exclaimed while running like a girl of ten until she discovered that her wedge sandals were slowing her down. Reaching down, she removed them and called out, "Chicken!" when she noticed that he was not trying to keep up with her. At the center of the boardwalk, she whirled around and peered back at him, uncertain of which way to go. His darkened figure, silhouetted against the aura of a lamppost, was all she could see of him as he strolled silently toward her, swinging the bottle of wine at his side as he walked along. "Which way?" she yelled.

Mark used his thumb to gesture to his left as he called out, "Past the next live oak. First dock near the bridge."

Lined with live oak trees, lampposts, and benches, the boardwalk snaked around the waterfront district from the Roanoke Marshes Lighthouse to a staircase and bridge leading to a tiny island directly across from the marina. Arching three hundred feet over the water, the bridge was both a vehicle roadway and a pedestrian crossing to the Roanoke Island Festival Park, an interactive historic site depicting the first English settlement where the *Elizabeth II*, a replica of a sixteenth-century merchant ship, sat moored along the shoreline. Attached to the handrails of the pedestrian walkway were flags snapping briskly in the fresh breeze amid the glowing radiance of several lampposts lining the bridge.

The marina consisted of several piers extending out from the boardwalk, three of them providing dock space for private slip holders and a few shorter piers used by the commercial boats. The private piers contained enough slips for about twenty boats, ten on each side, with the larger vessels moored near the ends. Most of the berths had short boarding platforms extending out from the docks as well as pilings set farther out in the water, weathered wooden posts to which the watercraft were secured with dock lines. Mark's boat floated in its slip midway down the first dock, the one nearest the bridge arching over the water to the Roanoke Island Festival Park.

Most of the moored boats in the marina had their bows facing the pier, but Mark preferred to back his sailboat into its berth. It was a thirty-five foot Beneteau Oceanis, specially rigged for single-handed sailing. Unlike most Beneteaus of that size, it had a shortened keel, which was an available option for that model year, one the previous owner had selected because of his plan to cruise the shallow waters of Florida before crossing the Gulf Stream on his way to St. Thomas. The shorter keel also aided Mark, making it easier for him to maneuver around the shoals of the Albemarle, Pamlico, and Roanoke Sounds in the Outer Banks.

Mark continued signaling the girl, guiding her to the boat via hand signals. When he finally arrived at the slip, he found her standing on the dock near the stern of the boat staring up at the mast and rigging. Approaching her from behind, he said, "It's not as big as that fishing boat I showed you, but it's very comfortable."

"I think it's wonderful," she replied with a grin.

Everything was relatively quiet at that hour except for the flags flapping on the bridge and the shackles clanking against the aluminum masts, echoes of a maritime lullaby played to the accompaniment of sailboat riggings humming in the breeze and water lapping against the hulls of the boats. The young girl's expression made it apparent that she found the whole scene mesmerizing as she gazed starry-eyed across the marina, observing the various types of watercraft rocking gently on their moorings.

The waterfront marina played host to many sailboats as well as power boats, cabin cruisers, and houseboats. Additionally, several commercial craft operated out of the marina, boats such as Captain Johnny's Outer Banks Dolphin Tours, *The Cypress Queen* Luxury Yacht Cruise, the *Downeast Rover* topsail schooner, and the Gypsy IV pirate ship; all of them berthed several yards away along the boardwalk. Directly across from the marina, along the darkened shoreline of Roanoke Island Festival Park, the *Elizabeth II* floated serenely in the night, its colorful hull and complex rigging brightly illuminated by several powerful floodlights. Framed in yellow pine and planked with juniper, the sixty-nine-foot square-rigger represented the type of ship used by Sir Walter Raleigh to transport colonists to that region of the New World.

"Well," Mark said, motioning to his boat, "shall we board?"

"Where?" she asked. She had been on a sailboat before.

Reaching out and releasing the lifeline cable at the aft end of the cockpit, Mark seized one of the dock lines and pulled the boat closer to the boarding platform. The girl did not wait to be told what to do but promptly threw her shoes over the coamings and jumped onboard. She then climbed under the Bimini top and plopped herself down on the teak-inlaid seats encircling the cockpit, her face clearly displaying her excitement and wonderment as she sat there staring back at Mark.

Following her onboard, Mark said as a means of instruction, "The number one rule for boats is *one hand for you and one hand for the boat.*" As he spoke, he demonstrated how she should support herself by always maintaining a grip on the boat with at least one hand, never releasing it until gripping another part of the boat with the other hand. "You should move around like a monkey," he said with a smile, "although I would never consider you a monkey."

"I don't know," she said. "You haven't seen me in action yet." She was beaming a broad smile as she spoke, but it was too dark under the Bimini for her to see if Mark was smiling back at her. Suddenly, a thought crossed her mind, and she asked, "What's the name of the boat?"

Her question caught Mark off guard, and he reacted as a stumped child exposed for not having done his homework. The name of the boat?—he thought. He had no idea, but before he could say anything, the girl began crawling across the cockpit seats, remembering that she had seen lettering on the back of the boat. Dangling herself over the stern of the craft, she attempted to read the upside-down letters with the aid of light from the bridge lampposts shining onto the dock. She called out, "*Amazing Grace.*

The boat's name is *Amazing Grace*. That's nice. I like that name. It makes me feel safe."

Mark did not respond, but his previous bemused expression grew into a smirk as he removed the hatch boards from the companionway and climbed down the steps into the darkened salon. Once inside, he began throwing switches on an electrical panel to brighten the interior. Reaching toward the cabin roof, he popped open a few of the smoked Lewmar hatches to cool the stuffy salon, an action that also released bursts of light into the air, narrow shafts resembling miniature search beams projecting deep into the blackened sky. The light emanating from the hatches and companionway caught the attention of his first mate, who promptly abandoned her station at the stern of the boat and scurried down the steps into the salon.

"Wow, this is nice," she said, her face radiating an Alice in Wonderland expression. "And there's really a lot of room down here." Noticing that Mark could not stand upright in the salon, she giggled and said with a smile, "Well, I guess there's plenty of room for *some* of us." Raising her hand, she tried to touch the cabin roof with her fingertips but was unable to do so until she stood on her toes.

"Yeah," he said with a slight tone of embarrassment. "It's something I've had to deal with all my life. Nothing is ever quite big enough, but you get used to it after a while." He grinned while looking at her through his sunglasses.

She began roaming through the interior of the boat, gliding her hand along the finely polished teak of the salon table and grasping the stainless steel support post directly below the mast in which she saw her distorted image staring back at her. Besides her face, the convex surface of the pole also contained the deformed reflections of everything else in the salon—everything, that is, except for Mark. She did not seem to notice his absence in the warped reflection of the support post as she turned and stepped into an alcove by a stainless steel sink and gimbaled stove. "I love this little kitchen," she said.

Sporting a smile, he corrected her gently, "We sailors call it a galley."

With a playful sneer on her face, she continued her tour. "Is this one of the bedrooms?" she asked while opening a door and glancing into the aft cabin where she saw a couple of iron dumbbells lying on the teak and holly floor, one dumbbell crisscrossed over the other. She found it amusing that he would pump iron even on the boat, but she made no comment about it as she opened another door next to the aft cabin. "Oh, the bathroom," she remarked. "A little cramped, but I guess it will do." He did not respond to any of her observations but merely watched her walk through the salon on her way to the bow where she opened the door to the forward V-berth and smiled. "Oh," she said, "the *master* bedroom." Turning back to the master of the ship, she commented lightheartedly, "Close quarters, but I could live here."

"Okay, but if you're going to live here, you need to get the terminology right. It's not the bathroom; it's the *head*. The bedrooms are called *cabins*—or *berths*." Pointing toward the front of the boat, he continued, "That direction is *fore*." Swinging his arm around in the opposite direction, he said, "And that direction is *aft*. The *stern* is the back of the boat, and the *bow* is the front—the pointy end."

"Aye, aye, captain," she said with a salute. She then motioned to the bottle of wine still in his hand and asked, "Are you just going to stand there holding that, or are we going to drink it?

"Oh, no, no, no," he said with a glance down at the bottle. "Not here. We're heading out onto the water first; maybe find a nice, dark place to anchor away from all the riff-raff." Because of his Ray-Bans, she could not see his eyes, but she got the impression that he had just winked at her. Placing the wine in the refrigerator chest, he ordered, "Now get yourself topside while I turn off the lights. I don't want to attract a lot of bugs down here."

"Aye, aye, captain," she said again before scurrying up the steps to the cockpit.

Mark then shut off the cabin lights and threw several switches for the outside steaming and running lights. Immediately, the stern light flicked on, its bright incandescent bulb illuminating the dock directly behind the boat. Similarly, the bow lights ignited and began shimmered off the water in vibrant shades of red and green. Gnats began collecting around the white steaming light halfway up the mast as Mark emerged from the darkness of the salon and slipped around a large stainless steel wheel to the controls on the side of the pedestal. He turned the key in the ignition switch, and the thirty horsepower Yanmar diesel chugged to life, emitting a syncopated thumping that excited the hearts of both the captain and his first mate. Adjusting the RPMs to the desired setting, he then abandoned the wheel and climbed across the deck to the forward peak of the boat where he released the bowlines from the pilings before moving swiftly along the side deck to step over the lifelines and hop onto the dock. "Sit back and relax," he called to his mate, who by then was resting comfortably in the cockpit. "I'm just going to cast off these lines, and we'll be free to go."

The wind was blowing from the stern, so he freed the aft spring line followed by the stern line at the far corner of the boat. Grasping one of the remaining dock lines, he then used his incredible strength to pull the boat toward him as he released the forward spring line and last bowline before stepping onto the deck. Swiftly and nimbly, he slipped behind the wheel where he jammed the engine into forward gear while increasing the throttle just enough to gain steerage. Gliding past the pilings that had previously held him fast, he wheeled the boat out into the water toward the floodlit *Elizabeth II*, using the historic ship as a navigation beacon for guiding him toward the channel leading into Shallowbag Bay.

As they motored past the brightly lit square-rigger and the other sleeping boats in the marina, the young girl fell into a dreamlike state. It seemed so unreal to her—so delightfully, fantastically unreal. She watched as the boat chugged toward shimmering red and green markers, points of light that meant nothing to her but which played an important role in getting them safely into Roanoke Sound. Some of the lights she saw flashed while others glowed brilliantly with uninterrupted constancy. Feeling the lure of their hypnotic beckoning, she turned to ask Mark about them but then became distracted by the lighthouse. "Oh, look at the lighthouse!" she exclaimed. "How pretty it looks at night, especially with all the sparkling lights lining the dock."

"That's the Roanoke Marshes Light," he said. "It used to be at the southern end of Roanoke Island near Wanchese, but they moved it here." He spoke without taking his eyes off the water and the navigational markers ahead of him.

She was going to ask him a question, but the noise of the diesel made it hard to hear, so she just stared at the Fresnel lens of the lighthouse until they passed farther out into Shallowbag Bay following the glowing red and green breadcrumbs left behind by previous explorers. Despite the loud rumbling of the engine, they seemed to travel at only a snail's pace, leaving her to conclude that speed was not a key aspect of sailboats. The slowness, however, did not disturb her because she found the whole experience incredibly relaxing.

Once outside the bay, they veered left into Roanoke Sound where she had a clearer view of the opposing shoreline along the backside of the Town of Nags Head. Under the light of a waxing gibbous moon, she was able to discern Jockey's Ridge State Park a short distance away by the shimmering moonlight reflecting off the sand of the giant dunes. She also observed the headlights of several cars traveling along the bypass as well the lighted windows of houses were people were still awake at that late hour. As the boat chased the red and green flashes through the blackness of the sound, she looked farther into the distance at the illuminated tower of the Wright Brothers National Memorial, its dim, distant image capturing and holding her attention while she rested her head against one of the Bimini support posts and gazed sleepily into the night.

Awakened from her trance by the unexpected dialing back of the engine, she heard the noisy rumble of the diesel reduced to a subdued patter as the boat slowly drifted to a stop. Glancing up at Mark, she saw him slide past her and climb onto the rail where he began walking toward the bow of the boat. In the darkness, she could not clearly discern his actions and did not know what he was doing up there until she heard the clanging of chain followed by a loud splash as the anchor quickly descended to the bottom of the sound. Upon his return to the helm, Mark shifted the engine into reverse and tugged a few times on the anchor before pulling out the fuel shutoff lever to stop the motor, triggering a high-pitched whine from the oil pressure alarm that continued sounding until he switched off the key. At that point, everything became deadly quiet except for the lapping of water against the sides of the hull.

Mark had anchored the boat in open water off the northwest point of Roanoke Island near Fort Raleigh and the Elizabethan Gardens, well within view of the outdoor amphitheater that played host to nightly performances of the symphonic drama *The Lost Colony*. At that late hour, the actors and audience had long since retired to their homes, but the curtain was just rising on a different theatrical performance, this one a modern tragedy involving Mark and his prey.

Continuing to stand at the helm, Mark said nothing as he stared down at the girl sitting close to him in the cockpit. She was again gazing over the side, still lost in the magic of the moment.

"I love that sound," she said.

"What sound?" he asked.

"I don't know. The water against the boat. The wind snapping those little flags on the cables. The whole experience of the night, I guess. It's calling us." She turned and gazed up at him, her eyes sending him a tacit message.

"You're right about that," he said softly as he reached down and gently stroked her cheek. She made no further comment but merely closed her eyes and tilted her head, giving his hand better access to the side of her face, until he lightly tapped her cheek and touched the tip of her nose while whispering, "I'm going to get the wine. You make yourself comfortable." He then disappeared below deck.

Finding a boat cushion, she made herself a pillow and reclined near the back of the cockpit while listening to the sounds of Mark opening and closing cabinet doors in the darkened salon. He had not turned on any lights, but she could hear him throwing electrical switches, loud clicks that coincided with the extinguishing of the white navigation light behind her and the red and green ones near the bow of the boat. With her head resting on the cushion, she could see over the back of the Bimini to the very top of the mast where a white anchor light flicked on in response to the last audible click that sounded below. It twinkled and glowed brightly like an alien planet burning in the night sky above.

Mark emerged from below with the bottle of wine and two stemmed glasses, both made of pewter. Standing near the companionway, he withdrew a corkscrew from his pocket and opened the wine while she watched him from her prone position at the back of the boat. Waiting until he had finished pouring the wine and had placed the glasses on the cockpit table, she jumped up and ran across the top of the cabin seats toward him, exhibiting the joy and abandonment of a child on Christmas morning. The change in elevation brought her eye-to-eye with him as she wrapped her arms around his neck and kissed him violently. "You were right," she chirped happily. "I've been swept off my feet." Not waiting for him to reply, she leaped from the seat and flew into his arms.

Lost in the passion of the moment, she forgot about her mundane life and allowed her emotions and dreams to control her thoughts and actions. The beautiful sailboat, the salty sea breeze, the sparkling distant lights, and Mark himself, all had an anesthetizing effect on her already mellow state. She grasped him very lightly, allowing him to grip her firmly, fully supporting her body in his powerful arms.

Mark easily held her, and he moved carefully around the cockpit table to sit down near the rail of the boat with her still in his arms. She leaned closer to him, placing her cheek next to his while tenderly stroking the back of his head and gazing dreamily over the side of the boat at the surrounding waters, musing on what lie beneath them. Extending her outspread fingers toward the horizon, she longed to grasp and hold the night, hoping to prevent this moment from ever slipping away, but she quickly drew back her hand when a fish unexpectedly leaped high into the air near the side of the boat.

"What was that?" she gasped in a tone that was almost a shriek.

Feeling her body tense, Mark replied with a smile, "My heart. Couldn't you tell?

"No, seriously," she said. "Something jumped out of the water?"

He paused several moments and then proceeded to speak in a manner that portended danger. "There is something that I didn't tell you," he said slowly. "I was afraid you wouldn't come along if you knew the danger, but I guess I should tell you now. We're not alone out here."

She sensed the seriousness in his voice, a dire tone that alarmed her slightly and caused her grow somber. "What do you mean?" she asked.

"You see," he continued darkly. "Legend has it that there exist other forms of life around here, creatures quite different from us, born and raised in the world beyond our everyday view, a hostile and alien environment that is quite unwelcoming and lethal to human beings. It is a place utterly devoid of morality or, rather, any enforcement of morality. Survival of the fittest is he Golden Rule there, a world where the strongest take what they want and what they need."

"Yeah, right," she said. She could sense that he was toying with her again.

"No, no. Hear me out before you dismiss what I have to say." His voice bore a tone of gentle admonishment. Looking directly at her through the lenses of his dark glasses, he continued, "At times, these creatures find their way into our world, but their time here is short due to a basic need. To survive, they require liquid sustenance elemental to their home environment, something they find scarce in ours, and it forces them to seek out artificial sources of this life-giving nectar or perish if they are unable to find it. Their only other recourse is to return quickly to their own world in order to save their lives and go on living. You see, they find our environment as inhospitable as we find theirs. The ancients had a name for them, but I believe you know them as ... *fish*."

With his utterance of the word "fish," he was no longer able to contain himself and began laughing with more passion than he had shown the entire evening. She reacted by lightheartedly pounding his chest until the rock hard surface of his pectoral muscles began hurting her fist. With a feigned look of disgust, she said, "I was about to tell you that you hadn't made one mistake in your seduction of me, but forget it. You just made your first mistake." Not waiting for a response, she leaned in and kissed him again.

When they separated, he asked, "Does that mistake mean I'm not going to get where I want to go?"

Taking a moment to gather her thoughts, she said with a broad grin, "I said you made your first mistake. I didn't say you lost the whole ballgame. Let's not be hasty now." Just then, a small splash sounded in the water not far away, causing her to cast a serious glance over the rail and ask, "You don't think there are any sharks out here, do you?"

He tightened his grip on her and pulled her closer to him. Speaking in a seductively soft tone, he whispered in her ear, "Why worry about sharks when you have me to contend with?"

"You might not know this," she said coyly, "but I've always had a thing for dangerous men." While she was speaking, he began kissing her just below her jawline, eliciting the total surrender of her body. With her eyes closed, she tilted her head sideways to expose more of her neck while whispering softly, "The sharks could take a few lessons from you."

Her desire swelled with each erotic kiss, and she drifted into a swoon where her body was no longer her own. Trapped in a state of total submission, all she could do was open her eyes and gaze dreamily at the eastward shoreline while Mark continued his sensual assault on her neck. Her attempts to speak became futile, especially after he discovered a particularly sensitive area just below her left ear, but, between her unrestrained moans and sighs, she managed to string together enough words for a single sentence. She said in a low, sensuous tone, "Maybe we should go down below ... or perhaps we could do it up here and watch the sun—" She never got a chance to complete her proposal due to an involuntary tremor that surged through Mark's body with a sudden, unexpected fury, a shocking jolt that caused her to pause midsentence.

The violent shudder had its origins in fear, starting in the tendons of his neck and spreading to the muscles of his shoulders before descending through the rest of his body as a wave of strain and tautness. He reacted anxiously by clutching the girl's shoulders with both hands while shoving her sideways like a ragdoll, craning his neck to view the eastern horizon. The sun had already crossed the halfway point on the other side of the earth, and the subtle, almost imperceptible glow of the eastern sky foretold an approaching dawn. For the first time that night, he reached up and removed his sunglasses, using his ultra-sensitive eyes to confirm what he thought he was seeing: the barrier island silhouetted against the backdrop of a slightly illuminated sky.

Casting aside any pretense of a lover and assuming the role of an executioner, Mark began his grim task without the slightest hint of care or remorse. Dawn was still several hours away, but he needed to finish his work and return to shore before it arrived. Springing into action with the deliberate intent of a monster, he grabbed the girl's hair at the back of her head while reaching out with his other hand to snatch the corkscrew from the cockpit table. Taking little notice of her shocked expression, he exposed the smooth young skin of her neck into which he cut a small incision in her carotid artery using the sharpened tip of the corkscrew. Plunging his mouth down onto the wound, he then began morbidly extracting the blood from her body like a hungry baby suckling its mother's breast. He performed the unnatural act so skillfully and precisely that not a drop of blood was spilled or wasted.

The girl died as effortlessly as she had lived, and it took only a second or two for Mark to rob her of all her life-giving fluid. It happened so quickly that she could not resist, and the speed at which he consumed her blood left her dead before she was even aware of her impending demise. Mark then dropped her lifeless corpse onto the cockpit seat and descended the steps into the darkened salon.

When he emerged from the lower deck, he carried with him one of the two dumbbells from the aft cabin along with some Dacron dock line. Pausing a moment, he picked up a wine glass from the cockpit table and took a sip as he stared grimly at the eastern sky. His movements were now more meticulous and measured than before with an enhanced sense of urgency guiding his actions. Putting down the glass and grabbing the dock line, he adeptly tied the girl's ankles and legs to the lead dumbbell before lifting her weighted cadaver and tossing it unceremoniously over the side.

She sank rapidly through the depths while Mark watched passively from the side deck of the boat. Little, if any, emotion showed on his face as the makeshift funeral came to an end. Just then, the dorsal fin of a bull shark appeared above the water's surface about twenty feet away. It moved in a straight line toward the hull of the boat where it sank from view at the spot of the girl's untimely passage from this world. Seeing the carnivore began its cruel descent, Mark raised his wine glass in a toast and said coldly, "*Bon appétit*, my friend."

CHAPTER 5

What was it his wife had asked him to do? Perhaps it something she wanted him to buy for her? Unfortunately, he could not remember. Upon disembarking the ship, he had known exactly what it was, but that was hours ago, long before Tommy had given him those two drinks. Bushwhackers, he called them.

Reaching into the pocket of his baggy shorts, he grabbed the business card of John and Shirley, the nice couple who had engaged him in conversation earlier that afternoon, and he began smoothing it out on the bar with the side of his hand, trying to remove the creases from it. While talking to the friendly couple, he had thoughtlessly jammed it into his pocket, crumpling and wrinkling it in the process. Shirley had since gone back behind the bar while John sat chatting with some customers at a table in the corner, so he decided to take a closer look at the card. He assumed that John and Shirley were the owners of the business because their names were printed prominently on the front of the card along with the name of the place, Coconuts Bar & Grill, displayed boldly under a banner declaring it to be the "Home of the Backstreet Bushwhacker." That was the real reason he wanted the card; the back of it contained the recipe for the drink Tommy had served him.

Flipping over the business card, he examined the drink recipe and muttered to himself, "Man, hell of a lot of liquor in those things. Good thing I can handle my booze." Downing the last swig of beer from a longneck bottle, he shoved it forward, signaling for another one while thinking once more about his wife, trying again to remember what she had requested of him. Unfortunately, it was no use; the beers and Bushwhackers had completely erased that memory from his brain. Glancing once more at the Bushwhacker recipe, he then tucked the card into his wallet, deciding that his wife would have to be satisfied with the new island drink he had discovered for her. Knowing how much she liked chocolate milkshakes, he was sure she would like it because it tasted just like one. When they got back to Pittsburgh, he would break out the blender and whip up a batch of them on the deck for his wife and the neighbors to sample.

After getting off the tender boat earlier that day along Veteran's Drive in downtown Charlotte Amalie, he had walked one block in the suffocating heat to Main Street where he had met a local guy who then directed him down an alley and told him to follow it to Back Street where he would find a nice, hospitable drinking establishment. With no reason to doubt the black fellow, he followed his directions and found Coconuts right on the corner where the native said it would be. That was around noon, and he had been there ever since.

It had been unbearably hot and muggy on the street that day with tourists cramming the narrow roads and alleys of St. Thomas, so he was relieved to have found such a welcoming oasis. Tommy, the bartender, knew exactly what he needed when he spotted him waddle through the door. Noticing the sweat pouring off his face, the young bartender immediately presented him with the bar's signature frozen drink, the Backstreet Bushwhacker. It tasted good and hit the spot, so he ordered a second one; however, the heat of the day and the five liquors contained in the drink set his head spinning. Therefore, he asked Tommy to bring him a double order of conch fritters to fill the void in his oversized belly, counting on the food to sop up the alcohol and counter the effects of drinking on an empty stomach. Switching back to his drink of choice—beer—he had to settle for Budweiser because Coconuts did not carry his usual brew, Iron City Beer.

Ron, or Ronnie as everyone knew him back home at the Elks Club, was vacationing with his wife. She had nagged him for the longest time about taking a cruise, so he finally relented and agreed to go. When he learned from his fellow Elks that he could get a better deal during hurricane season, he scheduled the trip for August despite the threat of unsettled weather. They had been lucky so far, but Hurricane Kim was barreling down on them. It was predicted to pass close to the island late tomorrow, but that was okay with him because this was the last stop on the cruise; his ship would be safely at sea tomorrow heading back to Miami. Thankfully, his wife had met those two sisters who had taken her shopping with them because he could not have endured another day of that crap. Instead, he got to sit in this wonderful island bar enjoying the company of like-minded drinkers. With his wife shopping in town, he had no reason to hurry to get back to the ship, so he decided to wait and catch the last tender scheduled to leave the dock at four-thirty.

Because the hurricane was striking St. Martin that day, some cruise lines had diverted their ships to St. Thomas, filling up the cruise ship terminals at Havensight and Crown Bay. As a result, Ronnie's ship had been left with no place to dock upon its arrival late that morning, forcing the captain to anchor outside St. Thomas Harbor and tender the passengers into the downtown area, leaving them off at the pier alongside Veteran's Drive. Many of the passengers were upset about tendering off the ship rather than disembarking at the cruise ship piers outside of Charlotte Amalie, but Ronnie liked the idea of traveling by tender boat because he avoided spending money on taxis to and from town. Instead, they dropped him off right in the heart of things.

Being free of his wife and her incessant shopping, he had planned to do a little exploring in town, but those plans quickly changed when he arrived at the pier and saw what awaited him there. With so many cruise ships in port, the city was in utter chaos with tourists clogging the streets and alleys in search of deals on electronics, perfume, and booze. Ronnie preferred his booze served in open containers directly over a bar, and that is exactly what he found when he stumbled into Coconuts. Once inside the place, he never left.

He had been able to claim a seat right at the bar because a young man was leaving at the very moment he walked through the door. Plopping himself down on the chair, he felt right at home in the drinking establishment amid the sound of recorded music mixing with the voices and laughter of the people coming and going in a continuous stream. The inside of the place was not large, wide enough for only three or four tables in addition to the bar and a tiny kitchen in which a native girl was cooking burgers, fish, and other dishes. Neon signs, beer advertising, and other paraphernalia covered the interior brick and mortar walls of the small restaurant and bar with portions of the walls papered with dollar bills on which customers had written their names and other messages. Additional seating was available outside in a narrow alleyway and in a small adjoining patio where tables and chairs had been set up. The restroom was also outside, adjacent to the patio. To use it, you had to get the key from Tommy.

After several hours, Ronnie noticed that there were fewer voices in the room because he could more easily discern the melody of the music playing in the background. Looking around, he spotted only a few people left in the place. There had been a lot of talk earlier about the hurricane, and he remembered someone mentioning that the storm had altered course and was now taking direct aim at St. Thomas. He also recalled hearing that it had picked up speed and strength, a fact that did not concern him. He and his fellow passengers would sail away long before the hurricane hit; all he had to do was get himself back to the ship. Glancing down at his watch, he saw that he still had plenty of time before the last tender departed.

Ronnie was a retired steel worker with a long thin nose that hung down almost to his upper lip. When he drank out of a glass, the tip of his nose would touch the beverage; therefore, he always made it a point to drink straight from the bottle. He had lived and worked his entire life in the Pittsburgh area, and, other than a short stint in the army as a young man, this was the farthest he had ever traveled from home in his seventy years. His two primary interests in life were his local sports teams and spending time with his buddies at the Elks Club.

An avid sports fan, he always dressed in licensed sportswear of a professional Pittsburgh team. Today it was a white Pittsburgh Steelers' jersey bearing the number twelve along with his last name emblazoned across the back—Bradshaw—just like the former quarterback Terry Bradshaw. Due to his hair loss and the need to protect his scalp from sunburn, he always wore a black Pittsburgh Pirates' baseball cap, which he had removed and placed on the bar beside his beer. He thought he had overheard John and Shirley telling another customer that they were originally from New England, perhaps Boston, and he saw a New England Patriots' flag hanging on the wall, leading him to wonder, but not ask, what they thought of his Steelers' jersey.

At one point, long after Ronnie had lost count of the number of beers he had consumed, it struck him that he no longer heard any customer voices around him. Additionally, the music had stopped playing so that the only audible sound in the room came from a television screen above the bar broadcasting a report about

Hurricane Kim. Looking around, he could not find the cook, and he noticed that everything in the kitchen had been neatly packed away. Tommy was also missing, and he wondered if John and Shirley had sent the two of them home, possibly due to the approaching storm. It was only then that he became fully conscious of being the only customer left in the place.

John and Shirley were incredibly busy, scurrying about making last minute preparations, but they did not seem to mind the fact that he was still there. As Shirley walked past him, he asked for one final beer and offered to pay his tab. It was then four o'clock in the afternoon, one half-hour before the last tender was scheduled departed and one hour before the ship was supposed to sail. He told himself that he had ample time to drink one more beer and still make it to the waterfront in time to catch the last tender.

Downing his last beer in one massive gulp while simultaneously rising to his feet, he almost tumbled to the ground as a surge of vertigo swept over him, making him weave like a tightrope walker reeling on a line a little too slack. Teetering on the brink of falling, he redistributed his weight and regained his equilibrium by using his exaggerated beer belly like a balancing pole. Feeling confident that he could safely navigate, he then placed his baseball cap over his thinning white hair and waved goodbye to his hosts as he shuffled through the doorway into the late afternoon heat. The door had barely slammed shut behind him when he heard the click of the deadbolt echo sharply in the deserted alleyway. The sound of a locking door heralding his departure made him smile. It was something he had heard and experienced many times before, but never at four-fifteen in the afternoon.

The world outside was very different from the one he had encountered earlier in the day. Gone were the crowds and sunshine of the late morning and early afternoon. Thick, heavy clouds now filled the sky, creating feelings of angst that stifled all hope and optimism. Additionally, the pedestrian alleyway appeared dark and gloomy with the businesses closed and the outside tables and chairs of Coconuts stacked and secured in the patio area by the restroom.

Reaching Main Street, Ronnie found it almost as deserted as the passageway outside of Coconuts, nothing like it had been earlier in the day when it had been nearly impassable due to the heavy vehicle traffic clogging the roads and the throngs of tourists jamming the sidewalks. He now found the streets entirely empty and all the shops closed, their wares secured behind enormous iron and wooden doors, weathered portals known as "slave doors" on which hung huge padlocks. These ancient, heavy hinged doors that had once imprisoned people inside, now functioned solely to keep Ronnie and others out.

Something about his surroundings deeply disturbed him, although he was only partially aware of it due to the numbing effect of the alcohol. The thing he found most bizarre was the macabre, ghostly silence—the deadness—that hung in the air and permeated everything around him, a type of stillness he had never experienced before and which he could not fully identify or explain. More than a silence, it was an alternate reality with a pervading sense of emptiness, almost like an alien world absent of the normal trappings of life.

As he trudged along the deserted street in search of the waterfront, he saw only one car pass by him. It looked like a taxi without any passengers and a driver uninterested in offering him a ride. All day long, he had heard about the hurricane, but he had not given it much thought, not grasping why everyone took it so seriously. Standing in the middle of the empty street, he finally understood their trepidation, and he began seriously considering his own precarious situation.

The captain of the cruise ship was also giving serious thought to the circumstances unfolding before him. Like many others that day, he had made a miscalculation, basing his decisions on predictions that proved to be wrong. Believing the hurricane tracking reports, he had prepared a float plan that called for a five o'clock departure; however, the hurricane then took a sharp and unexpected turn with a new trajectory placing St. Thomas directly in its path. Instead of a glancing blow, it would now be a direct hit with an earlier than expected landfall due to the increased velocity of the storm. He needed to weigh anchor and get out of there a soon as possible, but he first had to get all his passengers back onboard. Unfortunately, he had announced that the last tender would not leave the dock until four-thirty, a decision he had made before receiving the updated hurricane report. That announcement had been a regrettable mistake but something he could not change at that late hour. The other ships had already departed; his was the last one remaining. To expedite embarkation and facilitate a quick escape, he had already weighed anchor and was pointing the vessel into the wind, holding it stationary with the aid of propellers and side thrusters. As soon as the last tender unloaded and cleared the ship, he intended to speed away at full throttle.

Ronnie, however, was not running at full throttle. He had consumed far too many beers and Bushwhackers to hurry or move quickly, but he was aware that he must get to the pier and catch the last tender before it left. A sense of urgency began to weigh on him like a heavy overcoat as he pushed himself to walk faster. Although the dense overcast kept the sun from beating down on him, the humidity was as thick as pea soup, making him gasp for air and perspire profusely. Stumbling along Main Street, he stopped briefly by a stone and mortar building, supporting himself with an extended arm while wiping the stinging sweat from his eyes. Mentally, he tried to retrace his steps back to the waterfront.

With the hurricane's landfall just hours away and the streets deserted, he could not rely on others to assist him with directions. He saw two black youths carrying a large piece of plywood ahead of him, but they were too far away to offer assistance. A shop owner was affixing boards over some uncovered windows, but he looked sullen and unapproachable, so Ronnie staggered past him without speaking, the metallic clinks of the shopkeeper's hammer the only sounds he heard as he plodded down the street.

He came across a pedestrian alleyway that looked like the one he had traversed earlier that day, but he could not be certain because they all looked alike. Fortunately, with the businesses closed, he could see straight through the passageway to the end where it intersected Veteran's Drive. The alley was long and dark, but the brighter hue of the clouds over the water in the harbor created an illuminated target at which he could aim. With hope in sight, he launched himself full-bore down the narrow alleyway toward his deliverance.

It was a long, slow slog down along the cobblestones with numerous stumbles and plenty of rest stops along the way, but he emerged unscathed onto Veteran's Drive close to where the tender had docked on the opposite side of the divided street. The wind had been negligible as he journeyed through the back streets and alleys, but, upon exiting the passageway, he felt a powerful onshore breeze slam into his body. Noticing a white uniform about fifty yards away on the opposite side of the street, he attempted to call out, but his voice was too weak to counter the effect of the wind gusts blowing away his words. Frantically, he picked up his pace, waddling unsteadily along the sidewalk while waving wildly at the young officer who had yet to see him. The awkwardness of his hand gestures knocked him off balance and impeding his progress, so he dropped his arms and lowered his head like a charging bull, trudging onward against the wind at a slow but steady pace.

The junior officer eventually spotted Ronnie on the other side of the street when he was about a block away, and he motioned for him to hurry up. Sensing that his salvation was at hand, Ronnie did his best to speed up, but the Backstreet Bushwhackers, beers, and conch fritters held him back. Earlier in the day, it had been a nightmare trying to cross the divided lanes of Veteran's Drive, but, with the town now empty, Ronnie charged straight into the street without so much as a casual glance in either direction looking for oncoming cars.

By the time he reached the pier, he was so winded could barely speak, so he quietly followed the instructions shouted at him by the officer and the crew of the tender. With his mind impaired by alcohol and stress, he was unsure if anyone had asked to see his boarding pass, but it did not seem to matter because he ultimately found himself sitting safely onboard the small transport boat, still breathing heavily from the exertion of sprinting across the street. It was not until then that he took notice of his surroundings, especially the angry seas sloshing and churning around the boat. Driven by the wind, the waves mercilessly thrashed the hull of the tender, repeatedly hurling it against the cement dock, crushing the inflated protective fenders almost to the point of the exploding as they strained and moaned under the enormous pressure produced each time the boat slammed into the reinforced concrete of the pier.

Earlier in the day, when the weather conditions had been sunny and pleasant, the cruise line had erected a small tent on the pier along with a folding table on which they served water, ice tea, and lemonade to arriving passengers and those awaiting transport back to the ship. Looking across the deck of the boat, Ronnie saw the table and tent lying side-by-side on the floor, stowed securely beside the empty refreshment containers. Three Filipino crewmembers dressed in dirty white coveralls sat next to the gear. They glared sullenly in his direction while conversing with each other in Spanish, all three of them acting a little edgy and hostile in the way they looked at him. The only other people on the boat were the young officer from the ship, the captain of the craft, and a hired deckhand. The captain and the deckhand were both native islanders and employees of a local company that operated the tender service.

Once the boat departed the dock and motored into the harbor, it became vulnerable to the full force of the wind and waves. As each wave smacked the bow, a fine mist of salt spray washed over the boat to moisten Ronnie's face. Additionally, the wind buffeted his ears so that he could no longer hear the Spanish conversation of the three Filipino crewmembers. Turning back to glance at Charlotte Amalie, he found it incredible how things had changed since his arrival earlier that day. The island no longer appeared inviting and attractive but bleak and lusterless as it squatted beneath an ominous canopy of clouds. The lush tropical vegetation had become gray and lifeless, and the vibrantly colored roofs and homes dotting the mountainsides now seemed dull and ordinary.

Pivoting around to look at the cruise ship laboring to hold its position outside of the harbor entrance, he was shocked at how tiny it appeared against the backdrop of the unsettled sea, looking no bigger than a toy boat bobbing in the vast, unwelcoming waters raging around it. The thought that a massive ship like that would find the ocean conditions challenging served to awaken him to the danger he and his shipmates faced on their tiny craft struggling against the wind and waves. It also caused him to turn his attention toward the eastern horizon where he witnessed something so startling and horrifying that he almost questioned its reality, an ungodly vision that pierced the bubble of his inebriation to produce a temporary and undesired sobriety.

The spine-chilling sight he observed was that of the sky, black and foreboding, appearing as he had never seen it before. It depicted a portentous omen that shook him to the core of his spiritual being, a shock that triggered an internal alarm as well as an interior prayer leading him to cast his eyes away from the sky and direct them back toward the cruise ship in a visual plea for help. His supplication—his prayer—was for a sign of hope, a heartfelt request granted to him in the form of a small spark of light emanating from a tiny door positioned low on the hull of the ship. It was the deliverance he had sought—an open, welcoming hatchway that awaited his return. Unfortunately, however, it was still a long way off through some very rough seas.

The tender endeavored to reach the ship, gallantly fighting the relentless onslaught of the waves and wind thrashing its bow, while Ronnie kept his eyes fixed on the open portal of the ship off in the distance, watching it grow larger and larger with each passing second. Holding tightly to the brim of his hat, he used his other hand to maintain a death grip on the rail while the small craft rocked and lunged against the elements. Feeling a slight tingling of seasickness welling up inside of him, he swallowed hard several times, trying to keep everything down while maintaining his view of the ship and the open hatchway that had come to represent his salvation.

As the small boat motored closer to the cruise ship, the larger vessel turned broadside to use its enormous mass to shelter the struggling tender from the wind, a maneuver that also calmed the waters around the open hatchway. With the young officer on the radio coordinating operations with the bridge, the native captain steered the boat into the wind shadow created by the massive ship, restoring peace and tranquility to the waters separating the two crafts, something that also helped alleviate the queasiness in Ronnie's stomach. With the re-establishment of calm and order on board, Ronnie rightly concluded that he had dodged another bullet and that he would live to drink again, preferably sooner rather than later. He then issued an internal "Thank you" as he breathed a final sigh of relief and glanced toward the hull of the gigantic ship where he could see members of the cruise staff standing in the open hatchway manning heavy dock lines as thick as their arms. Watching them cast the lines from the ship to the tender, he smiled and turned once more toward the darkness engulfing most of the eastern sky. The old adage is true, he thought to himself. God really does protect drunks and fools.

CHAPTER 6

Dave was barely visible in the shadows of the late afternoon sun. It was shortly after six o'clock on Tuesday, and he appeared to be waiting for someone while sitting beneath the yellow Mulligan's sign along the beach road at the corner of East Soundside Road, a side street running between the bypass and the beach road. Resting his back against one of the wooden support posts, he sat partially concealed behind a sprawling juniper bush growing under the sign. About three hundred feet away, directly across the parking lot, people had gathered on the upstairs Tiki Deck of Mulligan's Raw Bar & Grille to eat and drink while listening to live music performed by a guitarist and singer. Due to the number of cars in the paved portion of the parking lot, Dave had parked his hearse in the unpaved section closest to a gravel exit lane leading to the beach road. Having then planted himself under the sign by the juniper bush, he was invisible to anyone traveling along East Soundside Road but in plain view of everyone sitting on Mulligan's deck or standing just inside the glass-paneled door of the upstairs bar.

"What the hell is he doing?" Sally asked while staring through the door panel.

Travis heard her question but ignored it, choosing instead to continue talking to Gary, a local high school English teacher who regularly spent his summer days at the bar in Mulligan's. Gary normally sat at the bar consuming large quantities of beer while silently reading the books he intended to use in his English Literature class the upcoming school year, but he would occasionally interrupt his studies to converse with Travis, whom he considered a close personal friend despite Travis having named him the "Professor."

"Travis, what the hell is he doing out there?" This time, Sally's question was louder and more insistent.

"Who?" Travis asked reflexively without ending or interrupting his conversation with Gary.

"Buddy," she said shrilly while continuing to stare out the window of the door.

The sound of his friend's name caused Travis' ears to perk up. "Buddy?" he asked with a grin before walking around the bar to see for himself. Gary, likewise, became intrigued upon hearing Dave's name mentioned, so he too wandered over to observe the melodrama unfolding near the road. They could see Dave's hearse sitting in the parking lot, but Dave, himself, was barely visible on the ground, hiding in the shadows under the sign. From their perch high on the second floor of Mulligan's, the three of them watched with great amusement the comic antics of their friend.

"He looks like a damn hermit crab," Travis said. "I knew he was eating too much clam chowder. It's gone to his head."

"Oh, leave him alone," Sally said brusquely.

Knowing all too well that Sally never stopped at just one sentence, Travis looked at Gary and rolled his eyes while awaiting Sally's follow-up.

"Can't you see he's waiting for someone," she continued without taking her eyes off Dave whose body remained motionless under the sign.

"Who could he be waiting for?" Travis asked. "We're all here." He then began taking attendance while pointing a finger at each of them. "You, me, the Professor—everybody's here." He paused a moment before resuming. "You know," he said, speaking frankly, "Buddy's doesn't have a lot of lasting personal attachments. Sad as it seems, we may be the only family he has." With a twinkle in his eye, he then added, "But, of course, who could ask for more?" To punctuate his last remark, he spread his hands and looked around the room with a panoramic turn of his head.

While Travis continued playing to his audience in the upstairs bar, Dave remained seated on a scattering of spent oyster shells spread beneath the sign, unaware that the others were watching him. Boredom had dulled his senses, lulling him into a state of semi-consciousness where, if he had been more alert, he would have discerned the sound of something striking the pavement a short distance away, a rhythmical percussion that increased steadily in volume until it was directly on top of him. By then, however, it was too late, leaving him dazed and surprised when a blonde flash rounded the corner of East Soundside Road and sped past him so quickly that he nearly missed it.

She was there and gone in less than a millisecond, but it was long enough to jar his senses, nudging him back to reality and reawakening him to his surroundings. He may have missed her approach from behind him, but he caught all of her departure down the beach road, telling him that he must hurry or she would get away before he had a chance to catch her. Lunging to his feet in one frantic bound, he started running after the young girl as she jogged effortlessly ahead of him, her ponytail bouncing with each stride she took, swishing back and forth like the pendulum of a clock. Inside the bar, far outside his range of hearing, his loyal fans were chanting in a cheerful, melodious tone, "Run, Buddy, run! Run, Buddy, run!"

Although he could not hear his friends' voices resonating inside the barroom, he followed their instruction to the letter, sprinting after the girl with all his strength, running harder and faster than he had ever run in his life. However, just when he was about to catch her, she unexpectedly bolted across the road and dashed up the driveway of a vacant cottage where she banked around the structure and veered onto the beach. Her sudden burst of speed startled him, leaving him dumbstruck that a woman could actually move that fast.

He tried his best to follow her, but his lack of training and proper jogging gear made it difficult for him to keep up. Unlike Nikki, he had not dressed for the occasion, neglecting to outfit himself with running shoes, wearing instead a pair of worn Sperry Top-Siders, the only footwear he owned. They provided sufficient traction and stability while running on the street, but they instantly filled with sand and hampered his ability to run once he ventured onto the beach. Hopping on one foot and then the other, he quickly removed them and charged barefoot down the beach, clutching one shoe in each hand.

The beach was exceptionally wide in that area, more so than normal due to the occurrence of low tide. It was also entirely devoid of sunbathers at that hour with only a few children playing on the beach, some of whom were building sand castles while others chased seabirds across the sand. Most of the beachgoers at that hour were couples splashing through the shallow surf at the water's edge plus a few joggers trudging along the shoreline. The brutal heat of the day had eased, but the air remained humid with a warm sea breeze blowing in off the water. It was relatively quiet except for the sound of seagulls crying overhead and the heavy panting of Dave struggling to catch the fleeting figure of Nikki sprinting ahead of him.

Luckily for Dave, he was able to close the gap when Nikki altered course and began running closer to the water, providing him a better running surface that enabled him to catch up with her. He marveled at how effortlessly she soared across the wet, hard-packed sand while he lumbered along, barely able to catch his breath, nursing an intense pain in his side that made it increasingly difficult to continue. Additionally, the high humidity took its toll on him, making it even harder for him to breathe as he choked down air at irregular intervals while trying to coordinate both his respiration and strained leg movements. The sounds of his puffing and wheezing were what caught Nikki's attention, prompting her to look over her shoulder where she saw him struggling behind her. The sight of him made her smile as she addressed him without breaking stride.

"Mr. Rasputin, I'm surprised to see you here." Her voice did not quaver or betray the least amount of fatigue or exertion.

Upping his pace, Dave positioned himself next to her, sprinting alongside her near the water's edge close to the small waves of the breaking surf. The image they conveyed was that of a dysfunctional jogging couple, a comical duo running side-by-side down the beach with her wearing a sleeveless V-neck tee shirt, Spandex racing shorts, and expensive Nike running shoes; and her barefoot companion dressed in cargo shorts and a wrinkled tee shirt. Like Dave, Nikki was wearing sunglasses, the tinted wraparound kind with mirrored lenses, plus she wore a lanyard around her neck onto which she had clipped a ring of keys that softly jingled as she ran.

"That's funny," Dave said with a halting, labored voice. "I was about to say the same thing to you. My friends call me Buddy, by the way. You don't have to be so formal." As he spoke, he used the back of his hand to wipe the sweat from his brow.

Glancing over at him with a comical smirk on her face, one that made her dimples more pronounced, she said, "Ah, yes, but I find that my patients' owners expect a reasonable amount of formality as a sign of respect, the same way I—or anyone else—would expect a fair share of honesty as a sign of respect. Wouldn't you agree?"

Her question required too much thought on his part at a time when he was more concerned about satisfying his need for oxygen. "What? Oh, yeah, of course" he muttered between breaths.

Recognizing the look of fatigue on his face and accepting that her last remark had passed right over his head, she smiled sympathetically and asked, "Do you run this beach often?"

"Oh, yeah, every day. Well, normally not this late ... usually earlier in the morning." His leg muscles were starting to cramp, and he was beginning to feel as if death were imminent. His only consolation was that he would get to die in her arms; at least, that is what he told himself.

"That's why I haven't seen you here before," she said in a relaxed manner. "On the days when I work until six, I like to jog the beach here before going home. I guess that explains why we haven't run into each other before."

"Yeah," he said. His answers were getting shorter and more succinct as he struggled to maintain their Olympic running pace. By then, perspiration had completely saturated his shirt, but Nikki seemed fresh and cool, looking as if she had just emerged from an air-conditioned room.

"Well, since you're clearly a seasoned runner," she said, "I guess it's not necessary to warn you about something." His little charade amused her, and she decided to play along.

"Warn ... about what?"

"I was going to suggest that if you intend to do a lot of running, you should invest in a good pair of running shoes, but, obviously, you have yourself conditioned to run barefoot. If I tried that, my calf muscles would be so sore tomorrow that I doubt I'd be able to walk."

Her words had a powerful effect on him, transforming his fatigued look into one of sickened apprehension, leading Nikki to offer a partial truce upon observing the change. "I hope you don't mind," she said while slowing down to a leisurely jog. "I need to stop and rest for a while. This pace is a little fast for me ... but don't let me hold you back." Coming to a complete halt, she immediately turned away and looked out at sea to keep from laughing.

An act of kindness—he thought. "No, no," he said, coming to a stop beside her. "That's all right. I could use the rest myself." For a few seconds, he delighted in the sea breeze striking his overheated body. "Ah, you know," he continued a little hesitantly. "What I said before about running here each day—"

"Look!" she said while pointing toward the surf.

Dave raised his eyes and peered out at the ocean, directing his gaze just beyond the breaking waves. Up until then, the sea had been relatively calm with small rollers pushing their way to shore, but the water now churned and bubbled with tiny fish jumping near the surface. The boiling of the ocean extended up and down the beach for about thirty yards in both directions, luring in gulls and terns attracted by the marine activity. The enticed seabirds then soared in circles above the agitated water before dive-bombing down for an easy meal.

Nikki had used the disturbance on the water to change the subject, hoping to spare Dave the shame of confessing his lie about being a runner. Although she enjoyed toying with him, she was extremely kindhearted and did not like putting anyone in an embarrassing situation. Standing beside him while watching the animated fish roil the water, she observed two dorsal fins pinwheel out of the ocean near the frenzied school. "Look," she said again. "Dolphins. Aren't they beautiful? How I'd love to swim with them." Sliding down onto the sand, she began stretching the muscles of her legs as she watched the two marine mammals feed on the small fish. Suddenly, three new fins emerged from the sea as more dolphins came to the feast.

Dave, feeling a little awkward standing on the beach while Nikki stretched her hamstrings on the ground beneath him, thought about dropping to the sand as well but quickly dismissed the idea, knowing that a clumsy attempt to stretch would only make him appear even more awkward. Therefore, he stood stoically beside her, ignoring his aching muscles while shifting his eyes back and forth between Nikki and the dolphins. Although the interplay between the dolphins and the fish intrigued him, he could not stop looking down at the golden hair of the girl beneath him, a woman-child who appeared mesmerized by the watery performance playing out before her. He agreed with her that the shiny gray creatures were beautiful and graceful, but he felt the same way about her. Somehow, he sensed a part of them within her.

"Last week I sailed with a whole pod of dolphins," he said after a long silence. Enough time had passed that he was now able to breathe and speak normally again.

Leaning slightly to one side, she tilted her head and gazed up at him, happy to see him fully recovered from the grueling jog down the beach. With a warm smile, she asked, "What kind of boat were you on?"

He took the occasion of her question to move closer, slipping down beside her while stretching out his legs. The sand, still imbued with the heat of the afternoon sun, felt soothing against his cramped calf muscles. "Not a boat," he said, "a sailboard. I was windsurfing off the beach not far from here." Looking out at the ocean as he spoke, he too found himself mesmerized by the performance of the dolphins. "It was wonderful," he continued, speaking in a slightly romantic tone. "I was right there among them, but they wouldn't let me get too close. Still, they were curious enough to stick around. I now wonder what would have happened had I dropped the sail and jumped into the water with them. You know, there's a place in the Florida Keys where you can swim with them, the Dolphin Research Center or something like that."

Concluding his observation of the sea mammals, he turned and saw the distorted image of his face in the reflective lenses of Nikki's sunglasses. She was staring directly at him, so he smiled shyly at her, becoming increasingly uncomfortable the longer she maintained her visual scrutiny, analyzing him as she would a wounded animal on her examination table. Her cool, unflappable expression made him nervous, so he turned his attention back to the dolphins, concluding that they were at least predictable and less likely to ask him disturbing personal questions. Hoping to end Nikki's optical probe of him, he tried to distract her by saying, "I once saw a TV program that highlighted the work of a Sea World whale trainer. It showed footage of him swimming with killer whales. That's what he did all day, swim around with those giants. It was incredible."

She did not respond to his comment but continued probing him in silence while hiding behind the tinted lenses of her sunglasses. Although he could not see her eyes, he could feel them passing over his body like optical scanners, searching for imperfections and irregularities. For that reason, he was reluctant to turn back toward her, preferring instead to gaze upon the gray dolphin fins as they sliced the water in tight spinning arcs. The synchronized dance of the dorsal fins offered a hypnotic escape from his nervous anxiety until the watery scene changed dramatically with the emergence of another fin, one larger and different from the others, an odd-looking fin with a configuration unlike anything he had ever seen before. It rose unexpectedly from the depths before receding beneath the surface of the water while tracking the same arcing path as that of a dolphin fin but looking quite different, having an alien appearance, one he would describe as prehistoric. "What was that?" he blurted out.

"What?" she asked with a quick turn of her head toward the ocean. Her visual probe of him had caused her to miss what was happening in the water.

"It was a fin," he said, "larger than a dolphin fin but shorter in height and wider at its base. It rolled through the water just like the dorsal fin of a dolphin, but it didn't look anything like a dolphin fin—or a shark fin for that matter." He used his hand to simulate the movement of the stunted fin through the water. With a bewildered look, he added, "It also had bumps on its back."

Glancing over at her, he found her intently searching the water with a surprised, child-like smile on her face, an expression that captivated him even more than the sea creature he had just observed. Unable to pry himself away from her, he fixed his eyes on her profile, taking note of every detail, even the five strands of golden hair feathering softly across her eyes. The lure of catching another glimpse of the strange fish in the distance was no match for the enticement of the lovely vision sitting just inches away from him.

"It was probably a whale," she said while brushing back her hair and sliding her sunglasses onto the top of her head. Her beaming smile exposed incredibly white teeth as she turned and asked, "Was the dorsal fin considerably shorter and less defined than a dolphin fin?"

"Yes."

"And were the bumps behind the fin?"

"Yeah."

"Sounds like a humpback whale," she said while turning back to look for the whale. "Those bumps would be the dorsal ridges. Humpbacks like to feed on the menhaden around here."

When she turned and smiled at him again, he could see in her eyes that she enjoyed sharing this moment with him. He also sensed the thrill surging through her body over encountering the whale, a joy and elation that animated his own passions to where he found himself dropping his defenses to share in her excitement. Normally, he did not let other people's emotions affect him as such, but she seemed capable of penetrating that barrier and pushing him into unfamiliar territory.

Directing her attention back toward the sea, she continued, "I hope it surfaces again. I've never actually seen one here, but we get them now and then. It's unusual for one to be so close to shore. It's even stranger that—" While she was speaking, the whale initiated a feeding lunge, launching itself into the air with the precision of an expert acrobat. "Whoa!" she exclaimed as it ascended high into the air. The sight of the giant going airborne brought Nikki to her feet in an equally graceful motion. She then stood in awe as the mammoth sea creature made a vertical plunge, slapping the surface of the water with the flukes of its tail, only to resurface seconds later to expel a blast of air through its blowholes that created a misty rainbow over its jagged, humped back.

"Oh, my goodness," she said. "That was wonderful ... and yes, it is a humpback." Playfully glancing down at Dave, who was still sitting on the sand beneath her, she said, "See what happens? You start talking about whales and one magically appears. You're not some kind of magician, are you?" Her eyes sparkled as she spoke, their alluring strength seizing his soul, challenging his long-held notions about what mattered most in life.

By then, everyone on the beach had begun watching the spectacle of the whale in the ocean. Some people pointed out to sea while others ran down from the beach houses to get a better look. A swimmer on an inflatable raft became alarmed after seeing the beast's spontaneous vertical lunge, so he started paddling closer to shore.

Dave rose and stood beside Nikki on the edge of the water where they spent the next twenty minutes whale watching in silence. During that time, the giant creature made one more lunge and surfaced several more times before following the school of menhaden down the coastline toward Jennette's Pier. The crowd that had gathered to observe the whale then broke up and wandered away while the children trailed the dolphins and the whale down the beach. Although the show had ended, Nikki and Dave continued staring out to sea without speaking.

Finally, Nikki turned toward him and said, "It's strange, you know." She spoke to the side of his face because his eyes remained fixed on the waves gently rolling in across the sea. Once again, her studied gaze made him feel uncomfortable. It was as if she possessed X-ray vision capable of peering into the darkness of his soul, reading his private thoughts and exposing his hidden fears.

"What?" he asked while continuing to stare at the waves.

"Somehow I knew I'd see you again," she said, dropping her head slightly when he turned to face her. "I will admit, though, there was a time—like that night at Mulligan's—when I hoped that I'd never see you again." Without commenting, Dave watched her slowly lift her head and brush the hair away from her eyes. "But somehow I knew I would." She punctuated her words with a warm smile.

"Are you sorry you did?"

"I don't know yet," she declared with a relaxed grin that dimpled her cheeks. "I'm withholding judgment on that question until ..." Her expression changed as she allowed her statement to trail off. Appearing indecisive, she sank onto the sand and wrapped her arms around her knees, saying nothing more as she stared silently at the breaking waves filling the air with their soft, melodious roar.

Following her onto the sand, Dave stretched out his lean body and reclined on one elbow. "Until what?" he asked.

Her appearance was that of someone deeply immersed in thought, struggling internally with a matter of grave importance. When she finally spoke, it was not with the same self-assurance he had come to expect from her. It was more apprehension and uncertainty than anything else, expressed with a halting inflection in her voice when she said, "Until ... no ... wait. Would you do me a favor? No ... I don't mean it that way ... never mind."

She seemed confused and frustrated as well as emotionally distraught as she grew silent and meditated quietly for several minutes while Dave patiently gave her all the time she needed. When she emerged from her contemplative state, she projected a regained confidence, and she spoke with resolve. "First, I want you to tell me about yourself, and then I'll decide whether or not to ask a favor of you. You seem like you'd be perfect for the part, but I first want to learn more about you before I ask for your help."

Now, he was the one confused. "I don't understand," he said. "If you want something, just ask. I'll probably say yes."

She looked at him, this time with eyes that appeared sad. "You're right; you don't understand. So just do me a favor and tell me about yourself and then—maybe—I'll ask you to help me."

Deep down inside he knew he would do whatever she asked of him regardless of what it involved; however, he thought he should stop appearing too eager—it was bad for his image. "Wow," he joked. "I've never had so much trouble getting someone to ask me for a favor."

"Well, it's not so much a favor," she said, unclutching her knees and digging her hands into the sand. He could tell that she was having trouble finding the right words. "What I mean to say is that you will also benefit from it." She made the assertion without looking at him, focusing her eyes on the fine grains of sand slipping between her fingers.

"Oh, like I'll get paid for it?" he asked glibly.

"Well ... yeah," she answered while staring at the cascading sand falling from her hand.

"In other words, you want to hire me." Now he was toying with her.

When she raised her head, her expression was that of an annoyed schoolteacher. She said rather brusquely, "Will you just do me a favor and tell me who you are? Then I promise to explain everything, even if I decide not to impose on you. Fair enough?"

"Fair enough," he responded with a subdued chuckle. "Now what do you want to know about me? I don't snore; at least, I don't think I do."

"That's not what I mean."

"Well, what do you mean?"

"You know."

"No, I really don't. If you would just tell me what this is about, perhaps I could tell you what you want to know."

She looked at him sternly. "Okay, let's try it this way. I'll ask the questions; you give the answers. Now, where are you from?"

He stared at his right foot buried in the sand and responded, "Not from around here."

"That tells me a lot," she said with a grimace.

Dave became instantly animated and sat upright. "Really, it does," he said, "if you look at it the right way. It tells you that I have no lasting connection with this place … in case you're looking to hire me as a hit-man. I'll then have no qualms about making the hit and blowing town right after the job is done."

She wondered if she should take him seriously, but he did not give her an opportunity for questions, immediately continuing with his discourse. "Considering where we are and the time of year, it could also mean that I'm a tourist on vacation. You know, just a guy soaking up the sun in the Outer Banks." She opened her mouth to say something, but he hushed her with a raise of his hand. "But then," he said, "I told you that I jog here every day, which is a lie, by the way. I'm only here because I knew you'd be here, and I wanted to see you again. In any case, it's quite possible that I'm a new resident who moved to the Outer Banks to start a whale watching business on the beach. Is any of this making sense?"

"No," she said, "but continue." Seeing that he was on a roll, Nikki decided to sit back and let him talk. She found it amusing how he had subtly admitted his runner charade, and it impressed her that he had even confessed it at all. It revealed to her a certain character, one she found lacking in most of the men she had met over the years.

"I would continue," he said with a hint of embarrassment, "but I'm not sure where this is going, and I feel as though I'm making a total ass of myself. Therefore, I think I'll just shut up now. How about that?"

"That might be wise," she said with a grin, "but I don't want you to shut up entirely. I still have a few questions to ask you, and I'd appreciate answers of substance with a little less rambling." Standing and brushing the sand off her legs, she said with a nod of her head, "Why don't we walk up the beach while we talk? "Your legs have to be tight if you're not used to running."

"What would give you that idea?" he asked with a groan as he labored to stand up. Plodding forward with a pronounced limp, he said, "My car is parked at Mulligan's. I can give you a ride back to the Animal Hospital when we get there."

They then began slowly strolling up the beach, walking beside the small waves crashing onto the shore several yards away. Because of her running shoes, Nikki stayed back from the water, remaining on the wet, hard-packed sand, while Dave, still in his bare feet, occasionally waded into the surf. Sandpipers raced before of them, pecking at the ground as they skated across the sand just ahead of the breaking waves, their long, fragile legs propelling them forward in brief spurts of kinetic energy.

The region of Nags Head in which they found themselves was the old Cottage Row Historic District comprised of cedar-shake homes sitting on stilts through which the glowing orb of the setting sun showered them in a soft, warm light, its color changing from a bright yellow to a phosphorescent orange. Nikki loved this part of Nags Head, and that is why she chose to run here rather than near her home on Roanoke Island. Walking along the beach, her tall, slender figure cast a long shadow across the sand as she moved with grace and poise while Dave hobbled along at her side, his cramped legs and sore ankles affecting his gait.

"Okay," he said, feeling that his legs had now limbered up, "let's hear those questions. I promise to give you straight answers. However, I can't guarantee that they'll be truthful answers. You see, I tend to shy away from probing personal questions." As he made that disclosure, an unexpectedly large wave sent him scampering out of the water.

"I've noticed," she said while smiling at his boyish antics.

Due to the dark glasses shielding his eyes, she was uncertain if he was looking at her or sunset behind her, but his next words provided the answer to her unspoken question. He said with a surprising softness in his voice, "Beautiful sky isn't it?"

The luscious yellows and oranges emitted by the waning sun bathed the smooth skin of Nikki's face when she pivoted westward to view the sky while Dave looked at her glowing countenance and said, "Too bad we're not on the west coast where we could watch the sun set over the ocean." Turning back, she stared intently at him but was still unable to see his eyes because of his sunglasses. This time, however, he did not shy away from her gaze but held it for several moments until they both turned and started walking slowly up the beach as the sun continued it descent toward the horizon, the fluorescent glow of the flaming sphere obscured only by the sea oats protruding above the crests of the dunes.

"So what is it you want to know?" he asked her.

Glancing over her shoulder, she brushed back the hair that had blown loose from her ponytail and asked, "What are you doing here? I mean, why are you in Nags Head?"

He could not help but notice the seriousness of her expression and the sincere manner in which she had asked the question. Regrettably, however, he answered impulsively. "Talking to you," he quipped, cringing the moment said it, instantly detecting the annoyed look in her eyes and remembering his promise not to be evasive. "I'm sorry," he said. "I'm here because of the water sports: surfing, windsurfing, kitesurfing. That's all."

"Oh, you're on vacation."

"No, not exactly." For the first time in his life, he felt uneasy about admitting his vocation, a lifestyle that involved simply playing around in the ocean waves. Something then caught his attention, and he tried to use it as a ploy to change the subject. "You know," he said, "I could have sworn that your eyes were blue, but now they appear green, a pale green but definitely green."

"They're changeable," she said. "They appear differently depending on the surrounding light, but you're not going to sidetrack me that easily."

He ignored the last part of her statement and continued on the same topic, "My eyes were blue when I was younger, but not anymore." He reached up and briefly lifted his sunglasses to expose his steel gray eyes. "There are still some hints of blue somewhere in there if you look close enough."

"You're continuing to dodge the question," she said with the voice of a disciplinarian.

"You're right," he conceded. "Okay, I'll tell you the truth. I'm not here on vacation. I'm just here. I travel up and down the east coast until I find a place where the surf conditions are good and the people are friendly. I usually stick around for the summer or until the novelty wears off, usually about the time the surf and the wind conditions die down, and then I move on. Regardless, I never stay past the first signs of winter. That's when I head south to Florida to escape the cold weather.

"I have a widowed aunt in Cape Coral, Florida—Aunt Antonia—who is a real saint. She does all sorts of volunteer work in the community, taking care of everyone when she should be taking care of herself. I show up in time for Thanksgiving and stay through Christmas before moving down to the Ft. Myers Beach area for the remainder of the winter. The windsurfing is great off the Sanibel Island Causeway at that time of year. There are also plenty of marinas where I can find work if necessary. However, before I can do any of that, I first have to complete all the home maintenance chores my aunt saves up for me during the year while I'm roaming around the eastern seaboard. There, now you know more about me than any other person in the world except for my aunt."

She acted as if she did not believe him. "And you just surf and windsurf?"

"Mostly windsurf, and I'm pretty good at it too."

"But—" She held her remark and looked at him square in the face. "I don't know if I should believe you or not. Take off those glasses so I can see your eyes." Once again, she hoped to rely on her poker expertise to assess his credibility despite the fact that it had failed her during their first meeting at Mulligan's.

Graciously, he accommodated her request, but he immediately returned the sunglasses to his face once she seemed satisfied.

"But how do you support yourself? How do you eat? There's not much money in windsurfing around here or anywhere else for that matter?" She was clearly perplexed.

"I know," he said matter-of-factly. "I came here for the first time as part of a national windsurfing championship, but that was many years ago, back when I was competing. However, I liked it here, and that's why I returned this summer. Grave seems to like it here too, but let me get back to your question." He peered diffidently at her through the shaded lenses of his glasses, trying hard to determine her reaction.

"It takes very little for us to live on," he continued. "I stay in a small cottage just down the beach, out near the road." He pointed in a direction opposite from the way they were walking. "One of the realty companies lets me stay there in exchanged for work I perform on Saturdays and Sundays. I'm one of the guys they employ to inspect the beach houses once the renters leave and the cleaning crews complete their work. That provides me with shelter, and I pick up some money giving surfing, windsurfing, and kitesurfing lessons arranged through the surf shops here in Nags Head and the ones down around Hatteras. I also have a deal with them where I can earn commissions on any outside sales I generate. It's not much, but it's a living, and I'm comfortable. I should add that Grave is comfortable too, but he's comfortable no matter where he is. If things ever get tough, though, I can always find temporary employment over in Wanchese."

If there were two character traits Nikki possessed, they were drive and ambition, and it frustrated her whenever she did not encounter those same qualities in other people. "Yes, you may be comfortable," she said, "but don't you want more out of life?"

"More? Like what?"

"Well, a good job, for instance, perhaps even a successful career."

With that comment, Dave knew he had won the argument. This was not the first time someone had been critical of his hedonistic lifestyle. In fact, he had defended his way of life so often that it had become second nature to him. She may have been uncertain where their discussion was heading, but he already knew its course and its likely outcome. He could predict her words almost verbatim, and he was prepared to offer a rebuttal to whatever point she tried to make. Adding to his amusement was the fact that Nikki had begun proselytizing in her argument, attempting to convert him to her work ethic, but he had heard it all before. Little did she know that it was almost impossible to tempt a comfortable man of simple means with the lure of material gain, power, and security through the sacrifice of his contentment.

"Why do people have good jobs?" he asked, not giving her time to answer. "So they can have the things they want in life, do the things they want to do, and live comfortably. Isn't that right?" Once again, he did not allow her time for a response. "Well, you see, I already have those things. I'm doing what I want to do, and I am comfortable doing it. Oh, yes, there is something else I have that others don't; I can do whatever I want, whenever I want, wherever I want, with whomever I want—and I don't have to wait until after work or plan a vacation to do it. I hope you're in an occupation that provides you the same satisfaction and contentment that I have discovered. After watching you on the job yesterday, I think it's safe to say that you are."

There was a kernel of truth in what he had to say—Nikki decided—even if she disagreed with it, but she chose to let the issue drop rather than argue with him. Despite his self-identification as an irresponsible surf bum, she perceived something more to him, a sense of purpose and character that made her reluctant to debate him further. In truth, she doubted that she could counter his logic, especially at this emotional time in her life, and she thought it best to learn more about him before challenging him further on this matter.

"What? Now you're not going to talk to me?" he said with an engaging smile when she did not immediately respond to his comments.

"No, I'm sorry. I was just thinking."

With a mild chuckle, he said, "No, no, no. We'll have none of that here on the sand. You're on my turf now, and I strictly forbid any serious thought taking place near the ocean. Only sun and fun down here. That's the *Code of the Beach* among us surfers."

She looked at him sideways not knowing what to think. "You're a hard one to figure out, David Rasputin. Do you know that?"

"I told you already, that's how I prefer it. So why don't you go ahead and ask that favor of me?"

Once again, she grew somber. Reaching down, she removed her shoes and strolled slowly into the shallow surf with Dave following close behind, their tanned legs splashing through the small breaking waves. They then walked side-by-side down the beach with the salty water lapping at their knees and the setting sun dropping lower in the western sky, its subdued rays creating a dazzling display of color above the pitched roofs of the antique cottages. Out over the water, a pervading dimness was approaching from the eastern horizon as the last rays of the sun reflected off the bleached sail of a lone sailboat gliding effortlessly over the undulating sea.

Speaking without looking at him, she said softly but distinctly, "It really bothers me that I'm about to tell you something very personal, and, yet, you haven't reciprocated. In fact, you've managed to divulge very little about yourself." She turned and peered sternly at him, her furrowed brow signaling her displeasure. Although he hid his eyes behind his dark glasses, she knew that he was looking straight at her.

"The reason I'm willing to do this," she continued, "is because I need to have something done, a task I cannot perform myself. If my friends knew what I was planning, they'd scold me and tell me I was crazy, but I don't care; this has to be done because I need to know … for my own sanity and peace of mind. That's where you come in. I think you can help me because you seem perfect for the part; you're new to the area and probably don't know many people around here, especially my friends." Glancing awkwardly at him in an attempt to discern his reaction, she then asked, "You haven't been here long, have you?"

"About three months," he answered, grinning at her as he did so. Becoming frustrated at her indecision, he tried to prod her along with some humor. Squinting at her through his sunglasses, he said, "You're going to ask me to kill someone, aren't you?"

"No, silly," she replied with a lighthearted wince. "Well, if you must know. It has to do with my boyfriend."

She spoke softly, but the word "boyfriend" resonated in his ears like a clanging gong, producing no change in his outward demeanor but wreaking internal havoc on his mental and emotional states. His confidence sank faster than an anchor plunging to the depths of the ocean floor, and the neurons in his brain began firing chaotically in random spurts of energy, creating panicked thoughts that ignited a plethora of pessimistic doubts and fears. The disturbing doubts combined with the unfounded fears to overtake his dreams, shattering his once comfortable lifestyle and morphing it into a dispirited existence of fatalistic anxiety.

Pausing briefly, as if she expected to hear one of his smart-alecky remarks, she continued speaking when it became apparent that he intended to remain mute. "What I should have said," she continued, "is that it concerns my *former* boyfriend. We were supposed to travel to Hawaii—actually, we should be there right now—but something happened to change all that."

She then went on to tell him the same story she had told her friends at Mulligan's on Sunday night, relating all the sordid details including Mark's failure to pick her up, the attempted phone calls, the unreturned voice messages, and her subsequent visit to his house looking for him. When she got to the part about seeing him the following night at Cahoon's, where he pretended not to know her after purchasing a bottle of wine, she became misty-eyed and hesitated a moment to collect herself before resuming her story. Dave could sense the incredible sadness she was experiencing at that moment, but he said nothing, choosing instead to listen to her describe her painful reaction to what had occurred outside of Cahoon's Market that Saturday night. He then walked beside her in silence, sloshing through the shallow water while reflecting on what she had said and how it related to him.

"What could I do?" she asked. "I couldn't call the police. He seemed all right when I saw him, even though he acted like he hadn't seen me—or even knew me." She again grew quiet for a moment before continuing, "When I drove to his house that first night, I spoke to one of his neighbors who said he had seen Mark leaving earlier that evening. He told me that he had waved to Mark and that Mark had waved back as he always did. Nothing appeared wrong, according to him. Maybe nothing was wrong. Maybe we were just wrong."

Dave did not say anything to Nikki, and she did not look over at him but kept her head down instead as if she were thinking of something else she wanted to add. After a few moments of silence in which the only audible sounds came from a few gulls crying overhead, she said in conclusion, "On Sunday night, my friends took me out to dinner to try and cheer me up. That's when I met you." Upon mentioning their meeting, she turned and looked at him.

"Okay," he said. "That explains it."

"Explains what?"

"Your fondness for straight Tequila shots." He said it lightheartedly with the hope of raising her spirits, but he was uncertain how she would take it.

Her lips formed a partial smile as her face reddened slightly, and he could tell that she was still a little embarrassed about their first encounter.

"I hope you didn't talk about me too much after I left," she voiced with a downward cast of her eyes as she kicked lightly at the surf.

"You mean after you ran away," he countered.

Lifting her head, she smiled at him but did not say anything as they both splashed silently through the water before stepping onto the wet sand where they continued strolling up the beach. It was apparent from her expression that retelling the story had been hard on her because she now seemed drained of all joy and enthusiasm. It had only been four days since her unexpected breakup with Mark, so it was understandable that her emotions would still be raw. To Dave, the breakup scenario seemed the classic case of someone wanting out of a relationship but lacking the guts to end it face-to-face. He really could not agree with the guy's methods, but he had seen worse. He also knew that if he got himself involved in this lovers' quarrel, he most likely would end up being the villain or the chump; however, when he looked over at Nikki's sad expression, he realized that the potential payoff was well worth the risk.

Dave opened his mouth to say something but hesitated when he heard stomping sounds resonating from behind him. Nikki also heard the thumping, and they both turned to glimpse a jogger charging up the beach, approaching them on a collision course. The harried sprinter was a shirtless middle-aged man sweating from every pore of his body. Running with a lit cigarette in his mouth, he snorted and strained as he ran straight at them and then swerved slightly to his left at the very last second to continue plodding up the beach. As he passed by, he left in his wake the sound of heavy breathing and the smell of tobacco wafting through the air. Speechless, Dave and Nikki burst out laughing as they watched the winded runner trudge up the beach, smoke contrails rising above him toward the sky. Dave used the moment of levity to get her talking again. "So where do I come in?" he asked.

Nikki's eyes were still locked on the receding figure of the smoking jogger, but, at the sound of Dave's question, she glanced down and began kicking the sand with her foot. Speaking earnestly, without raising her head, she asked, "Could you find out what's going on? He knows all my friends, so I can't involve them. I'd be too embarrassed to ask them anyway. I thought if you could follow him for a few days, you might learn ..." Her words drifted off before she could finish the sentence.

"Learn what?" he asked.

"Well," she responded, her eyes still cast down, "you might be able to discover if he is seeing someone else. That is all I really want to know. If he wants to be with someone else, that's fine. She can have him, but I, at least, want to know. You don't think that's too much to ask, do you?" She ventured a shy glance in his direction.

His reply was sympathetic yet straightforward. "There are easier, more direct ways to learn these types of things, you know ... such as asking him."

"No," she said adamantly. "I can't—I won't. Please, I want it done my way, and I'll pay you to do it. Let me find out the going rate for a private detective, and I'll pay you that fee. It's worth that much to me to have him followed for a few days. He doesn't know you, and my friends don't know you; therefore, nobody will be the wiser."

He found her offer to pay sweet but unacceptable. "The going rate with this detective," he said, "is a date with you, perhaps dinner somewhere. Extend that offer to me, and I'll accept." He heard the words coming out of his mouth, but he could not believe he had spoken them.

"No, I'd feel better paying you," she said assuredly.

"And I'd feel better if you didn't," he countered with a degree of tenacity. His demeanor then turned serious. "The only way I'll accept this assignment is on my terms, and my terms involve no compensation other than a dinner date with you."

Upon hearing the ultimatum, she stared obstinately at him, hoping to persuade him with a determined glare; however, the shielding provided by his sunglasses blocked her penetrating gaze, preventing it from striking its target. Conscious of his resoluteness on this matter, she ultimately conceded to his wishes. "Okay," she said, "you win, but you must allow me to pay for dinner."

"You're the boss," he said with a satisfied grin.

By then, they were near Mulligan's, so they trudged toward a vacant cottage as the glowing orb of the sun sank below the dunes along the bypass, its waning rays casting long shadows on the surrounding landscape as the couple walked around a beach house and down the driveway toward Mulligan's parking lot on the opposite side of the road. High above them on the outside Tiki Deck, customers watched the colorful sunset as they ate and drank cheerfully, their voices mixing with the amplified guitar music filtering down into the parking lot.

The inside bar was also crowded with customers demanding drinks from Travis, forcing him to scurry up and down the bar as he tried his best to keep up with the surge of orders. Consequently, it allowed him little time think about his friend or watch for his return. The bustle of the restaurant also diverted Sally, who had forgotten about Dave and his outdoor escapades as she frantically waited tables. Gary, likewise, had returned to his previous activity at the end of the bar, his reading of Herman Melville's *Moby Dick*.

With his reading glasses perched low on the bridge of his nose and a scowl on his face, Gary sat immersed in the classic tale of the White Whale while leaning back in his chair with the book held in one hand and his free arm resting on his well-nourished stomach. Suddenly, he twitched and shivered in response to an unseen impulse that plucked him from his mythical sea adventure and caused him to squirm uncomfortably in his chair. With no change in expression, he abruptly placed the book on the bar and lumbered to his feet, shuffling toward the restroom but pausing briefly to glance out the window toward the parking lot. There, in the waning light of dusk, he saw Dave and Nikki crossing the beach road toward the parked hearse. Wiping his hand across the stubble of his neatly trimmed beard, he smiled internally as he turned and descended the stairs to the first-floor men's room without saying a word to Travis or Sally about what he had seen.

"When would you like me to start?" Dave asked as they entered the parking lot.

"Tonight … or tomorrow?" she replied questioningly. With raised eyebrows, she maintained her inquisitive expression until he gave an affirmative nod. "His place is close by," she said. "I'll show you where he lives before you drop me off at my car."

Motioning with his hand toward the crowded parking lot, he said, "Sure, my car is over there. We can swing by your buddy's place, and then I'll take you wherever you want to go." Speaking rather quickly with a hint of urgency in his voice, he let his eyes furtively glance up toward Mulligan's deck to see if anyone was watching him. Tightly clasping Nikki's arm above her elbow, he tried to hurry her along, hoping to evade the stares of his friends that would invariably lead to teasing comments and uncomfortable questions. He disliked drawing attention to himself and absolutely loathed being the brunt of anyone's joke.

Nikki was immediately cognizant of his efforts to nudge her along, but she did not say anything even though she could tell he was nervous about something. It was only when his paranoia became even more apparent, that she spoke up. "What's wrong?" she asked.

"Uh, nothing," he said nervously while shooting glances up at the deck, still trying to assure himself he had avoided detection. "Just practicing some private eye strategies—stealth tactics, you know." He mustered a contrived grin, but she saw right through it.

Still unsure of him, Nikki found herself questioning his odd behavior and wondering if she had been too impulsive in recruiting him for this endeavor. Her feelings of uncertainty then soared when she saw where they were heading. Stopping dead in her tracks, she exclaimed in near disbelief, "You drive a hearse?" Searchingly, she looked over at him. "Is there something you're not telling me?"

"My Mercedes is in the shop," he said while opening the passenger door and motioning her inside, once again glancing up at the bar to see if they were being watched.

Nikki had yet to overcome her misgivings about him, but her mind became distracted the moment she slid onto the bench seat of the old hearse and found herself surrounded by artifacts from a different era. She had never before sat in a vintage automobile, and she found the interior fascinating, especially the antiquity of the accessories. For its age, the hearse was very well preserved. Being a top of the line 1965 Cadillac, it also had several features taken for granted in today's modern automobiles such as power windows and air conditioning. She admired the softness and quality of the leather covering the dashboard and seats, and, aside from the dog hairs, it impressed her how clean and neat everything appeared; that is, until she glanced over her shoulder and looked into the back compartment at the chaotic collection of surfing and sailing equipment jammed into every square inch of available space.

Meanwhile, Dave ran around the back of the vehicle and jumped into the driver's side without putting on his deck shoes, preferring to drive shoeless, the soles of his feet toughened by years of barefoot windsurfing. It was not until the door slammed shut that he found himself able to relax, feeling secure in the knowledge that the people in Mulligan's could no longer see him. Taking notice of the look on Nikki's face while she inspected the mess in the back, he commented, "Now do you understand why I drive a hearse? Try carrying all that stuff in a Subaru."

Nikki gave an understanding nod before turning back around to examine the dashboard. "This thing is pretty old," she said.

He answered proudly, "Yeah, 1965. A Cadillac Miller-Meteor hearse. Only one hundred and sixty-seven were made."

"How do you keep it running?"

"Prayer," he said with a smile. "I pray a lot about it."

Pointing toward the rearview mirror above the dashboard, she asked, "What's hanging from the mirror? It looks like a noose."

Turning the key only far enough to provide accessory power, he used the buttons on the driver's door to lower both side windows. Then, while gazing at the reflection of Mulligan's in the rearview mirror, he said in response, "You're right, it's a noose—a macramé noose." Reaching up with his hand, he tapped it lightly, hitting it just hard enough to send it swaying back and forth.

"Let me guess," she said. "Because you drive a hearse, you thought you needed a noose hanging from your rearview mirror. It all fits: a dog named Grave, a car that's a hearse, and a noose hanging from the mirror instead of fuzzy dice. I'll ask again: Is there something you're not telling me?"

"Yes, as a matter of fact, there's a lot I'm not telling you. However, the last time I revealed more about myself to someone, I ended up with a macramé noose." Once again, he tapped the dangling noose with his fingertips.

Dave was beginning to intrigue her. She detected something in his voice indicating that this might be the right moment to extract additional information from him, so she pushed forward, hoping to learn more about his personal life. "How is revealing yourself to someone related to this noose?" she asked.

"Well," he said tentatively, "back in my hometown—"

"Which is?"

"Niles, Michigan," he said. "Satisfied?"

"Yes," she replied with a smug look on her face. "Please continue."

Glancing sternly at her over the top of his glasses, he visually signaled that he would not tolerate interruptions. This was a rare and unprecedented moment of self-disclosure on his part, and, if she wished for it to continue, she would have to adhere to the ground rules. He then went on to describe the tales and legends circulating about him back in his hometown along with a factual accounting of what really had happened.

"According to the legends," he said, "I supposedly drive around with a noose hanging from my rearview mirror. I once shared this information with another girl, and she made that noose and hung it there." He stared at the noose swaying back-and-forth in a light breeze wafting in through the open windows. "I never bothered to take it down." His voice trailed off in conclusion of his story.

Nikki did not know what to say after listening to him recount his tortured past, especially the part about his deceased siblings and the way the people in the community had ostracized him. Fearing the deadening silence that had crept in like an unwanted houseguest, she quickly changed the subject. "I should give you my cell number so you can get in touch with me if you learn anything about Mark."

The sound of her voice broke him out of his trance, preventing him from falling prey to the onset of melancholy after talking about his past. "Oh … yeah," he replied. Pointing toward the dashboard, he said, "There should be a pen and a pad or something in the glove box."

Reaching down, she pushed a button that released the hinged door of the glove box, dropping it onto her knees and igniting a small internal light that revealed its contents. "Oh, my God," she said. "This is as cluttered as the back of the hearse!"

He made no reply but merely shrugged his shoulders and glanced uncomfortably at her while she rummaged through the messy collection of seemingly unrelated items. Finding an old envelope on which to write, she dug deeper into the mess but failed to locate a pen or pencil. "Here is something that might help you in your surveillance work," she said as she pulled out a small pair of binoculars that she placed on the seat beside her. Diving back into the clutter, she found several compact discs, one featuring the greatest surfing hits of The Ventures and three containing the music of the Beach Boys—*Pet Sounds*, *The Beach Boys in Concert*, and *Holland*. She said, "You truly are a beach boy, aren't you?" She then examined the cover of the *Holland* disc with an air of curiosity.

"*Holland*," he said. "That's my favorite Beach Boys CD."

A shake of her head signaled that she had never heard of it before. She then held up the cover of another disc, one she found even more intriguing. Her questioning look communicated that she expected an explanation.

"That's the *Tommy James and the Shondells Anthology* CD," he said with a confident grin.

It was immediately apparent to him that his explanation had not satisfied her and that she required additional clarification of why he preferred songs from an era long before his time, music that she considered almost ancient.

"Tommy James lived in my hometown," he said. "You know, local boy makes good. Even though it was a long time ago, I still have to do my part to further the legend and help keep it alive."

"Okay," she said with a tone of acceptance as she pulled out two more music discs, both recordings of Jack Johnson. "Well, at least, you have something from this century, but you still can't break out of that surfer theme. Can you?" Reaching back into the glove box, she picked out and examined the plastic cover of Bob Marley's *Legend* CD, which she accepted as being contemporary despite the fact that the reggae singer died in 1981.

During all of this, Dave sat calmly while watching her rummage through most of his worldly possessions. Aware that he had never before permitted anyone to do what she was doing, he found it odd and shocking that he had no compunction about allowing her to sift through the contents of his life. That recognition both pleased and disturbed him.

At one point, Nikki pulled out a large bronze medallion, which she placed under glove box light for a better look. Studying the image and reading the inscription on it, she asked curiously, "Is this what I think it is? Is it real?"

"Yeah," he said softly, almost shyly, "but that's another story."

"I have time," she said while pressing the medallion between the palms of her hands.

He waited several seconds before speaking. "What you hold in your hands," he declared with a sigh, "represents my mother's proudest moment."

"Well, if that's the case, you should take better care of it." She opened her hands and examined it again. "How did you get it?"

"Doing what I do best," he said. "Windsurfing." After speaking, he paused briefly to study her soft but strong features as she examined the bronze medal.

Glancing over at him, she signaled by her expression that she wanted to hear more.

"As I mentioned," he continued, "I grew up in Michigan, about a half-hour from Lake Michigan. Because of its close proximity, I spent a lot of time on the lake, vacationing there each summer with my family, and I developed a love of water—warm water, that is. I hate cold water, and Lake Michigan was so damn cold. That's one of the reasons I decided to leave and why you now find me in the south where the waters are a little warmer.

"Anyway, after the deaths of my brothers and sisters, I was the only child remaining, so my family moved to Chicago to get a fresh start and escape the bad memories. My dad took a job as a long-haul trucker, which meant he was away from home much of the time. I started hanging out in the marinas close to our house where I met a crusty old sailor who lived on a sailing trawler, a thirty-nine-foot steel-hulled Bruce Roberts design." From the look on her face, he could see that his description of the vessel meant nothing to her, so he continued.

"The old sailor was a funny guy. He had a cat that guarded his boat, a nasty feline he liked to call a 'watch cat' but which I referred to as an 'attack cat.' He also owned a life-sized manikin fitted with carpeted eyes. The cat loved to spring at the manikin and claw at its eyes, seeing it as a game that the sailor encouraged it to play. After he had thoroughly trained the cat to attack the manikin, he then began leaving one hatch open at all times so the devil cat could climb out onto the deck. If anyone ever tried to break into his boat, well, you can guess the rest."

"You're making that up," she said to him.

"No, I'm not. He really did have an attack cat—and a manikin with carpeted eyes. The manikin was always sitting on a chair in the corner, and I'd watch the cat lunge at it without warning, clawing frantically at its eyes. I never trusted that damn cat. Hell, I'm still paranoid of cats even now. That's why I started wearing sunglasses all the time. It didn't matter whether it was day or night. Whenever I was on that boat, there was a pair of sunglasses on my face."

Nikki was skeptical of what she was hearing, but she found his tale entertaining. She sensed a change his demeanor, one considerably more carefree and less guarded than before, and she found herself experiencing a greater level of comfort around him as well, especially while listening to him narrate his life story.

"With my dad gone much of the time that first year in Chicago, I spent most of the summer with the sailor. My mother liked him and didn't mind that I was on his boat all the time. She seemed to consider him a good substitute father figure, but, at the time, I couldn't understand why. He seemed so old and gruff that I found her approval of him mystifying. Looking back now, I can see that he was a good influence on me. He taught me how to maintain marine engines, and I'm a pretty good diesel mechanic now, good enough that I can usually pick up work in a marina when necessary. He also did something else for me.

"Lashed to the side of his boat was an old sailboard, an original Hoyle Schweitzer-Jim Drake designed Windsurfer from the 1970s. I once asked him about it, and he told me that I could have it if I learned how to sail it. It turns out that the old guy was a pretty good windsurfer in his youth, and he taught me how to do it. It came naturally to me, and I really enjoyed the sport. Afterward, he introduced me to someone from the local yacht club who taught me how to sail and race Laser sailboats. That's something else that came naturally to me, but I always preferred windsurfing.

Fortunately, I was able to combine the two to become an exceptional racer in the windsurfing class. Despite my youth—I was only seventeen—I made the tryouts for the U.S. Olympic team, and that's how I earned the bronze medal. That was the only Summer Olympics in which I ever competed. That's why I say it was my mother's proudest moment."

Nikki was silently impressed and started to think that she had misjudged this skinny kid. "Whatever became of the sailor?" she asked.

Dave's demeanor changed as if her question touched an emotional void deep within him. "I went to see him one day in the early fall," he said, "and he was gone."

"Gone?"

"Yeah, he just pulled up anchor and sailed away, probably headed south for the winter. Never said goodbye or anything—just left." After a brief silence, he added, "He and I are a lot alike in that respect, so I really can't complain or fault him for what he did."

Throughout Dave's discourse, Nikki had been facing him with her left knee resting on the bench seat, but she turned back toward the glove box after he finished speaking. From the tone of his last sentence, she understood that he would be offering no more insights into his personal life, at least not then, so she carefully returned the bronze medal to the glove box. Just then, she spotted a pen lying in the remaining clutter, so she grabbed it and began recording her address and phone number on the envelope. "I only have a cell phone," she said, casting her eyes up at him, "but you can also reach me at work." She smiled and added, "I'm sure you remember where I work."

As she handed him the envelope, the keys jingle on the lanyard around her neck. "Oh, yes," she said. "Let me give you this." Fumbling with the split ring at the end of the lanyard, she removed a key and gave it to him saying, "Here's the key to Mark's house ... in case you need it."

Looking at it, he replied, "What? Are you also trying to turn me into a cat burglar?"

"No," she said, "but you never know. Perhaps."

By that time, the sun had dropped completely behind the dune, sharply reducing the level of lighting both inside and outside the hearse, prompting Mulligan's to switch on the overhead strings of lights across the deck. Just then, the guitar player returned from a short break and began playing again, his summer melody drifting in through the open windows of the hearse.

"Well," Dave said as he jammed the key into one of the many

pockets of his cargo shorts, "let's go find the door this key unlocks." He then reached down and fired up the engine, after which he yanked on the headlight lever but winced when saw no light reflecting off a wooden post near the front bumper of the hearse. Annoyed at what he saw—or failed to see—he pushed in and pulled out the plunger of the light switch several times without success, quietly swearing under his breath when the headlight refused to illuminate.

"What's wrong?" she asked.

"Damn headlight again," he said in disgust. "I'll be right back." With the engine running, he hopped out and rushed to the front of the hearse, leaving open the door while grumbling under his breath about the temperamental headlight. Nikki could only shake her head as she watched Dave's shadowy figure comically strike the glass lens several times with the side of his fist, hitting it harder each time until the headlight surged to life, exploding with a blast of illumination that exposed him in a sea of brilliant white light. Upstairs in the bar, Travis happened to be walking by the window at the very moment the headlight poured forth its light, and he easily recognized his friend spotlighted in the parking lot. With the inside dome light brightening the interior of the hearse, Travis also saw through the open door where he could discern the lower torso of a female passenger. "Score!" he exclaimed with a triumphant lifting of his arms, unaware that no one else in the place understood his inference.

As Dave jumped back in the driver's seat, Nikki asked playfully, "Does that happen often?"

"Only when I'm in a hurry—or trying to impress someone," he said offhandedly. "Damn, now I'm night blind from that headlight."

"Are you trying to impress me, Mr. Rasputin?"

"What?"

"I asked, 'Are you trying to impress me?'"

"Of course," he said with a boyish grin. "How am I doing?"

"Do you really want to know?"

He paused a moment and thought before answering, "Probably not."

Staring out the windshield while Dave wheeled the hearse through the parking lot toward the beach road, Nikki reflected on their time together, admitting to herself that she was, indeed, impressed with him. That awareness left her with many unanswered questions, the most prominent one being what she intended to do about it. At her direction, Dave turned right onto the beach road and then drove southward before cutting over Dune Street just before Surfside Plaza to continue heading south on the bypass. As they drove through the twilight, she asked him, "Whatever ever became of the girl who made the noose?"

Dave did not immediately respond to Nikki's question but sat quietly on the seat, his hands loosely gripping the steering wheel as he silently pondered an appropriate response. He found it amusing and slightly telling that she had remembered the brief mention of his former girlfriend, and he liked the fact that she had asked about her. He was not entirely sure what it meant, but he was anxious to find out.

Just when he was about to answer her question, he sensed a rising tension in Nikki's body a split second before she shrieked, "Look out!" Her cry had the tone of near panic, and it instantly reawakened him to the road ahead of him. He had become so distracted formulating an answer to the girlfriend question that he had not noticed a bicyclist attempting to cross the highway directly in front of them. Fortunately, however, Nikki had been watching the road and alerted him in time to swerve past the cyclist, missing him by barely an inch. The young man's terrorized expression was apparent to both Nikki and Dave as they careened past him.

"What about the girl?" Nikki asked once they were safely past the cyclist.

"No, I think it was a guy," Dave replied, craning his neck to look back at the bicycle, its rider now safely on the other side of the highway.

"Keep your eyes on the road," she ordered with a grin. "I'm not talking about the kid on the bike. I'm talking about the girl and the noose. What happened to her?"

The conversation was now starting to intrigue him. "Oh, her, I don't know. I knew her briefly a few years ago in Georgia, but either she or I had to leave; I can't recall which. All I know is that I haven't seen or heard from her since."

"So, that's how it works," she said. "You blow into some resort town, spark up a summer romance, and then you're gone, leaving the poor girl with a broken heart. I see how you operate." Despite their brief association, she knew how to get him on the ropes.

"No, no. You've got it all wrong."

"Have I?" The scowl on her face was not something he had seen before. "Oh wait," she said suddenly. "You want to turn here."

Pointing to the right, he asked, "Here?"

"No, no," she said, "at the light after the Outer Banks Mall. Slow down after you make the turn." She was becoming anxious, and he could sense it.

The signal was green so he was able to turn without stopping, after which he slowed down to a crawl once they were on West Seachase Drive. With no other cars behind him, he crept slowly down the road while Nikki studied the lights of the homes silhouetted against the glowing western sky directly ahead of them. Although she had not indicated which house belonged to Mark, he could sense her mounting trepidation as they drew closer to the first cluster of homes, and he felt himself becoming anxious as well.

"What are you looking for?" he asked in a near whisper.

"Shhh," she said to silence him.

He did not ask anything else but increased his speed slightly until they approached the first intersection in The Village at Nags Head development. The residential plan sat on a higher elevation than the bypass, allowing it to receive the final rays of the sun setting over Roanoke Sound, but most of the light was blocked by the houses, rendering the streets gray and shadowy. Despite the darkness, Dave managed to navigate the hearse without removing his sunglasses, which by then had lightened to a subdued tint.

"You want to turn left on this first street," she said in her best tour guide voice. "His house is off to the left." She craned her neck and squinted into the shadows as Dave slowed down in preparation for turning. "Wait," she cried, "there's his car in the driveway—oh my God!"

"What?"

"It's him!"

Without warning, Nikki flung herself across the front seat, resting her head on Dave's thigh as he wheeled the long hearse through the ninety-degree turn. The binoculars from the glove box were still lying on the seat, digging deeply into her ribs, but she gritted her teeth and remained paralyzed in her prone position, desperately trying to make herself as inconspicuous as possible. Reaching down, Dave placed his right hand on her shoulder to reassure her and help hide her presence.

The moment that Nikki had spotted him, Mark was stepping off his front porch, and he reached his car in the driveway just as the hearse coasted past his house. Despite Nikki's anxious behavior, Dave had not increased his speed after the turn, choosing instead to creep along at a snail's pace, hoping to get a good look at his competition. He sought only a glimpse of the man but received much more than that. His first reaction was that of shock— followed by dread and intimidation—at the sheer size of Mark, but a quick glance at the golden hair of the girl resting her head uneasily on his lap filled him newfound confidence and courage, enabling him to dispel most of his fear and apprehension. Coldly and callously, he peered through the twilight at the larger man opening his car door.

A hearse cruising slowing through a residential development at night is not a common sight, and it instinctively caught Mark's attention, causing him to pause and observe the strange phenomenon. He could see the face of the driver looking at him with a hardened expression, so he stood his ground and stared back at him, matching the unprovoked glare with a menacing scowl of his own. Appearing calm and determined, both he and Dave locked onto each other's gaze and held it for several seconds without moving or blinking, both experiencing an unexplained air of recognition as they peered through the lenses of their sunglasses at the divergent reflections of themselves, silently and dangerously passing one another in the tranquil twilight of the warm summer evening.

CHAPTER 7

Scattered leaves littered the front lawns of the middle-class neighborhood as a looming chill foretold the approach of winter. At the far end of the street, the sun performed a dramatic death scene in spectacular reds and oranges, but the contorted branches of the barren trees lining the avenue blocked the view of the young man plodding down the sidewalk, his cumbersome burden tucked securely under one arm. The only sound in the neighborhood came from a dog howling forlornly in a backyard kennel, a melancholy lament giving voice to the residents of this depressed industrial town, all of whom huddled in their homes awaiting the approach of nightfall.

The sole occupant of the desolate street continued onward at a slow, deliberate pace, carrying a large cardboard box that he unconsciously shifted back and forth from one arm to the other. Using his breath to warm his free hand, he wiggled his fingers before tucking them into the front of his jacket while staring woefully at the steps of another unwelcoming home, this one a massive structure constructed of dirty bricks held in place by cracked and crumbling mortar. The old house loomed dark and heavy in the twilight, much like the despair and despondency weighing on the young man's soul, a tortured soul teetering on the verge of collapse—emotional collapse.

Light emanating from the windows confirmed the presence of

people inside the house, and the style and pattern of the window curtains suggested that the residents were of advanced age. Resigning himself to the unpleasant chore, the young man dragged himself onto the porch and rang the doorbell, not attempting to hide his apathy or the disgust he felt, visual markers that miraculously vanished the moment the porch light flicked on and an elderly woman opened the door.

"Hello-o-o," he said with feigned enthusiasm. "This is your lucky day because I'm here, and I'm … the light bulb man!" As he spoke the words, he mechanically reached into the cardboard box to retrieve a package of light bulbs that he strategically placed alongside his cheek. The twinkle in his gray eyes and the electrifying smile on his face were enough to make any actor envious. Drawing on some hidden power, he had shed all traces of discontent to execute a total personality change that was nothing short of phenomenal. Unfortunately, however, his talents went unacknowledged and unappreciated by the old woman who slammed the door in his face.

"Best thing I ever did was to get my ass out of that miserable town," Dave announced to the empty interior of the hearse while shaking off the invasive memory. Fidgeting in the front seat, he yawned sleepily as he glanced up at the house he had been watching since early morning. It was almost noon, and no one had entered or left Mark's place the entire time he had been there.

In an attempt to remain hidden, he had stationed himself in the parking lot of the Outer Banks Mall in front of the Food Lion grocery store adjacent to the Outback Steakhouse. That placed him about fifty yards away from West Seachase Drive but close enough to see into the residential development of The Village at Nags Head. From his concealed position, he had a clear view of the upper rear portion of Mark's house rising above the pines and shrubbery of the golf course, but the tightly drawn shades of the second-floor windows prevented him from seeing into the house despite his binoculars. With only two ways in or out of the residential development, Dave had positioned himself in the parking lot of the strip mall because he believed it to be the route Mark would probably take when leaving the house; however, the big man had not ventured out all morning.

Dave passed the time reading several chapters of two worn paperback books he had brought with him from his cottage, and he occasionally turned on the car radio to listen to the weather updates, especially the ones pertaining to Hurricane Kim that was skirting the northern coast of the Dominican Republic that Wednesday morning. Ultimately, however, boredom—that great enemy of comfort—crept in to claim him as one of its victims. By noon, the monotony had become intolerable, so he used his urge to find a bathroom as justification for leaving.

"That's it," he said in desperation. "This guy's not going anywhere." As he spoke those words, he cut short his surveillance by pulling out of the parking lot and driving up to the stop sign on West Seachase Drive where he glanced at Mark's house to deliver his apologies. "Sorry, Mark, old boy," he said, "but if I don't find a bathroom soon, I'm going to explode. Do me a favor and stay put until I get back."

Dave's cottage was nearer to his stakeout, but he instead sought relief at the Animal Hospital of Nags Head where he found an empty waiting room and no one sitting behind the counter. Not bothering to announce himself, he made a mad dash for the restroom, only to be shocked to find by Nikki waiting for him when he walked out. Standing with her arms crossed, she asked, "Is this what I'm paying you for?"

Surprised at seeing her, he grinned and said, "You need to understand, there are some things in life that can't wait. Besides, that creep hasn't budged from his house all day."

"He didn't go out at all?" She seemed perplexed. "Normally, he schedules client meetings in the morning."

Dave shrugged his shoulders and wiped his hands on his pants while voicing a mild complaint, "Do you know you're out of paper towels in there?" Construing from her expression that she was not interested in restroom-related issues, he continued, "No, he never left. He hasn't even opened the window blinds. I've been sitting there all morning while he's been sleeping or doing whatever it is he does in there."

Nikki was unwilling to accept this assertion. "Are you sure he didn't leave before you got there? He jogs every morning about seven o'clock. He's obsessive about things like that. He also likes to run on grass because it's easier on his knees, so he goes out the back and runs up the fairway of the golf course."

"Not unless he left or went running before the sun came up. I had a clear view of the back of his house as well as the fairway and green, so I would have seen him if he had run up the course. Also, his car has been in the driveway all morning, so he didn't drive anywhere. I've been sitting in the hearse watching the back of his house, and, a few times, I walked up the road and checked the front as well. My vehicle is a little conspicuous, so I've had to park down by the Food Lion in the mall parking lot."

"You're telling me the truth? You were definitely there early, and you are absolutely sure he didn't go anywhere?"

Dave was not used to having his veracity questioned. "No," he said with some annoyance, "he didn't leave the house, and yes, I was there early. In fact, the last seven hours I've been sitting on my ass watching my life waste away."

She threw him a dubious glance that only served to increase his frustration.

"Hey," he said. "Remember me? Buddy Rasputin, windsurfer, surf bum—not Sherlock Holmes. Responsibility is not my bag, but I'm always willing to do a favor for a friend. I never claimed to be a private eye, and, frankly, I really don't know how to be one; so maybe this whole thing was a mistake. Maybe you should find a professional who can give you the quality service you demand at commensurate prices." After his exasperated outburst, he boyishly shrugged his shoulders and turned to go.

"No, David, wait. Please. I'm sorry. This thing still has me upset." At that moment, one of the vet technicians emerged from the back and glanced curiously at the two of them standing in the waiting room. Nikki looked at Dave and said, "Come with me to the kennel area where we can talk. I have a lot of work to do, but we can discuss things while I work."

They both walked through a doorway leading back to a room stacked from the floor to ceiling with animal cages. However, before getting there, Nikki ducked into an office and yanked Dave into the room with her where she closed the door and said, "First things first." She then lifted the phone receiver and began dialing a number. "This is a private line," she said while punching the numbers into the keypad. "It's blocked from caller ID, so he won't know who's calling." Instead of raising the receiver to her ear, she thrust it against the side of Dave's face and commanded, "When someone answers, ask for Mark Allen."

"What?" Her actions startled him, and he instinctively backed away only to be stopped by the wall directly behind him. "And then what?" he asked incredulously.

"Just pretend to be an investor."

"How? I don't know anything about money or investing."

"Just fake it," she said sternly with an annoyed scowl on her face.

He did not want to argue with her, so he grudgingly complied and stood quietly by the desk while the phone clicked off several rings. Mentally, he tried to come up something to say if Mark should answer, but it was not necessary because the call jumped to voicemail after about five rings. Relieved, he reached down and pressed the button of the phone carriage to terminate the call before the recording beep sounded.

Nikki started to say something, but he quickly hushed her. "Voicemail," he said softly.

She then dialed the number of Mark's landline as Dave took the phone receiver from her hand and pressed it to his ear. "Try this one," she said to him.

Again, he nervously pondered what he would say if someone answered the call, but the only thing he heard at the end of the line was a recorded announcement of Mark's vacation plans along with a suggestion that he call back later. The line then terminated without offering him an opportunity to leave a message. He made no comment but simply hung up the phone and stared at Nikki.

"Well?" she asked impatiently.

"Just a message saying he is on vacation and that I should call back when he returns."

"Vacation," she moaned angrily. "Yeah, some vacation." She then became glassy-eyed as she stared woefully at the blank wall, her expression that of an abandoned little girl, the identical look that had persuaded him to help her in the first place.

"You know, that's not such a bad idea," he quipped.

"What idea?" she muttered under her breath. Lost in introspection, she had responded reflexively without an awareness of having spoken.

"A vacation!" he said loud enough to snap her out of her trance. "Maybe you should take some time off. Look at you. Can't you see how rattled you are? Why don't you follow through on your vacation plans and go somewhere?"

"Now you sound like my girlfriends." Her tone was dismissive, but then she grew strangely quiet, pausing a few moments as if she were seriously considering his suggestion. Shaking her head, she said with renewed determination, "No, I couldn't."

"Why not?"

"Well, I don't know. I just can't see spending a lot of money traveling to some exotic place when I know I won't be able to enjoy myself. I've already discussed this with my friends. When I go away, I want to be in a good frame of mind so I can have fun. I don't want to be in a funk while I'm there. A vacation should be more than just therapy for depression."

He could see that she had thought this through and had already dismissed the idea. Thinking quietly for a moment, he smiled and said, "Well, then, why not just a day or two—or even an afternoon?

Join me at the beach. I'll teach you to surf … or windsurf … or even kitesurf if you want. Have you ever done any of those things?"

"I've water skied before, but I've never tried the others. I've always wanted to give windsurfing a try, thinking it might be easier to learn since I'm pretty good at waterskiing, but I've never had the opportunity—or the time." Her expression softened as she thought more about it, and he sensed that she was warming up to the idea when she did a sudden about-face and said, "Wait a minute! How can you teach me to windsurf when you're going to be following Mark around? Oh, I see your plan."

Observing her through his sunglasses, he was thankful she could not see his eyes because he knew how expressive they were and how easily they betrayed what was in his heart. Consequently, he always concealed them to shroud his intentions and gain an edge in any negotiation. "Well," he said. "I just figured that if you were taking a day off, then I deserved one too."

Stone-faced, she tried to scold him with one of her schoolmarm glares, but it had no effect. "I wish you would take off those glasses," she said in frustration. Dave's only response was to shake his head, indicating that he was not about to surrender his only defense shield. "Come with me and we'll talk about it," she snapped as she shoved him out of the office and into the room with the kennel cages.

The room they entered was flooded with harsh fluorescent lighting that reflected coldly off the stark white walls, and it had a strong antiseptic smell hanging in the air, one tinged with the scent of wet pet hair. Lying on a blanket on the floor was a small beagle puppy that began yapping and struggling to its feet the moment it saw the door open. Nikki smiled at the puppy while handing a leash to Dave. "There's a dog over there," she said. "Bring him here to me."

"The beagle?"

"No," she said, pointing her finger. "There's another dog in a large cage on the end. You can't miss him." She said it with a peculiar smile on her face as she stooped down and began attending to the squirming puppy.

A plaster cast on the beagle's hind leg hindered its ambulation, but the puppy still managed to wag its tail frantically, inducing a swaying motion that sent it tumbling onto its side. Nikki reached down and began examining the soft, wriggling patient, laughing playfully as it spastically licked her hands and gnawed on her fingertips. Gently lifting the animal, she moved it to one of the cages where it began crying and yelping loudly.

Dave watched the interplay between Nikki and the puppy while walking backward toward the end of the room where he stopped and turned to view the largest dog he had ever seen in his life. Sitting erect in an oversized cage, the dog neither barked nor displayed the least amount of interest in Dave or anything else for that matter; it just sat there panting in long, deep breaths with a blank, impassive expression on its face. "You've got to be kidding," he called out. "I wouldn't reach in there unless I was armed with a stun gun."

"Oh, you baby," she said, coming to his rescue. "Give me the leash." She yanked it from his hands and unbolted the gate. "C'mon Godzilla," she ordered.

"Godzilla?" he questioned with a smile.

Shrugging her shoulders, she remarked, "It's his name."

The enormous dog lumbered to its feet with the slow, deliberate movements of a sedated elephant. It then plodded out of the cage at a labored pace, gradually overcoming inertia until it gained enough momentum to sustain its forward progress. Nikki tightened her grip on the leash and braced herself against the tug of the beast, knowing how hard it would be to stop it once it got moving. She then directed it toward the door at the end of the room.

"What kind of dog is he?" Dave asked.

She replied to his question without taking her eyes off the dog, concentrating instead on the trajectory of the hulking canine. "Our friend here has a lot of things going on inside of him," she said. "Mastiff, Great Pyrenees, Newfoundland, Great Dane, St. Bernard, and unquestionably the real Godzilla." Rapidly approaching the end of the room, she cried out, "You better open the door or he might go right through it."

Dave slid around them and propped open the door just in time for beauty and the beast to pass through. "We're heading to the examination room over there," she said, and he ran ahead to open that door as well. As luck would have it, the dog was not averse to going into the examination room, so it voluntarily strode through the open doorway. Once inside, however, it proclaimed an end to its compliance and immediately collapsed onto the floor in a heap of fur.

"Now for the fun part," Nikki said with a smile.

"What do you mean?"

With a playful sparkle in her eye, she said, "Now we have to put him on the examination table."

Glancing over at a stainless steel table, Dave saw that it was a standard tabletop model without a mechanical lift, so he said while looking down at the huge dog drooling on the floor, "Wouldn't it be easier to bring the mountain to Mohammed?"

"Maybe you're right," she said with a quick glance at the animal now resting comfortably on the floor. "Perhaps I can examine him down there. After all," she said with a smile, "we wouldn't want you to get a hernia lifting him."

"A hernia is not what worries me. It's those large white teeth and his questionable disposition."

"Oh, he's harmless," she said while dropping cross-legged onto the floor where she began poking and probing the docile dog with her fingertips. Holding open its mouth, she peered down its throat and examined its teeth. Afterward, she listened to its heart and then probed the pads of its feet. No matter what she did to it, the dog complied and yielded to her touch, appearing to enjoy the attention showered upon it.

Dave watched in awe. He could not help but admire the control she wielded over the beast and her natural skill in performing this type of work. It was truly a gift, which he had first seen during her examination of Grave. On the beach the previous day, he had spoken about her career choice, expressing his hope that she had chosen the correct one, a career that satisfied her spiritual and emotional needs as well as one that provided her both comfort and contentment. What he observed in the examination room at that moment confirmed that she had indeed selected the right vocation, her true calling in life.

"You have a gift," he said. "It's incredibly obvious. Do you have a dog of your own?"

"No, it wouldn't be fair," she answered while continuing her examination of Godzilla.

"What do you mean?"

"It wouldn't be fair to the dog. I put in long hours here, and I volunteer at the Humane Society. In addition to my normal working hours, I'm on-call like a regular *people* doctor. That means I'm liable to be called out in the middle of the night to deliver a calf. So, you see, it wouldn't be fair to the dog, but I definitely would love to have one. You are very fortunate to have Grave. He's such a beautiful animal despite his repulsive name."

Godzilla appeared to grow weary of the examination, and he began rocking back and forth in an attempt to stand up. "Down, citizen," she ordered, and the giant canine sank back to the ground. Halting her probe of the animal, she stroked its head while staring across the room as though pondering some pressing matter. Still sitting cross-legged on the floor, she glanced up at Dave and looked at him with a spirited look on her face. She said, "I'll tell you what. Maybe I will take you up on your offer of some beach time and windsurfing lessons—tomorrow. That might be exactly what I need, and it will give you a legitimate excuse not to follow Mark."

Dave liked what he was hearing, especially the part about no longer having to shadow that muscle-bound klutz.

"I'll make you a deal," she continued. "You do your surveillance work today and tonight, and then tomorrow we'll play. Depending on what you see or learn today, maybe I'll call the whole thing off, and you won't have to follow him anymore. Is it a deal?"

"It's a deal!" he said emphatically. That was the best offer he had received all day.

"Then don't you think you better get back over to Mark's place and hold up your end of the bargain?"

"Ah, yeah, of course. Are you sure you don't need me here for anything?"

"I can manage," she said with a broad grin. Rising to her feet, she brushed the dog hairs off her white lab coat while adding, "Give me a call later tonight to let me know what's going on."

He had already started to leave but stopped abruptly upon hearing her request that he phone her later. "Sure," he said with a glance in her direction. "I'll give you a call and let you know what's going on. See you later. You too Godzilla—and don't let her push you around." At the mention of its name, the great beast looked in Dave's direction and yawned deeply in affirmation that it let no mere mortal push it around.

Since Dave had not yet eaten lunch, he decided to swing by Sam & Omie's to grab a quick bowl of clam chowder served "Hatteras-style," but those plans were instantly scuttled when he received a phone call from Travis whose car had broken down in the vicinity of Kelly's Restaurant. Without hesitation, he wheeled his hearse onto the bypass and sped off to his friend's rescue. Knowing that Nikki would not approve of another diversion from his surveillance duties, he nevertheless jumped at the opportunity, feeling safe in the knowledge that she would never find out. After a few minutes of traveling up the bypass, he spotted his friend trudging down the side of the road in front of the Secret Spot Surf Shop near the sixteenth milepost, so he pulled into the lot and parked facing the highway.

"Damn, it's hot ... and humid," Travis moaned while climbing onto the passenger's seat. "Doesn't this antique have air conditioning? Close the windows and turn it on. I'm dying here!" With perspiration streaming down his cheeks, the overweight bartender wiped his face on the front of his Mulligan's tee shirt while panting profusely, barely able to catch his breath.

Dave used the switch on the door panel to close all the windows and then reached for the air conditioning controls. "I'm trying to save some money," he stated grudgingly while complying with his friend's request. "It's expensive running the AC."

Travis slumped in his seat and gently closed his eyes. "I'll write you a check," he said serenely as his panting subsided. "But, first, let me cool down and rest."

Dave looked down the bypass but saw no sign of a disabled vehicle. He asked, "Where's your car?"

"It's farther up the highway, about a half-mile on the other side of the road near Kelly's. Actually, it's right across from Dirty Dick's Crab House. That's where it broke down. I thought I could walk to Mulligan's, but it's too damn hot for that. After a half-mile, I said, 'Forget it,' and I called you." With a smile widening across his face, he opened his eyes and rolled his head in his friend's direction.

Dave looked at him and said, "Wow, you walked a whole half-mile. So that's how you stay so slim and trim."

"Screw you," Travis said lightheartedly while massaging his Buddha-like belly. "You're just jealous of my Adonis physique."

After studying his friend's beer gut for a few seconds, Dave shook his head and asked, "Do you want me to stop back and take a look at your car after I drop you at work?"

"Hell, no!" Travis said with a playful glint in his eye. "Buddy, I know you're good at keeping this old heap running, but I called a *real* mechanic—a professional. I called the Mayor."

"You called the Mayor?"

Travis started laughing uncontrollably. "Yeah, I called him and told him that my car had broken down on the side of the road. It gave him a thrill knowing that I was stranded—an even bigger thrill when I asked for his help. He was absolutely ecstatic knowing that I was at his mercy, but I let him have his fun. I laid it on thick too. I spoke so meekly and humbly; it was pathetic. It was all I could do to keep from laughing as I sucked up to him. Trust me, Buddy, it was not pretty. Be glad you weren't there to hear any of it. On second thought, maybe you should have been there. My performance was Oscar-winning."

Dave again shook his head. "I can't believe you called him … I can't believe he agreed to help you."

"That's the beauty of it, Buddy. The Mayor's ego is so massive that he's easily manipulated. I've known him longer than you have, so I know the right buttons to push when dealing with him. Here's the thing you need to understand about the Mayor: if some piece of machinery is not functioning properly anywhere in the world, he views it as a disturbance in the cosmos and a direct affront to him. He then feels obligated to set things right by repairing it—even if it is owned by me! The fact that I let him know there is a disabled vehicle requiring his assistance means he will become obsessed with it until it's running again. He even told me that he'd get his truck and tow it to his shop if he can't fix it on the road, but he doesn't anticipate having to do that. On the phone, he acted as if he already knew what was wrong with it, telling me he could probably repair it onsite." Travis then chuckled while reclining his head and again lowering his eyelids.

"Oh, one other thing, Buddy," he said without opening his eyes. "If you find yourself down here later today while the Mayor is working on my car, you better wear your shades because the glare of the sun reflecting off his chrome-dome might cause a driving hazard." He then sat upright and beamed an enthusiastic smile. "Perhaps we should post warning signs along the highway?"

While they continued talking about the Mayor, an old motorcycle with a sidecar whizzed past them heading north on the bypass. The sight of it surprised both Dave and Travis, leaving them slightly dumbstruck and somewhat amused. The motorcycle was a two-toned red and white 1950 Indian Chief Blackhawk with a signature fringed saddle, skirted fenders, and an ornamental Indian head mounted on the front fender. It had a hand shifter extending up along the fuel tank and two fishing poles protruding from chrome tubes on either side of the rear wheel. As the antique motorcycle roared up the highway, the fiberglass fishing rods curved backward like whip antennas bending in the wind.

The biker was a man in his early fifties sporting a graying goatee, his face a weathered patchwork of lines carved so deeply that they resembled scars. He wore a black tee shirt, camouflage cargo shorts, and biker boots in addition to a highly polished chrome skull lid cinched tightly over a fluttering Confederate flag bandana protruding from beneath the helmet. Gripping the handlebars tightly in his powerful hands, he stared straight ahead, his eyes shielded by extremely dark wraparound sunglasses. Sitting next to him in the sidecar, clad in goggles, was a basset hound panting excitedly, its long tongue blowing off to the side and its enormous ears flapping in the wind. Both Dave and Travis craned their necks to view the unusual sight as it zoomed past them.

"Did you see that?" Travis eventually cried out in astonishment.

"Yeah," Dave replied, still a little dumbfounded.

"I can't believe it! His Honor, the Mayor, right on cue!" Travis' voice had a gleeful tone to it as he bounced merrily on the seat like a child unexpectedly catching a glimpse of Santa Claus on Christmas Eve. "And where did he get those dog goggles?"

Dave still had a look of incredulity on his face. "I'll be damned if I know," he said. "The Mayor told me that he planned to pick up Grave and take him with him today, but I never—" He turned to Travis, "You know; that damn dog won't even let me cut his toenails. How the hell did the Mayor get him to wear those goggles?"

"I'm not sure who is stranger, Buddy, the Mayor or that dog of yours. I'll tell you one thing, though; I wouldn't let my dog ride with the Mayor, not on a bike with a suicide shifter. I don't think those things are safe."

"The Mayor's bike doesn't have one of those," Dave said. "Those shifters are low on the side under your butt. They also call them ass wipers. I think the 1948 Indians had them. The Mayor's bike is a 1950 model with a three-speed hand shift transmission, rock-a-bye foot clutch, six-volt ignition, and an eighty cubic inch engine—a real classic."

"Damn it, Buddy, now you're starting to sound like the Mayor. Just don't start acting like him—*if you know what I mean.*" Travis grinned at his friend and then continued, "The Mayor might not like many things, Buddy, but he sure likes that dog of yours. You better be careful, or he might steal him away from you."

"Nah," Dave said. "Grave would never—" He paused a moment. "Hmm, on second thought. Nah, he wouldn't."

Travis glanced over at him skeptically. "You're probably right," he said, "but we better get moving, or I'm going to be late for work. By the way, what's up with you and that blonde? I caught your little escapade in the parking lot last night. As a matter of fact, we all did."

Dave ran his fingers through his dark hair as he tried to formulate an appropriate response. Travis' question had taken him by surprise, and it triggered a slight surge of embarrassment that he suspected his friend could sense. He knew that any hesitation in answering would only add fuel to Travis' prying nature, so he jammed the hearse in gear and pulled out onto the bypass. "Long story," he said. "I'll tell you about it when I come in tonight. What about you and what's-her-name?" He brought up another subject he thought would steer their discussion away from his relationship with Nikki, and the ploy seemed to work because Travis took the bait and sat up straight, waving his arms like a maniac. Travis may have been a master at manipulating the Mayor, but Dave knew how to play Travis.

"That crazy chick!" Travis exclaimed. "I think she's the reason my car broke down. At first, I thought she had dumped sugar in my gas tank, but I don't think she's smart enough to do that. Besides, the Mayor told me it couldn't be sugar in the gas."

Dave smiled. "What's up with you two? I haven't seen her for a while."

"Ah," Travis remarked with a disgusted wave of his hand. "She's history—History ... *if you know what I mean*." He calmed down and again flashed his boyish grin.

"You don't keep them around long, do you, Travis?"

"About as long as you do."

"You've got a point there," Dave said as he reached over and inserted his Tommy James CD into the slot of the disc player.

Travis immediately switched it off and said, "You and that damn music. I think History is into that old stuff too. Maybe I should get the two of you together."

"No thanks," he said. "I've got enough trouble as is."

"I don't know, Buddy. She's got some large assets that could keep you warm at night, especially during those long winter months. By the way, where do you hide out in the winter? I'm sure you go farther south to escape the cold weather, but where?"

"Southwest Florida—Fort Myers, Cape Coral, Sanibel Island area. There's some great sailing by the Sanibel Causeway Bridge, and there's a watersports shop near the bridge called Ace Performer where the owner lets me give windsurfing and kiteboarding lessons out of his store. On the whole, my winters down there are pretty much like my summers up here."

Travis chuckled and closed his eyes again. "You've got the life, Buddy. You've sure got the life."

When they arrived at Mulligan's, Travis opened the door and asked, "You coming in?"

"Later," Dave said as he watched his friend get out. "I've got something to do right now."

Travis leaned against the open door and stuck his head back inside the hearse. "Hey, Buddy, don't think I've forgotten about that blonde. I still expect a full accounting of everything. You're not getting out of this one, at least, not that easily."

"Okay," Dave said in submission while flipping off the air conditioning. "I'll tell you all about her tonight."

Travis smiled and pointed his finger at his friend. "I'm going to hold you to it ... *if you know what I mean*." He then closed the door and chuckled to himself as he shuffled toward the restaurant, mumbling something about the Mayor as he walked across the pavement.

Dave knew he had wasted too much time already, so he ditched his plan of stopping at Sam & Omie's for chowder and opted instead to get something from Dune Burger to take with him to the stakeout. Fearful that Mark might have slipped out during his absence, he first drove by the house to check on things, breathing a sigh of relief upon finding Mark's car parked in the driveway and everything buttoned down tight. Telling himself that nothing had happened while he was gone, he then drove back to reclaim his parking space in front of the Food Lion, smiling internally as he congratulated himself on his good fortune. Nikki would not have been happy with his dereliction of duties if Mark had escaped unnoticed, but now she would never know. Having sidestepped that potential problem, he eased back on the seat and enjoyed his Dune Burger in the comfort of his hearse.

The afternoon passed slowly with Dave becoming more and more frustrated with each passing hour. He was incredibly bored with the whole endeavor and uncomfortable sitting inside the hearse all day. The sun beating down on the shiny black finish of the vehicle raised the interior temperature to that of a blast oven, making him feel like an overdone baked potato. He tried to keep the doors open for ventilation, but he frequently had to close them whenever shoppers insisted on parking beside him. All day long, he listened to the clanging of shopping carts and the snippets of conversations as people passed by. No one seemed overly concerned about the sinister-looking hearse parked all afternoon in the same spot or the slender, sweating man in sunglasses trudging up to the stop sign each hour to peer at a house in the distance before spinning around to walk back to his vehicle. Then, in the evening twilight, just after sunset, something unexpectedly happened.

The first sign of change came when Dave abruptly awoke from one of his brief, unscheduled slumbers. Becoming aware that he had nodded off again, he rubbed his eyes and said to himself, "Sleeping on the job—not a good idea." As he reached down to massage the calf muscles of his legs still sore from running on the beach, he glanced drowsily at Mark's house where something caught his attention in the approaching darkness. There, in the murky distance, he noticed that Mark had fully opened the vertical blinds of the sliding glass doors on the second floor. It was a minor alteration in his perception, the first sign of life all day, and he was aware of it only because it contrasted significantly with the static image of the house seared into his brain from hours of non-stop observation.

No lights appeared in any of Mark's windows, although his neighbors had already turned on their inside lamps. Additionally, his next-door neighbor had flipped on his two large floodlights, one of which illuminated the side of Mark's house. Dave considered trekking up the street to have a closer look, but something made him remain in the hearse. Shortly afterward, he observed a pair of headlights emerging from Mark's street to turn onto West Seachase Drive and move in his direction. Even in the pale shade of evening, he recognized the approach of Mark's storm gray sedan.

Parked some two hundred feet from the road, there was no need for Dave to hide, but he found himself unconsciously slouching down on the seat as Mark's car drew closer to the strip mall. Knowing that efforts to avoid detection would be futile due to the conspicuous nature of his vehicle, he kept his head down anyway, peeking through the steering wheel as the car drove past the entrance to the parking lot and proceeded to the intersection with the bypass, stopping at the traffic signal when the light turned red.

Having confirmed that the car was indeed Mark's Infiniti and that Mark was alone in the car, Dave started the engine and began slowly backing out of his parking space, creeping up to the stop sign at West Seachase Drive where he waited to see which direction Mark would turn when the traffic light changed. Observing him head south, Dave then barreled full bore toward the intersection where he negotiated a hard right turn onto the bypass just as the signal was transitioning from green to yellow. That put him directly behind Mark's car but far enough back to remain unnoticed.

His pursuit of Mark took him two miles down the highway to Whalebone Junction where the gray sedan veered into the left lane beneath a sign for the Cape Hatteras National Seashore and the Nags Head beaches. Reluctantly, Dave followed him into the turning lane, knowing that he faced the likelihood of having to stop behind him at the traffic signal. Fortunately, however, the light changed just as Mark approached the intersection, and both of them were able to make the left hand turn without getting too close to each other.

Instead of proceeding south into the Cape Hatteras National Seashore, Mark continued past the Holy Trinity by the Sea Catholic Chapel and turned right on South Old Oregon Inlet Road into the South Nags Head District. Through the many turns, Dave was able to keep Mark in sight, but, once they got off the highway and onto the beach road extension, he was only able to track him by means of his glowing red taillights.

They traveled just a few miles down the dark, two-lane road from the sixteenth to around the eighteenth milepost where Mark's car made an abrupt left-hand turn onto a short street lined with beach houses. With no cars behind him, Dave slowed down to a crawl as he approached the place where he had lost sight of the taillights because he did not want to turn onto a street without knowing what awaited him there. As luck would have it, another car was approaching from the opposite direction, so he brought the hearse to a full stop and waited for the car to pass him by, using those few moments to assess the situation. Sitting on the road with his left turn signal flashing, he was neither nervous nor frightened, and yet he felt his heart thumping vigorously, keeping time with each audible click of the pulsating signal. It led him to surmise that his body was sensing a danger that his conscious mind had yet to recognize.

Peering through the darkness toward the end of the street, he spotted Mark's car sitting outside a beach house about one hundred feet away. It would not be possible for him to drive down there and remain hidden, so he decided to hide in the driveway of another house, one closer to the road. Fortunately, the first rental house near the corner appeared to be unoccupied, so he turned onto the street and immediately pulled into the driveway of a small stilted cottage, parking beneath its porch so that only his taillights were exposed. Jumping from the hearse with his binoculars in hand, he agilely ascended the stairs to the porch where he had a clear view of the street all the way to the end.

The house where Mark had parked his car was a typical cottage-style beach house with a pitched roof and slatted railings surrounding its wraparound porch. Located precariously close to the sea, the weathered home sat enveloped on three sides by enormous mounds of drifting sand that limited the number of parking spaces in the driveway to two. Mark's Infiniti occupied one of the spots with another car parked beside it. Because the house faced the beach, Dave could not see into the living area, his view limited to the darkened windows of the bedrooms on the back of the house. He thought about walking down to get a better look but decided to wait a few minutes to see if anything happened. He did not have to wait long.

The first thing that caught his attention was the sound of laughter, the bright, sweet timbre of a young woman's voice. Looking through the binoculars while sitting on the railing of the porch, he was able to confirm that she was indeed young as she strolled out the door of the beach house, tightly clutching the arm of a towering man in sunglasses. She appeared to be in her early twenties, but it was hard to tell in the murkiness of the night and the weak glow of the single light fixture positioned above the door. "Oh, so that's what's going on," he said aloud as he watched the two descend the stairs and get into Mark's car.

As the gray sedan moved slowly up the road toward the stop sign, Dave remained hidden in the shadows while sitting in a wooden Adirondack chair on the porch. He waited until Mark had turned onto the beach road extension in the direction of Whalebone Junction before springing to his feet and charging down the stairs, clearing the last three steps in a single bound. Hastily backing out of the driveway, he was in pursuit of the couple within seconds, speeding down the road with Mark's taillights in view.

At Whalebone Junction, he saw Mark veer onto the beach road and then turn into Cahoon's Market beside Jennette's Pier. Rather than follow him into the store's parking lot, Dave hid in the shadows by Sam & Omie's Restaurant on the opposite side of the road where he could watch in secret everything occurring at Cahoon's. He did not have to wait there long because Mark was only in the store a few minutes, emerging with a bottle of wine that he handed to the girl through the car window before climbing back into his Infiniti and speeding away. Pulling out a short distance behind him, Dave raced down the road, beginning the chase anew.

It was astonishing how quickly he had mastered the technique of shadowing someone, and he began thinking it might prove a lucrative career for him if he ever decided to give up the surfing life. He had no problem maintaining visual surveillance of Mark's car while remaining undetected despite driving around in a circus wagon that practically advertised his presence, and he looked forward to telling Nikki about his newfound skill along with all he had learned about Mark's secret life. Yep, he thought to himself, his discovery of Mark's affair would be just the thing to cement the deal with Nikki. Once he told her how the jerk had dumped her for someone else, it would be clear sailing for him. Observing Mark race down the road, moving farther and farther away from Nikki, he felt himself drawn even closer to her.

He followed Mark and the girl onto the causeway where the two vehicles crossed the Washington Baum Bridge to Roanoke Island. Driving past Pirate's Cove Marina and Condominiums at the end of the bridge, Dave smiled as he thought about Nikki, finding it astonishing how everything was unfolding practically on her doorstep. Tailing Mark's car past the Roanoke Island Marshes and through a right-hand turn toward Manteo, he pursued the big man and his date all the way into town being especially careful to maintain enough distance to remain unseen. At an intersection several streets beyond a banner advertising nightly performances of *The Lost Colony*, Dave followed Mark onto Sir Walter Raleigh Street where they traveled down the narrow road through several picturesque neighborhoods lined with flowering crepe myrtle trees spilling their sweet fragrances into the warm night air.

Despite Mark's substantial lead, Dave seemed unconcerned because he knew that the street continued only as far as the town square, a confined area where it would be easy to spot and observe the couple once they parked the car and began walking around. Upon reaching the end of the road, he turned left onto Queen Elizabeth Avenue and motored just one block before spying Mark's car in the tiny lot beside The Tranquil House Inn. The parking lot was too small for him to enter without being seen, so he drove past it and turned onto the bridge leading to Roanoke Island Festival Park. Glancing to his right as he crossed over the water, he was able to glimpse the waterfront and the many boats moored in the marina, but he could not see Mark or the girl anywhere on the boardwalk.

There was a parking area at the end of the bridge, so he pulled into it and abandoned the hearse under some Loblolly pines teeming with fireflies. Running back across the bridge via the pedestrian walkway, he took little notice of a young man approaching him from the other side of the bridge, an actor dressed in sixteenth-century Colonial garb. Upon passing each other, the young actor addressed him in character, speaking with an early Euro-American dialect. "G'd evenin', sir," he said.

Dave did not respond to him, ignoring his greeting and sprinting to the center of the bridge where he stopped by one of the lampposts and peered over the side. Attached to the handrail on either side of him were American and North Carolina flags swirling lazily in the gentle breeze as if waving to the boats in the marina and the people on the boardwalk below. Off to his left, he could clearly see the *Elizabeth II* spotlighted in the darkness amid the trees and marsh grass, but historical displays and tourist attractions were not what he was there to observe.

He did not advance beyond the arch of the bridge because he immediately spotted Mark and the girl on the first pier extending out from the boardwalk. Unwittingly, he had stumbled upon the perfect place from which to continue his surveillance. Because it was a peaceful summer night, many people were walking onto the bridge, trying to gain a better view of the marina, so he appeared no more than an average tourist casually observing the activities of the couples milling around the waterfront. In truth, however, he was focused on one couple and one couple alone.

Over the course of the next fifteen minutes, Dave watched Mark and his girlfriend board a sailboat and disappear below deck. The Bimini cover over the cockpit prevented him from seeing into the main salon despite the open companionway, but he could distantly hear the voices of the couple although he could not make out what they were saying. The one thing he clearly discerned, however, was the coquettish laughter of the girl, indicating the nature of the activity occurring unseen in the salon of the boat. Eventually, Mark and the girl reappeared topside, and, shortly after that, Dave heard the familiar sound of a Yanmar marine diesel firing to life. He next observed the illumination of the boat's steaming and running lights followed by the scampering of Mark's large, shadowy figure across the deck to release the dock lines. A few minutes later, the boat lurched out of the slip and began chugging slowly in the direction of the channel.

Dave did not leave his post even after the sailboat had departed its slip, choosing instead to watch the craft motor slowly away from him, praying that it marked an end to this whole fiasco. The intensity and urgency that had gripped him during his pursuit through Nags Head and Manteo had dissipated, leaving him relieved and thankful that it was finally over. From his vantage point, he still could see into the cockpit of the boat but only dimly. The outline of the girl reclining on a cushion against one of the coamings was barely visible, but he had no problem distinguishing the massive hulk standing behind the wheel of the helm, a figure that appeared intimidating yet absurd—intimidating due to its colossal size yet absurd for wearing dark sunglasses in the gloom of night.

At one point, Mark turned and looked up at the bridge with something other than a casual gaze. It was more a challenging glare than anything else, and it lasted a little too long for Dave's liking, evoking an internal reaction that he could not explain. Because of the darkness and distance, he believed it improbable that Mark could clearly discern him in the night, and yet he sensed the large, antagonistic man looking directly at him, impaling him with his shaded eyes. A cold chill ran through his body, and he experienced a feeling of dread that he could not shake. Even when Mark redirected his eyes back to the boat, the sense of foreboding remained, leaving his defense mechanisms on high alert. By then, all he could do was focus on the white stern light of the boat as it passed by the *Elizabeth II* on its way through the marina.

Mark never turned around again, and Dave eventually diverted his attention toward the other watercraft in the marina in a deliberate attempt to distract his mind and banish the unfounded fear that had seized him. It worked, too, because, the moment he cast his eyes across the tops of the sailboat masts, he observed a startling sight that commanded his full attention, one that pushed from his mind all other thoughts. At the end of the dock on the far side of the marina was something that touched a familiar chord deep within him, a triad of notes comprising a bittersweet melody known only in his memories and dreams, a lonesome song containing a one-word lyric—*home*. Without thinking, he raced across the remaining length of the bridge and practically leaped down the stairs to the boardwalk where he ran with abandon past the metal benches, lampposts, and live oak trees lining the waterfront. Oblivious to the disapproving glares of the people ambling along the wooden planks of the walkway, he sprinted past them, concentrating only on the implausible hope swelling within him. His mind and purpose were singularly driven and directed toward one location, one slip, one boat.

The uplifting vision he had spotted from the bridge was that of a tall mast with two furling headsails: a jib sail and a staysail. Multiple headsails are quite common, and many boats carry them; however, this boat also had a wishbone shaped boom suspended over the cabin roof of a pilothouse. Silhouetted against the glowing lights of the bay, it looked familiar—too familiar—wonderfully familiar—and it spoke to him of his youthful days spent in a Chicago marina. He felt certain that it was the boat owned by his former mentor, the crusty old sailor who had left without saying goodbye.

Tiptoeing down the dock as if fearful of spooking the sailing trawler, he moved slowly and tentatively toward it, appearing hesitant to learn if he had been too impulsive in assuming that this was the same boat owned by his old friend. With the light of the shore power pedestal illuminating the stern of the craft in a yellowish glow, he was able to read the name of the boat, but it was not what he had expected to see, triggering a small wave of disappointment that threatened to plunge him into a state of melancholy. Not only was the name different, but so too was the color of the hull; however, under closer examination, he noticed raised lettering beneath the colored surface, hard edges of a hidden name decal covered over with a fresh coat of paint. Smiling to himself, he remembered applying the decal years ago after pestering the old sailor to give the boat a name, insisting that every boat deserved a name. Eventually, his mentor acquiesced to his request and purchased a custom-made name decal, handing it to Dave and telling him to apply it to the stern. This certainly was the same boat, he assured himself, but with a fresh coat of paint and a new name.

While standing at the stern of the boat, his ears perked up when he heard a familiar sound coming from offshore, prompting him to turn his attention to the water. What he heard was the joyous sound of laughter coming from a boat passing by the end of the dock, the same laughter he had heard earlier that evening at a beach house in South Nags Head. Unbeknownst to him, his wild race down the boardwalk had outpaced Mark's departure through the marina, and it placed him on the last dock just as Mark's sailboat was motoring by. Standing quietly in the shadows amid the moored boats, Dave's presence remained hidden from the couple in the cockpit as they joked and laughed while cruising slowly toward the navigational markers leading into Shallowbag Bay.

"Can I help you?" asked a soft, warm voice.

Dave turned to face a woman in her mid-fifties standing along the rail at the back of the sailing trawler. He made eye contact with her but then promptly pivoted back to follow Mark's progress out into the bay.

"Is that a friend of yours?" she asked in a pleasant tone.

"Actually, a friend of a friend," he said, glancing once more in her direction before again peering at Mark's receding stern light.

"Well, don't wait up for him," she said. "Since we arrived a week ago, we've seen him go out several nights, but he never comes back before we go to bed, which is usually pretty late. However, his boat is always back in its slip by morning when we take a stroll down the boardwalk with the boys. I think he's more interested in late night entertaining than he is in sailing … if you know what I mean." Upon making her innuendo, she gazed at him with a matronly smile.

Dave responded with a grin of his own and said, "Can I ask you about your boat?"

Before she could answer, a minor disturbance erupted on the dock not far from the boat. It consisted of growling, snorting, and whimpering followed by scratching and clawing as a small tidal wave approached Dave in the form of three pugs swirling around his ankles.

The woman began laughing effortlessly. "I see my husband is back with the boys. Don't worry, they won't hurt you."

The three pugs continued snorting and jockeying for position around Dave's feet while jumping and clawing at his legs. Dropping down on one knee, he tried to pet them, but their squirming and nipping at each other made it hard to scratch or caress any of them. The woman's husband came walking across the dock and tried to herd them away while saying, "C'mon boys, leave the poor guy alone."

"That's all right," Dave said, still trying to pet all three at once. "They probably smell my dog on me."

"Honey," the woman said to her husband. "This gentleman wants to ask us something about our boat."

"Yeah," Dave said while rising to his feet. "I knew the former owner."

Upon hearing Dave's claim, the man started chuckling. "You mean Captain Ahab?" he said. "That's what my wife called him."

Dave found himself laughing along with him. "He is quite a character. Do you know where he is now?"

"That's anyone's guess," the woman said. "Why don't you come aboard, so we can talk about Ahab. You tell us your stories, and we'll tell you ours."

Dave and the husband stepped around to the side of the boat followed by the dogs. The distance between the boat's deck and the pier was too great a distance for the pugs to cross on their own, so the man boarded first while Dave handed the dogs over one at a time. Once everyone was safely on board, the husband took Dave on an extensive tour of the boat, proudly showing off some of the modifications he had made since purchasing the craft. Despite the changes, Dave easily recognized the sailing trawler as the one on which he had spent many hours as a youth learning valuable life lessons, but it was not exactly the way he remembered it. All the wood had been sanded and refinished, and the brass trim and fixtures were now polished to a high sheen. The new owners had dumped some serious money into the restoration of the old trawler, and it was absolutely gorgeous. The J-brackets on which had hung Dave's original Windsurfer were still in place, but fishing poles and several boat hooks now occupied its space. Upon finishing the tour, they retired to the back deck and sat on expensive teak furniture while the man's wife blended some boat drinks in the galley. When she offered Dave a tall glass filled to the brim with a thick, creamy beverage, he took a big gulp of the sweet concoction and told the couple about the old sailor's attack cat.

"That explains the dogs' reaction to certain places inside the boat. They still smell the cat," the wife said.

"That could be," Dave said. "It was always slinking around

somewhere, looking for an opportunity to pounce. It used to scare the hell out of me, but I tried not to let the cat know—or his owner. So what became of my old captain?"

The husband set his glass down on a teak table and said, "Well, we live up in New Jersey along the shore, and we bought this boat from him up there. You see, he won the Power Ball and bought himself a new boat."

"He what?" Dave could not hide his astonishment, and he almost choked on his drink upon hearing what the man had said.

"Yeah," said the wife. "He became a millionaire overnight and bought himself another boat. We saw pictures of it. It's quite beautiful. What is it, Honey? A Seaward?"

"A forty-six-foot Seaward; they call it a Seaward 46RK, one of those boats with a retractable keel and a pilot station inside the main cabin. The pilot station was the big selling point for him because he wanted to be able to sail in heavy weather without getting wet. He ordered it with twin diesels and had it rigged for single-handed sailing. I guess you can get whatever you want if you have the money. That helped us too—the fact that he didn't need the money—because we were able to buy this boat for next to nothing. Of course, it needed a lot of work."

"But what about the captain? Where is he now?"

The man looked over at his wife, enlisting her aid in answering Dave's question. She shrugged and said, "Like I said before, that's anyone's guess. When we last saw him, he said he was heading south to Florida to pick up his boat. From there, who knows? He just told me that he planned to avoid the temperate zone and finish out his days in the tropics. He was tired of cold weather and never wanted to see snow again."

The husband then interjected, "He did say, though, that he'd like to sail over to Spain at some point. But who knows? When we left New Jersey, I mentioned to my wife that we might run into him. We're thinking about sailing as far as Florida where we plan to spend the winter."

Upon hearing that the couple did not know the captain's whereabouts, Dave felt a stab of disappointment, one that dulled his elation over his friend's good fortune. He missed his old mentor, and he found that sitting on the deck of the trawler surrounded by so many pleasant memories only intensified his sentimental longing to see him again. The salty old sailor embodied a part of his past that was truly joyful, and he dreamed of reconnecting with him at least once more in his lifetime. Although they remained separated, the information provided by the couple about the old-timer's travel plans offered a glimmer of hope, a chance that their paths might cross someday while Dave was down in Florida escaping the cold himself.

For the next hour, the three new friends sat on the back deck drinking and relating stories about their mutual acquaintance. The boat owners were friendly people, and Dave enjoyed being in their company. He also enjoyed talking to them about his past, something that was quite unusual in its own right. Ultimately, however, he decided that he should get back to Nikki and things that dealt more with his present and future, a future that looked much more promising now that Mark had sailed away. Bidding his adieus and wishing his hosts a safe journey, he unclasped the gate of the lifeline and climbed off the sailing trawler.

Just being in the marina had triggered nostalgic memories of his youthful time in Chicago, remembrances that lingered while he listened to the sound of his feet slapping against the wooden planks of the dock. Moving farther away from the boat, he experienced a sense of closure, a feeling of finally having said goodbye to his old friend. A few times along the way, he stopped and glanced back at the vessel floating serenely in the darkness, remembering doing the same thing in Chicago whenever leaving the sailor to return home each night. However, when he reached the end of the dock and turned onto the boardwalk, he marched straight ahead and never looked back.

Near the end of the boardwalk by the stairs leading to the bridge, he stopped under a lamppost and pulled out his cell phone along with the envelope on which Nikki had written her telephone number. Holding up the envelope to the light, he read the number and punched the digits into the phone before plopping himself down on a bench to await her answer.

She picked up the call on the fifth ring. "Hello!" she said.

"Is this the veterinarian from the Animal Hospital of Nags Head?" Dave asked in an altered voice.

"One of them, yes."

"I really hate to bother you at this hour, but my cow is about to give birth to her calf. Do you think you could help me?"

"Believe me," she said, recognizing the farce. "No one can help you."

His charade exposed, Dave smiled in response to her comment. "I'm over here at the waterfront in Manteo," he said. "Your boy just set sail on his boat, and it will take the Coast Guard to follow him any farther tonight."

"What boat?"

"I don't know. I assume it was his boat. He got onto a large sailboat, started the engine, and motored into Roanoke Sound."

"He hates the water," she said. "He doesn't swim. Actually, I think he's afraid of the water. He wouldn't set foot on a sailboat if his life depended on it, and, if he did, he'd insist on wearing at least three life jackets."

"Well, he wasn't wearing a life jacket tonight, and he seemed pretty comfortable around the water. It appears as if you don't know him as well as you think you do." Dave did not mention the girl with whom Mark had set sail because he was unsure if it was the right time to divulge such information.

"It seems you're right," she declared, almost in a whisper.

"Listen," he said. "I haven't eaten yet, and I was going to go to Mulligan's to get a sandwich or something. Why don't you join me, and I can fill you in on what happened?"

There was a pause at the end of the line.

"I can pick you up," he continued. "It's right along the way, and I have to drive by your place regardless." He held his breath while awaiting her answer, counting the seconds that felt like hours.

"Okay," she said in a sudden outburst, indicating she had been holding her breath as well.

With a gratifying sigh, he told her, "I can be there in about five or ten minutes."

"Okay, I'll be ready. My address in on the envelope I gave you. You just need to turn left once you enter Pirate's Cove and go through the guard station. Just say you're coming to see me if anyone asks. That will put you on Pirate's Way where you'll find my building. I'm on the second floor. You'll also see my Jeep Patriot parked in front of the building, and I'll keep an eye out for you."

"Sounds good. I'll see you in a few minutes." As he ended the phone conversation, he jumped to his feet and ascended the stairs leading to the bridge, clearing the six steps in a single bound to set off jogging across the pedestrian walkway while glancing over the railing at the *Elizabeth II* floated serenely in the warm summer night, its framed planks glowing iridescently in the darkness. Farther across the marina, he observed the burning illumination of the Roanoke Marshes Lighthouse, its reassuring light offering guidance to mariners in search of safe harbor, and he found himself wishing anything but safe harbor to Nikki's ex-boyfriend, the one mariner he hoped never to see again.

When Dave and Nikki arrived at Mulligan's, the festivities were well underway. There had been a surfing competition earlier in the day, and all the participants were enjoying themselves at an awards party on the Tiki Deck. Dave had skipped the contest because of his surveillance commitment to Nikki, but he still wished to attend the celebration. He had not yet decided what to tell her about Mark, and the uncertainty of it weighed heavily on him despite the celebratory nature of the night. Nikki had refrained from questioning him about Mark while they were at her condo and in the hearse on the way over there, but he knew the questions were coming, surmising that she must be saving them for dinner conversation. As they ascended the stairs, he grappled with how he would break the news to her until the sound of his name rising above the din of the crowd jarred him from his quiet deliberations.

"Buddy!" Travis roared the moment he spotted them at the top of the stairs.

Dave did not respond but merely nodded to his friend as he and Nikki walked past the bar toward the deck, stopping to speak to the hostess at the door who told them to take any vacant table they could find outside. Travis stood dumbfounded, repeatedly looking down at Dave's usual spot at the bar until his friend finally got the message. Glancing uncomfortably at Travis, Dave leaned closer to Nikki and whispered, "If I don't go over there now, he'll badger us all night. I'll order a couple drinks while you find us a table. What would you like?"

"Just a glass of white wine—Pinot Grigio, Riesling, anything," she said.

He touched her lightly on the arm as she turned and walked onto the deck while he stood watching her for a few moments through the glass panel of the door. The way her clothes enveloped her tall, slender frame made her appear incredibly elegant even though she wore nothing more than a simple sleeveless white top and light tan shorts. Peering down at himself, recognizing that he looked more like an unmade bed than anything else, he cinched tight the belt of his baggy shorts and walked to the end of the bar where Travis stood waiting for him.

"Buddy, what's wrong?" the bartender asked. Aren't we good enough for you anymore?" Travis then feigned a wounded look that was a phony as he was, glancing briefly in Gary's direction to see if he was paying attention. With his vintage reading glasses perched low on the bridge of his nose, Gary sat nearby at the bar. He appeared to be reading his book amid the noise and chatter of the crowd, but he was keenly aware of everything occurring in the place, especially matters involving his two friends at the end of the bar.

With an admonishing glare, Dave retorted, "Just get me a beer and a glass of white wine and cut the crap or I'll call History and have her stop in here to see you."

At the mention of his estranged girlfriend, Travis twitched and displayed a mischievous smile before scurrying away to fill his friend's order. In his absence, Dave relaxed for a moment and leaned against the bar as he glanced in the direction of the Tiki Deck. He was surprised to find Sally standing nearby in a quiet corner of the room. She had been there for several minutes taking a break from waiting tables, but he had not spotted her until that moment. A foul, bitter look contorted her face, announcing to everyone that something was bothering her. "What's wrong, Sally?" he asked.

With a disdainful grimace, she snapped, "Don't push me!"

"What?"

"Ah, never mind," she groaned. "I've just got a bug up my ass." Suppressing a smile on her lips, she walked away and began waiting tables again.

Travis had returned with the drinks just in time to catch the exchange between them. He said nothing when Dave shot him a questioning glance, merely shrugging his shoulders and rolling his eyes in Sally's direction before hurrying away to fill other drink orders despite his desire to stay and hear about Nikki. With Travis too busy to probe his love life, Dave happily grabbed the wine and beer off the bar and walked out onto the deck where he spotted Nikki sitting at a picnic table on the upper level under a string of incandescent light bulbs. Ascending the four steps to the upper deck, he had barely reached the top when he heard his name rising above the music of a two-man band performing in the corner.

"Buddy!" a young bartender called out from the corner bar while flashing a "hang loose" sign with both hands. His booming voice also caught the attention of a table of surfers who, until then, had been unaware of Dave's presence. One of them reached up and grabbed Dave's arm just as he was taking a step in Nikki's direction.

"Buddy," he said, "we missed you today."

Looking down at the group, he smiled and addressed them, "Hi, guys. Yeah, I've been busy."

The seated surfer spotted the beer bottle and wine glass in his hands and then looked in the direction he had been walking. "Yeah," he said with a crooked smile upon eyeing Nikki at a distant table. "I can see that." He then turned and glanced over at his fellow surfers, all of whom were now grinning and gawking at Nikki as well.

"Don't even think it," Dave said to the four of them, none of whom were paying him any heed. Instead, they continued ogling Nikki until he stepped in front of their table and used his body to cut off their view while walking off in her direction.

Mulligan's had set up a buffet table on the deck with a large assortment of food and two covered stainless steel serving trays, both heated with flaming Sterno canisters. While passing the table, Dave put down the wine glass and lifted one of the covers to examine the contents of the tray, becoming instantly aware of his folly when steam billowed out from around the sides of the lid to scald his forearm while the searing heat of the stainless steel handle blistered his fingers. His initial impulse was to cry out in pain and throw the lid to the ground, but he managed to control his outburst and carefully returned the cover to the warming tray, a pan containing nothing more than boiling water. Quickly picking up the wine, he soothed his injured fingers on the cool surface of the chilled glass as he slinked over to the table, trying his best to hide his discomfort from Nikki.

"You're pretty popular around her, aren't you?" she asked jokingly.

"Well," he said, "you have to consider the venue. It's a surfing party." He set her wine before her and then placed his wounded hand around the cold beer bottle. As the moist, frigid glass provided relief to his blistered fingers, he closed his eyes for a moment and sighed softly.

"What's wrong?" she asked when she detected the unusual expression on his face.

"Nothing. Why?"

"No reason." She looked at him sideways and asked again, "Are you sure nothing's wrong?"

"No, no. Everything's fine," he declared with a forced grin.

Looking as if she still did not believe him, she picked up her menu and began reading it while commenting, "It's a little late. I think I'll just have a salad."

Peeking over his shoulder at the buffet table, he warily eyed the warming tray that had inflicted the burns on his hand, after which he turned his attention to the second tray, noticing that it also had a flame under it, wondering if it was empty as well. Although curious about its contents, he decided not risk finding out. Still, he questioned if the scalding trays were someone's idea of a sick joke, a way to get people to burn themselves.

Turning back to Nikki, he noticed that she was still studying the menu, so he once again directed his attention to the serving table. Just then, a man and woman walked onto the deck and moved in a direct line toward the buffet table. From their appearance and the amount of leather they wore, he surmised that they probably had ridden in on motorcycles. Pivoting his body slightly to get a better view, he became so absorbed in the drama unfolding at the buffet table that he failed to notice Nikki staring at him.

As if following a script written by Dave himself, the woman biker pointed to the warming trays and said something to her burly companion, who compliantly lifted the cover of the first tray, the same one that had inflicted Dave's wounds. By that time, the temperature of the water had increased to where it was boiling with even greater ferocity, and Dave winced and squirmed on his seat in response to the tortured expression of the biker standing motionless with the red-hot lid clutched tightly in his large hand. Machismo prevented the guy from wildly overreacting or openly expressing his discomfort, so he gingerly lowered the lid onto the tray without a sound. The only betrayal of his agonizing burn was the sporadic rubbing of his hand on the back of his jeans. As was the case with Dave, he decided to forego investigating the second tray as he ushered his girlfriend back into the bar. Upon their departure, Dave felt a slight twinge of disappointment along with an increased desire to know what lay beneath the lid of the second warming tray. Turning back to the table, he was a little shocked to find Nikki studying him with genuine curiosity.

"What are you looking at?" she asked.

"Oh, nothing," he said with a smile. "Just sharpening my surveillance skills."

Although it was nighttime and the only available light came from strings of overhead bulbs slung across the deck, Dave still wore his sunglasses, which had lightened to a softer tint. Nikki noticed the change in the lenses and asked, "Are those prescription glasses?"

"No," he said. "I've got twenty/twenty vision."

"But aren't those transitional lenses? They seem to get lighter when it's dark out."

He took them off and placed them on the table. "Well, to be honest," he said with a grin, "they *are* transitional—or photochromic as they should be called. You've probably noticed that I tend to wear them all the time, a habit that used to annoy a girl I once dated. She claimed that she needed to see my eyes to know when I was telling her the truth."

"I know how exactly how she felt," Nikki said with an empathetic nod.

"As it turns out, she worked for an optometrist, so she made me this pair of transitional sunglasses. It allowed her to see my eyes at night or whenever we were inside."

"Let's see, you have a former girlfriend who made you a noose, and now one who made you a pair of sunglasses. Are there any more discarded females lurking around out there?" She sat waiting for an answer but did not really expect one.

Fidgeting in his seat, he looked skyward through the strings of lights and said, "Wow, look at the moon. It's almost full." Reaching down, he then grabbed the menu and continued, "We really need to order. I'm hungry." Nikki did not respond but simply grinned at his attempts to avoid her stare. Fortunately, he was rescued from the uncomfortable situation by the arrival of the waitress, a petite young girl in her early twenties.

"Hi, Buddy," she said. "I see you've got your drinks. Are you ordering food?"

"Yeah," he said. "I didn't pay Travis for the drinks, so you'll have to put them on my tab."

"No problem," she said with a smile. Turning to Nikki, she asked, "What can I get you?" The waitress then wrote down Nikki's order—a classic Caesar salad topped with a crab cake—after which she spun around and started to leave.

"Wait," Nikki called out. Looking at Dave, she asked, "Aren't you getting anything?"

The young waitress glanced casually in Dave's direction. "You're getting the usual, aren't you, Buddy?" He nodded his head affirmatively while the server smiled at Nikki and pointed her pencil at Dave. "Mr. Predictable," she said before turning and walking toward the door.

"The usual?" Nikki asked a little astonished. "You really are famous around here, aren't you?"

"Clam chowder," he said with a shrug. "It's my staple diet."

Examining his lean figure, she said, "You might want to start doubling up on it or, at least, adding a little more protein to your diet."

"What? You want me to get fat?"

"I don't think you'll ever be fat," she commented. "And while you're at it, feed Grave a little more too. He's starting to look like you."

"Well, don't people usually look like their pets?"

"That's true," she acknowledged with a grin.

Unconsciously, he slid his hand across the table to grab the stem of his sunglasses, but she stopped him by putting her hand on top his. She then snatched the glasses with her other hand and moved them closer to her. "You can have these back when we leave," she said. "You have such lovely eyes. Why must you always hide them?"

Just then, the musicians ended their song, and, in the brief lull, Dave heard a disturbing noise coming from behind him, something that sounded like a groan. Spinning around, he saw a woman standing by the hot serving trays with her fingers jammed into her mouth. Like the biker before her and Dave before him, she then bypassed the second tray and moved quickly away without looking under the cover. "Damn!" he said under his breath.

"What?" Nikki asked, rising slightly from her seat to look around the deck. "Just what is so interesting over there?"

"Nothing," he said with an impish grin.

"You are a strange one, Mr. Rasputin. I will say that." Her demeanor then became less playful and more serious. "Now tell me what you found out today ... and tonight."

"Okay," he said, "but you're not going to like it."

The waitress then returned with their orders, setting the salad in front of Nikki and reaching across the table with Dave's clam chowder.

"Pretty good chowder here," he said, pointing to the bowl with his spoon. "This is New England style, but my favorite is still the black grouper chowder I used to get at the Hurricane Seafood Restaurant in Pass-a-Grille, Florida—also the conch chowder from the Twisted Conch in Cape Coral, Florida. It's spicy with a good bite to it."

"You were saying that I'm not going to like it?" She was not going to let him sidestep the issue by distracting her, something at which he was quite adept.

"Yeah," he said, blowing lightly on the hot soup before swallowing a large spoonful of it. He then proceeded to tell her about Mark and his romantic rendezvous with the young girl that included an after-hours sailing excursion on Roanoke Sound. He also told of meeting the couple on the sailing trawler who reported having seen Mark on other nights cruising out of the marina with different women.

Nikki's usually bright expression imploded like a collapsing star when Dave mentioned the existence of another woman and the likelihood of multiple other women. She had expected this outcome and had even prepared for it, but hearing it presented in such a blunt fashion was far more devastating than she had ever imagined.

Dave immediately sensed her change in mood, but he did not know what to do about it or how to cheer her up.

"Where does she live?" she asked matter-of-factly.

"He picked her up at a beach house in South Nags Head around Milepost Eighteen."

"Oh, yes," she said, as if familiar with that particular area, although she knew no one who lived there. Becoming aware of how the tone of the evening had changed, she made an effort to restrain her emotions by donning the false armor of contrived acceptance. "I guess that's that," she said, downing a big gulp of wine.

"Yep," he said, unsure of what else he could say to ease the tension. Fortunately, Nikki saved him from commenting further.

"Oh my God!" she said with a disturbed shriek. "You should have seen the face of the man behind you. What a horrible expression!" She tried to mimic his grimace, but her soft, well-developed features would not allow it.

Turning around, Dave observed a man standing beside the first warming tray, his hand clamped tightly beneath his armpit. Smiling inwardly, he anxiously awaited the man's next move, wondering if he would walk away or go for the second tray. With the suspense building, Dave began rocking rhythmically on the edge of his seat, thrusting his head and shoulders forward, psychically trying to nudge the injured man toward the second tray lid. In the end, however, his projected telepathy missed its mark, and the man walked away, cooling his fingers in his drink.

Dave and Nikki then finished their meals amid a lengthy procession of maimed customers who ventured too near to the warming trays on the buffet table. While they ate, Dave longed to ask Nikki if she was ready to call off the surveillance of Mark, but he held his tongue after seeing how his initial report had affected her mood. It was apparent to him that she was making a gallant effort to appear upbeat, and he did not want to say anything that might upset her again. They talked for a long time, touching on a variety of subjects, but no further mention was made of her ex-boyfriend.

It was not until the end of the evening after Dave had paid the bill and the waitress had returned with his change that Nikki said, "You don't have to follow him anymore. Enough is enough." Then, in the same breath, she added, "I'll come by your place tomorrow at ten, and we can go to the beach."

That was exactly what Dave had hoped to hear, and he did not try to hide his delight. He smiled softly in appreciation and prepared to say something when a disturbance erupted near the buffet table, one that caught the attention of all those sitting nearby.

"Damn it! Son-of-a-bitch!" a longhaired surfer yelled at the top of his lungs as he cast the tray lid from his hand, sending it crashing to the floor with a resounding clang. Not attempting to hide his pain, the kid then began shaking his hand like a maniac while blowing on his fingers. Everyone on the deck saw and heard what had happened, but only those in the vicinity with newly blistered fingers truly understood the outburst. Based on his overreaction to the burn, Dave guessed that the kid would not be investigating the other pan, leaving forever in doubt what lay beneath the lid. Resigned to the fact that he would never know the contents of the second serving tray, Dave left the waitress a tip on the table and then drove Nikki back to her condo at Pirate's Cove.

CHAPTER 8

The Cuban youth sprinted through the darkened streets with an unrestrained swiftness that only a twelve-year-old boy knows. His thin frame and youthful agility allowed him to soar effortlessly over the obstacles in his way as he navigated the flooded pavement and dodged the pools of mud swamping the sides of the road. Soaked to the skin by the unrelenting rain, he relied on the weight of his saturated shirt and pants to counter the effect of the driving wind, tethering him to the earth but creating aerodynamic resistance that hampered his forward progress, making it even more difficult for him to reach his intended destination. It was only his feeling of adolescent invincibility—combined with his great love—that propelled him onward, driving him forward through the gloomy streets despite the deteriorating weather conditions. Without a second thought about having undertaken such a dangerous yet noble mission, he charged headlong into the storm, unimpeded by concerns or doubts, quite aware of the danger he faced but accepting of his fate—too young for regrets, fear, or soul searching.

Earlier that morning, the government meteorologists had predicted that Hurricane Kim would strike the island nation during the night, and their forecast proved to be correct. The weather conditions had deteriorated throughout the day with the storm making landfall that evening, maliciously pounding the island with unbridled fury while holding the inhabitants in a lethal stranglehold.

Unable to remain in their home because of the storm, the boy's parents, along with his infant sister, had sought shelter at a Havana hotel, the same hotel employing their son.

His father had once held a good paying job in a sugar factory, but that was prior to the family incurring the wrath of Fidel and his brother, Raul, over something the boy did not fully understand. It involved the disappearance of his uncle's family and rumors that the family had left for America. The young boy missed his uncle and his cousins, and he wished he could have joined them in America because it was after their departure that bad things started happening. That was when his father lost his job and began laboring on the city streets, performing the only work permitted by the government—shining the shoes of those with power and influence, the ones with money and prestige. The government officials had also forced his family to give up their home and move into a shanty community on the outskirts of town. Fortunately, however, a very distant cousin then secured employment for the boy at one of the hotels catering mainly to Canadian citizens. What little money the boy earned, he gave to his father.

At his young age, Francisco was not interested in money. His real passion in life involved soccer, and he hoped to play for the Cuban Olympic Team someday, practicing long hours to achieve that end. Most of his friends preferred baseball, but he liked to play soccer. Baseball was too sedentary; soccer was continuous action, pure adrenaline. He loved the competitive nature of the sport, especially the demand for quickness and endurance, things that came naturally to him, mainly because he was so fast and agile. That was why he knew he would be successful in his endeavor that dismal night despite the many impediments in his way. Dodging the flying objects in the air and sidestepping the obstacles in the street were akin to fighting his way down the soccer field toward the goal. Now, finding himself in pursuit of a different type of goal, he drew upon those same soccer skills as he soared through the filthy, empty streets of his neighborhood.

His parents had sought shelter at the hotel because it was too dangerous to ride out the storm in the hovel they now called home. They brought with them only Francisco's baby sister and nothing more. The few possessions they had retained after moving into the shantytown, they left behind in their makeshift house. One of those possessions was the boy's puppy, a shorthaired mongrel hound.

Francisco was beside himself when his family arrived without the dog, but his parents tried to explain that they had feared the hotel manager would turn them away if they showed up with an animal. The boy loved that dog more than anything in the world, and he lashed out at his parents for leaving it behind. It was the first time in his life he had ever challenged either his father or his mother. The elder man sensed his son's passion while listening to Francisco insist that he had the speed and stamina to race back to the neighborhood to retrieve the dog, and he realized that his son was going to go with or without his permission. Therefore, he gave his blessing to the boy and turned him loose, a decision that incensed his wife.

When Francisco spotted his home at the end of the muddy road, he was relieved to find it standing with its corrugated roof still intact. Many of the other shacks lay in rubble, their sheet metal roofs swept away to other parts of the island. Several times along his journey, he had dodged their sharp edges as they soared through the air like deadly kites or skated along the pavement like unforgiving harvesting sickles mowing down everything in their way.

Pushing harder against the wind in a struggle to make his way past the empty dwellings, homes normally filled with other indigent families, he discerned a ghostly stillness in the village resulting from the flight of the occupants, a perceived quietness amid the clamorous mayhem of the raging storm. Mindful of the folly in remaining in their flimsy structures, the residents had abandoned their shanty community to seek shelter elsewhere. The usual sound of their voices was noticeably absent, displaced by the deafening roar of the wind and the cacophonous clatter of twisted metal and crumpled newspaper blowing through the deserted neighborhood. A tiny sound, however, managed to cut through the clamor of the chaos to reach the ears of the young man, tweaking his consciousness and stirring his soul. Straining to hear and then identify the high-pitch cry of an animal, he became euphoric and energized as he waded with renewed vigor through the mud and debris toward the frightened sounds of a forsaken puppy.

Exploding through the door with a fury equivalent to that of the hurricane, he startled the anxious little dog and sent it scampering into a corner of the shack. Standing in the open doorway, drenched and exhausted, Francisco appeared no more than a shadowy specter in the terrifying night until the puppy recognized his scent and charged at him with uncontrollable yapping, its tail wagging with unrestrained jubilation. Scooping the dog into his arms, Francisco allowed the puppy to lick his face while he used his shoulder to restrain the storm by forcing close the door, thereby restoring a measure of serenity to the inside the shanty. Due to the blowing rain penetrating the gaps in the walls, the tiny brown dog was almost as rain-soaked as its master, but Francisco hugged it tightly nonetheless, unoffended by the foul odor given off by its dirty, wet fur. Once again reunited with his one true friend, he refused to allow anything to upset him or rob him of this newfound joy.

The dark-skinned boy wiped away the dripping strands of hair from his face as he peered through the darkness at what used to be his home, taking note of the blown-out windows and the dirt floor that had become a sea of mud. Knowing that he held in is arms the only thing of value in the place, he tightened his grip on the dog and ventured back into the blustery night. Conditions were growing worse, and he knew he must move quickly, or he would never make it back to the shelter of the hotel where his family awaited his return.

Battling the wind, he sloughed through the ankle-deep mud to a paved section of road where he shook the heavy, wet muck from his feet in preparation for running. He would now be moving with the wind, something that could hasten his return to the hotel, but the journey would be much more challenging due to the deteriorating weather conditions and the small burden he carried in his arms. So far, the puppy had offered no resistance despite the mayhem swirling around it, and Francisco prayed that it would remain serene once he began sprinting through the streets. Resetting the dog in his arms, he looked down the road and prepared to set off running until something caught his attention.

What he glimpsed was nothing more than a flicker of light coming from one of the hovels a short distance ahead, a dull, glowing shimmer in the window of a broken-down shack. He found it unbelievable that anyone would have chosen to remain behind during the storm. Even at his young age, he knew the utter foolishness of trying to survive a hurricane in any of the fragile structures comprising the shantytown. Additionally, he was aware of the grave danger he and the dog faced if they did not leave immediately. Common sense told him to ignore the light in the window and run straight to the safety of the hotel. Common sense also warned him against going into the shack once he had climbed over the debris and reached the front door.

A collective shriek sounded the moment Francisco and the dog burst into the house. They brought with them all the violence and savagery of the storm until Francisco restored tranquility to the one-room shanty by forcing close the door. Turning toward an oil lamp sitting on a small table, he followed the beams of light across the panicked faces of an elderly woman and her four-year-old granddaughter. The harsh shadows of the flickering flame emphasized the embedded lines in the old woman's forehead and cheeks as well as the sagging bags under her eyes. The light also highlighted the colors of her hand-painted headscarf, a garment made of the same material as her ragged dress, and it revealed the crucifix and rosary beads she wore around her neck, plastic beads strung together on a thick hemp cord.

Francisco had seen the old woman before, but he had never spoken to her. She was a cripple who needed a cane or a single crutch to support herself. Her granddaughter was a mulatto child with large brown eyes and black hair braided up in short spikes covering the entire top of her head. She clenched her grandmother tightly and looked on with eyes full of wonder and nervous anticipation of what would happen next. Both the girl and the grandmother sat atop a rug on a dirt floor in the center of the shack.

Upon recognizing Francisco as a boy from the neighborhood, the disabled woman beckoned him closer, an order he obeyed by repositioning the dog under one arm while dropping to his knees in front of the old woman. What happened next shocked him beyond belief when, without warning, the woman shoved her granddaughter into his free arm while signaling that he should carry the girl to safety. Dumbfounded, he stared back at the old woman who continued waving him away with both hands. Seeing the lamplight glisten off the tears in her eyes, he gave an understanding nod and rose to his feet with both the girl and the dog folded in his arms.

Amused by the puppy's playful licking of her face, the little girl did not comprehend what was happening; however, when Francisco turned to go, she began wailing and screaming while stretching out her hands toward her grandmother. Unable to control the little girl's violent kicking and squirming, he had no choice but to release her and allow her to claw her way back onto the old woman's lap.

Francisco knew that he could not carry the girl to safety, not if she refused to go, but he also understood that he must leave immediately if he had any hope of making it back to the hotel. The strength of the hurricane had increased significantly, and he knew it would be far too dangerous to be on the street if he delayed much longer. Nevertheless, he sensed in his heart that he could not abandon the girl and her grandmother to the night, leaving them alone to face their inevitable destruction. His twelve-year-old mind was not equipped to handle moral considerations of that magnitude, and he found himself bewildered and stymied by the fear and emotion welling up inside of him. The old woman knew the quandary he faced and the internal struggle raging in his soul, so she cast her eyes away from him so as not to influence his decision. Likewise, she forced her granddaughter's attention elsewhere, leaving Francisco alone to wrestle with his conscience.

Standing pensively in the center of the room, he glanced around the inside of the shabby cottage while trying to decide the right and proper thing to do. It surprised him that the woman's home exhibited none of the damage sustained by his house or the other dwellings on the street that night. Her dirt floor was still bone dry, and the windows were all intact. The rain had not breached the structure even though he could see gaps in the planks of the clapboard walls. In fact, the whole interior seemed remarkably dry other than the ground beneath him where water continued dripping from his rain-soaked clothing. Despite the devastation and destruction all around it, the house appeared dry, secure, and serene—a sheltered oasis of peace.

Francisco looked down but saw only the back of the woman on the floor with her granddaughter cradled in her arms. Gazing upon them with sympathy, he felt the warm breath of the puppy against his neck, and he smiled in response to the pleasing sensation. Glancing down at the helpless puppy, he felt an incredible, unexplained calmness wash over him in the form of an enormous outpouring of compassion that gently shepherded him onto the floor beside the old woman and her granddaughter where he added his shadow to theirs on the wall of the dingy hut. The little girl then turned to look at him, so he handed her the dog, allowing her to hug it tightly while he slid closer to her grandmother, positioning his body around them as a protective barrier against the perils of the night.

The old woman stretched out her crooked fingers to grab an eight-inch resin statue of the Virgin of Guadalupe from a nearby table that she tucked into her granddaughter's arms, fitting it snugly between the girl's breast and the wet puppy. It was a cream-colored Marian statuette trimmed and accented with sepia staining, the type of religious item sold to tourists as souvenirs. Francisco, likewise, reached out to extinguish the flame of the oil lamp, acting on the fear that it might fall during the storm and start a fire. Instantly, the one-room shanty was plunged into total darkness.

The loss of light triggered an immediate rush of panic that spread throughout the boy's body due to the perceived sound amplification of the walls heaving and shuddering under the enormous pressure of the wind. Fearing the inevitable destruction of the fragile home, he struggled with his fright and thought lovingly and longingly of his family as a way to divert his mind from the danger he faced until the sensation of something lightly touch his hand eased his anxiety. It was the fingers of the old woman, delicate and comforting, as she reached over and placed into the palm of his hand the rosary beads she had worn around her neck. Gently folding his fingers around them, she withdrew her hand to await the uncertain outcome of their ordeal.

Outside the ramshackle shack and across the entire island, the storm raged with all its destructive might while the kindred souls huddled together on the floor of the decrepit structure piously praying the rosary, knowing that the only thing standing between them and total annihilation was their faith, hope, and love.

CHAPTER 9

Dave jumped out of bed that Thursday morning feeling energized and excited to be alive. After whipping up some breakfast in a blender—a bizarre concoction of bananas, raspberries, orange juice, flaxseed oil, and raw eggs—he decided to take a walk on the beach before it got too hot and muggy. Strolling along the water's edge, he watched the gulls and sandpipers pick through the wet sand while Grave frolicked in the frothy tidal pools of the retreating waves. Due to the lack of people on the beach at that hour, he ignored the rules and allowed his furry friend to run free without a leash.

They walked about a half mile down the beach before crossing over to the beach road where they stopped at the Cavalier Surf Shop. It was about eight o'clock, and the store had not yet opened, so Dave tapped lightly on the window to get the attention of Marty, who he could see standing behind the counter checking an inventory sheet. Although he regularly surfed with their son, Jerry, it had been a while since he had visited with Marty and Ken, so he stayed a little longer than he had planned, putting him way behind schedule once he left the shop. Walking along the road with Grave, he came to the Surfside Plaza where he noticed the Mayor's motorcycle parked outside of the Harley-Davidson shop. He was tempted to stop by and say hello but decided against it because it was almost time for Nikki to arrive at his house. He also jettisoned his plan to drive up to Cap'n John's Marine & Nautical Consignment to check on a surfboard he was trying to sell. That could wait for another day, he told himself. Instead, he and the dog marched straight home where Dave jumped into the shower and Grave crashed on the couch.

When Nikki pulled up to the tiny cedar-shake cottage and emerged from her Jeep, the first thing she heard was the sound of water gushing from a spigot on the side of the house. Glancing around the corner, she spotted an outside shower as well as two exposed feet standing inside the wooden enclosure. Without announcing her presence, she grinned and climbed the few steps onto the small porch where she heard the lively sound of reggae music drifting through the screen door. The song was an old Bob Marley tune that she knew well, so she mentally sang along with the refrain while letting herself into the cottage.

Inside Dave's modest home, she found Grave asleep on the upholstered couch, exhausted from his long walk down the beach. He slept lying on his back with his long body curled to one side, his head almost touching his hind leg and his front paws folded tightly against his chest. Disconnected and unconcerned, he did not twitch or even raise his eyelids when awakened by the opening and closing of the screen door.

Nikki smiled at the slumbering basset hound as she crept over to the couch and slid down beside him, careful not to sit on his tail. With the palm of her hand, she began softly stroking his broad chest as it expanded and contracted with each breath. Already awakened by the door but quite comfortable in his relaxed pose, Grave had not yet opened his eyes, but he did so in response to her light touch. His reaction was immediate; a frantic struggled to right himself upon realizing that it was not Dave sitting next to him. Remembering her scent, he ferociously attacked her cheeks and chin with his wet tongue, making her laugh joyously as she yanked on his oversized ears to keep him from consuming her entire face. After calming him down, she began caressing his soft, smooth coat, running both hands over his head and down along his ribs, putting him into a state of total bliss until he collapsed back onto the couch. She then gently patted him several times on his side and rose to have a look around the place.

On the coffee table were two dog-eared paperback books that she picked up and examined: *Zen and the Art of Motorcycle Maintenance* by Robert Pirsig and *The Teachings of Don Juan: A Yaqui Way of Knowledge* by Carlos Castaneda, each one bookmarked with a small scrap of paper. Returning the books to the table, she then walked into the kitchen area, finding her eyes drawn to several items lying on the kitchen table: car keys, a thin wallet, and a money clip holding several dollar bills. Additionally, she spied a knife among the items, one that appeared to be quite old, a folding model that looked to have received its share of use over the years.

She first picked up the knife and studied it closely. Folded, it was about three and a half inches long with a blue Delrin stag handle and a strong, sturdy carrying loop. On one side of the grip was a diamond-shaped inlay covered with a transparent plastic coating. Closer examination revealed that the inlay contained two raised images: a wolf's head and a paw print. Lettering between the two images spelled out *CUB SCOUTS B.S.A.* She found it interesting and amusing that he had once been a Cub Scout and that he still carried his scout knife. Closing her eyes, she tried to picture him as a boy in his uniform.

Putting down the knife, she assessed Dave's financial state by furtively counting the dollar bills in his money clip. Made of brass, the money clip replicated a horse race ticket with engraved lettering that was practically unreadable due to the years of wear. It denoted a one hundred dollar bet on the seventh horse in the seventh race held on July 7, 1977. Appearing even older than the Cub Scout knife, she assumed that it had belonged to his father or grandfather, suggesting that he was the kind of person who placed great sentimental value on objects from his past.

What served as his wallet was just a business card carrier holding only two items: an ATM bank card and a driver's license. Giggling at the "mug shot" photo on his license, she noticed an out-of-state address, a residence located on Avalon Drive in Cape Coral, Florida, something that explained the Florida license plate on the back of his hearse. Just then, the song that had been playing in the background ended, and she heard the sound of creaking floorboards out on the porch, prompting her to shove the cards back into the wallet and quickly turn around to face the door. Leaning back with her hands tightly gripping the edge of the table behind her, she tried to project a sense of casual disinterest.

Dave had already seen her car outside when he stepped through the doorway wearing nothing but a beach towel wrapped around his waist. His hair was wet and disheveled, and he had a peculiar grin on his face, appearing neither embarrassed nor concerned about his state of partial undress. His appearance did not bother Nikki either. In fact, she enjoyed it immensely. Without conscious effort, she found herself attempting to absorb as much of the scene as possible: his broad shoulders, gristly biceps, lean torso, and slender waist. She even found herself unconsciously counting his clearly defined ribs.

"Isn't this cottage a little close to the road to be parading around outside like that?" she asked.

He grinned at her but waited a few moments before answering. "I only wrapped myself in this towel because I knew you were coming. If I hadn't expected you, well then ..." He never finished his statement before walking toward the bedroom. "Make yourself at home while I get dressed." Glancing down to see his wallet sitting on the table next to her hand, he shook his head slightly as he continued to the bedroom only to re-emerge a few seconds later still wearing the towel but now carrying some clothes. "I'm going to shave first," he said while moving toward the bathroom. Looking over at Grave, once again sleeping on his back, he smiled at Nikki and said, "Some watchdog, eh?"

Upon returning to the living room, fully dressed and freshly shaven, Dave found Nikki sitting on the couch beside his droopy-eyed friend, gently kneading Grave's long velvety ears and allowing him to lick her cheek. Hesitating briefly at the sight of them together, Dave turned and tossed his wet beach towel into the bedroom before plopping himself down onto the chair near the wall. "Some guys have all the luck," he said while watching the dog nuzzle Nikki's face. Dressed as usual in a worn tee shirt, cargo shorts, and deck shoes, he had with him a pair of swimming trunks and a dry beach towel, both of which he hung over the arm of the chair.

Despite the reggae music blaring from the compact disc player, Nikki felt an uncomfortable silence in the room as Dave reclined in the chair and peered smugly at her. He sensed her discomfort and grinned in response to it, recognizing his natural ability to unnerve her. Nikki, totally conscious of his skill in that area, sensed her own uneasiness but possessed enough discipline to restrain it before it got the best of her.

"I didn't know you lived along Cottage Row," she said with an air of confidence, letting him know that she was back in control. "There's a lot of history in this area."

It had never occurred to him that some of the crazies living in the neighborhood could be relatives of Travis' ex-girlfriend, History, and the disturbing thought sent a chill down his spine.

"They also call this area the Unpainted Aristocracy," she said while rising from the couch. Looking down at him, she asked, "Are you an aristocrat, Mr. Rasputin?"

He returned her gaze with a chuckle. "I've been called many

things in my life, but never an aristocrat." He rose to his feet and faced her eye-to-eye. "By the way," he added with a quick scan of her apparel, "is that any way to dress for windsurfing?"

Nikki glanced down at her clothes. She wore khaki shorts with the cuffs rolled up and a white cotton tee shirt. "I have my swimming suit on underneath," she replied before stepping forward, moving much closer than necessary for normal conversation. Leaning toward him, she put her cheek near the side of his face in a manner that gave the impression she was about to whisper something in his ear. She said nothing and stood motionless with her head just inches away from his face, an enormous grin spreading across her lips. Surprised and a little dazed, Dave also remained still, unsure of what was happening.

"I need to investigate something," she said before quickly turning and dashing into the bathroom. Laughter then echoed from inside the bathroom preceding a cry of "Just as I thought!" before she emerged carrying a bottle of aftershave lotion. "I knew it!" she exclaimed.

"What?"

"Old Spice," she said while holding up the bottle. "You smell like my dad."

"Is that a bad thing?"

"No," she answered cheerily. "I like my dad."

Picking up his swim trunks and beach towel, Dave shut off the music and grabbed his belongings off the kitchen table while Nikki took Grave out to the hearse. Nikki wanted to stop and purchase something for her nephew's upcoming birthday, so they first drove to Kitty Hawk Kites before heading to Roanoke Sound for their windsurfing lesson.

Kitty Hawk Kites operated out of a shopping complex known as Jockey's Ridge Crossing located directly across from the dunes of Jockey's Ridge State Park on the bypass between the twelfth and thirteenth mileposts. Marking its location along the highway were blowing windsocks, banners, and flags, as well as twirling windmills, all made of Sun Tex fabric. The shopping center was a long yellow building trimmed in blue with white ramps and staircases connecting the floors of the two-story complex. Perched high at the north end of the building was a crow's nest with a flagpole on which flew an enormous black and white bovine windsock, a cartoonish Holstein that fluttered and bounced happily in the constant breeze.

In addition to Kitty Hawk Kites, Jockey's Ridge Crossing also housed a number of other stores that included The Fudgery, Salty

Paws Biscuits, Scoops Ice Cream Parlor & Deli, Natural Life, Kitty Hawk Surf Company, Kitty Hawk Hammocks, and Life on a Sandbar; but Kitty Hawk Kites was the largest of the retailers, occupying both levels of the north end of the shopping complex. Not only did the store sell kites, flags, windsocks, and all sorts of wind-related merchandise, it also offered hang-gliding lessons on the adjacent sand dunes. Nikki chose to enter the kite store through the second level entrance while Dave waited outside on the covered deck.

Positioning himself at the top of the ascending ramp, Dave was able to observe Nikki through the glass doors of the shop. Additionally, he could see out beyond the parking lot to the other side of the highway where an eighty-foot dune rose from the earth like a giant sandcastle. At that hour, many people were struggling to climb the enormous sand mound while others stood along its crest flying kites in a variety of designs. He enjoyed watching the soaring kites, delicate wings of fabric diving and swirling through the air in a rainbow of blending colors, some creating buzzing and whizzing sounds that he could hear from his high perch on the second-level deck. Although an accomplished kiteboarder, he had no memory of ever having flown a kite just for the fun of it, not even as a child.

Farther along the ridge of the main dune, protruding partially above its peak, he noticed two hang-gliders poised to plunge down the backside of the massive sand mound. With the dunes extending all the way to Roanoke Sound, Dave knew that there must be more hang-gliders on the secondary dunes behind the one fronting the highway. The existence of the larger dune and the smaller ones behind it intrigued him, mainly because they were such a contradiction. Despite their illusion of permanency, they were always in flux, change being their only constant. Continually in motion, they marched forward or receded backward depending upon the vagaries of the wind that drove them here or there. In that respect, he and the dunes were very much alike.

The shopping center was active that morning with many children and families scurrying from store to store. He seemed unaware of their presence as he leaned against the railing at the top of the ramp, passively watching the activities on the dune. After about ten minutes, though, he started getting antsy, so he peeked over his shoulder through the shop door where he saw Nikki still milling around inside. By then, it was starting to get hot, but he had parked his hearse under the shade of the building with the windows down so Grave could sleep comfortably while waiting for them. Directing his vision away from the store, he glanced down the ramp to observe a black man walking up from the ground level. Appearing hairless, the man's highly polished cranium glistened with reflected sunlight. It was not until the gentleman neared the top of the wooden ramp that Dave noticed a light dusting of gray stubble along the sides of his head. Another "commode-head"—he thought to himself. Suppressing a grin, he wondered what Travis would say if he were there.

Although he did not know why, Dave found himself shocked to see a Roman collar on the man, an obvious indication that the stranger was a cleric. Reaching the top of the ramp, the black priest looked Dave straight in the eye and flashed him an engaging smile that exposed a mouthful of unblemished white teeth. "*Good* morning to you," he said in a manner indicating that he sincerely meant it. Dave did not reply but instead acknowledged the priest with a nod of his head while focusing his attention on the clergyman's accent. It sounded African.

The priest then stepped around Dave and peeked through the shop window while walking past it. Something he saw there caught his attention, making him stop and promptly enter the store. As the door sprung shut, Dave heard him address someone inside, "My dear Nikita—" The slamming door muted the rest, and Dave turned to see Nikki rush over and embrace the priest, giving him a huge bear hug and an exceptionally warm smile. Watching the priest straighten his back to increase his stature, demonstrating to Nikki that he was as tall as she was, Dave chuckled; it was something he had done more than once himself when in her presence. He then watched the two friends talk for the next ten minutes, laughing and giggling as they did so. The priest was quite emotive, and, when something struck him as funny, he would stamp his feet in excitement and clap his hands. It was like watching a silent movie without subtitles, and Dave longed to know what they were saying. Finally, Nikki embraced the priest again, and the black clergyman turned and walked out of the shop.

"*Good* morning to you, again," he said upon exiting the store. "How are you today?"

"Good," Dave answered, his response delivered mechanically without much thought.

The priest stopped and looked him dead in the eye. "Are you sure?" he asked with a mischievous grin on his face before proceeding on his way. Walking in a casual manner, he offered a parting observation, "Yes, it is going to be a *good* day."

Dave made no reply but simply observed the priest stroll across the deck toward the other shops, moving briskly with a relaxed gait and a measured tempo. He swung one arm in a steady rhythm as he walked along, creating the impression he was quietly singing to himself or mentally listening to a song playing in his head. For some odd reason, Dave felt compelled to watch the receding figure of the priest until Nikki emerged from the store and they both returned to the hearse.

Their destination was the Harvey Sound Access area on Roanoke Sound at the sixteenth milepost next to Miller's Waterfront Restaurant. Grave had claimed the seat beside the window to enjoy the fresh breeze on his face, so Nikki sat in the middle beside Dave as they traveled down the bypass. He was extremely conscious of her thigh against his leg and the way his arm would brush against her whenever he turned the large steering wheel of the Cadillac. He was also aware that she made no attempts to pull away from these light physical contacts, and he found himself driving slower than normal to savor the closeness of her presence a while longer. Eternally grateful to his four-legged companion for having nudged her closer to him, he made a mental note to reward him later on with a special treat.

"Is Nikita your real name," Dave asked as they drove along.

"Yes," she said. "How did you know?"

"The priest. That's what he called you when he entered the store."

"Father Andal. Yes, he always calls me by my proper name. Did you talk to him?" she asked rather hopefully.

"No, he just acknowledged me as he walked by."

"That's too bad," she said. "He's such an incredible man." Thinking quietly for a second, she added, "I think he might possibly be the happiest man alive. He continually sings, and he makes us sing in church. Even at Mass, when he is on the altar, you can hear him humming to himself at the consecration. It's as if he has so much joy inside him that he can't contain it." She turned and glanced in Dave's direction. "I'll have to introduce you to him someday. It would be good for you." She bit her bottom lip and looked back at the road without saying anything else.

"I should warn you," he said. "I'm not the church-going kind."

She did not respond but stared straight ahead with a twinkle in her eye and a shrewd smile on her lips.

Entering the driveway shared by Miller's Waterfront Restaurant and the Harvey Sound Access area, Dave veered into the parking area on the right. Since the lot was deserted, he pulled as close as possible to the water, parking in the loading zone between the restaurant and a large community pavilion. Erected on stilts, the peaked-roof pavilion contained several wooden picnic tables and two austere restrooms. Slats of horizontal lattice covered the railings of the stairs and ramps as well as the lower portions of the structure. At the base of the pavilion, a narrow boardwalk stretched across a sandy lawn to a tiny beach on the edge of the Roanoke Sound Estuary. Beyond the beach, farther off in the distance, stood the Washington Baum Bridge leading to Roanoke Island where Nikki could see the condominiums of Pirate's Cove appearing as a hazy outline on the horizon at the end of the bridge.

Dave jumped out of the hearse the moment it stopped, but Nikki remained inside, quietly scanning the horizon to identify her condo on the distant shoreline until something struck her flush in the face. It was the soft tail of the excited basset hound prancing and wriggling on the front seat in anticipation of escaping the vehicle to begin exploring the terrain. Having been there before, he knew where to find the best smells and was eager to experience them again.

"Okay, boy, there you go," she said, opening the door so they both could exit the hearse.

Grave's paws had barely hit the ground when his nose dropped to the sandy soil, and he began zigzagging about in a fit of frenzied sniffing before charging for the cordgrass near the water. Nikki watched him in amusement until he disappeared into the reeds, but she knew his exact location at any moment by the sound of his snorting that grew louder and deeper the further he retreated into the tall grass. Walking to the back of the hearse where Dave stood fumbling with his car keys, she noticed two decals on the window of the oversized door, one from the American Sailing Association and the other a sticker from an organization known as U.S. Sailing. He saw her looking at them and said while unlocking and swinging open the enormous door, "I'm a certified sailing instructor through ASA and a certified windsurfing instructor with U.S. Sailing."

With the rear door open, the back of Dave's hearse lay fully exposed, revealing to Nikki the totality of disorder she had only glimpsed from the front seat. Seeing it as a metaphor for his entire life, Dave felt a surge of embarrassment sweep over him as he internally chastised himself for not following through on his pledge to organize the ungodly mess. With a sheepish glance in her direction, he then began moving items around in a futile attempt to make things a little more presentable while, at the same time, gaining access to the windsurfing equipment he needed to begin the lesson.

He first grabbed a rechargeable four-thousand-lumen spotlight that was lying loose on top of the mess, and he tossed it carelessly into a wooden box containing small sailing items. Although the spotlight had been driving him crazy for days, rattling around in the back of the hearse, this marked his first attempt to secure it. Picking up a short spade shovel that had also been banging around, he threw it into the box as well.

While Dave worked in vain to bring order to the clutter of sails, masts, booms, and boards, Nikki studied the interior of the hearse with a discerning eye. Noticing the pleated curtains on the windows, soiled and weathered with age, she wondered how many trips to the cemetery the old hearse had made over the years transporting poor souls to their final resting place. Closely examining the open rear door, she said in surprise, "There's no handle on the inside of this door."

"That's right." The sound of the muffled affirmation came from a body half covered with a long surfboard. Having found what he was looking for, Dave extracted himself from the back compartment and continued with a grin, "There aren't handles anywhere inside the hearse except for the doors of the front seat." He added with a quirky expression, "Anyone riding in the back of a hearse really doesn't need a door handle."

After a momentary pause, Nikki smiled and said, "I guess you're right. I hadn't thought of that."

"You're not alone. My dad didn't think of it either. One day, shortly after purchasing the hearse, he allowed the rear door to slam shut on him while he was inside the back compartment. That's when he learned there aren't any internal door handles. At that time, there was a glass panel behind the front seat. It had a small sliding window, but my dad was too big to squeeze through it. That meant he had to wait for someone to find him. It took about an hour, but my mother eventually wandered out of the house looking for him. Of course, when she found him trapped inside the hearse, she had to torment him a few minutes before setting him free. Right after that, he removed the glass panel." Reaching back into the heap of cluttered equipment, Dave began rummaging through it again while adding, "Being locked in here is kind of like being buried alive, I guess."

"Oh, don't even say that," she said with a grimace.

To remove the largest of his sailboards, the one more suitable for instruction, he first needed to first pull out his custom fiberglass board, which he placed on the ground with great care. Fascinated with the pattern and colors, Nikki knelt down beside the board and remarked, "Such beautiful colors! I also love the intricate design. It looks like a work of art. Are those elaborate decals or paint?" She slid the palm of her hand over the board's smooth surface, trying to determine if the design was part of the fiberglass or glued onto it.

"Neither," he answered. "The color and design are glassed right into the board."

"It's very intricate work. I wonder how they do it."

After a brief pause, he smiled and said, "Hell if I know. A guy named Roy Massey made it for me. He owns Ace Performer near Sanibel Island in Florida." With a chuckle, he added, "Roy claims that he was named after Roy Rogers, but I don't know if that's true or not. He does, however, have a life-size cutout of Roy Rogers in his store along with the Lone Ranger, Tonto, and a few others." Glancing down at the board, he said, "I don't think he makes glass boards like this anymore because they're not cost-effective—too work-intensive to be profitable. Selling production boards makes more sense from a retail perspective, but you can't beat the aesthetics of something like this. Roy made this board for me as a favor." Gently caressing the smooth fiberglass finish with his hand, he added sweetly, "She sure is a beauty, isn't she?" His warm smile and tender caress gave the impression he was comforting an old friend.

"It's almost too pretty to sail," she said.

"Don't worry," he replied with a gentle tap on the board. "You're not using this one, at least not yet. For learning, you'll need a bigger board, my original Windsurfer." Reaching into the hearse, he yanked out a twelve-foot sailboard that he placed on the ground beside the fiberglass board. Besides being longer, it was also considerably heavier than the shorter board.

Nikki looked through the open rear door at the remaining clutter of equipment. "You know, if you were to add some organization to this mess, it would be a lot easier to manage."

"Are you talking about my gear or my life?" he asked jokingly.

"Both," she said. "I'm a stickler for organization. Hang around long enough and I'll straighten you out."

Pulling out the booms and a sail, he droned loudly, "Hmm, I don't know. Perhaps I could use a little more structure in my life."

"Be careful what you ask for," she quipped while taking the sail from him and carrying it closer to the water.

After they had finished unpacking the equipment, Dave moved the hearse from the loading zone to the parking lot, returning immediately to begin assembling the windsurfing rig near the edge of the tiny beach, explaining to Nikki what he was doing at each step in the process. The outhaul line of the boom had frayed, so he reached for his Cub Scout knife while Nikki watched in amusement. She smiled but made no comment about the knife or his days as a Cub Scout, glancing instead at Roanoke Sound while he trimmed the line. The water was relatively calm except for some slight rippling ahead of an onshore breeze blowing out of the southwest. The wind felt refreshing on her face and arms as she knelt next to Dave by the sailboard, happy that she had taken him up on his offer of windsurfing lessons that day. The conditions were perfect for learning the sport: warm but not too hot with a steady light breeze blowing across the flat shallow waters.

Dave assembled the parts of the sailboard in short order but continued tinkering with the rigging, making one minor adjustment after another. Dissatisfied with the shape of the sail, he attempted to modify it by tightening the downhaul and then adjusting the outhaul, after which he began playing with the battens. Because beginners frequently fall on their sails, he had chosen a Dacron sail of an older design because it was less brittle and more forgiving than the higher aspect sails made of laminates such as Mylar, Kevlar, and other composite materials. While he fined tuned the sail, Nikki spread a beach towel on the ground and stretched out on it after removing her shorts and tee shirt. Rolling onto her stomach, she then rested her head on her hands while watching Dave make his sail adjustments. Observing him work, she learned that he was not entirely carefree, that he took some things in life seriously, and attaining proper sail shape appeared to be one of them. Not only was he serious about sail tuning; he was a perfectionist.

Finally satisfied with the shape and tautness of the sail, Dave positioned the windsurfing rig near the water and then sat down on the ground beside Nikki. It was the first time that day he had closely observed her. Except for their time together jogging down the beach, all their meetings had been in a more conventional setting where she had been appropriately dressed and well-groomed for the occasion. Running with her on the beach that day, he had been too exhausted and nervous to scrutinize her appearance; however, observing her now, it was like seeing her for the first time. Stretched out on the ground in a white one-piece bathing suit, she looked seductively relaxed. No tattoo or piercing defaced her body, and she had again pulled back her hair into a ponytail, giving her a little girl appearance. With everything stripped away, she looked so ... so clean. Yes, that was it! She looked clean as if nothing sordid had ever touched her body. Glancing down at himself with his clothes wrinkled and Band-Aids covering the burns on his fingers, he wondered what she saw in a drifter like him.

Noticing that he was watching her, she twisted her body to look up at him, smiling with such tenderness that he abandoned trying to figure out why she was there. Grinning back at her, he decided to accept their unlikely pairing and enjoy it for as long as it lasted. He then moved his vision across her long, slender figure and stopped to rest his eyes on her tanned forearms and hands, perceiving them to be the same nutty shade of brown as the teak wood of his antique Windsurfer booms. The dusky tone of her skin also emphasized the pearl-white brilliance of her bathing suit and the fine blond hairs on her arms that normally would have been unnoticeable. Plucking a short blade of grass from the ground, he used it lightly to stroke the skin of her wrist, causing the tender hairs of her forearm to stiffen slightly in response to the light stimulation.

"Why are you looking at me that way?" she asked.

"I think you're pretty," he answered without hesitation, being totally honest and sincere for a change.

That type of candor was the last thing she expected from him, so she gave him a funny look and then glanced out at the sound without responding to his gracious admission, choosing instead to study the movements of a woman on a stand-up paddleboard rapidly approaching their beach.

"Buddy," the woman called out from the water. "What are you doing here?"

Dave looked up to see Sally standing on a paddleboard along the shoreline wearing a short farmer john wetsuit. In her hand, she held a long wooden oar that she had used to propel herself to the beach. Grinning back at her, he responded, "This is my office. I thought you knew."

"Yeah, I know," she said while dismounting the board and stepping onto the sand. "But I thought you'd be surfing in the ocean with the other guys today, not here in the sound. I heard that the waves are pretty good over there."

"Normally, I would join them, but I'm giving lessons today. No good trying to teach windsurfing in the waves—much easier here in the sound." He motioned to Nikki. "I don't think you two have met."

While smiling at Nikki, Sally winked at Dave, letting him know her true reason for rowing up to the beach.

After the introductions, Dave asked her, "By the way, what are *you* doing here? And what's with the wetsuit? The water's not cold, and neither is the air."

"I rented this paddleboard from Kitty Hawk Water Sports," she said with a nod toward the place on the other side of the restaurant. "And you know me. I'm always cold." Glancing over at Dave's windsurfing rig, she added, "I probably should try that someday too. Maybe I'll ask them about lessons when I return the paddleboard."

"Well, what about me?" he asked. "I could teach you."

Climbing back onto the paddleboard, Sally replied with a smirk, "Listen, Buddy, I discovered long ago—back when I was learning to drive a car—that you never take lessons from a relative ... or a friend. They have no patience." As she said that, she glanced over and smiled at Nikki.

"But I am a professional," Dave said in disbelief.

Sally only laughed and started paddling away while calling back over her shoulder, "Nice to have met you, Nikki. Good luck with your lesson."

Remembering Sally's complaint at the bar the previous night, Dave yelled to her, "By the way, how's that bug?"

"It's still up there," she answered without turning around. "And with this wetsuit on, it's never getting out!"

Dave could only laugh while glancing at Nikki, who did not understand the joke.

"Well, Mr. Professional," she said. "Are you going to have any patience with me?"

"It's a well-known fact," he asserted, "that most of my students end up as patients ... sooner or later." Just then, Grave stuck his head out of a patch of marsh grass, his fur thoroughly soaked and his long ears dangling in the shallow water. "There you are," Dave called out to him. "I wondered where you were hiding."

"Will he be okay while we're in the water," Nikki asked.

Dave glanced at the wet dog now sniffing around the windsurfing rig. "No," he said. "I'll tie him to the pavilion when I change into my swimming suit. If we don't restrain him, he'll follow us into the water, and basset hounds don't swim well—at least not for very long."

Unlike Grave, Nikki was at home on the water. She was also an excellent student who listened attentively to everything Dave told her, paying close attention to his instructions and the information he shared about sailing, such as what it means to "tack" and "jibe" and how to apply those principles to windsurfing. He explained how the sailboard was just a simple sailing craft consisting of a wishbone-shaped boom and sail along with a mast attached to a board with a universal joint that enabled the mast and sail to rotate freely around the board as well as fall and rise when lifted out of the water using a rope called and "up-haul." He also described how her body would act as "standing" and "running" rigging commonly found on sailboats. Instead of employing ropes and cables to hold up the mast, she would use her arms and legs supported by her muscles to perform those crucial functions. By tilting the mast fore and aft, she would steer the board, and by pulling in on the boom and easing it out, she would control her speed.

He compared the sail to an airplane wing standing on its end and explained that the board's movement through the water would result from "lift" generated by the air moving across the sail. In effect, she would be flying across the water. With the sailboard capable of skimming across the water's surface like a flat stone, the flying analogy was not far from the truth; however, the breeze that day was too light to make anything like that happen. She would have to wait until another day to experience that kind of speed and exhilaration.

Before moving into the water, Dave had her practice on dry land, standing on top of the board near the water's edge while Grave barked at them from the steps of the pavilion where Dave had secured him. Once Nikki had demonstrated her mastery of the basics, Dave dragged the rig into the sound about twenty yards offshore. He had chosen that area of Roanoke Sound to teach her because the water depth was mostly knee to waist deep except for a few low spots farther out and some deeper areas in the dredged channel closer to Roanoke Island.

Once in the water, Nikki immediately climbed on the board and struggled clumsily to her feet while Dave stood beside the sailboard, steadying it with his hands. He then released his grip the moment she pulled the sail out of the water, but her erratic movements sent her tumbling backward on top of him, plunging both of them into the brackish water of the sound with the sail falling down to cover them like a blanket, creating a tight seal over the surface of the water with both of them trapped beneath it.

Forced underwater, Dave relaxed his body as he lay on the sandy bottom with Nikki on top of him and the sail covering both of them. He could feel the panic in her body as she hardened her muscles in response to the weight of the heavy sail and rigging lying on top of her, so he wrapped his arm around her waist and pulled her closer to him, shielding himself from being kicked and elbowed if she were to begin thrashing. The strain of her body was intense, but he held her tightly while turning slightly to poke his free arm up into the sailcloth, creating a hollow of air into which he quickly thrust her head. With her breathing restored, the tension of her muscles eased, but Dave maintained a firm grip on her waist while encircling her body to emerge in the air pocket directly in front of her. Kneeling on the gritty bottom of the sound with their heads breaking the surface of the water, the two of them then stared at each other face-to-face under the canopy of the multi-colored sail.

"And that," he said, "is how you breathe when the sail falls on top of you. It's a trick you need to remember, especially when you're in deep water."

She was so close to him that she could almost taste the salt water trickling over the taut skin of his cheekbones as she peered deeply into his gray eyes. Feeling the intense, constant pressure of his arm around her waist, she glanced overhead at the colorful canopy supported by his extended arm pushing upward toward the heavens, sheltering her beneath the protective covering of the sail. Observing him just inches away from her, she realized that he offered her everything she needed at that moment, the air to breathe and the strength to go on living.

The world around them had grown quiet, even Grave's barking had ceased, and she felt totally cut off from the rest of humanity. Beneath the sail, it was a new and different world, a magical one created by him where only they existed. She wanted it to last forever but knew it would continue only as long as he chose to allow it—or until the strength of his supporting arm gave out. Right now, she thought, he is the one person sustaining my world, the fantasy one under the sail and the real one out there as well. She wondered how long he would choose remain and keep her safe in both worlds.

Gazing longingly into Nikki's eyes, Dave, likewise, wondered how long it would last. He found the proximity of her body intoxicating as he struggled like Atlas to support the firmament over her head, hoping to prolong the experience indefinitely. Feeling her hands resting on his bare chest, he was certain she could detect the thumping of his heart, a thunderous pounding that increased with each breath he took, and he wondered how she would react to the message it heralded. His awareness of such an obvious declaration made him slightly self-conscious, so he shyly lowered his head and released his hold on her, allowing her to slip free of his embrace and the magical water world he had fashioned for her.

After Nikki had escaped, Dave shoved the sail higher into the air and slipped out from under it while maintaining a firm grip on the boom. Settling back into his role of instructor, he said to her, "If you find yourself under the sail, just make an air pocket to breathe and then work your way to the edge of the sail where you can slip out from underneath it. It's not much of a problem until you get better at windsurfing and start wearing a harness. That's when you can find yourself tethered to the boom if the harness line twists and fails to release. In that case, you just need to keep your cool and create an air pocket until you can calmly unhook yourself." He grinned at her. "There's nothing to it."

From that point on, Nikki did remarkably well, better than any student he had ever instructed. Dave attributed her success to her natural athletic ability along with the fact that she was an accomplished water skier who instinctively knew how to lean back and trust the sail to support her weight. After only a few dramatic falls, she became acclimated to the rocking and tipping of the board, settling into a comfortable performance zone that took her out into the sound on a steady breeze. At that point, she was on her own, well beyond the range of his voice to call out advice or additional instructions. He had already informed her about the exhilaration she would experience once she started moving across the water, warning her about sailing away and not wanting to stop or even look back, a trap that often ensnared beginners who would get far from shore and have trouble returning to the beach. As he watched her skim across the rippled surface of the water, moving farther and farther away, he counted on her remembering his warnings because he had no desire to slosh halfway across the sound to retrieve her.

Fortunately, Nikki had remembered his warnings, prompting her to slow down and attempt a turn before getting too far away; however, an unexpected puff of wind sent her plunging into the water again. Wet, but more determined than ever, she climbed back onto the board and sailed straight for the beach where Dave stood waiting for her in the shallow water near the shoreline. Her resolve to master this new challenge was intense, and she demonstrated it by completing a smooth, successful tack that took her sailing back out into the sound. Realizing that he had nothing more to offer her, Dave returned to the beach where he retrieved his yelping basset hound from the pavilion and plopped himself down on a beach towel to admire the grace and beauty of the agile young girl on the water.

After more than an hour practicing her newfound skills, Nikki began showing signs of fatigue. She started falling more often and appeared to have a harder time pulling the sail out of the water. At that point, she decided to head to shore for a short break, giving Dave an opportunity to put on a performance of his own. The winds were too light for him to go screaming off toward the horizon, so he stayed close to the shoreline, showing off a bit with a selection of freestyle routines and maneuvers that he used to perform back in his competitive windsurfing days. His exhibition was nothing short of a windsurfing clinic in which he demonstrated the finer points of acrobatic sailboarding executed by a professional athlete.

Having tasted the demands of the sport, Nikki could better appreciate Dave's performance on the water. Sitting on the beach beside Grave, her arms wrapped around her knees, she watched in amazement as Dave moved across the smooth surface of the board as if he were walking on solid ground. Not once did he stumble or lose his balance. His speed and agility were incredible as he glided effortlessly around the mast and leaned backward on the opposite side of the sail while continuing to skate across the water under complete control with one elbow resting on the boom and his distributed weight determining his speed and direction. When he tacked and jibed, he would duck under the boom instead of slipping around the mast as he had taught her to do. Several times, he completely let go of the boom and pirouetted around to catch it before the sail fluttered even once, whirling with such speed and grace that she barely detected any movement in his body. None of his catlike acrobatics impeded his forward progress as the sailboard glided smoothly across the water on a straight-line course.

Dave's exhibition of on-water gymnastics attracted a group of spectators in the gazebo at Miller's Waterfront Restaurant. Even on the beach at Kitty Hawk Water Sports, Sally and some of the instructors stopped to watch the show. Dave impressed Nikki with his skill and precision, and she realized that his earlier statement about the beach being the equivalent of his office was not far from the truth; this was where he was at his best—out there on the water. Smiling to herself, she wondered whatever made her think she could turn him into a detective. Although it made no sense in her responsible, straight-laced world, this was where he belonged. As she watched him dance on the water, she could sense that she was beginning to care for him. There was something about him, both rugged and sensitive, that attracted her to him. She liked his callused hands, but she wished those calluses had come from work rather than hanging onto the boom of a sailboard.

The hours passed quickly with Nikki, Dave, and Grave enjoying their time together, but the day was not over yet. It was still afternoon, so Dave drove to the Sugar Creek Seafood Restaurant on the causeway instead of taking Nikki back to her car. He was hoping to find the outdoor deck open, and it looked like it was. Walking up the ramp with Nikki and Grave, he saw a young girl inside a small enclosed bar near an outdoor gazebo. She did not see him, so he tapped lightly on the screen door of the tiny barroom. "Anybody home?" he called out.

Hunched over a big white cooler, the young bartender was stocking it with beer bottles, but she raised her eyes in response to the question. "Buddy!" she cried out happily. In her voice was the slight twang of a Southern drawl.

"You open?" he asked.

"For you, Buddy, we're always open. Actually," she said, smiling at him through the screen door, "I've been here about fifteen minutes. You're my second customer." Nodding her head to the right, she directed Dave's attention to an old man sitting on a wooden stool along the rail by the gazebo. He appeared sloppy and sweaty as he sipped whiskey from a small plastic shot glass and chased it down with a swig of beer. The guy looked vaguely familiar, but Dave could not quite place him. If he had to guess, he would say that the old-timer probably worked on Roanoke Island, most likely in Wanchese.

Without giving the stranger another thought, Dave held open the door for Nikki and Grave to enter the tiny room, which was a miniature service bar large enough to accommodate only about four people. A whiteboard hanging on the wall listed the available frozen drink specialties along with a limited number of beers and wines.

Looking down at Grave, the bartender said, "There's my guy," to which the basset hound began shuffling his paws on the floorboards and wildly wagging his tail. "Sorry guy, I don't have anything for you right now." Looking at Dave and Nikki, she asked, "What can I get y'all?"

Dave stared up at the whiteboard as he spoke. "We've just been windsurfing, so I think we need some boat drinks." Turning to Nikki, he asked, "What do you think?"

She nodded her acceptance and pointed up to the second drink scrawled on the board. "I'll take the Heat Wave."

"Yeah," he said, "and give me the Gazebo." Glancing down at Grave, he added, "Sorry boy, you're not old enough to drink."

"I'll get him some water," the young girl said as she bent down to scratch Grave's long ears. "And maybe I can find something else too." She then grabbed two blender jars and filled them coconut rum, pineapple juice, orange juice, grenadine and numerous other liquors to create a couple of tropical concoctions. "Be careful, Buddy, these are pretty powerful," she said while pushing two plastic glasses toward him on the bar. "And here's Grave's water. Sorry, but I don't have anything else for him right now. I still have to go inside and get some change for the cash register. While I'm in there, I'll look in the kitchen to see what I can find. Wait until I get back before you pay me."

"Sounds good," Dave said as he grabbed the drinks and nodded for Nikki to pick up the plastic cup holding Grave's water. Stepping out of the bar, they then moved toward the gazebo but stopped abruptly before reaching the old man, unable to pass by him due to the stench of dead fish hovering around him like a toxic cloud. Making an immediate about-face, they then found two stools along the rail closer to the bar where the only scent in the air was the appetizing aroma of steaks wafting out of the kitchen vents on the outside of the restaurant. Nikki then placed the cup of water on the floor while Dave glanced over at the noxious smelling stranger, feeling more certain than ever that the old guy worked in Wanchese—on a fishing boat.

Sitting relatively close to the restaurant, they could see through the heavily tinted windows where ghost-like shadows of people moved around inside the dining room. Their seats also offered them a clear view of Roanoke Sound looking north, a vista that included the Harvey Sound Access area where they had just come from windsurfing. Spotting the location, Nikki reflected on her first-time sailboarding experience, and she recognized how therapeutic it had been for her, providing her the time she had needed to relax and refocus her life. As she sat on the stool beside Dave, the troubles of the past week seemed miles away, and she found herself hypnotized by the lapping of the water on the pilings and the gentle breeze blowing through the open deck. Sipping her drink, she smiled inwardly, wondering what role the alcohol was playing in lightening her mood and easing her mind.

Suddenly, she heard a different type of lapping sound resonating from beneath her seat, one that awakened her from her peaceful trance. It was Grave drinking noisily out of the plastic cup she had placed on the floor. Extending her leg down to touch him, she ran the bottom of her foot across the soft fur of his back while turning toward Dave. "I now understand your warning about sailing off in one direction and not wanting to stop," she said. "That could really be dangerous, and you could find yourself quite a distance away before you realized it. Yet, I'd love to jump on that windsurfer and sail off, clear across the sound, all the way to Currituck, maybe even farther—too far to ever come back." She gazed longingly across the water as she fantasized about escaping into the unknown.

Dave stared at her profile while her eyes pensively embraced the horizon. Tiny salt crystals still adhered to her cheeks, and he noticed more of them sprinkled across her forehead where they shimmered like uncut gems sparkling in the sunlight reflecting off the water. He loved the tacky feel of dried, saltwater on his own skin, and he longed to experience the sticky sensation on hers as well. Unaware that he had been watching her, she turned and looked at him as if expecting a response to her prior remark.

"You're right," he stammered, returning to the topic of her last comment. "Getting lost in the moment while under sail is an easy thing to do." Glancing out at the sound, he continued, "More than once I found myself doing exactly that, especially as a teen when I had first learned to windsurf. Each year, my family would vacation at a resort town in Michigan, usually near the end of August just before school started. Even after we had moved to Chicago, we still returned to the same Michigan town to stay at an old hotel. It sat at the top of a long grassy hill that led down to the beach. A few times, we rented cottages, but, mostly, we stayed at the hotel.

"Anyway, I'd rig my board and go windsurfing on the lake. With the right wind, I could get on a tack and head straight out. The feeling was intoxicating, and I wouldn't want to stop. I'd just keep going and going until I was in danger of losing sight of land. On hazy days, that would actually happen because the shoreline would dissolve into the horizon. Even on clear days, the whole shoreline looked the same, making it hard to spot the beach in front of the hotel. Some might consider that dangerous, being that far out, but it never really frightened me because I knew I had the strength and stamina to get back in."

"What would you do then?" she asked. She had not taken her eyes off him the entire time he had been speaking, but his gaze remained fixed on some distant point, almost as if he were back on Lake Michigan searching for safe harbor along a hazy shoreline.

"I would drop the sail and sit down on the board," he said with a contented smile.

"And then what?"

"Nothing."

"Nothing?"

"Nothing," he said, turning to meet her gaze. "The sail would fill with water and act as a sea anchor while I'd sit there amid all that emptiness. Nothing to do. Nothing to see. Nothing to hear—nothing except the laughing of a gull or the cresting of a wave. I'd float on the board with my legs dangling in the water, moving up and down on each wave, enjoying the seclusion and remoteness—the *nothingness*—of the moment. The phenomenon was especially powerful if a haze obscured the horizon, leaving me alone in the water to bob like a cork in the vast expanse of nothingness.

Thankfully, it was late August and the water temperature had warmed up, or it would have been a very cold nothingness," he added with a grin.

"What did your parents think about your disappearing into all that *nothingness*?"

His expression changed markedly as he redirected his gaze back to the water. "It really scared my mother," he said. "She didn't know how to swim, and water terrified her. She tried to hide her fear because she didn't want her children to share her phobia, but we all knew it. Whenever I would sail back to shore and catch sight of land, the first thing I'd spot would be this tall flagpole that stood outside the hotel. The next thing I'd see would be this lone figure standing at the top of the hill searching the water—searching for me. I knew it was my mother waiting there, acting as a sentinel, hoping that her maternal love would be enough to protect me out there on the water. When I'd reach the beach, however, the figure would always be gone, having retreated back into the hotel. She thought I didn't know she stood there guarding me at a distance whenever I was on the lake, but I did. Neither of us ever spoke of it."

Nikki listened attentively as she observed the tense muscles of his face slowly relax. She remained silent because she knew he had more to say.

"You know," he continued, "even now, when I'm windsurfing on the ocean or here on the sound, the moment I turn and sail back toward shore, I think I can see her lone figure standing on the beach searching for me—or I just find myself looking for her."

From his words and expression, she presumed that his mother was no longer around. "What became of your mother—and your father?"

"They were both killed in an airplane crash on the way back from the Summer Olympics," he said flatly without much emotion. "I left our home after the accident and never returned. No reason to." The tone of his voice indicated that he had finished discussing the topic. "My God, look at that!" he cried while pointing toward the water's edge near the restaurant. "That's the biggest rat I've ever seen in my life."

Nikki turned to where he had pointed and smiled. "That's not a rat."

"Sure it is. Look at the tail. It can't be a beaver with that long rat tail. Nah, it's a rat. Damn big rat too."

"No, it's not," she said, elbowing his arm. "It's a nutria. I didn't know there were still some around here."

"A what?"

"A nutria. They're native to South America. I think the Spaniards brought them here. They're just another invasive species, and they're bad news too. They destroy wetland areas—like the ones around here—by eating plants down to their roots. The soil in the sound is fragile, and it needs root mats to hold it in place. Once they're gone, the soil gets washed away. I thought the last hurricane got rid of the nutrias, but I guess one survived."

"I don't know," he said. "Still looks like a rat to me." He then called out to the rodent using an old Edward G. Robinson line, "You dirty rat!" Laughing aloud, he turned to Nikki and asked, "Who was the old movie actor who used to say that?"

Closing her eyes, she squinted and thought for a few moments but could not recall the name of the film star. "That was before my time," she said while lifting her eyes skyward in another attempt to tap her recollection. "Wait a minute," she said, "I think I know who it was." After a brief pause, she continued, "Ah, the name was right on the tip of my tongue, but now it's gone. I'm usually pretty good with things related to old movies—musicals mainly. Oh, that reminds me—" She again paused and smiled mischievously. Glancing away, she then peeked at him out of the corner of her eye.

"What?" he asked.

Playfully clenching her jaw and pursing her lips, she elected not to respond and directed her attention back toward the nutria. Observing her in silence, Dave wondered what she was up to until he heard her speak again. "I have a surprise for you," she said cryptically, directing her words at him but continuing to gaze at the large rodent that had slipped back into the water and was now swimming toward some marsh grass. "I'll give it to you later."

The promise of a surprise produced a wave of anticipation in him, cresting and breaking over his impressionable mind like a tsunami. Her surprise could be almost anything, but he thought it best to tamp down his expectations, thereby avoiding disappointment. Clearly, she was toying with him, hoping he would try to pry it out of her, but he was determined not to play her game. It was in his nature to resist manipulation, even in lighthearted matters such as this, so he reached for his glass and took a long swallow of the tropical drink while attempting to devise a plan that would turn the tables on her. His deliberations were cut short, however, when Grave began emitting a high-pitched whine while dancing in place under Nikki's stool as the young bartender approached them from behind.

Carrying with her a hotdog, the young girl said to Grave, "I guess you know who this if for, don't you, baby?" She broke the hot dog into two pieces and gave each one to him. "Now be gentle and don't bite off my fingers." The dog inhaled both pieces without chewing, and the girl smiled at Dave while saying, "Compliments of the kitchen staff. By the way, I've got plenty of change now if you want to pay for those drinks."

Dave started reaching into his pockets, but Nikki stopped him with a gentle touch of her hand. Raising an index finger, she silenced him before he could speak. "I'm still paying off a debt," she said. "Besides, you bought dinner last night." Cognizant that his cash reserves were low, he lodged no protest and graciously allowed her to pay for the drinks. Nikki then handed the girl a twenty-dollar bill and told her to keep the change.

After paying the bill, she said to Dave, "I still owe you a dinner for the work you performed for me, and I always pay my debts."

"If I recall," he said, "the price was a dinner-date with you. Isn't that what we had last night?"

"No, that didn't count. For one thing, I didn't pay for it, and, besides, it was too inexpensive."

He grinned at the way she overruled his insincere objection.

"I want to get dressed up and go someplace special where we can get a good meal," she said. "No clam chowder unless you have it as an appetizer. I want you to eat some real food tonight—and give Grave an extra helping too." She took a swallow from her glass. "I really like this drink," she said.

"So where are we going to eat?"

"I heard about a new restaurant up in Duck that just opened. It is supposed to be upscale ... and very expensive."

"Stiff joint!" A husky voice bellowed from over near the gazebo.

Both Nikki and Dave turned toward the crusty old man who smelled like fish. "Excuse me," said Nikki, biting her lip to keep from laughing.

"The place is a stiff joint," the old man said before drinking the remainder of his whiskey and chasing it down with the last of his beer.

"What do you mean?" Dave asked, unable to resist the urge to engage the funny old guy.

"Just what I said," the fisherman replied brusquely. "The place is a stiff joint!" He followed his comment with a clumsy hand gesture intended to add emphasis to what he had said. "You pay out your ass, and you're still hungry when you leave. A stiff joint!" He then motioned them away with a dismissive wave of his hand.

"Well, I guess that settles it," Dave said to Nikki in a subdued tone.

Leaning closer, she whispered, "Yes, now we're definitely going there because we know *he* won't be there." She smiled a devilish grin as she finished the last of her drink.

A few seconds later, they heard the scraping of a wooden stool across the floorboards as the old man struggled to his feet and began shuffling across the deck, trolling the stench of dead fish as he walked toward them. The smell forced Nikki to hold her breath, but Grave found the pungent aroma fascinating, causing him to follow the eccentric culinary critic with his upturned nose as the old guy trundled mutely past them on his way to the parking lot.

After he was gone and the virulent smell had dissipated, Nikki began breathing again and said, "I have to work tomorrow, so I don't want to stay out too late. Let's try to eat around six. Is that okay with you?"

"Yeah, sure."

"No, wait." She paused a moment to think. "Since we have to drive to Duck, we better make it seven, but pick me up at six. That gives me a couple hours to get ready."

"I don't know," he said. "You always look ready to me."

She responded to his compliment with a soft smile but then remembered something else. "Oh yes," she added, "this place is a little formal. I think it requires you to dress, meaning that men must wear a jacket—not necessarily a tie but, at least, a jacket."

"A dress code," he remarked, finding himself slightly taken back. "How long is that place going to stay in business around here?"

"You have a sport coat or something, don't you?"

"Oh, sure … sure," he replied with a blank, uneasy look on his face.

Dave flew down the bypass at breakneck speed, trying to get to Colington Island as quickly as possible. He did not know why he had been afraid to admit to Nikki that he owned nothing nicer than the clothes he wore on his back, but it was too late now to reveal the truth. Fortunately, he had been able to reach Travis, who said he could help. The only problem was that Dave had to get to Travis' home on Colington Island before the bartender left for work.

Nikki had not tarried long at Dave's place after they returned from Sugar Creek, so he was able to shove Grave into the cottage and dash off to Colington Island without much delay. Traveling well in excess of the speed limit, he slowed down only when he hit road construction on Ocean Bay Boulevard near the Wright Brothers National Memorial, knowing that the last thing he needed was a moving violation in a construction zone. After arriving at Colington Harbour and receiving a yellow day pass from the guard at the main entrance, he then drove around the development looking for Travis' house.

He had never been there before, but the directions provided by Travis guided him straight to the house, an elevated two-story cottage-style residence along one of the canals. At first, he was unsure if he had found the correct house because he did not expect Travis to own such an attractive home, especially one with direct channel access, but the presence of Travis' car in the driveway convinced him that he was at the right place. Walking around to the side facing the canal, he climbed the wooden stairs to find his friend lounging in a screened-in porch just off the living room.

"Buddy," Travis called out, "that has to be the fastest anyone has ever made the drive here. What's the distance, eight miles? You had to be soaring." He motioned him through the screen door. "How about a beer?"

"I can't believe you own this house," Dave said in astonishment. "How can you afford this place on your salary?" Plopping himself into an Adirondack chair, he looked out at the dock along the canal and added, "I'm surprised there's not a yacht sitting there."

"Oh, the yacht?" Travis said casually as he sipped his beer. "Yeah, it's out of the water for maintenance." Dave glared at him in disbelief, but Travis maintained his casual demeanor. A few seconds later, he started chuckling and pointed a finger at his friend. "Ha! Had you on that one, didn't I?"

Dave only grinned in response.

"Don't worry, Buddy. I don't own a yacht, at least not yet. A few more coins in the tip jar, though, and you never know. *If you know what I mean?*" He ended his remark with a wink and a nod as if communicating in some secret code.

"What about the house?"

"The house? Yeah, I actually own the house. I inherited it. You don't think I could afford something like this, do you? I'm an only child, and I got everything when my parents died. Of course, I've blown through most of the money already—that's why I'm working at Mulligan's." He downed the last of his beer and stood up. "You didn't say if you wanted a beer."

"If you're getting yourself another one—"

"I am."

"Well then, get me one too. But I can only stay a few minutes."

Travis got up and went inside. "C'mon in here, Buddy, and we'll discuss your problem."

Dave followed him through the sliding glass doors into the air-conditioned living room where the temperature was almost frigid. He saw Travis march into the kitchen, but he lingered a few moments in the living room to inspect the furnishings before wandering into the dining room where he approached a serving bay through which Travis handed him a can of beer. Travis then stood opposite him on the other side of the counter as if standing across the bar from him at Mulligan's.

"So what's with this mystery woman?" Travis asked. "I waited all night for you to introduce me, but you slipped out the minute my back was turned. We started a little pool at the bar, throwing money into a kitty to see who would be the first to rate an introduction."

"Who?"

"Me, Sally, the Professor, and a few others."

Dave just smiled. "I hate to tell you this, but you've already lost."

"What do you mean?"

"We ran into Sally this afternoon, and, well—"

"Damn bitch! I had plans for that money," Travis said disgustedly, curling his lip into a snarl as he spoke. His grin then returned, and he continued pressing Dave about Nikki, "So, you've decided to take your girlfriend to some ritzy joint, but you have nothing to wear. Getting a little extravagant on our limited budget, aren't we, Buddy?"

Dave smiled and said, "Yeah, I guess I need some new clothes … but she's buying tonight."

"That's my boy!" Travis exclaimed while raising his arms in triumph. "How come I never meet women like that?"

"What about History?"

Travis froze in place and pointed his stubby finger at his friend. "What did I say about mentioning her name in my presence—especially in my house?" He then smiled and rubbed his extended belly. "My clothes aren't going to do you any good. But—" Raising a finger, he shuffled around into the dining room where he grabbed his friend by the shoulders. "Stand up straight!" he ordered while measuring him with his eyes. "Yeah, you're about the same height as my father, and you both have the same build. Unlike me, dad watched his diet and kept himself pretty trim. A lot of good it did him." Tapping Dave lightly on his shoulder, he said, "Come with me," after which he turned and started for the stairs.

"What's upstairs?"

"Clothes, my son, clothes. Dad was a dapper fellow, and he owned a lot of clothes."

Following him up the steps, Dave asked, "When did he die?"

Travis paused at the top of the stairs. "About ten years ago, I think."

"And you still have his clothes?"

Glancing over his shoulder, he said, "What can I say? I'm sentimental."

"That's not what History used to say."

Travis tried to harden his expression, but his comical features would not allow it. "Hey, if you want my help," he said, "you have to play by my rules. *If you know what I mean?*" With that said, he playfully poked his finger into his friend's chest and then walked into one of the bedrooms.

In a walk-in closet filled with clothes neatly arranged on hangers, they found a lightweight oyster-colored blazer that looked brand new. Made of a delicate weave of linen and silk, it fit Dave perfectly. Even the sleeves were the proper length.

Travis queried him, "I assume you have some long pants to wear with this jacket."

"I have a pair of cargo pants that should look okay," he said shyly while glancing at his friend.

Travis shook his head in disbelief and moaned, "What am I going to do with you, Buddy?" He then turned and started rummaging through the closet again. Pulling out a pair of khaki slacks and a belt, he commanded, "Try these on."

Dave did as instructed, instantly dropping his shorts and slipping on the slacks. The waist size was just right, but the length was about a quarter-inch too long; however, they would do.

"Better too long than too short," Travis said with a laugh. Looking down, he asked, "Shoes?"

"These are all I've got." Lifting one leg, Dave exposed a beat-up deck shoe. "Maybe I can use a wet cloth to wipe them off a bit."

"You're hopeless, Buddy, simply hopeless. What does she see in you?"

"I've been asking myself the same thing."

Travis quickly scanned the floor of the closet and picked out a pair of tan deck shoes. They also looked relatively new. "What size do you wear?" he asked while peering inside one of them.

"Ten."

Pushing them into Dave's chest, he quipped, "Here, you'll have to make due with a half-size larger. Once again, better too big than too small." After that, he started shuffling through the closet again. "I'm not even going to ask this time." Pushing aside hangers, he pulled out a long-sleeved white pinpoint shirt and handed it to Dave saying, "Your neck size doesn't matter. Don't wear a tie, and leave the collar open."

Dressed in his new slacks with his hand-me-down deck shoes clutched in one hand and his new shirt held in the other, Dave looked slightly clownish, so much so that Travis began laughing hysterically. Between gasps of air, he managed to spit out a one-word question. "Socks?" he asked in a high-pitched squeal.

"I'm not wearing socks," Dave said adamantly. "I draw the line at socks."

"Have it your way," Travis answered, still chuckling over Dave's comical appearance. "Now put your shorts back on and come downstairs to finish your beer. I feel like the damn Salvation Army here." Travis started for the door but stopped briefly to deliver a heartfelt message to his friend. "And, Buddy," he said, "you can keep the clothes. If anyone is going to wear my dad's stuff, I'd prefer it be you. I've kept everything in the closet because I couldn't bear to give it away to Goodwill, but he would have liked you—and he'd be happy knowing you're wearing his clothes." In a more lighthearted tone, he added, "Old dad was also quite the ladies' man, so who knows? You might get lucky!"

After Travis had walked out, Dave changed back into his shorts and neatly folded his new wardrobe before returning downstairs. By then, Travis had gone back out onto the porch, speaking up when he heard Dave step through the doorway, "Buddy, you've only been in town what? Three or four months? And you're already on your way to becoming a legend around here. Do you know that?"

Dave grinned and sat down on a chair with his newly acquired booty resting on his lap. "I thought Mojo Collins was the Living Legend of the Outer Banks, at least, that's what he told me."

"When did you see Mojo?"

"Last week. The Mayor and I had lunch at Sam & Omie's, and he told me that Mojo was playing at the Tale of the Whale that night. Of course, I had to go over and pester him a little. I arrived early while he was still setting up in the gazebo. When I started down the ramp, he was sitting there tuning his guitar, so I yelled at him, 'Hey Mojo, there's nobody here!' You know his sense of humor. He just growled at me saying, 'Well, you're here ain't ya.'"

Travis laughed. "Everything in life changes, but not Mojo."

Dave gulped down the last of his beer and continued, "We talked until the dinner crowd showed up and he started singing. He told me that he's playing at the Outer Banks Brewing Station a week from Saturday, so I told him I'd stop over. You should come too if you're not working."

"I'll have to check my schedule," Travis said. "I'd enjoy seeing Mojo again. I get tired of using my best material on the Mayor. The only problem is that Mojo is a lot quicker on his feet. His comebacks to my barbs are more expressive and pithy than what I get from the Mayor."

"Yeah, but, unlike the Mayor, Mojo actually likes you."

"The Mayor likes me. He fixed my car didn't he?" As he said that, he chugged down his beer and spied the long shadows on the houses across the canal. "I hate to tell you this, Buddy, but it's getting late. You should hurry, or you'll miss your date. And I need to head off to work."

"Damn!" Dave said. "I've got to get going. Thanks for the clothes." Grabbing his things, he raced through the screen door and down the stairs.

Travis called out to him as he left, "I expect a full accounting of everything that happens tonight … *if you know what I mean!*"

Dave stood a few steps inside the doorway of the Gaslight Saloon, the bar and lounge of the Port O' Call Restaurant located on the beach road between the eighth and ninth mileposts. Nikki had modified their dinner plans upon learning that the restaurant in Duck would be hosting a special event that evening, deciding instead to dine at the Port O' Call. Her first inclination had been to pick Kelly's Restaurant because of their sweet potato biscuits, but she chose the Port O' Call after remembering her plans to dine at Kelly's on Saturday with her girlfriends. She also wanted Dave to sample the she-crab soup at Port O' Call while she, being a true southern belle, savored their cornbread with honey-laced butter. When Dave discovered that they would not be going to the "stiff joint" in Duck, he considered shedding his blazer but then decided to leave it on after Nikki commented on how handsome he looked wearing it. Although it was a little warm outside for the jacket, he found the temperature inside the restaurant quite cool and comfortable.

Standing alone in the doorway of the saloon, he waited patiently for Nikki, who had disappeared into the gift shop located directly off a Victorian-era vestibule containing antiques and collectibles tucked into every nook and cranny. The Gaslight Saloon also reflected the Victorian theme with richly carved hardwood fittings and walls adorned with colorful paintings set in heavy wooden frames. Crystalline chandeliers hung from the high ceiling of the dimly lit saloon, casting soft light into the upstairs lounge known as the Captain's Lounge, an elevated area that encircled the room like a loft.

Directly to Dave's right was a dance floor set before a low stage on which stood a wrought-iron spiral staircase. In addition to the iron staircase, there was a carpeted stairway at the back of the room leading upstairs to the Captain's Lounge where customers enjoyed excellent views of the lower bar and stage area. The views were especially keen when seated at the lounge's most distinctive table at the corner of the loft, a partially enclosed booth similar to that of a box seat in an opera house. Surrounded by a wrought-iron railing, this exclusive booth held but a single round table and some low cushioned chairs set amid other antique couches and furniture arranged throughout the upstairs that allowed for drinking and socializing in a Victorian atmosphere surrounded by classic paintings displayed in thick, heavy frames. Everything in the place was for sale.

Dave sauntered out onto the dance floor and glanced up at the corner booth in the Captain's Lounge. He could see two couples sitting around the table having drinks, and he heard the sound of their laughter and conversations amid the modern music playing in the background. They were the only people in the saloon at that time other than the bartender. With his jacket unbuttoned and both hands in his pants' pockets, Dave looked relaxed and at home, the epitome of casual elegance. His new clothes hung well on his lean figure, giving him a smooth, graceful appearance as if he were dressed in his usual attire, although he could not recall the last time he had worn anything other than a tee shirt and shorts. Rotating slightly to his left, he strained to see through the subdued lighting toward the back of the room where a set of sliding doors stood partially open, exposing the dining room where he and Nikki planned to eat dinner. Never before in his life had he dined in such elegant surroundings.

He had only been at the Port O' Call on one other occasion to hear a popular band perform in the saloon, so he did not know the bartender, a young man of roughly the same age who was busy inventorying the liquor bottles on a shelf behind the bar. For several minutes, Dave watched the young bartender perform his monotonous chore before turning and strolling back into the lobby in search of Nikki. The lobby, like the saloon, contained antique furniture, paintings, and a multitude of archaic collectors' items. Through the glass windows of the gift shop, he could see Nikki standing at the jewelry counter, so he amused himself by viewing the scrimshaw knives in a tall, freestanding display case positioned against the wall between the two restrooms. The dining room hostess, sitting on a red Victorian loveseat, saw him looking into the display case and said, "If there is anything you would like to see, just let me know."

Inclining his head in her direction, he replied, "Thank you," before returning his attention to the knives. After a few moments, he pointed toward one of the shelves inside the case and said, "I would like to see this knife if you don't mind."

"Sure," she said as she rose from the loveseat. Walking to the cabinet with a key she kept in her pocket, she asked, "Which one?"

"That one right there," he answered while pointing to a medium sized folding knife with an intricately carved bone handle. The inscribed images on one side of the handle were those of a lighthouse and a compass rose with carvings on the other side depicting a whale's tail along with a bearded sailor wearing a Sou'wester fisherman's hat. The whale flukes reminded him of the humpback whale he and Nikki had observed two days earlier on the beach, and the bristled mariner looked much like his old mentor from Chicago. Holding the knife in his hand, he nodded approvingly while squeezing it tightly in his strong grip. Upon unfolding the blade, he was surprised to find it scored with etchings incised with the same artisanship as the carvings of the bone handle. A quick glance at the price tag, however, made him wince, and he reluctantly gave it back to the hostess.

She took the knife from his hand and smiled. "Are you sure you don't want to buy it?" she asked before returning it to the case.

Grinning sheepishly, he replied, somewhat disheartened, "I'd like to, but I can't afford it." Pulling out his Cub Scout knife, he showed it to her, adding, "I guess I'm stuck with 'Old Faithful' here." Just then, he caught the whiff of an enticing fragrance, an alluring scent suggesting the attar of flowers with just a hint of seduction, an elegant bouquet that alerted him to Nikki standing directly behind him.

Turning to meet her gaze, he made no effort to hide his delight. As he had done upon arriving at her condo to pick her up that evening, he gasped for air at the sight of her tall figure standing firm yet vulnerable in a sleeveless silk dress, pure white with flowing folds of liquid fabric gliding loosely over the curves of her slender body. She no longer pulled her hair back into a ponytail but allowed it to hang down in golden strands to the tops of her shapely shoulders, and she wore only a few pieces of jewelry: a diamond tennis bracelet, diamond stud earrings, and the same gold pendant she had worn at the Animal Hospital on the day she had examined Grave. Attached to a delicate gold chain, the pendant lay hidden beneath the graceful neckline of her dress. She neither wore nor needed any makeup except for the slight sheen of gloss on her lips. Facing her again in the lobby of the Port O' Call, he was as speechless as he had been earlier while standing on the doorstep of her condominium.

"Are you ready to eat?" she asked.

"I am if you are," he said after catching his breath. With his hand pressed lightly against the lower portion of her back, he guided her to the hostess' station, savoring the feel of the silk beneath his hand, especially the way it glided gracefully over her skin. She, in turn, enjoyed the gentle pressure of his soft touch on her back. "We're ready for our table now," he said to the hostess.

The dining room was a large open space with subdued lighting provided by Tiffany chandeliers and table lamps in a variety of colors. The walls were made of oak on which hung large, heavy framed paintings similar to those in the bar and lobby. Upholstered chairs constructed of dark cherry complemented the wooden tables draped with white linen tablecloths and adorned with place settings of folded napkins, crystal water glasses, and pewter bread plates.

While being seated at a table near the wall, Dave glanced over his shoulder at the doorway leading into the bar, the same one he had noticed while standing in the saloon. The sliding doors were now wide open, and waiters and waitresses were coming and going through the doorway carrying glasses filled with wine and spirits. One of the passing servers, a young girl of college age, stopped to ask what they would like to drink. When it was Dave's turn to order, he glanced at Nikki and smiled before saying, "I've recently developed new tastes, even in my choice of beer. What I truly desire is … Carolina Blonde." Holding Nikki's gaze for a few seconds after ordering, he detected a slight blush on her tanned cheeks.

"That's actually an ale," the waitress corrected him. "I'll see if we carry it." She then disappeared into the bar through the open doorway.

The place was crowded with couples and several large families occupying most of the tables, but Dave saw only Nikki in the room.

He never took his eyes off her throughout the evening as he listened to her talk about her life and the things that interested her. For a change, she did not pry into his past but, instead, freely divulged information about herself, her family, and her goals in life. When the topic turned to him, her questions were less invasive and her observations more complimentary about his ability to endear himself to other people. Nikki encouraged him to cultivate that natural talent to better himself personally as well as professionally. She pointed out that he had made more friends and acquaintances in his brief time in the Outer Banks than she had garnered in her years living there. "That's a skill that is highly marketable," she told him, "and you should find ways to profit from it."

Underlying their dinner conversation, especially when Dave was the focus of the discussion, was a subtle effort on Nikki's part to extol the value of hard work and personal betterment. He knew what she was trying to do, and he did not object to it as long as he could remain in her company, delighting in her presence while listening to her words. He found her voice incredibly soothing, even when it encouraged him to act more responsibly by adopting a productive lifestyle. With loving patience, he remained attentive and receptive to all she had to say, reacting with grace and deference born of genuine affection.

Not only did Dave enjoy conversing with Nikki in such a relaxed and sophisticated setting, but he also relished the culinary delights served up by the restaurant. Upon Nikki's insistence, he ordered appetizers and she-crab soup in addition to his dinner entrée and all the accompanying side dishes. Nikki also coaxed him into choosing the king-sized portion of prime rib when she noticed his enthusiastic reaction upon seeing it on the menu. She even told the waitress to bring him an extra-large cut—the biggest one available—because she was trying to fatten him up. When it arrived, however, the sight of the oversized portion on his plate made her cringe.

She had never seen such a large and rare cut of meat in all her life. Ringed with a thick layer of fat and oozing blood from every pore, the enormous slab of beef was almost too much for her to bear. Dave, however, found it utterly delightful, attacking it like a predator falling upon its prey. At one point, Nikki began shaking her head in wonder as she watched him consume every last bite of meat, gristle, and fat as well as everything else placed before him. Feeling quite satiated, he raised his hand at the end of the meal, signaling that enough was enough when Nikki suggested that he order dessert. He had not eaten that much in one sitting since dining at his aunt's house in Florida the previous Thanksgiving.

When it came time to pay, Nikki kept her word by picking up the check when the waitress dropped it in front of Dave, waiting until the young girl had walked away before grabbing it. Jamming six twenty-dollar bills into the leather folder, she set it back on the table in front of Dave and said, "Tell her to keep the change." She then smiled at him while placing her napkin on the table and adding, "I'm going to the ladies' room."

As she stood to leave, Dave found himself rising from his chair. He thought it odd that he would instinctively react that way because he was not one who ordinarily subscribed to proper etiquette. "It must be the clothes," he whispered to himself after she had left the table. Upon sitting down, he peeked into the billfold to see what the dinner had cost. The sight of it chilled him to the bone. It was not something he could ever afford, and it brought into clear focus much of what Nikki had been addressing that evening. He then concluded that he would have to find a way to earn some real money if he wished this relationship to continue.

When the waitress walked by, he reached out and handed her the leather wallet containing the money, telling her to keep the change, but she returned a few minutes later to give him a printed copy of the bill. "Here's a dinner receipt," she said. "It will get you into the bar tonight without paying a cover charge if you come back to hear the band." Dave smiled and unconsciously jammed the receipt into the inside pocket of his jacket while Nikki approached the table. Once again, he politely rose to greet her.

She did not sit down but reached over to straighten the lapel of his blazer. "Let's go back to my place and I'll fix you some coffee or tea," she said. "I still have that surprise for you." Once again, a mischievous twinkle appeared in her eye, the same one he had observed at Sugar Creek when she had first mentioned the surprise.

"Well, then, let's go. I wouldn't want to miss my *surprise.*" He spoke the words close to the side of her face as he gently grasped her arm above the elbow and led her toward the exit.

Night had fallen, and the full moon was rising over the eastern horizon as they crossed the Washington Baum Bridge after having stopped by Dave's place to pick up Grave. Because of their attire that evening, they had taken Nikki's Jeep Patriot instead of Dave's hearse, but he had insisted on driving. It was the newest model of car he had ever driven in his life, and he enjoyed the handling as well as the interior comfort of the vehicle. Grave also enjoyed the SUV, especially the uncluttered rear compartment that gave him plenty of space to roam while investigating the many new scents and smells. Additionally, he enjoyed exploring Nikki's condominium once they arrived at Pirate's Cove, immediately disappearing into the inner confines of her residence where he moved from room to room, revealing his location only by the echoing sounds of his snorting and sniffing.

Nikki's home was a lovely place, tastefully decorated in light colors and soft pastels. The pale tint of the walls blended exquisitely with the colorful floral patterns of the upholstered furniture as well as the delicate hues and tones of the lamps and drapery. A luxuriously long couch sat in the center of the living room facing a fireplace over which hung a wide flat-screen television mounted to the wall. Recessed ceiling lights, controlled and managed by electronic timers, softly illuminated the interior space.

The few times that Dave had been there, he had never been beyond the entryway, but he now found himself free to roam and explore the place, although not as openly and obviously as his furry friend. Removing his jacket, he hung it on the back of a chair in the dining area and then strolled into the living room, rolling up his shirt sleeves as he walked along, exposing the charred bronze of his forearms that appeared even darker when contrasted against the brilliant white of his shirt. Upon reaching the center of the room, he found his eyes drawn to a framed picture sitting on a table at the end of the couch. A closer look revealed that it was not a photograph but a framed magazine cover featuring a female water-skier on a slalom ski carving a radical turn while gripping the towrope with only one hand. The cover was from *WaterSki* magazine, and the female skier was Nikki looking a few years younger. He lifted the frame from the table for a closer examination. "That explains her knack for windsurfing," he said aloud.

Having been in the kitchen, Nikki was unaware that he was looking at the picture. "Oh," she said a little embarrassed when she walked into the living room.

Turning when he heard the sound of her voice, he grinned and said, "Very nice." Without breaking eye contact, he reached down and returned the framed picture to the table where he had found it.

"I don't want you to get the wrong idea," she said. "I'm not that much of a narcissist. My sister framed that magazine cover for me as a gift, so I keep it on display for whenever she comes to visit." She glanced down at the picture and then looked back at him, still a little embarrassed. "I used to model in college to help pay my tuition." She said it matter-of-factly before walking back into the kitchen.

From out in the kitchen, she called out to him saying, "Have a seat on the couch, and I'll show you your surprise," after which she filled a bowl with water and placed it on the floor for Grave. "Do you want any coffee, tea, or anything?" she asked.

"No, thanks. Not right now."

"Beer?"

"No, nothing. Thanks."

Plopping himself down onto the couch, he leaned against the cushioned armrest to await his surprise. The first thing he noticed was the sheer comfort of the couch. It was far more luxurious and comfortable than that rickety old thing in his cottage, softer and more restful than even his bed. Leaning farther back, he peacefully closed his eyes and wondered what she had in store for him. Her obsession with this surprise was starting to intrigue him, but he refused to let his imagination get the best of him. Better to wait and see what happens rather than be disappointed, he told himself. However, it was hard not to wonder.

Nikki then walked into the living room and positioned herself directly the front of the couch with something concealed behind her back. She smiled without saying a word, making him wait a few moments before finally asking with a hint of delight in her voice, "Are you ready for your surprise?"

"Hit me," he said.

The words had barely passed his lips when Nikki eagerly revealed the hidden item. With blinding speed, she whipped her arm around to display a plastic video case bearing the images of a man and a woman imprinted on a background of red Scottish plaid. The woman stared blissfully at the heavens while resting in the arms of the man who gazed lovingly at her face. The woman was Cyd Charisse and the man, Gene Kelly, with the word *BRIGADOON* emblazoned above their heads.

"Brigadoon?" he asked with the same facial expression he had exhibited at Mulligan's on the night they had met. This was not what he had expected and definitely not the surprise he had desired.

"Yeah," she said with a grin. "It's the story of how we met. You like musicals, don't you?"

Not waiting for a reply, she turned and began fiddling with the DVD player while he nervously pondered how he should answer her question. Then, after a short pause, he blurted out, "Actually, I have seen some musicals—or I guess you would call them musicals."

She stopped tinkering with the video equipment and glanced back at him, her face bearing an inquisitive look.

In answer to her expression, he continued, "Near the end of my grandfather's life, he moved in with us. He was a big Frank Sinatra fan, so I would buy him videos of Sinatra movies on his birthday and at Christmas. I guess you would call them musicals since Frank always sang in them, at least most of them. Of course, I would then have to watch the videos with him, and he would tell me stories about the songs and the actors in the movies. I actually began to enjoy them, but one I really liked. It was the story of Joe E. Lewis."

"I know that one," she cut in. "He played some reprobate playboy singer. I think Kim Novak was in it too."

"No, that was *Pal Joey*," he said. "This was a different one."

"You really do know your Frank Sinatra movies, don't you?"

He shrugged his shoulders. "Hey, what can I say? I've seen them all, and more than once. Anyway, the name of this movie was *The Joker is Wild*, and he played Joe E. Lewis, a nightclub singer who ran afoul of the mob. In the movie, they try to kill him by cutting his throat, but he survives, although he is no longer able to sing. Instead, he becomes a comedian. He also becomes an alcoholic and screws up his whole life because of the booze.

"The final scene in the movie is the one I really like. After he has alienated his wife, his friends—everyone—he is walking down the street at night on his way to a performance. The stores are all closed, but their darkened picture windows reveal his reflected image as he walks down the sidewalk. At one point, his reflection stops walking and begins talking to him, reprimanding him for his drinking and all the screw-ups in his life, advising him to straighten up and turn things around before it's too late. Acknowledging his shortcomings and mistakes, Frank then agrees to give it a try, at which point he turns and continues walking down the street toward the nightclub. Because of that movie, I often expect my reflection to start talking to me whenever I see it a window or a mirror."

Her eyes narrowed, and her face grimaced. "That's kind of creepy," she said.

"No, no. It was a great scene, and it really capped off the movie. You ought to watch it sometime."

"Well, I'll think about it," she said while sliding down beside him on the couch. Slipping under his arm, she folded her legs beneath her and rested her head against his chest. "In the meantime," she said, "we'll watch this movie. I guarantee there won't be any talking reflections, but there is magic involved." She pointed the remote at the DVD player to activate it but then hit the pause button and asked, "Were you serious when you said you haven't seen this movie before?"

"Yes, absolutely."

"Well, then, let me fill you in on a few things. Brigadoon is a village in Scotland that appears for only one day—a single twenty-four-hour period—every one hundred years. When the residents go to bed and wake up the next morning, one hundred years have passed. To them, it feels like one night, but to the rest of the world, it's been a hundred years. That's all I'm going to tell you."

"Intriguing," he said, trying to sound sincere.

Pointing the remote at the screen, she clicked the play button. "Oh, by the way," she said, "I'm driving to Norfolk after work tomorrow for my nephew's birthday party. I'll be back on Saturday, probably late afternoon or early evening. I'm meeting my friends for dinner at Kelly's; that is, if the hurricane doesn't head this way. Jan's brother's band is playing there later that night, and I promised I'd go. You should join us after dinner to hear the band. I'd like you to meet my friends." She glanced up at him expectantly.

"Okay," he answered with a smile.

"Good," she said, settling snugly under his arm. "And now that I know you like musicals, we can go see *The Lost Colony* over at the Waterside Theatre sometime. It's not really a musical but a symphonic drama. It highlights Virginia Dare, the first English child born in the New World, and it tells the story of the Roanoke Colony that vanished without a trace."

"Vanishing without a trace? I'm pretty good at that myself," he said lightheartedly.

Ignoring his remark, she continued, "I haven't been to that play in a long time. Have you seen it?"

"No, but I've heard things about it from people who have seen it."

"What did they say?"

He chuckled before responding, "They told me that there were lots of mosquitos." He quickly added, "You know, maybe those colonists didn't leave. Maybe they just disappeared from sight only to reappear sometime in the future, just like the people in Brigadoon."

Lifting her head from his chest, she glanced quizzically at him while he stared stone-faced at the television screen displaying the FBI copyright warning. She found his speculation about the whereabouts of the missing colonists fascinating, and it surprised her how adeptly his mind had recognized the parallels between the two stories. But what she found most impressive was the speed at which he had synthesized and processed the information to proffer an entirely new hypothesis. Once again, she wondered if she might not be underestimating this skinny kid.

Just then, the introductory music began playing, so she lowered her head and snuggled closer to him to watch the film. With her ear pressed firmly against his chest, she could hear his heart keeping time with the orchestrated theme music resonating from the Bose speakers in the four corners of the room. She told herself that as long as she could hear his strong, steady heartbeat, he would not be vanishing from her sight anytime soon.

Neither one of them spoke as the screenplay unfolded with the singers and dancers performing their upbeat songs and well-choreographed Highland dance routines. Through it all, Nikki heard the continuous background thumping of Dave's heart until she began detecting a slight slowing of its rhythm along with a change in his breathing pattern. Softly and gently, she turned to gaze upward at his face, affirming her suspicion that he was sound asleep. With a mild shake of her head, she said, almost inaudibly, "I guess that means we're not going to *The Lost Colony.*" As she quietly spoke those words, she unobtrusively used the remote to stop the video and turn off the television before easing her head back onto his chest to drift slowly off to sleep.

Dave awoke with a mild jolt to find the television turned off and Nikki lying on the couch next to him. She moaned slightly in response to his awakening but remained undisturbed, quietly lost in a deep sleep with her head buried in a pillow on his lap. His arm now rested on her hip, and he could feel the contour of her figure against the underside of his forearm. As she breathed deeply, his arm floated gently over the flimsy barrier of her silk dress, and he marveled at the total absence of tension anywhere in her body, especially in her face that was now void of all lines and creases. Even the dimples on her cheeks had vanished.

He wished he could remain there forever, but an intense need to use the bathroom meant that he had to get up. Moving slowing and carefully, he gently slipped from beneath the pillow and lowered her head onto the cushion. His attempt to free himself evoked involuntary groan from Nikki as she squirmed and rolled onto her side while he stepped lightly away from the couch. In his search for the bathroom, he discovered her bedroom where he found Grave sleeping on his back in Nikki's bed, his legs splayed and his nose buried beneath one of the pillows. Shaking his head at the sight, Dave continued down the hallway toward the bathroom.

The clock on the wall was striking eleven when he walked back into the living room. Aware that Nikki had to rise early for work and drive to Norfolk the next day, he decided to leave so she could go to bed. Sitting on the edge of the couch near her head, he gently stroked her hair, prompting her to move slightly as she drifted in and out of consciousness. In a quiet whisper next to her ear, he said, "It's late, Nikki. I'm going to take Grave and go home." With a chuckle, he added, "He's sleeping in your bed right now."

She did not open her eyes but sighed sleepily, "Let him stay tonight. I'll drop him off on my way to work tomorrow." With that, she appeared to drift back to sleep while hugging the pillow to the side of her face.

"Lucky bastard," he muttered quietly while shooting a wayward glance toward the bedroom. Bending down, he tenderly kissed her on the cheek, whispering timidly, almost soundlessly, "Thank you," before standing and walking into the dining room. A deft smile formed on Nikki's lips as she heard his footsteps carrying him away from her. Although fully conscious of his movements, she remained motionless on the couch with her eyes closed. Grabbing his jacket off the chair, Dave then walked out the door without saying goodbye to either Nikki or Grave.

Since it was just past eleven o'clock and Mulligan's had not yet closed, he decided to swing by bar to visit with Travis. After being on the receiving end of his friend's charity, he knew he must fulfill his obligation of sharing the details of his date; however, he had already decided to leave out the part about *Brigadoon*. It only took him about ten minutes to reach Whalebone Junction and drive up the bypass toward the restaurant under the light of an incredibly luminous moon. The newscasters that week had called it a "super moon," one having a perigee of just under two hundred and twenty-three thousand miles. He swore it was the biggest full moon he had ever seen in his life with a radiance almost as bright as the yellow Mulligan's sign where he turned onto East Soundside Road. Then, just as he was about to swing the hearse into the parking lot, he looked ahead at the intersection where he saw a storm gray Infiniti Q70 zoom past him on its way up the beach road.

The shock of seeing the vehicle caused the muscles of his body to harden, but he quickly dispelled the tension and eased off the accelerator, allowing the hearse to move forward under its own inertia. The speeding sedan looked very much like Mark's Infiniti, but he could not be sure because the dazzling light of the super moon was powerful enough to reveal the make and model of the vehicle but not bright enough to identify the driver. Deep down inside, he felt a burning desire to follow the car if only to discover if it was, indeed, Nikki's ex-boyfriend, but he also heard an internal voice telling him to let it be. In the few moments he spent grappling with what to do, the hearse made the decision for him by drifting past the parking lot entrance and heading straight for the intersection. It was then that he committed himself wholeheartedly to the endeavor by completing the turn onto the beach road and soaring up the asphalt at breakneck speed. "I can't believe I'm doing this," he groaned while racing through the night.

Up ahead in the distance, he saw the taillights of the sedan plainly visible in the gloom of the night. Despite its excessive speed, the Infiniti had not traveled that far up the road during Dave's moment of indecision, giving him an opportunity to close the gap between the two vehicles. He then slowed down and stayed back a considerable distance, remaining just close enough to discern the glowing red tail lamps in the darkness ahead. With each passing second, he became more and more convinced that it was Mark's Infiniti. He could easily have solved the mystery by pulling closer to the car and checking the license plate number, but he wished to remain hidden if it turned out to be Mark; therefore, he maintained a safe distance and bided his time. Not only did he want to confirm that it was Mark he was pursuing, but he also desired to know if Mark was cheating on Nikki again and, moreover, if he was doing so with the same girl or a different one this time. It did not take him long to find out.

After about four miles, the Infiniti signaled left and then pulled into the parking lot at the south end of the Port O' Call Restaurant. Astonished by the fact that he had come full circle, finding himself right back from where he had started only a few hours earlier, Dave drove past the restaurant and entered the parking lot on the north side of the building in an effort to remain hidden from view. Reaching for his jacket on the seat beside him, he rummaged through the inside pockets until he found the dinner receipt the waitress had given him. The spot where he had parked the hearse did not provide a clear view of the front entrance, so he waited patiently inside the vehicle, giving his quarry sufficient time to enter the restaurant.

Despite the simplicity of his plan, the first part of which involved walking over to the other parking lot to check the license plate number of the car, he found himself hesitant to act, stymied by an uncomfortable feeling that something was not right. Although he could not explain his reluctance to solve the mystery, he knew that he would ultimately act, spurred on by his desire to end the suspense. Deep down inside, he hoped that he was just chasing ghosts, telling himself that the car most likely belonged to someone else; however, his wishful desires were quickly dashed when he stood at the rear bumper of the familiar gray sedan and recognized the plate number of his adversary. Although uncertain why he harbored such uneasy feelings, he knew exactly what he would do next; he would enter the restaurant if only to satisfy his need for closure.

The inside of the Port O' Call appeared no different than when he had been there several hours earlier except for a younger crowd jamming the lobby and the loud, disjointed music playing in the Gas Light Saloon. The deafening volume inside the place did not surprise him because he had already heard the din of the raucous metal band while still in the parking lot. Studying the crowd in the hallway, he failed to spot Mark, so he ducked into the men's restroom where the only occupant was a slightly intoxicated kid leaning against the wall by the urinals. Completing his sweep of the restroom, a search that included the bathroom stalls, he then returned to the lobby, confident that Mark must be in the bar.

Handing his dinner receipt to the bouncer in lieu of a cover charge, Dave stepped into the saloon near the dance floor, finding it filled with people his age or younger, mostly girls jerking and gyrating to the heavy metal beat. Those not on the dance floor were milling around the bar or sitting at the rear of the room, but he could not distinguish their faces due to the low lighting and the flickering of multiple strobe lights distorting their features. Unable to search using facial recognition, he instead scanned the crowd based on body shapes; Mark was huge and would be easy to spot. A quick pass of his eyes around the room, however, did not reveal anything except someone vacating a seat at the end of the bar. Slithering through the crowd as quickly as he could, he succeeded in claiming the empty chair that provided him an excellent location from which to observe the crowd. From his seat beside the waitress station, he was able to view the entire downstairs and see anyone going up or down the carpeted staircase directly behind him.

When the bartender came over to take his order, Dave merely pointed to an orphaned beer bottle on the bar rather than shouting over the music, tossing money to the young man when he returned with the beer. Dave then tilted back his head to take a long swig from the bottle but found himself rendered motionless by the disturbing sight of Mark reclining on a chair high above him in the corner booth of the Captain's Lounge. Sharing the exclusive booth with the oversized brute was a petite young girl sitting on his lap, the fabric of her short white dress clinging tightly to her thin frame. Her long flowing hair, red as an autumn leaf, confirmed for Dave that she was not the same girl he had seen last night on the boat.

"Well, that proves it," Dave said loudly and openly, although no one could hear him due to the earsplitting music of the band. "This guy's just playing around—and having a good old time doing it."

Discovering Mark with yet another woman raised his spirits, making him glad he had overcome his misgivings about following the car that night. This new discovery was sure to improve his chances with Nikki, he thought, or at least provide additional advantage should she consider reuniting with the big jerk. After some reflection, he decided to refrain from sharing this bit of information with her until he actually needed it. He then gulped down a swallow of beer in celebration, feeling secure and confident in his continued relationship with Nikki. "What a sleazeball," he said while glancing up at Mark, an insult that went unheard due to the blaring music coming from the stage.

Dave did not like crowds, and he was even less fond of loud music. Finding himself surrounded by both, he decided to finish his beer and get out of there. With his mission accomplished, there was no reason for him to linger, and yet he found himself dawdling at the bar far longer than necessary. Perhaps it was out of curiosity, he mused, although he could not say for sure. Whatever it was, it kept him glued to his chair, enduring the noise and people while occasionally glancing up at Mark and the redheaded girl on his lap.

About an hour passed and Dave still had not left, maintaining his observation post at the bar while listening to the amplified sounds of the heavy metal music booming from the giant speakers on both sides of the stage. He often wondered why musicians played at such a high decibel level, but, for once, he was thankful for it because it drowned out the conversations of a small group of girls standing nearby. During a brief interlude in the music, he heard portions of their banter, and it almost drove him crazy. Thankfully, the lead singer saved him by wailing out another song, overpowering their mindless, juvenile chatter. Now—he thought— if he could only find a way to insulate himself from the smell of their noxious colognes.

Eventually, it became too much to bear—the constricting crowd, the earsplitting music, the suffocating perfume—so he decided to end to his eavesdropping on Mark before it turned into a compulsion. As he prepared to go, he glanced up at the Captain's Lounge one last time, shocked by the sight of an unfamiliar couple sitting at the table previously occupied by Mark and his date. Swinging his head in a frantic search of the room, he found his vision blocked by the back of an incredibly large man in a blue Oxford shirt and khaki slacks who had stepped directly in front of him. The giant then moved toward the door, cutting a wide swath through the crowd, much like Moses parting the Red Sea, pulling along in his wake a petite young girl with long red hair. Chugging down the last of his beer, Dave moved quickly to pursue them across the floor, but the sea of humanity closed in around him, stymying his forward progress and pinning him in on all sides as he pushed and squeezed his way through the mob only to see the back of Mark's head disappear into the lobby.

When Dave finally succeeded in freeing himself from the crowd, Mark and the girl had already exited the restaurant, so he charged through the lobby and out the front entrance, oblivious to the disturbed looks on the faces of the people congregating in the doorway. Jumping into his hearse, he coasted without headlights toward the beach road, silently asking himself why he sought to continue the chase. No answer was immediately forthcoming because, at that very moment, he spotted the gray Infiniti exiting the parking lot on the other side of the building.

Caught up in the thrill of the chase, Dave surrendered to the adrenalin rush by flipping on his headlights and pulling onto the beach road, adjusting his speed to maintain a considerable distance between the two vehicles while keeping a visual lock on Mark's taillights. Once again, he asked himself why he was stalking the brute, especially at that late hour when he could be home sleeping comfortably in bed. This time, however, his mind offered a possible explanation, one rooted in a primal masculine trait: the irrepressible urge to proceed along a course of action, stubbornly advancing toward a predetermined goal regardless of the consequences.

Both vehicles traveled south along the beach road at a pace well in excess of the posted speed limit until Mark suddenly veered off the road, turning right into a parking lot just before the Jockey's Ridge Crossing shopping complex. The concrete lot sat next to the shopping center, directly adjacent to Kitty Hawk Kites, and it provided parking space for two business establishments, Sooey's BBQ & Rib Shack and Life is Good, both closed for the night. Caught off guard and uncertain of what to do, Dave slowed down to assess the situation. His first inclination was to stop and weigh his options, but that was out of the question due to the approaching traffic from both directions. In the end, he had only two choices: turn blindly into the darkened lot without knowing Mark's whereabouts, or give up and go home. Despite the late hour and his desire for sleep, he still could not bring himself to abandon the hunt, so, with palms sweating, he leaned hard on the oversized steering wheel, sending the hearse careening into the parking lot.

As his headlights panned the pavement, he saw no other cars until he spotted the Infiniti parked off to the side near Kitty Hawk Kites. Uncertain if Mark and the girl were still inside the darkened sedan, he felt too exposed and conspicuous to slow down, so he continued at a steady pace through the vacant lot, driving toward the exit lane leading to the bypass. Coming to a stop before entering the highway, he glanced left and marveled at the unexpected sight of the couple running across the road under the light of the ominous super moon. Their destination appeared to be the great sand dune of Jockey's Ridge State Park on the opposite side of the highway.

Sitting quietly in the hearse while watching Mark and the girl cross the bypass, he waited until they began climbing the dune before pulling onto the highway and quickly turning onto West Soundside Road, an intersecting street that paralleled the state park. Knowing that the road skirted the sandbank all the way to Roanoke Sound, he hoped to find a location nearby where he could scale the side of the dune and observe Mark and his date from a covered position on their flank. The dense roadside thicket near the intersection, however, forced him to drive an additional six hundred yards down the road where he found a more accessible spot with less obstructive growth. Pulling the hearse onto the berm, he then grabbed his binoculars off the seat and began running toward the thicket at the base of the dunes.

Plodding through the brush and thicket, Dave struggled valiantly, trying his best to make up for lost ground. Having traveled a greater distance down the road than he had intended, he knew that he must pick up the pace or he would be too far away to observe Mark and the girl once they cleared the top of the dune. Emerging from a thick growth of red cedar, he started climbing the soft sides of a dune ridge, but he found his progress hampered by his oversized shoes filling with sand as well as his cramped legs still sore from his run on the beach two days earlier. Fortunately, however, the ground hardened once he reached the top of the ridge, improving his footing and alleviating the muscle fatigue in his legs.

Having scaled the dunes before, he was familiar with the terrain and knew what to expect. During his previous undertakings, the scorching sun had been the chief irritant. But he was now climbing at night in temperatures only slightly cooler, and he began experiencing even more discomfort due to the added exertion of being in a race. The landscape also appeared different, no longer bathed in bright sunlight but blanketed in a ghostly lunar radiance that gave it the appearance of a lost and distant world.

The topography flattened out somewhat once he cleared the ridge, enabling him to run swiftly and effortlessly up and down the sand valleys amid sparse patches of grasses and growths of yaupon, wax myrtle, and bayberry. His goal was to get closer to the couple before they reached the top of the dune, and he seemed to be making progress toward that end while jogging steadily in the hot, sticky air, his eyes focused intently on the peak of the giant sand hill some five hundred yards away. Just then, in the distance ahead, he saw two figures cresting the sand mound, their darkened outlines silhouetted against the bright starless sky as they stood side-by-side along the upper ridge. Their sudden appearance triggered an involuntary response in him, causing him to dive onto his stomach like a soldier collapsing to the ground upon spotting an enemy patrol.

Despite the distance that separated them, Dave worried that his white shirt would make him too conspicuous, so he rolled several times across the sand to seek cover behind an outcropping of beach grass that camouflaged his presence but allowed him a clear view of the couple. Aided by his binoculars and the Sturgeon Moon, he saw everything on the distant dune with incredible clarity, even to the point of discerning the facial features of Mark and the girl. She was unfamiliar to him, but there was no mistaking Mark's mug. Exposed by the lunar light, it was identical to the face he had seen up close on the night he and Nikki had driven through The Village at Nags Head. Everything was the same, right down to the sunglasses Mark wore then and now.

While continuing to watch the couple through the small but powerful field glasses, he heard an internal voice questioning his motives, asking him why he was there and what he hoped to achieve in the end. Rather than lie to himself, he thought it best to answer honestly, admitting that his actions were indeed sick but beyond his control, simply a voyeuristic urge that was too strong to resist. "I'm a sick puppy," he said aloud while refusing to lower the binoculars for fear of missing something on the far dune.

When Mark and the girl had first come into sight, they were walking hand-in-hand, but that soon changed when she broke free and began charging down the side of the powdery mountain, kicking up sand as she ran. Extending her arms, she leaped high into the air, mimicking the take-off of one of the hang-gliders she had seen there during the day, only to fall unsteadily back to earth, stumbling several yards but avoiding a nasty tumble to the ground. It was apparent from her behavior as well as her lack of balance that she had consumed a large quantity of alcohol, but Mark made no attempt to catch her or curtail any of her antics. He merely followed her to the bottom of the dune, walking steadily at an even pace.

While still lying on his stomach, Dave grew increasingly uncomfortable. Not only was he hot and sweaty, but the sandflies had begun biting him, causing him even more discomfort. He tried sitting up, propping his elbows on his knees while holding the binoculars to his eyes, but that position proved equally distressing. "Buddy, just get up and go home," he said aloud, confident that Mark was too far away to hear him. "It's too late to be doing this."

Lowering the binoculars, he looked around the area, first at the moon and then over toward Roanoke Sound, wondering how he could escape without exposing himself. A discreet departure would be difficult because Mark and the girl were closer now after having descended the dune, and they would certainly see him if he stood and began walking away. Despite the fact that he would be unrecognizable at that distance, he still preferred to remain unseen.

Uncertain about what to do, he resumed his eavesdropping and watched the girl make another leap into the air, this time reaching out to wrap her arms around Mark's neck, dangling in front of him with her feet off the ground and her long hair flowing over her shoulders. The big man caught her with one arm and held her like a rag doll, glancing down at her before kissing her slowly and gently, a tender action that rendered her motionless. He then raised his head and began unobtrusively scanning the terrain.

Grinning broadly, Dave found it amusing that Mark would worry about privacy in such a remote location or be concerned that someone might spot him necking with his date. His amusement waned, however, when he noticed Mark's massive hand reaching up to engulf the back of the girl's head, an action that appeared more ominous than affectionate. Although too far away to observe such details, Dave could sense a tightening of Mark's fingers as they sank deep into the thick mat of red hair. Then, in a split second—the equivalent of a heartbeat—he saw Mark yank back on the poor girl's head, tugging and twisting with such force that he completely separated her skull from her delicate shoulders. Without a knife or cutting instrument of any sort, the brutal behemoth had decapitated his innocent young companion using only his bare hands. And it did not end there.

Still clutching the limp, headless torso of the girl in a one-armed embrace, Mark then thrust his mouth down between her shoulders, spreading his lips like a serpent to cover the entire void of her neck. It all played out before Dave like a silent movie, shocking his visual sensibilities but sparing him the auditory agony of having to listen to the gruesome sounds of Mark emptying the girl of her life-sustaining blood and bodily fluids. Bathed in moonlight, the giant fiend stood on the shimmering sand, feasting on his victim with the savagery of an animal, holding the girl like a vessel while dangling her head at his side, suspending it by its long red hair.

Able to maintain his sanity only by mentally detaching himself from what he was observing, Dave watched in horror the tragedy unfolding several hundred yards away from him. Disgusted, yet paralyzed and unable to turn away, he remained sentient only by convincing himself that the whole thing was nothing more than a staged scene from a slasher film—total fiction. It seemed unreal; therefore, it could not be real. Things like this were not possible, he assured himself, as he sat like a statue, unable to move, watching in utter disbelief what resembled grotesque Siamese twins sharing the same head.

Mark's mouth stayed tightly attached to open wound of the girl's neck until he had drained every ounce of fluid from the shell of her body. At that point, he dropped her carcass onto the sand like a discarded piece of trash and tossed her head onto the mangled heap of human remains. Standing visibly relaxed on the desolate landscape, he wiped his mouth with the back of his hand while gazing down at the remnants of his consumed meal. Then, without warning, he spun around and began furiously digging in the sand, much like a dog preparing to bury a bone. His actions were an incredible display of speed and power in which he used nothing but his bare hands to send plumes of sand soaring high into the air, creating a fog so dense that Dave temporarily lost sight of him. The result of his labor was an astonishingly deep hole, hollowed out entirely by hand in just a matter of minutes, into which Mark crammed the girl's body along with her disembodied head. Filling in the makeshift grave, he then smoothed its surface with the side of his forearm before sprinkling fresh sand over the murder site to hide the few traces of spilled blood.

Stunned and detached, Dave watched the revolting spectacle in the role of a passive observer. Since it all seemed impossible and unreal, he was unable to react in a rational, moral way. As such, he experienced no fear, nor did he feel threatened by anything he saw. Even as he witnessed the morbid burial rite, he had no active participation in what his eyes observed or what his mind perceived until he noticed a minor irregularity in the overall scene, a feature of the environment he had overlooked until then—shadows.

The diffused light of the super moon painting the night with the impressionistic aura of daylight was causing long shadows to appear on the landscape, but Dave had been ignoring them, observing things around him without noticing their presence. Suddenly, he became conscious of shadows everywhere, dark patches on the ground caused by anything of substance. Sand mounds, shrubbery, grass, even his own body; everything cast a shadow—everything, that is, except for Mark.

Struck by this odd phenomenon, Dave used his binoculars to search the ground around the behemoth man, but he could not find a shadow anywhere on the sand. The bizarre nature of this circumstance made him even more determined to find a rational answer, and he again scoured the ground for the elusive lunar shade until he noticed the murderous fiend raise his head and gaze upward toward the sky, sneering in open defiance at the glowing orb reflecting light upon the earth. Seeing the shadowless villain scoff at the moon in such a manner, Dave half-expected him to thrust back his head and emit a bloodcurdling howl, much like a werewolf in a horror movie, but that was not to happen. Instead, a provocation more frightening and intimidating occurred when Mark carefully removed his sunglasses and peered directly at Dave from across the sandy terrain.

The shock of seeing the lethal man staring at him from the base of the dune was enough to shake him out of his disengaged stupor. It awakened him to the danger of becoming more than just a spectator in this deadly game of voyeurism, but he managed to tamp down his fears by reassuring himself that Mark could not possibly see him at that distance, not without some sort of optical aid, which he did not appear to have. The solace provided by his argument was only short-lived due to the feelings of uncertainty that bubbled up almost instantly, steadily increasing the longer the homicidal maniac maintained his menacing glare. With each passing second, Dave felt the ghostly eyes of the predator pierce the lenses of the binoculars to burrow straight into his brain, ultimately convincing him of the precariousness of his situation and the very real threat he faced. Holding his breath while attempting to restrain his growing sense of dread, he nervously watched the menacing figure scowl at him from across the sand where it stood entirely motionless, remaining as still as death itself, until, without warning, it began charging in his direction.

The anxious feelings he had tried to suppress now became a rational fear that swelled instantly into total panic and terror, upending his world and throwing his mind into utter chaos. He had no memory of getting to his feet, but he found himself running as fast as he could through the valleys of compacted sand toward the dune ridge where had parked the hearse. As he ran, he intoned with each breath, "Oh, my God! Oh, my God! Oh, my God!" until it became a marching cadence. He never once looked back, too fearful of what he would see, praying only that he would make it to his vehicle in time. Pumping his arms as hard as his legs, he noticed that he no longer carried the binoculars, although he had no recollection of having dropped them anywhere. It did not matter, though, because his only concern at that moment was making it back to the hearse and getting the hell out of there.

Reaching the final dune ridge, he hurled himself over the top of it and tumbled down through the soft, cascading sand to land in a massive clump of red cedar at the bottom of the dune. Emerging from the prickly bush with just a few scratches on his face and forearms, he charged toward the road and jumped into the hearse, gasping for air as he fumbled with the keys, barely able to hold them due to the quaking of his hands. Eventually, he found the right key and slipped it into the ignition slot, starting the old Cadillac on the first try and jamming it into gear, spinning his tires on the sandy pavement to make a U-turn that sent him speeding off toward the safety of the bypass.

Near the end of West Soundside Road, just before the intersection with the bypass, he slowed down and craned his neck to look over his shoulder. It was the first time he had glanced backward since taking flight, and what he glimpsed on the dune ridge behind him was enough to collapse his entire world. The vision was something he could not ignore but which he desperately wished to purge from his mind, the sight of an enormous man silhouetted against the sky, holding to his eyes a small pair of binoculars. Immediately recoiling from the disturbing sight, Dave plowed headlong into the intersection without stopping or again looking back. He then charged down the highway at breakneck speed, hoping to put as much distance as possible between himself and his deadly assailant.

CHAPTER 10

The storm raged violently outside an old mission church in a seaside community where an elderly priest knelt in prayer and quiet contemplation before the altar. More a chapel than a church, the mission served mainly as an outpost worship site for the celebration of Sunday Mass, a single service held for the convenience of those living in that area of Florida Keys, sparing them the long journey to the parish basilica each week. The aged priest, now living in residence at the parish house near the basilica, had been retired for many years, but he always volunteered to make the trek to the chapel every Sunday to say Mass because he liked it there. It felt like home.

Although small, the structure was nonetheless magnificent in its sacred simplicity. It had the architectural look and feel of a Spanish mission, which explained in part why the priest felt such affection for the ancient building. He could trace his ancestry back to the Spaniards, some of whom he expected to see very soon, and he felt a greater communion with them whenever he celebrated Mass within the confines of the old mission church. A cancer survivor— at least so far—he was entering the final stages of esophageal cancer. Not only was it difficult for him to eat, but it had become a challenge to speak as well; therefore, he said very little, saving what voice he had left for Sunday Mass. He recited his daily office internally as he did most of his prayers and spiritual meditations.

In addition to attacking his esophagus, the cancer cells had spread to his lymph nodes as well as his bones. Just recently, the doctors had informed him that his liver was now under assault. His time was short, and he knew it, but he had lived a long life and harbored no bitterness regarding his infirmity or anything else for that matter. He did not even feel animosity toward the hurricane currently ravaging the Florida Keys.

The authorities had issued a mandatory evacuation order once it became apparent that Hurricane Kim would strike the archipelago, but the old priest knew he could not bear the strain of a long, grueling drive back to the mainland over the congested Overseas Highway; therefore, he decided to remain behind. Having lied to his superiors, telling them he was evacuating with a member of the parish congregation, he instead drove himself directly to the old mission church to embrace his fate in the place he felt most comfortable. He hoped the sin would not be held against him.

Because of a power outage across the island, he had lighted two candles that sat on opposite ends of the altar, their burning flames softly illuminating the interior of the old church, creating stark shadows across the faces of two life-sized statutes concealed in the recesses of the sanctuary walls. One statue was that of the Sacred Heart of Jesus and the other the Virgin of Guadalupe, both painted in rich yet subdued colors. As icons of inspiration and intercession, the holy images held places of special significance in the life of the ailing cleric, spiritual repositories of strength and mercy especially in times of turmoil and need.

The mission church, like the priest himself, was low and squat in construction. It had weathered many a storm over the years, several of which had been powerful hurricanes. Lying directly in the path of Hurricane Kim, it stood ready to withstand one more. Like the Catholic Church itself, the ancient house of worship was built to endure. Many years before, the parishioners had replaced the panes of the small windows with heavier shatterproof glass to resist the pounding of the tropical storm winds, leaving only one window untouched, a tiny stained-glass window with a colorful depiction of St. Michael the Archangel.

Despite the eight rows of wooden pews, all of which contained kneelers, the old priest had dragged out an individual prayer kneeler, placing it directly in front of the wooden altar. There, he knelt in solemn silence while dressed in a white linen alb with the cincture cord tied loosely around his waist. Folded and draped neatly over the kneeler was the Humeral Veil that he had worn across his shoulders while exposing the Sacred Host in a monstrance on the altar. The monstrance was of a traditional sunburst design made of finely polished gold and silver. It was by far the most ornate object in the entire church.

Kneeling in humble reflection before the Blessed Sacrament, he gave no indication that he was even aware of the noise created by the harsh winds and torrential rains striking the stucco walls of the old church. For once, his diminished hearing was a Godsend, helping him tune out the unwelcome distractions of the storm so he could focus his mind and soul entirely on the gold and silver sunburst sitting atop the altar, its polished surface shimmering in the pale light of the quivering candle flames. Lovingly and adoringly, he stared at the pure white center of the monstrance without a word spoken internally or externally, knowing that, over the course of his eighty-seven years, he had said everything he needed to say.

He soon found himself reminiscing, remembering back to a time when he had attended a retreat in the Diocese of Pittsburgh. It was there that he met a fellow priest, Father Reginald, who had shared with him a personal story from his own priestly ministry. As a young priest, Father Reginald had been assigned to a parish with a perpetual adoration of the Blessed Sacrament, and he would see the same elderly gentleman there day after day for extended periods of time. Shaking hands with the man one Sunday after Mass, Father Reginald asked him what he said to the Lord during those long hours of adoration. "Nothing," the man replied. "I look at Him, and He looks at me."

At the time, he wondered why his fellow priest had chosen to share that story with him, but now, years later, on that perilous night in August near the conclusion of his long and productive life, he finally understood. So, with the wind and rain battering his beloved old church and mayhem raging all around him, with death appearing imminent and his final reward at hand, the noble old priest knelt in peaceful silence, staring lovingly and longingly at his Lord, who returned his gaze with a look of tenderness and consolation, assuring his good and faithful servant that he had nothing to fear.

CHAPTER 11

The glowing sphere of the early morning sun danced atop the ocean waves as they advanced from the eastern horizon toward the beach. Transitioning from ember red to brilliant yellow, the searing disc bathed the shoreline with its warm, buttery radiance, spreading its intense light across the barrier island to collide with the side of Mark's house, striking the tightly drawn window shades that prevented it from entering his living room.

Mark stood by the vertical blinds where he could feel the sun's heat radiating through the glass. He attempted to peer between the gaps in the slats, but the bright light proved too much for his ultra-sensitive eyes, forcing him back into the shade of the living room. Turning away from windows, he prowled calmly through the upstairs living space, moving like a cougar in search of prey, hunting for something but not knowing what. With his eyes uncovered, his dilated pupils saw everything in vivid detail as he made a deliberate and systematic sweep of the house in search of clues.

Clues—yes, that is what he sought. He told himself that he needed to discover clues and insights into his predecessor's former life to explain what was happening now. Ever since last night, he could not stop thinking about the man on the dunes, the one driving the hearse. Disturbing—he thought—especially since it was not the first time he had seen the unusual vehicle. He knew nothing about the stranger, but he understood the need to address the problem of the troublesome eavesdropper if he wished to continue existing in this time and place—in this form. Perhaps something in his host's past could shed light on the man's identity. His newfound desire to discover the underlying connection between himself and the stranger then became his primary focus as he slinked through the house.

Nothing in the upstairs living areas revealed anything new regarding Mark's former life. It was all so precise and orderly—too neat and clean. Even the wastebaskets and garbage cans were empty. In fact, the only discarded item he found anywhere in the place was an Amazon shipping box sitting on the floor in the kitchen, a twelve-by-twenty-inch cardboard container with nothing in it. Seeing the counter space free of junk mail and everything in its proper place, he concluded that his host's prior life had been as tidy and sterile as the house itself, utterly bland and vanilla.

Walking down the stairs, he started back toward the office, a room he had not visited since the night he had emerged from the mirror. If any place could offer some clues about Mark's former life, it would be his office, so he walked into the room and plopped himself down on the chair behind the desk. A tri-folding portfolio lay open before him, but none of the scribbled comments on the notepad seemed particularly significant or enlightening. Turning his attention to the papers tucked into the side pockets, he found them equally boring, so he switched on the computer to see what information he could find there. Just like the portfolio on the desk, the computer files held only investment strategies and little else other than a client directory containing the names of people he did not know. Frustrated and annoyed, he shut down the computer and sat brooding at the desk while glancing around at the sterile surroundings of the room. It was apparent—he concluded—that the old Mark Allen had been a superficial man of little depth, quite unlike the newly transformed Mark Allen, who had recently burst onto the scene.

With a menacing grin, he chuckled at how he had taken this boring, predictable klutz and had turned him into a dangerous force of nature in the course of just one week; however, he knew it could not last much longer. Eventually, the victims of his nightly outings would turn up missing, and people would begin looking for them. At that point, he would have to consider moving on or—pausing a moment, he pondered an idea that had been incubating in his subconscious mind—or he could find someone to take the fall. That emergent idea caused his thoughts to drift back to the hearse and the man on the dune.

Smiling internally, he ruminated on the matter for several seconds before coming to a firm resolution, punctuating his decision by flipping close the flaps of the tri-folder and pushing himself away from the desk, stopping the moment he spotted an inverted picture frame and a cell phone lying on the desktop. Pausing to stare at the two items previously obscured by the portfolio, he then scooted his chair back toward the desk and scooped up the cell phone, finding it inactive and completely discharged. Without even thinking, he began scouring the desktop and drawers for a phone charger, eventually finding one plugged into a surge protector on the floor. Connecting it to a port on the phone, he pressed the phone's power button to turn it on.

It took about a minute for the phone's operating system to complete its startup operation, at which time the cell phone sounded several beeps, audio alerts that denoted missed calls and voice messages. With his massive thumb, he clicked the message button but could not access the voicemail account because he did not know the password. His ignorance of the password, however, did not prevent him from viewing a log of recently missed calls along with their originating the phone numbers. With just one exception, the calls came from the same number, all made exactly one week ago. The lone exception was a call received a few days earlier from a restricted number.

Searching the list of contacts in the phone's directory, Mark was able to determine that someone named Nikki had made of all of the calls placed last Friday. He assumed that the unheard voice messages were also from her. A check of her profile revealed little more than her first name; however, it did list two phone numbers, a cell number and a business number. Glancing down at the picture frame lying upside-down on the desk, he flipped it over and set it upright, exposing a close-up photograph of an attractive young woman with blonde hair. The presence of sand and sea oats in the background led him to conclude that she was a local girl. Now things were starting to make sense, he thought. Perhaps his host was not so dull after all.

With a genuinely joyful grin, he hit the call button for the business phone number and waited to see who would answer. It rang only twice before a recorded message announced that the Animal Hospital of Nags Head was closed and that the caller should call back during regular business hours. Looking up at the clock, he saw that it was still quite early in the morning, too early for a veterinarian's office to be open, so he scrolled down to Nikki's cell number and prepared to hit the call button, stopping himself before completing the action. Putting the phone into sleep mode, he returned it to the desk saying, "No, not yet." He would wait until he learned more about this woman before making contact.

For a time, he sat staring at the bright, innocent smile of the girl in the picture, thinking that she looked familiar, too familiar. He knew that it could not be a lingering memory fragment of his deceased host. No, he thought, it was something more than that or, rather, something more recent. Yes, that was it! He had seen her recently, although she was not smiling at the time. Extending his large hand, he covered her smile with his fingers and gazed at only her eyes and forehead. The longer he stared at her face, the more the veil began to lift until he knew with certainty where he had seen her before; it was one night at Cahoon's Market when he had looked through the windshield of a car to observe the shocked expression of a blonde girl scowling back at him. Now things were becoming clearer, but they also were becoming more complicated. Instead of one unexpected problem, he now had two requiring resolution, two petty annoyances that would have to wait until after sunset to receive the attention they deserved.

Lying in bed, his face half buried in the pillow, Dave could feel the cold, emotionless eyes staring down at him. He did not move, pretending to be asleep, because he needed more time to gather his wits before facing the unwelcome intruder. Although it was late morning, he still felt exhausted after having grappled most of the night with what he should do, replaying the events of the previous night over and over again in his mind—the horror, the fear, the uncertainty. At one point, somewhere in the early hours of the morning, he had succeeded in banishing the troubling thoughts, but now, fully awakened by the intruder, he sensed them creeping back into his consciousness.

The eyes that had been carefully monitoring his slumber detected a change in his breathing pattern along with several involuntary ticks in his facial muscles, causing the unwelcome visitor to begin exhaling in short blasts of heated air. Leaning even closer to the pillow, the intruder then widened his jaws to expose numerous sharpened teeth clustered within a sizable oral cavity from which he extended a moistened tongue long enough to touch Dave's cheek.

"I see you made it home safely," Dave said to the basset hound hovering just above his head. "Did you and Nikki have fun last night? No, don't tell me. I don't want to know."

At the sound of Dave's voice, Grave began wagging his tail vigorously, rhythmically shaking the bed in time with the swaying of his hindquarters. Although Nikki had dropped him off earlier that morning, he had waited patiently for Dave to arise before taking matters into his own paws when it seemed like his master would sleep all day. "Woof," he barked brusquely, indicating that it was time to get up.

"Okay, okay," Dave said to his tricolored friend as he rolled onto his back and began rubbing his eyes. Feeling a stinging sensation on his face, he lightly touched several scratches on his forehead and a longer one extending from his ear to the side of his mouth, and he remembered tumbling into the red cedar last night. From the angle of the sun shining into the room, he knew it must be late, so he glanced over at the alarm clock. It was eleven o'clock.

"Ah, dammit," he said almost in despair as the anxiety of the previous night began creeping in again while he lay staring at the ceiling, focusing on the patches of peeling paint. Grave then distracted him by jumping off the bed, triggering a frenzy of motion that left Dave bouncing for several seconds on the worn-out mattress and squeaky box springs. Hearing the whining of the dog at the front door, he realized that he had no choice but to get up.

Forcing himself from the bed, Dave trudged into the living room to let Grave outside. "There you go, pal," he said, opening the door. "Stay off the beach. I don't want people stepping in anything you leave behind." Shirtless and wearing only a ragged pair of cotton shorts, he stood on the porch looking at the bright summer day. The weather was again beautiful with an abundance of sunshine painting the shoreline and hardly a cloud in the sky, nothing that would suggest the approach of Hurricane Kim currently wreaking havoc several states away. Similarly, there was nothing in Dave's outward appearance to suggest his deep despondency over what he had witnessed the previous night.

Disappointed with himself, especially at how he had run like a coward, he wondered what else he could have done. What could he do now? The fear surging through him last night was still present today, binding him like an emotional hostage, so his options seemed limited based on his inability to control his fright. Running, he concluded, was probably his best recourse, something that had served him well in the past. Perhaps it was time to run again. Seriously pondering the advantages of flight while charting out the best way to make a speedy departure, he vacillated when he heard a question crying out forcefully from within him, compelling him to consider someone other than himself. "What about Nikki?" he murmured softly, repeating the question he heard resonating internally.

He was never good at decision-making, especially in matters requiring responsible choices. Nikki, on the other hand, was the one who was adept at such things. It occurred to him that he should tell her everything and let her suggest a course of action, but that seemed so weak on his part. He was already ashamed of the way he had behaved on the dunes last night. Showing further weakness by throwing this burden onto her would only make him appear even more pathetic. Besides, what he had observed last night did not seem real, not even humanly possible, not by any measure whatsoever. No one, not even a brute the size of Mark, could completely decapitate another human being using only his hands. Moreover, there was the way in which he had buried the girl. That also seemed impossible, and it would not sound credible if he tried to describe it to anyone, especially if he told the police. After all, Mark was a respected businessman living in the area, and he was just—well—he was a transient, a drifter. Whom would they most likely label the murderer? The more he thought about it, the more running seemed his best alternative, especially since there was nothing at that point to tie him to the girl's murder.

Once again, he instinctively felt the presence of someone nearby, and he looked down to see Grave standing at his feet, whipping his tail back and forth with excited energy. "All done?" he asked while dropping to his knees. He then began caressing the dog's elongated ears while resting his cheek on Grave's head. "I'll tell you what, old friend. I'm in some big trouble, and I don't know what to do about it." In response to his soulful admission, Grave raised his snout and licked Dave twice across the bridge of his nose.

Remaining on his knees, Dave brushed his hand over the dog's muscular shoulders, hypnotically watching the motion of his hand while pondering his current dilemma, knowing that his options were limited. He worried about Nikki but felt confident that she would be safe at her sister's house that night. It was tomorrow that mainly concerned him, after her return to the Outer Banks. Whatever he chose to do, he decided—whether it be run or stay—he would first wait until he saw her again. For the life of him, he could not understand why Mark had stopped seeing her and why he had not contacted her for over a week. It did not make any sense, but he would not waste time trying to figure it out. Instead, he would focus his energy on keeping her from reconnecting with her murderous ex-boyfriend until he could devise a plan. Until then, he would not breathe a word of this to anyone. That, he concluded, was the best course of action for the time being.

Having developed at least a partial plan, he went back inside the cottage to shower, shave, and dress. After feeding Grave, he then struck out for Mulligan's to get himself something to eat. Perhaps— he thought—the secure, familiar surroundings of his favorite haunt would offer a brief respite where he could think clearly and concoct a better strategy.

Roars of laughter sounded in Dave's ears even before he reached the top of the stairs, letting him know that Travis was again holding court. The flamboyant bartender's voice rose high above the din, but it seemed slightly raspy, indicating that he had been speaking for quite a while; he would often get hoarse whenever he talked too much or too loudly. Still, the recognizable intonation of his friend's voice along with the laughter of the bar patrons helped to dispel much of Dave's anxiety.

"Will you just look at that!" the husky voice echoed from overhead in the barroom.

Travis and the others were watching a weather broadcast on one of the television screens over the bar. While Travis spoke, the program displayed a map of the United States created by the National Weather Service showing all the projected hurricane tracks drawn in lines of varying colors.

"Texas! Texas!" Travis screamed in disbelief. "The damn hurricane is now crossing Florida on a northeast track, and one of the predictions is for it to hit Texas?" He stopped speaking and turned to the customers at the bar. "Of course, these are the same geniuses who preach that phony man-made global warming nonsense to us. How dumb do they think we are?"

"Gary, sitting at the bar reading *Moby Dick*, raised his beer bottle in salute without lifting his eyes from the page.

"Thank you, Professor," Travis said politely before continuing. "You know, if you were to blindfold the Professor's students and give them a map of the United States along with a box of crayons, they could produce the same crap we just saw up there." He pointed toward the television screen as he made his assertion.

"Gary's students are in high school," Sally chimed in while passing by with a lunch order. "They don't use crayons."

"Hey," he said in her direction. "We're talking about the American education system here."

Gary stopped reading and looked up over the top of his glasses.

"Okay, okay," Travis said apologetically. "Let me rephrase that. If you were to give some crayons to a bunch of blindfolded Ivy-league college professors, they could produce the same crap we just saw on The Weather Channel. How about that?" He glanced over in Gary's direction. "I could have used blindfolded chimpanzees, but that cliché is so overused. Besides, it means the same thing."

Gary chuckled while making a notation on the page he was reading.

Just then, Travis noticed Dave standing at the top of the stairs. "Buddy," he said. "Have a seat and join our discussion about the hurricane. We were just making plans for a hurricane party if it heads this way."

"Seems like it might," Dave said while walking to his favorite spot at the bar. Pulling out his chair, he noticed someone sitting behind him at a table against the wall, a man he recognized instantly as Nikki's friend, the black priest who had talked to her yesterday at Kitty Hawk Kites. Dave glanced at Travis, who was also looking at the priest, and he saw the bartender rub the top of his head several times while quietly whispering, "The new Mayor." With a grin, Dave took his seat two places down from Gary while Sally stopped at the table to deliver the priest his lunch.

Looking at Dave a little sideways, Travis said, "You don't look so good today, Buddy. Is anything wrong?" He had barely asked the question when he noticed something. "Whoa," he said leaning a little closer to examine the long scratch on Dave's cheek, "I guess someone was partying hard last night. She must be a wildcat, that one!" He made his comments loudly with a sly glance at the others sitting around the bar before spotting additional scratches on his friend's forearms. "Oh, I can't wait to hear this story," he added with a smirk.

Dave did not respond but stared passively at him.

"What's the matter, Buddy? No sleep last night? No wonder you look like Grave." Leaning over the bar, he said in a more subdued tone "Seriously, Buddy, if you don't want to say anything in front of the rest of them, I understand. We can talk later." He then shot Dave a wink and continued in his customarily loud tone, "But, just for the record, you look like death sucking on a LifeSaver."

"What's that supposed to mean?"

"I don't know. It's something I heard once. And speaking of hot dates and LifeSavers, I've got a new honey."

Dave appeared genuinely surprised. "What's History got to say about that?"

"Screw her," Travis said with a grimace before grinning broadly. "Besides, I think almost everyone around here has. And what did I tell you about mentioning her name in my presence?"

Dave kept his mouth shut and glanced over at Gary who appeared too absorbed in his book to pay attention to the antics of Travis or anything else happening at the bar.

"But honestly, Buddy, I've got this new girl," Travis said sincerely with a deadpan expression that made Dave want to believe him. "Oh, wait a minute," he said while patting the pockets of his shorts. "Come to think of it, I've got a picture of her. Do you want to see it?"

"Where's the picture? On your phone?"

"No, no, here in my wallet. See?"

Dave studied Travis's face as the bartender handed him a small portrait-style photograph. He asked him skeptically, "How is it that you didn't mention her yesterday when I was at your place?"

"I just met her last night."

"And you already have a photo of her?"

"Yeah," he said, prodding him on. "What do you think?" He motioned for Dave to inspect the girl's image and then stood back to await his friend's verdict.

Giving into Travis' request, Dave glanced casually at the picture, raising his sunglasses to get a better look at the girl. The photograph was an authentic portrait, professionally done, and it contained the legitimate likeness of a girl, the homeliest girl he had ever seen in his life—not painfully ugly, just incredibly homely. It was obvious that she had tried to make herself as presentable as possible for the picture but to no avail. She was at her best and still unappealingly plain.

At first, he thought it was a joke, but, because it was an actual portrait of a girl attempting to appear photogenic, he briefly dismissed the suspicion until he noticed Travis suppressing a smile, the same one he saw shared by everyone at the bar. With no change expression, Dave lowered his sunglasses and laid the photo on the bar. "Better stick with History," he said flatly, his candid advice delivered in a monotone voice.

Travis immediately burst out laughing and grabbed the photograph from the bar. "Isn't she great?" he cried. "Have you ever seen anything so unattractive and dull in all your life?" Dave tried to respond, but Travis gave him no time to answer. "She's not so ugly as to appear a fraud, but just repulsive enough to make you cringe at the thought of getting close to her."

The bartender then peered intently at the picture while continuing to talk, interrupting himself with short bursts of laughter. "I pulled this on Sally last night, and she said, 'What an attractive girl.' Can you believe that? She called her an attractive girl! I looked her in the eye and said, 'You're such a liar!' That's why she's pissed at me today—because I called her a liar in front of everyone."

While his friend continued hurling insults at Sally and the poor girl in the photograph, Dave asked, "Who is she ... really?"

Travis hesitated briefly and looked around the room, stumped by a question he had not anticipated. Then, with widening eyes, he cried out, "The Mayor's daughter!" He could not contain his laughter as he walked toward the opposite end of the bar where a customer had been impatiently waiting for a drink.

Shaking his head, Dave removed his sunglasses and began rubbing his bloodshot eyes before signaling to Travis to bring him a beer on his way back, dropping his hand when he saw the bartender showing the girl's photograph to another unsuspecting customer. Once again, he shook his head in acknowledgment that his screwball friend was one of a kind.

While awaiting Travis' return, he stared blankly at the television screen and allowed his thoughts to wander freely. The horrors of the previous night instantly shot to the forefront of his brain, and he found himself stymied by his immediate problem, a moral quandary for which he had no remedy or answer. The fight or flight response had again kicked in, and the choice of flight seemed the most viable option as it always did. It would be in his nature to surrender to it but for one thing—Nikki. He had never before met anyone capable of preventing him from pulling up stakes and leaving whenever he saw fit, and he wondered how he could break the gentle bonds of this sweet obsession. Unfortunately, he was no more prepared to deal with her than he was with all he had witnessed the previous night. Sitting for a time, he stared into space with his mind completely blank, praying for something to point him in the right direction, until Travis stepped in front of him and placed a beer on the bar, jarring him back to his senses.

"You're really out of it today, Buddy," his friend said with a note of concern.

Dave just nodded his head.

"Do you want something to eat?" Not waiting for a reply, Travis signaled to Sally, who was nearby clearing dirty dishes off a table. "Hey, Sally," he yelled. "Get my boy here some nourishment!"

She did not respond but glared coldly at the bartender and then marched down the stairs to the lower dining room.

"Whoops," Travis said. "Still pissed I guess. Well, Buddy, who knows if you'll get your chowder." Nodding over at the couple sitting to Dave's right, he then asked, "Did you meet Jim and Carol? They're from …"

"Indiana," the man said, extending his hand to Dave.

"Yeah, Indiana," Travis echoed before becoming extremely animated. "Quick, Buddy, tell me who he looks like!"

Still shaking Jim's hand, Dave looked directly at his face and examined his features for a few seconds before saying, "I don't know."

"Sure you do! Look at him again."

This time, Dave turned his chair to get a better view. After studying him further, he smiled at the guy and then turned back to Travis. "I still don't know."

"Charles Manson," the bartender said. "Charles Manson! Can't you see it?"

Jim began laughing and shaking his head while his wife patted him on the back and said, "We just call him Charlie for short."

Travis picked up a pen from behind the bar and pointed it at the man. "I asked him if I could draw a little swastika on his forehead, right above the bridge of his nose, but he wouldn't let me do it. If I had done that, I'm sure you would have recognized him."

Subdued chuckling resonated from a table near the wall, and both Dave and Travis turned toward the priest, who sat with a broad grin on his face while munching on his Mulligan Burger.

Returning his attention to Dave, Travis said, "Many people don't know this, Buddy, but there is a little-known connection between Charles Manson and the Outer Banks. You should check it out sometime."

Dave looked at him questioningly. "How do you know that?"

"The study of serial killers is my hobby," he answered proudly.

Travis' admission caused Gary to stop reading his book and raise his head slightly, but Dave's reaction to the subject of serial killers was much more apparent.

"Yeah, I've been reading about them for years now," Travis announced boldly, unaware of the surprised expressions on the faces of the bar patrons or the fearful look in Dave's eyes. "I'll tell you one thing you never want to do," he continued, "and that is to trust anyone with two first names such as Bill David or Rick James." As he made the pronouncement, he nodded emphatically like a schoolteacher imparting a profound truth to his class. The only name Dave could think of at that moment was Mark Allen.

"And what's even worse," Travis said, "are guys who go by three names. Take for instance your typical serial killer: John Wayne Gacy, John Eric Armstrong, Derrick Todd Lee, Vickie Dawn Jackson, David Allen Coe. Oh wait, David Allen Coe doesn't belong on the list. Other than a song lyric or two, he's never killed anyone."

Once again, chuckling arose from the table by the wall.

"And let's not forget the most famous three-named serial killer of all," Travis added. "Jack *the* Ripper!" He concluded his lesson with a smile.

At the mention of Jack the Ripper, the priest laughed even louder, causing Dave and Travis to look at him again. Always happy to have an audience that appreciated his humor, the bartender said to the priest, "Parson, why don't you come and join us," to which the black cleric immediately stood and began moving toward the bar, carrying with him his lunch plate and glass.

While the priest was approaching, Dave said to Travis, "Let's get back to guys with two first names. Can they also be notorious killers even though they don't go by three names?"

"Of course. Don't forget Sirhan Sirhan."

The priest placed the remainder of his Mulligan Burger and ice tea on the bar as he climbed onto the empty chair between Dave and Gary.

"So, what shall we call you, Padre," Travis asked rather pleasantly.

With a thick African accent, the bald priest answered, "My first name is Andalwisye, pronounced 'ahn dal WEES yeh.' It means 'God has shown me the way.' They call me Father Andal for short."

Travis grinned. "What about your last name?"

The black priest flashed a huge smile and said, "You could not pronounce it." He then let out a boisterous laugh.

"So, I take it you're not from around here," the bartender asked while surreptitiously winking at Dave.

"No," Andal said. "Is it not obvious? I am from Norway!" Once again, he gave out a bellowing laugh that caused everyone at the bar to join in.

Dave understood why Nikki liked the priest. From his brief exposure to him, he also found him affable and engaging. Smiling at the priest, he asked him, "So where are you from, really?"

Father Andal turned and peered deeply into Dave's eyes with an intense stare that was more an exploratory probe than a casual gaze. The cleric then said, "I am from the village of Wassa Nsuta in the western region of Ghana." After delivering his response, he prolonged his visual scrutiny for several seconds, eliciting in Dave feelings of both consolation and agitation.

There was a brief pause before Dave asked, "Oh … ah … so you found my friend's lecture about mass murderers amusing?"

Andal grinned broadly. "I am always interested in stories about good and evil," he said.

Travis then interjected. "You know, Father, I was watching the movie *The Exorcist* the other night." He paused briefly after noticing Dave roll his eyes and Gary stop reading to listen to the question. "Yes, as I was saying," he continued with an annoyed expression, "I watched *The Exorcist* the other night, and I would like to know something. Is the Devil real?" Satisfied that Travis had not made a total ass of himself, Gary returned to his book but kept one ear open to hear the priest's answer.

Andal chewed his last bite of his burger and took a sip of tea before replying. Instead of answering Travis, he seemed to speak to Dave. "Yes, Satan is real, and his greatest weapon is that people do not believe he exists. We do not hear much about him these days, not like in the past—as in ancient writings—because he does not need to be as visible and prominent in these modern times. In fact, Satan projects more power hiding in the shadows. But let there be no doubt about it, evil exists today as much as it did in the past." As he talked, he noticed his words stirring something in the younger man sitting next to him.

Dave turned and saw the priest watching at him, so he asked, "If evil is hiding, how do we spot it?"

"Excellent question, my friend. Evil has taken many forms over the centuries, some of them outrageously shocking and others quite obscure. At times, it can be a chameleon, disguising itself as good, while, at other times, it makes no effort to hide its hideous face, relying on fear to traumatize people into despair because they believe that nothing could defeat a monster so repulsive and dreadful. When confronting it in that form, it requires great courage and a strong will to survive. To achieve success, one must be grounded in truth and be extremely sure of oneself. One must also be willing to risk everything and, most of all, one must have faith— faith anchored in trust guided by love." He could see that his words troubled the young stranger. He asked him, "What is your name?"

"Dave—but everyone calls me Buddy."

"Well, young David, understand this. Good always recognizes evil—and good must always confront evil."

"Will good always prevail?"

Andal smiled another beaming grin. "Eventually, but it might not seem so at the time. Evil loves the darkness while good walks in the light." He then reached down and drank the last of his iced tea.

By this time, Jim and Carol had begun talking to another couple at the bar, and Travis had moved to the other end of the room. Gary remained seated in his chair with his nose buried in his book, pretending to be detached but completely engaged and fully aware of everything the priest was saying. It was only Father Andal and Dave who actively continued the conversation.

The priest wiped his mouth while staring intently at Dave, recognizing in the young man's expression that his mind was greatly troubled. Without comment, the African cleric reached across the bar and grabbed a paper napkin on which he scribbled something before folding it twice and handing it to his new friend. Sliding off his chair, he patted Dave on the shoulder while speaking, almost in a whisper, "I will tell you one more thing about good and evil. Besides recognizing evil, good also always recognizes other good." He then placed money on the bar to pay for his lunch before turning to leave, saying in a louder voice while descending the stairs, "You have a *good* day, my friend." Unfolding the napkin on which the priest had written only his name and phone number, Dave refolded it and crammed it into the pocket of his shorts just as Sally arrived with his bowl of chowder and some crackers.

When Travis wandered back, he found Dave sitting alone quietly eating his soup. "Where'd your new friend go?" he asked. "That polished scalp of his would have made the Mayor jealous. I don't think the Mayor's chrome-dome is nearly that shiny."

Dave looked up from his meal. "He's a commode-head just like the Mayor."

"He is? I hadn't noticed. Maybe he can come back and we'll make him the new Mayor since the real one doesn't stop by anymore. We can call him the Pope or the Cardinal or something like that."

Dave grinned while stirring his soup. "The Mayor still comes here," he said. "He just stops in when you're not around, on your days off."

"No, he doesn't!"

"Yes, he does. Just ask Sally."

Travis searched the room until his spotted Sally at one of the tables taking a lunch order. "So, she's been holding out on me, has she?" He then noticed Gary pushing his beer bottle across the bar, so he hurried away to get him another one.

Blowing gently on a spoonful of hot chowder, Dave gazed

furtively in Gary's direction, observing the high school teacher strike his usual pose with his reading glasses slung low across the bridge of his nose while he leaned back in his chair, one hand resting on his stomach and the other one holding the novel close to his face. He appeared to be engrossed in his reading, but Dave knew he was conscious of everything going on around him, a classroom skill he had perfected over his many years as an educator. Watching Gary remove his hand from his belly to turn to the next page, Dave noticed that he was about one-third of the way through the classic sea tale of Captain Ahab and the Great White Whale.

In addition to his book, Gary always carried with him several other items: a pen, a yellow highlighter, and a small spiral notebook in which he recorded notes and passages too long to write in the margins of the paperback. While Dave continued watching him, Gary read halfway down the page only to stop and write something in the notebook before closing the novel and setting it down on the bar. Struggling off his chair, he smiled at Dave and then waddled toward the unisex bathroom near the top of the stairs.

During Gary's absence, Dave reached over and pulled the notebook closer to him, positioning it so he could read what Gary had written before heading to the bathroom. Scribbled in it was a passage from the book ... *all the subtle demonisms of life and thought; all evil, to crazy Ahab, were visibly personified, and made practically assailable in Moby Dick – Chapter 41*. Shoving back the notebook, he considered the plot of Melville's novel and how it related to his own situation. Was he Ishmael, caught up in circumstances beyond his control, or was he Ahab, obsessed with destroying what he believed to be a white demon? It was a distinction of real consequence because, in the end, only Ishmael and the whale survived; Ahab perished.

Just then, Gary returned from the restroom and promptly resumed his reading while Dave stared blankly across the bar, wrestling with what he should do. He drew inspiration from the priest's words about confronting evil, but he still feared Ahab's fate at the hands of the giant demon. It all seemed so perplexing and overwhelming. Despite the prodding of his conscience telling him to go to the police and explain everything, he resisted because of he knew that they would never believe him when he described how Mark had decapitated the girl using only his bare hands, also the way he had buried his face into the stump of her neck doing God knows what. No—he thought—he needed to get more information before involving law enforcement. Otherwise, he risked becoming the primary suspect and target of their investigation.

His thoughts then turned to the night he had observed Mark

sailing his boat out of the marina with a girl different from the one he had killed on the dune. Could she also have suffered the same fate? Should he even try to find out? Having followed Mark to her house that night, he knew where she lived. Perhaps he should return to the beach house and search for her there. But what if he discovered her missing? What would he do then? Did he really want to be seen snooping around the home of another murder victim? That would implicate him in two homicides and give the police even more reason to suspect him. Such a bleak and frightening scenario would surely lead to Ahab's fate.

Amid the fear and doubt swirling inside his brain, it was only the tranquil, lifesaving image of Nikki that kept him mentally afloat, offering safe harbor to his shipwrecked mind. She was his own private lighthouse, a secure beacon of hope, one more brilliant than even the Bodie Island Lighthouse projecting its guiding light across the treacherous waters of the North Carolina coastline. Recognizing the role she played in sustaining his sanity and well-being, he pledged to do everything in his power to ensure that she remained a part of his life.

Uncertain how to go about fulfilling that pledge, he knew only that he first needed to address the threat of Mark, so he quickly finished his chowder and downed the last of his beer. Needing money to pay the bill, he dumped the contents of his side pocket onto the bar and began sorting through it, pulling out some loose change and removing several crumpled bills from his money clip. While smoothing out the wrinkled money on the bar, he stared vacantly at the other objects from his pocket until a faint glimmer of light caught his attention when it reflected off the keys of his hearse. The sight of it triggered a misplaced memory, and it sparked in him a surge of activity in which he began cramming his hands into the other pockets of his shorts until he found the item he sought, something Nikki had given him three days earlier, the key to Mark's house.

Dave waited in the hearse under the porch of a vacant rental home in The Village at Nags Head. Well concealed in the shadows beneath the stilted structure, he had a clear view of the houses on the other side of the street, their facades bathed in the crimson glow of sunset. Twilight was nudging the smoldering ember below the horizon, spreading darkness across the region, until a final spurt of sunlight burst forth to brighten the front of Mark's house, briefly illuminating the fierce sun god Tonatiuh in the center of the Aztec calendar stone hanging on the outside wall. The stone had escaped Dave's detection while hidden in the shadows; however, once exposed, its disturbing image commanded his full attention, haunting his thoughts as he sat alone in the hearse while nightfall descended over the Outer Banks.

No lights were visible inside of Mark's house despite the encroaching darkness, but Dave knew that he in there because his car was still in the driveway. Expecting Mark to venture out for the evening, perhaps to claim another victim, Dave planned to slip into the house and have a look around. If he could just find something to take to the police—he told himself—some piece of incriminating evidence that would link Mark to the murder of the redheaded girl, then, maybe, he could end this nightmare. Of course, he had no idea what that evidence might be. He only hoped that he would recognize it when he saw it.

When he had first arrived, he was feeling calm and quite sure of himself, but that quickly changed once nightfall descended on the neighborhood and apprehension began chipping away at his confidence and conviction. To make matters worse, Mark's neighbor had neglected to switch on his two floodlights, leaving the entire street shrouded under a pall of darkness, something that only added to his growing sense of doom. He had never before considered himself afraid of the dark, but a lot had changed since last night.

For a long time after the onset of evening, Dave sat quietly in the tomb-like quietness of the hearse, giving himself more time to consider the wisdom of his intended actions, making him wonder if he had the aptitude to carry out such a plan. With fear building and resolve waning, he found himself on the verge of abandoning his mission when the front door of Mark's house suddenly opened, bringing to an end all introspection and tentativeness.

Dave did not move or duck when he saw a large man step onto the porch, believing himself to be far enough away to avoid detection; however, that was the same mistake he had made last night. Recalling that miscalculation, his pulse rate jump and sweat began forming on his brow. Both mentally and emotionally, he was back on Jockey's Ridge at the very moment the murderer had peered at him from across the terrain despite his presumed concealment. This night, however, clouds were building over the eastern sky, preventing the rising full moon from spreading its light across the neighborhood to expose his hiding place.

He watched nervously, straining to see through the murkiness of the night as the hulking man locked the deadbolt of the house before descending the stairs to the car, pausing by the driver's door to make a visual sweep of the neighborhood, his eyes once again shaded by sunglasses. Detecting nothing unusual or suspicious, the man opened the car door and climbed into the vehicle where the illuminating glow of the interior courtesy lights fully revealed his identity. A few seconds later, Mark backed the gray Infiniti out of the driveway and sped off toward the bypass.

Retrieving a small pen-sized flashlight from the glove box, Dave then patted the side pocket of his shorts to assure himself that he was still in possession of the house key. As he readied himself to go, he paused a second to collect his thoughts before taking three deep breaths and quickly exiting the hearse, opening and closing the door as fast as possible to prevent the dome light from drawing attention to his location. Hunched over, he ran down the street and climbed the stairs to Mark's front porch where he gently slid the key into the deadbolt slot, silently rotating it while simultaneously turning the doorknob to crack open the door. It was only then that he considered the possibility of a home security system, and the distressing thought threw him into a mild panic. Holding his breath, he braced himself for the blare of an alarm or the sound of a buzzer demanding a passcode, eventually relaxing and exhaling quietly when nothing happened. Feeling confident that electronic security did not protect the house, he opened the door a little farther and slipped inside.

Standing motionless in the entranceway with the door closed behind him, he waited a few moments to give his eyes time to adjust to the interior darkness. With his temples pulsing in time with the rapid-fire compressions of his heart, he struggled to remain calm as he briefly flashed the tiny penlight toward the wall to confirm the absence of a home security keypad. He then took a few steps into the foyer where he stiffened with fear the moment his peripheral vision detected something slightly behind him, an indistinct specter hovering in the corner by the door. A tilt of his head and a backward glance of his eyes then confirmed the presence of the unknown assailant whose legs and shoes were the only things discernible in the darkness.

Aware of the danger he faced and the need to act quickly, he found himself encumbered by a perplexing question: Who was standing behind him near the door? Mark had driven away, so he knew it could not be him. That knowledge helped dispel some of the fear, but it did not quell all of the panic paralyzing him at that moment. His status as an illegal intruder entrapped by an occupant of the home also heightened his anxiety, but he still managed to act within a split-second of detecting the shadowy figure in the corner.

From the time when he had first recognized the danger until the moment he fully committed himself to action, everything moved in slow motion, giving him the chance to think and plan his next move. He had experienced the same sensation once before during a catastrophic fall while kitesurfing when, within in a millisecond or less, he had analyzed the entire situation and prepared himself for a hard landing in shallow water. Now, standing motionless in the darkened foyer, he performed a similar analysis of the situation and decided on a course of action that he executed with incredible speed and agility. Springing explosively with the nimbleness of a cat, he whirled around in a defensive posture to face his unknown opponent while simultaneously switching on the flashlight, finding himself shocked and stunned when the only thing confronting him were a pair of rubber-spiked golf shoes and a bag filled with drivers and irons.

Despite the overwhelming adrenaline rush, his heart slowed its frantic beating once he recognized the absurdity of the situation. Switching off the penlight, he tried to calm himself. "Okay," he whispered between breaths. "Take it easy. Take it easy." His words offered sedation while providing the reassurance he needed as he began exploring the darkened home, turning on the small flashlight only when necessary.

The first room he entered was the office lying directly ahead of him where everything appeared neat and clean, a spotless setting with nothing out of the ordinary, nothing except for Nikki's picture sitting prominently in the center of the desk. The sight of her smile sent a shudder down his spine, bringing into clear focus the danger she faced. Although conscious of the threat posed by Mark, he had been so concerned with his own safety that he had neglected to recognize the greater danger faced by Nikki, one she did not even know existed. Seeing her framed photograph on the desk, he felt the urge to take it and run, hoping to eradicate the threat by removing her image from the house but knowing that it would make no difference. Shining the flashlight on her joyful expression, he concluded that absconding with the picture would only put her in greater peril, so he did his best to ignore it while continuing to search the room.

Recognizing that what he sought would not be found in the file folders of Mark's desk, he did not bother combing through them. Instead, he quickly scanned the objects on the desktop and then sifted through the wastebasket, searching for something substantive—a physical item—one that would link Mark to the murdered girl. Perhaps—he thought—if he could find an article of clothing, preferably bloodstained clothing, something like the shirt or pants Mark had worn the previous night, it would provide him the proof he needed, evidence he could take to the police. With that in mind, he walked into the bedroom and began looking around in there.

Due to the darkness, it was difficult for him to identify things directly in front of him, but he was reluctant to turn on the flashlight for fear it might alert the neighbors to his presence. Without the benefit of light, he did his best to search the bedroom and the adjoining bathroom but discovered nothing pertinent. That placed him back in the foyer where he merely glanced down the steps toward the guest bedrooms before going upstairs to investigate the living area.

Moving around the living room, he accidentally bumped the coffee table and knocked over the ship model sitting there, which he managed to catch at the last minute before it tumbled onto the floor. Next, his leg brushed against the ornamental fireplace tools, causing the wrought-iron poker to clang against the shovel and tongs, producing a metallic resonance similar to that of a wind chime. Passing straight through the dining area, he then entered the kitchen where the only thing he found was a discarded twelve-by-twenty-inch cardboard box sitting on the floor beside an empty trash can. Baffled by the total lack of normal human clutter and waste, he said in frustration, "Does anyone actually live like this?" Compared to the disorder of his own life, what he observed in Mark's kitchen seemed sanitized and unreal, no more than a stage prop.

Standing in the empty kitchen, confounded by the lack of incriminating evidence, he saw a flash of light streak across the interior walls of the house the moment a car motor sounded in his ears. His response was automatic as he darted straight through the dining room to the front of the house where he peeked between the slats of the blinds at a car sitting in the driveway below, its motor still running and its tail lamps glowing brightly. Listening nervously to the rumble of the engine, he stood frozen by the sliding glass doors, peering anxiously at the back of the vehicle until the taillights dimmed and the house went as silent as a tomb.

Finding himself at a moment of zero consciousness, lost and vulnerable, he had no idea what to do. It was not until he heard the creaking of the porch steps that instinct took over, and he found himself bounding toward the back of the house, dashing through the living room where he performed a fluid shoulder roll over the loveseat. Separating the vertical blinds, he silently unlatched the sliding glass doors and quietly slipped out onto the deck. A quick glance down the stairway at the deck outside the bedroom made him rethink his intended escape route. He knew that it would be too easy for Mark to ambush him there, so he opted to go over the railing where he hung from the floorboards and dropped straight to the ground, running in place even before he hit the sandy soil. He then scampered over a grass-covered dune to the green behind the house where he raced down the fairway and circled around to his hearse.

Out on the front porch, Mark prepared to enter the house by inserting the key into the deadbolt slot while simultaneously turning the doorknob. Lacking any resistance, the door moved slightly in his hand, causing him to stiffen his body and cease all physical movement. Realizing that someone had breached his house, he quietly withdrew the key and returned it to his pocket while silently pushing open the unsecured door. Then, in a quick and agile motion, he stepped into the entranceway and immediately closed the door behind him, resting his back against the doorframe as he peered into the darkness of the home's interior. Removing his sunglasses, he surveyed everything with a single sweep of his eyes before inching forward a little at a time, moving his massive body with cat-like grace and balance. Slowly sliding one foot in front of the other, he came to an abrupt stop when something stimulated his olfactory senses, causing him to lift his nose and arch his back as he sniffed the air like a hungry predator.

His nose still elevated, Mark followed the scent back to his office where the trail branched off in two divergent directions: one tracking into his bedroom and the other one leading upstairs. Pausing a moment while deciding which path to follow first, he heard the sound of an automobile racing past the front of his house just as its headlights glistened in the cut glass around the doorframe. Without hesitation, he sprang to the entranceway where he yanked open the front door, arriving in time to see a long black vehicle make a reckless turn onto Seachase Drive at the end of his lane.

With his tires squealing loudly throughout the turn, Dave regained control of the fishtailing hearse and directed its trajectory down the road toward the traffic light by the Outer Banks Mall. Drawing that kind of attention to himself was the last thing he needed or wanted, but he was far too distraught to consider such things. Panic was the order of the day, the only thing driving him at that moment, and he made no effort to restrain it. As he had done the previous night while escaping the madness on the dune, he did not stop at the intersection but barreled headlong into the traffic along the bypass, dodging and swerving around several cars before flying down the highway at an unrestrained speed. The frenzied nature of his flight, underscored by his erratic and dangerous behavior, was on full display to the darkened figure of Mark, who stood quietly on the upper deck of his house watching the receding taillights of the same vehicle he had observed on two other occasions.

Overcome by fear and despair, Dave drove around the Outer Banks for over an hour; it took him that long to calm down. Except for his encounter with Mark the previous night, he could not recall having experienced that level of terror in all his life. Once again, he was glad that no one had been there to witness his cowardice. Winding his way through the darkened streets of Nags Head, Kill Devil Hills, and Kitty Hawk, he traveled throughout the region, unaware of his surroundings or even himself, his mind incapable of cognitive operations; he just drove and breathed—that was the best he could do under the circumstances. Ultimately, he found himself sitting in the parking lot of Jennette's Pier where he came to his senses and began thinking coherently about what he should do. With few options available, he jumped at the first one that popped into his head; he put the hearse in gear and drove straight to Mulligan's.

Arriving a little before eleven o'clock that Friday night, he found the place fairly crowded, yet he still managed to secure his regular seat at the upstairs bar. Travis immediately set a cold beer in front of him and moved quickly away, rushing to the end of the bar where the orders were stacking up. With the Tiki Deck filled to capacity, many of the servers were bringing Travis their drink orders instead of waiting outside at the smaller Tiki Bar. That left the affable bartender little time to chat, something Dave found disappointing because he really needed someone to talk to that night. Glancing down the bar, he searched the crowd for Gary but failed to find him anywhere, forcing him to deal privately with his burdensome dilemma.

As he thought more about it, he concluded that it was probably best to keep the details of his predicament to himself. Too risky, he thought, to involve Travis and Gary. It would only place them in jeopardy, and he did not want to be responsible for what might happen to them; he was in enough trouble himself and should avoid spreading it around. Altruism was not one of his strong points, so it surprised him greatly that he would be concerned about protecting the wellbeing of others, especially at his own expense; and he found the novel mindset slightly perplexing because the notion of self-sacrifice ran counter to the way he usually lived his life.

Scraping the legs of his chair over the distressed wooden floor, he pushed back from the bar and slid off his seat just as Travis walked by with a handful of beer bottles. "You're not leaving, are you, Buddy?" he heard him ask. "No, just going to the head," he responded with a nod to the other side of the room.

Starting down a short hallway toward a unisex bathroom, he noticed a girl entering it, so he did an immediate about-face and headed downstairs to the men's room located on the first floor near the kitchen. It was a modest sized restroom containing a small sink and a framed mirror attached to the wall directly above it. Additionally, the room had a partition next to the sink that extended toward the door, a partial wall forming a privacy screen for the urinals in the corner by the toilet stall. Although unable to see past the partition, Dave assumed that he was alone in the room when he entered it because the only thing he heard was the mechanical hum of the ventilation fan.

Pushing closed the door, he stepped over to the sink and stared at his reflection in the mirror. Facing him was the visual echo of a man bearing little resemblance to the one he typically saw in the glass. Instead of the handsome projection of carefree vitality he had come to expect, the mirror displayed the beleaguered look of someone in great turmoil. Removing his sunglasses, he closely examined his eyes, bloodshot and weary, unchanged from how they had appeared that morning, so he leaned down and splashed water onto his face, thinking it might wash away some of the uncertainty and improve his pitiful look. Drying his face with a paper towel, he again shielded his eyes with his shades and walked toward the urinals, stepping around the partition just as the door to the restroom opened and closed behind him. Glancing over his shoulder, he felt his face go flush and his heart rocket up the back of his throat.

Stone-faced and defiant, Mark stood with his back pressed firmly against the door, the heel of his shoe resting along the doorsill to prevent anyone else from entering the room. Dressed similarly to the previous night in a long-sleeved Oxford shirt and tan twill slacks, his shoes appeared dusty as if he had been walking through sand. In the small confines of the restroom, his tensed, oversized presence was even more apparent as he occupied the entire entranceway and most of the area in front of the sink. His reach was such that he could almost touch the mirror on the wall, but he could not reach Dave without taking a step forward. Towering like a mountain in his Ray-Ban sunglasses, he glared down at Dave, who stood frozen by the door of the toilet stall, totally in shock.

Without a word, Mark raised his nose and drew in a long silent breath followed by two quick sniffs of the air. Having confirmed that Dave's aftershave was the same fragrance he had detected in his house, he displayed a gleaming set of white teeth behind an enormous grin. Satisfied that he had succeeded in locating and trapping the intruder, someone he judged as non-threatening, he relaxed his overall demeanor, finding it unnecessary to remain in such a heightened state of preparedness. Seeing that there was nowhere for Dave to go, Mark began his discourse in a casual manner.

"So, you're the fellow who's been following me around in a hearse." He paused briefly while continuing to stare at Dave, his face utterly expressionless. "But the real question is," he continued, "why are you doing it? By the way, what type a person drives a hearse anyway?" He did not wait for an answer before adding, "Perhaps someone just *dying* to ride in one?" He found his remark amusing and began chuckling.

Dave neither responded nor reacted to any of the questions, finding himself too shocked and frightened to utter a word. He remembered in excruciating detail how Mark had murdered the girl on the dune, ripping off her head as if it were nothing, and he wondered if he, too, would suffer the same fate. Although he believed himself to be in grave danger, he did not think that Mark would try to kill him there in the restroom, not in so public a place—certainly not in Mulligan's—but he had no way of knowing for sure. With no plan of attack or any idea whatsoever about what he should do, he did nothing other than stand there and listen to the words of the giant.

Mark continued addressing him in a relaxed tone. "It appears that you like scampering around in the dark at night. Well, I can't blame you." He grinned down at him. "So do I."

"Actually, I prefer the daytime," Dave replied, the lump in his throat having vanished. He was uncertain why he said it or why he had said anything at all.

Mark seemed delighted that Dave had decided to engage him in conversation rather than stand there quivering in fear. "Ah, but there is power in the night!" he said. "All great predators hunt at night."

Raising his head slightly, Dave said insolently, "There's more than just power in the night." As his apprehension began to fade, he found himself becoming more confident and defiant.

Mark started laughing and leaned back against the door. "Don't tell me you believe in ghosts and goblins!"

Dave mulled the question for a few seconds before responding, "You left out vampires." After making that comment, Dave removed his sunglasses to rest his steely gray eyes upon his interrogator.

Mark, likewise, grabbed the stem of his own sunglasses but quickly relented and dropped his hand to his side. "Ah, yes, vampires," he said, "an interesting phenomenon. But how much do you know about them? Let me tell you where they come from. Porphyria. Do you know what that is?"

"No."

"It's a rare metabolic blood disease that results from a deficiency of certain enzymes in the production of heme. Heme is a blood component that carries oxygen, as in hemoglobin. Are you with me so far?"

Dave said nothing, never once taking his eyes off the larger man.

"I guess you are," he answered himself. "Some porphyrics need periodic heme transfusions, and others become severely scarred if exposed to sunlight. Additionally, their gums recede, revealing their roots and creating the appearance of fangs." He snapped his teeth several times like a rabid animal before smiling and continuing, "So, you see, as usual, folklore has its basis in fact. That's how legends get started."

"Interesting," Dave said. "But what's the point? Halloween is not for a couple months."

Mark's relaxed demeanor vanished, and his face became as hard and cold as ice. "Halloween is a lot closer than you think, David Rasputin." He delivered the warning harshly in a guttural growl.

Just the sound of the killer saying his name sent a chill through Dave's body, reigniting the fear he had temporarily tamped down. He found it disconcerting that Mark knew his name, and he wondered what else the murderous fiend knew about him; more specifically, if he knew about his relationship with Nikki. He did not respond to Mark's comment but, instead, stood his ground and defiantly mirrored the big man's expression until Mark reached up and withdrew the sunglasses from his own face, revealing for the first time the dark voids of his inky black pupils floating ghoulishly in the creamy whites of his eyes. Caught off guard by the alarming sight, Dave took a step back in revulsion while Mark glared at him from behind the morbid portals of his heightened vision.

Dave's startled reaction and the fear in his eyes seemed to amuse Mark, who found the harsh lighting of the room distressing without the armor of his sunglasses. From the moment he removed the darkened shades, he began squinting, although he tried to sustain his glare for as long as possible because he saw that it frightened Dave. After a few seconds, however, he found the light unbearable and quickly returned the protective eyewear to his face, something that did not escape Dave's awareness despite his elevated state of anxiety at that moment.

Once again relaxed and comfortable behind his Ray-Bans, Mark quietly gazed down at Dave just as someone pushed against the door in an unsuccessful attempt to enter the room. The outsider then shoved a second time, giving up when he could not dislodge Mark's heel that remained firmly fixed against the base of the door. Mark smiled at Dave but made no comment about the brief interruption, choosing instead to divert his attention toward the adjacent the wall. Something on that side of the room seemed to fascinate him, but Dave could not make out what it was due to the obstruction of the privacy partition blocking his view. Edging ever slowly to his right, Dave moved to where he could see around the divider, unaware that what awaited him there was a sight so bizarre and incomprehensible that his rational mind would be incapable of processing it.

Tilting his head slightly forward to view that side of the room, he gasped and did a double take when he saw in the mirror the reverse image of the doorway with no hint of Mark anywhere in the reflection. The polished glass clearly revealed the far corner of the room along with the classic Guinness Beer poster of the Ostrich and Zookeeper hanging on the opposite wall, but it lacked any trace of Mark within the confines of the mirror. The Laws of Physics dictated that the poster should not even be visible due to the immense presence of Mark standing in front of it, and yet there it was in all its nostalgic detail. The murderous giant, however, was nowhere to be seen—at least not in the mirror. Dazed and confused, Dave directed his eyes back toward Mark, who stood directly across from him, staring down at him with a broad grin on his face.

"Light is an amazing thing," Mark said after a few seconds. "It can illuminate and expose, but it can also bend and deflect, thereby distorting reality." Taking a half step toward the sink while keeping one heel planted solidly against the door, he extended a hand toward the mirror and asked, "How is it that a mirror turns back light? Have you ever thought about it?" He then slid his fingernails along the outer edge of the wooden frame surrounding the mirror as if preparing to pry it off the wall. "More importantly," he continued, "what lies on the other side of the glass where even light cannot enter?" Pulling back his hand, he turned and asked, "Have you ever pondered that question? What exists on the other side of the mirror?"

Dave did not answer but looked on in disbelief, his eyes darting back and forth between the giant and the unmistakable void in the center of the mirror. He then observed Mark straighten his back and extend his hand to within an inch of the glass, pausing just long to ensure that Dave was watching him before he lightly touched the mirror, turning it into a sea of clear liquid into which he plunged his fingers, going only as far as the second knuckle. Dave's response was one of shock, but Mark's reaction was entirely different. Standing before the mirror, the ends of his fingers immersed in the silvery liquid, he allowed his body to go limp while placidly closing his eyes as if lost in ecstasy. While observing Mark's odd reaction to the sensation of having his fingers submerged in the swirling fluid, Dave struggled to process all he was seeing, finding it too bizarre and unreal to believe.

"Smoke and mirrors," Mark said after regaining his senses. "They'll fool you every time." As the euphoric sensation evaporated, he said, almost to himself as if fighting the urge to plunge his entire body into the mirror, "No ... not yet ... but soon." He then withdrew his fingers, and the glass surface again became as hard and as brittle as ice. Despite its transformation back to a normal state, the mirror still failed to reflect the deadly anomaly standing directly in front of it. Turning his attention away from it, Mark then began addressing Dave in a calm, almost docile manner.

"You see, my bothersome friend, you spend your time watching television and playing video games, while we spend our days watching you. We do it quite openly, I must admit, while you stumble blindly through your pathetic, wasted lives, totally unaware of our existence—unaware of your own true existence. Headstrong, you think yourselves alone in the universe. You even believe that life is one dimensional when, in fact, there are countless worlds and numerous dimensions out there, all interconnected with windows— or portals—yet you remain ignorant of any of them." Motioning to the mirror on the wall, he then dropped his hand and declared brusquely, "You busy yourselves with delusions of grandeur, believing that you are changing your climate while you ignore the real truths of existence, even those staring you in the face. Change the climate? You can't even pick your nose without help let alone alter an entire ecosystem. You are truly a stupid and arrogant species."

Seeing Dave turn and stare curiously at the mirror, Mark paused briefly, thinking that a question might be forthcoming, only to continue his discourse when Dave said nothing.

"I incorrectly said that we are watching you. Actually, we are studying you, something we have done for quite a long time. We study your culture, your language, your history—your weaknesses. We know more about your species than you do." Nodding again toward the mirror, he said, "Normally, these portals are impassable barriers; however, under the right set of circumstances, at the right time, with the right host, they become permeable and can be breached. That is when we enter your world. Having discovered their cycle, we can predict their accessibility, permitting us to come and go as we please whenever the time is ripe. Another noteworthy feature of the portals is that they remain open after we have passed through them, staying that way until we return, at which time they slam shut again—until the next time.

"Although we are unable to control the visiting schedule, we can see through the portals whenever we wish. That is how we can blend in with you, and why we know so much about you. There are those in my world who devote their entire lives to watching and studying your kind. Then there are those, like me, who take that knowledge and come-a-calling." He chuckled at his last remark and then cast a curious gaze in Dave's direction. "*Sprechen Sie Deutsch? Parli italiano? Parlez-vous français? Вы говорите по-русски?*" he asked. "No? What a shame." Grinning down at his small rival, he continued, "I probably shouldn't tell you this, but I will anyway. The portals work both ways, you know. But your species is too ignorant to recognize what is hiding in plain sight. Just as well, though, because we don't need any interlopers from your side crossing over into our world.

"You realize, don't you, that this has been going on for centuries? In the past, you created legends to hide your ignorance, using myth and superstition to explain what you did not understand. Now, you use science, but it remains nothing more than myth and superstition. Don't forget what I told you about vampires and how your science explains them away with porphyria.

"Unfortunately," he said with a visible change in mood, "the only way we can remain outside of our own environment is by sustaining ourselves with nourishment. It takes a lot of energy to survive in your world, and we must obtain it in its purest, most basic form. That means consuming *you* in order to stay alive. Actually, we only need your blood; however, many of my predecessors preferred total consumption.

"Animal hosts were popular among my species in the past, particularly wolves to which your legends will attest. A tranquil, reflecting pool of water where animals gather to drink can offer as safe a passage between worlds as a finely polished mirror. Like I said before, light is an amazing thing. Anyway, animal invasion offered some advantages, such as being able to remain longer in your world because animal attacks and mutilations, at least in earlier times, were more accepted and almost expected, rarely causing a panic. It was so much easier then. Do you know that some of your supposedly great civilizations often viewed us as gods? Yes, they would willingly offer themselves and their children as human sacrifices. Ah, the good old days." He paused a moment as if savoring a blissful memory before pivoting to ask, "Want to know what actually happened to your Lost Colony?"

Once again, Dave remained mute with no hint of a reaction. He heard the words but found them incomprehensible.

"Then as now," Mark continued, "human-on-human attacks with their cannibalistic overtones would invariably cause upheaval unless there was a plausible explanation, such as a legend, or when there was someone available to take the fall." He stared intently at Dave as he made the remark. "Still," he added, "mutilations of humans always create hysteria, causing an uproar that triggers more caution and vigilance, but that's the price you pay. That's why many of my predecessors chose to appear in animal form, something that doesn't appeal to me because it's not as much fun. Personally, I prefer human hosts, and I don't care if people get upset because I don't plan on sticking around that long. I like to view this incursion as more of a holiday than anything else, and I think you'd agree that there's no better place to vacation than in the Outer Banks of North Carolina in the summertime!"

The idea of regarding himself as an average Joe on vacation struck him as diabolically comical, causing him to chuckle slightly, but Dave found no humor in it whatsoever. Easily reading Dave's expression, Mark decided that he had wasted enough time with this squirt, so he spoke to him as he would a condemned man with no control over his fate.

"It's always beneficial when you're in a position like mine to have a stooge, someone to whom you can channel all the hysteria and suspicion that inevitably arises when the community gets wind of what has been happening. By the way," he said with a deadly glare, "that stooge would be you. It's the perfect scenario: a drifter down on his luck with no future prospects—a misfit who drives a hearse of all things! That is why I am sharing this information with you, so you will sound crazy when you try to explain it to the authorities. But here is all you need to know and understand about my species: our greatest strength lies in the fact that people refuse to believe that we exist ... that I exist."

Dave remembered hearing something similar to that recently, but the shock of what he had just seen and heard prevented him from recalling where. Although he remained trapped in the corner of the restroom, he discovered that he no longer feared death as much as he feared being linked to the murders, something that would ultimately result in his incarceration for the rest of his life. The thought of losing his freedom was too overwhelming, and it revived his desire to flee. Perhaps—he thought—he should run. Maybe there was still time.

Mark took another step toward the mirror, and, in doing so, he removed his heel from the base of the door. Using the fingers of his left hand, he preened the hairs of his flat top while pretending to see himself in the mirror. "I'm getting pretty good at playing this Mark fellow," he said, "although I'm not real enamored with his name." While he spoke, he grinned at the glass that displayed only the reflection of the framed beer poster on the wall behind him. "I've had better names in the past, names like Tonatiuh, Teach, even CRO, but I guess I'm stuck with Mark for the time being. Anyway, old Markie was a pretty dull guy before I came along, but he had an excellent credit rating and lots of money saved, which I'm now spending by the way." Turning to look at Dave, who continued standing with his back pressed against the bathroom stall despite the fact that he now had a clear path to the door, he said with a quirky look, "Did I tell you that I acquired a yacht? I'm thinking about doing some coastal cruising—perhaps even take an extended sea voyage." His smile became sinister as he added, "But I'd first have to provision the boat with several half-witted girls for when I get the *munchies.*"

Before Dave could say anything, the door opened, and a young man walked into the restroom, bringing with him the sound of music playing in the first-floor dining room. Immediately, Mark backed away from the mirror and quickly exited through the open door, leaving Dave pinned against the toilet stall by the young man trying to get to the urinals. Dave's first inclination was to follow Mark through the doorway, but he stepped over to the sink instead and slapped his open palm over the reflection of his face in the mirror. The glass felt cool against his skin, and it remained hard and brittle, neither rippling nor giving way under the pressure of his hand. Having satisfied his curiosity, he then bolted out the door in pursuit of the big man but ran straight into Sally, who had been walking toward the kitchen.

"Whoa, Buddy," she said as they collided.

"Sorry," he mumbled when he realized what had happened. The crazed look on his face told Sally that something was wrong.

"You okay, Buddy?"

"Yeah, yeah," he said, somewhat distracted.

She looked at him skeptically but then pretended to accept his assurance while saying, "I see you two finally met."

"Who?" he asked without looking at her, diverting his attention to the faces of the people sitting in the dining room.

"Mr. Muscles," she said.

Her answer jolted him to attention, and he asked again, "Who?"

"The big guy who just left the men's room. He stopped in a few hours ago asking about you. Actually, he was asking about your hearse. He said he wanted to buy it, so I gave him your name and told him to wait around because you'd be in sooner or later. So, are you going to do it?"

"What?"

"What do you mean, 'What'? Sell him the hearse. Are you going to do it?"

Dave stared blankly at her.

She interpreted his silence to mean that he had not yet decided, so she offered him some advice. "If you don't want to sell the hearse, then don't. But I'm not sure I'd want to tell that guy he can't have what he wants. My suggestion is to say no and then run."

"You're right," he said. "I probably should run." He made the comment offhandedly as he walked away, circling through the downstairs dining room in search of Mark. Sticking his head into the Gazebo Bar, he did not see him there, so he bolted upstairs and peered anxiously at those sitting at the tables and around the bar. Travis noticed his bizarre behavior but said nothing as he watched Dave charge onto the Tiki Deck and return a few minutes later displaying the same rattled look on his face but moving considerably slower.

Lost in the moment, Dave was barely aware of anyone else in

the place as he walked over to his chair and tossed money onto the bar next to his unfinished beer before turning and heading toward the stairway.

Travis called to him, "Buddy, you're not leaving are you?"

"Gotta go," was his only response as he disappeared down the stairs.

Sapped of all joy and vitality, he trudged through the paved portion of the parking lot in a semi-conscious state, unmindful of the music and laughter filtering down from the Tiki Deck above or the sound of the fluttering flags snapping briskly in the humid night air. Moving away from the lights of the restaurant, he entered the gravel section of the lot where it grew darker due to the clouds over the ocean obscuring the rising full moon, rendering his hearse almost invisible in the blackness of the night until the dome light flicked on the minute he opened the door and hopped into the vehicle.

His body had barely settled onto the seat when he received the shock of his life the moment his senses detected the presence of someone sitting beside him, a distorted image painted by his peripheral vision that scared the hell out of him, triggering a reflex action that propelled him through the door at near super-human speed. He then stood several feet away from the hearse, staring in through the open doorway at the bare, sand-covered legs of an unwelcome intruder. Bending slightly forward to get a better view of the front seat, he observed something that both frightened and sickened him.

The lurid scene that greeted his eyes made him gasp loudly and slam shut the door, an action that doused the interior light, preventing anyone else from seeing into the vehicle. He was now operating in full panic-mode as he directed a fright-filled glance up at Tiki Deck before turning back to glare through the open window at the gruesome sight, chastising himself for not having closed the windows and locked the doors while he was inside Mulligan's. Once again, his mind ceased functioning rationally as he paced back and forth beside the vehicle, frantically trying to comprehend what was happening.

"How is this possible?" he asked in desperation while bending down to peer through the open window, praying for a miracle that would erase what he had seen. The tragic scene, however, remained unchanged. If anything, it appeared even more horrific now that his eyes had adjusted to the darkness. Seeing with greater clarity, he could discern every detail of the girl's corpse sitting in a partial fetal position on the front seat, her headless torso leaning obtusely against the passenger door with granules of sand still clinging to her bloodstained dress.

Just then, the sound of voices echoed from behind him, and Dave spun around to see two couples exiting Mulligan's front door and heading down the ramp into the parking lot. Despite the overriding sense of revulsion that kept him outside the vehicle, he knew he could not remain there any longer, so he took two quick breaths and got into the hearse, climbing in through the open window to avoid engaging the interior lights. Firing up the engine, he then churned through the gravel parking lot and shot onto the beach road where he sped off in a southerly direction.

It only took him a second or two to regain his composure and slow his speed to the posted limit. He could not afford to have the police pull him over for speeding, not with a body in his car, but he also did not want to drive too slowly and appear like an overly cautious drunk driver. With a general idea of where he was going, he hoped to get there as quickly as possible because the idea of sharing the front seat with a headless corpse was more than he could bear. The only way he was going to survive this, he reasoned, was to pretend that she was not even there, but he doubted he could do that because of the smell. The rush of air surging in through the open windows helped dilute the stench somewhat, but it was not enough to kill it entirely. He still felt himself gagging at times as he struggled to keep from vomiting.

Hoping to reduce his travel time, he thought about crossing over to the bypass but quickly dismissed the idea because of the increased traffic on the highway and the risk it posed. No—he thought—too many chances for other drivers to see into the hearse at the traffic lights. He needed the darkness and seclusion offered by the beach road to get him there safely, even if it meant traveling at a slower pace and prolonging his time with the dead girl.

Despite the fear that someone would catch him before he could dispose of the corpse, he began experiencing a profound sense of guilt along with tremendous sadness over the girl's fate, especially the defilement she had yet to undergo. She did not deserve this moral outrage and desecration—he told himself—and he wanted to turn and apologize to her, but he was too afraid to glance in her direction.

Upon reaching Whalebone Junction near Jennette's Pier and Sam & Omie's Restaurant, he veered onto the beach road extension—South Old Oregon Inlet Road—because it was a safer, more remote route to his destination in the Cape Hatteras National Seashore. It also avoided the cars heading to Roanoke Island and the traffic signals near the main entrance to the national park. As he drove the five miles through the district of South Nags Head toward the spot where the road merged with the highway, he refused to look over at the girl, glancing instead at the shoreline where vacationers slept peacefully in their rented beach homes, blissfully unaware of the tragic drama unfolding just yards beyond their doorsteps.

His mind, for the most part, had ceased functioning properly, preventing him from holding a rational thought in his head for more than a second or two. Additionally, the internal voice that typically guided his actions had gone mute, and his ability to distinguish right from wrong seemed to have vanished, swept away by the buffeting sea breeze blowing in through the open windows, eroding his moral judgment but failing to stop the stench of decaying flesh from finding its way into his nostrils.

A short distance past a green water tower emblazoned with the words *Nags Head*, he reached the juncture with the main highway where he made a hasty left-hand turn and plunged headlong into the inky blackness of the night, increasing his speed from thirty-five to sixty miles-per-hour. The suffocating darkness along that stretch of national seashore then began pressing in on him, draining his spirit and robbing him of all hope until he looked ahead and spotted it hovering over the horizon just above the tops of the pines, burning as bright and radiant as a flaming star—the pure, sweet light of the Bodie Island Lighthouse.

The piercing white beam of the first-order Fresnel lens flashed twice every thirty seconds, winking at him with the assurance of safe passage to his intended destination. There were no words to describe his reaction upon seeing it. The experience was more emotional than anything else, much like that of a rescued sailor the sea, and he immediately sensed a restored confidence and optimism with each new burst of light that penetrated his soul with its cutting yet soothing illumination, a sensation that was both calming and invigorating. Rising before him in the darkness, the lighthouse stood stoically erect, impervious to the wind and weather—strong, secure, and glowing with hope—much like Nikki. He realized that both, in their own ways, were offering him guidance, providing clear direction on how to proceed.

Approaching an intersection that led to the Bodie Island Lighthouse on the right and Coquina Beach on the left, he slowed down before making the turn, his wheels slipping on the sand-dusted asphalt. Veering onto the road leading into Coquina Beach, he continued into the first parking lot where he stopped and carefully scanned the area for parked cars. Seeing none, he flipped on his high beams and looked again before proceeding into the second lot that also appeared empty. Coquina Beach was a recreational area with several paved parking lots, all of which had walking paths across the barrier dunes to the beach. Additionally, there was an expansive bathhouse facility with a wooden boardwalk providing beach access over the dunes. Dave's destination was the bathhouse where he parked the hearse in a handicapped spot, attempting to get as close as possible to the wooden access ramp.

The National Park Service operated the bathhouse complex that included restroom facilities housed within a large building constructed in the traditional Outer Banks style of architecture with a pitched roof and slatted wooden siding. The building faced the ocean with an open area in front of it, similar to that of a courtyard, in which stood four monolithic showers with multiple showerheads aimed in various directions. Arranged around the perimeter of the courtyard were individual changing rooms with unsecured doors that creaked noisily in the stiff breeze, flinging open and then slamming shut like diabolical doorways in an old gothic house. At that hour, the entire facility projected an eerie, unwelcoming aura, void of light except for that which spilled from the open doorways of the restrooms and the ambient glow of the light fixtures hanging above the haunted changing room doors.

The erratic banging of the doors unnerved Dave the minute he stepped from the hearse. Having already confirmed that the parking lots were empty, he found his confidence shaken by the creaking and thumping coming from the bathhouse area, so he raced up the ramp to determine the source of the noise, stopping abruptly when he saw four darkened figures standing in the courtyard. Without moving a muscle, he peered intently at them for several seconds until his eyes adjusted to the darkness, after which he concluded that they posed no threat, being nothing more than the shadowy outlines of the four shower towers in the center of the compound. Just then, a strong gust of wind blew shut one of the changing room doors, and the loud knock caused him to jump involuntarily, making him wonder if he could ever recapture that cool demeanor for which he had become known. Pulling himself together long enough to conduct a quick inspection of the complex that included both restrooms and all the changing booths, he convinced himself that he was entirely alone and returned to the parking lot to proceed with his gruesome chore.

His first task was to retrieve a shovel from the back of the hearse where he had stowed it a few days earlier while teaching

Nikki to windsurf. It was small, only about twenty-six inches long, with a pointed blade and a handle like a coal shovel, the perfect tool for such a morbid undertaking. Gripping it tightly in one hand, he slammed closed the back of the hearse and then walked around to the passenger side where he balked at opening the door. The internal torment raging inside of him had caused a temporary paralysis, preventing him from touching the door handle as he struggled with the morality of his intended actions. Morally speaking, he knew his behavior to be wrong, but he recognized that there was no other alternative. In actuality, he had already made up his mind; he was just allowing himself more time to build up the strength to act. He only hoped that he had the stomach to see it through to the end.

To get to the beach, he would have to carry the girl's body up the ramp, through the courtyard, and across the boardwalk that zigzagged a considerable distance over the dunes. He wondered if he could carry her the whole way in a single breath, but he knew he must try. Mustering all his strength, he partially opened the door while using his hand to prevent her headless torso from rolling onto the ground. A wave of revulsion assaulted his sensibilities the moment he touched her cold, clammy skin, but he maintained control and continued supporting the weight of her body while averting his eyes away from the gaping neck wound through which protruded her severed spine. Swinging the door fully open, he purposely unfocused his eyes while assessing the best way to lift her out of the car. With her body stiff due to rigor mortis, he concluded that her folded fetal position would actually aid him in carrying her sand-caked corpse to the beach.

It had become apparent to him that the only way he could accomplish this task was to stop thinking of her as a girl, or even a human being for that matter. If he had any hope of succeeding in this endeavor, he must purge himself all emotion and view her as nothing more than an inanimate object needing relocation to the beach—a gross, disgusting, odorous object requiring disposal as quickly as possible. Having been buried in the cool, wet sand since the previous night, her decapitated corpse had escaped the heat of the day, keeping the stench from becoming overpowering and wholly intolerable; however, the smell was pungent nonetheless, and it was becoming more so due to the accelerated decomposition brought on by the humid night air. Therefore, without further delay, other than the time it took to inhale a massive amount of fresh air, he grabbed the shovel and scooped the girl into his arms, holding her tightly against his chest as he raced up the ramp.

Running as fast as he could, he found it surprising how little she weighed, something he attributed to her small stature and the massive amount of blood she had lost—also the absence of her head that lessened her weight an additional ten pounds or more. Clearing the ramp, he experienced the first powerful urge to breathe as he charged across the courtyard and then onto the walkway where he slowed down to prevent the girl's body from snagging on the slatted railing of the boardwalk. In addition to the discomfort of not breathing, he also had to endure the heat and humidity of the night as well as the noxious smell invading his nostrils despite his self-imposed suffocation. Exploding onto the beach in one final effort, he promptly dumped his load next to an outcropping of beach grass before walking across the sand to catch his breath, pacing aimlessly back and forth as far away as possible from the disgusting corpse in the tight white dress.

Licking at the sweat streaming down his face, he walked about with his hands on his hips and his heart pounding like a sledgehammer. Tilting back his head to fill his lungs with air, he spotted the rising orb of the moon peeking above a cloud bank along the eastern horizon, its pale, morbid radiance pervading the coastline, tinting the sand and waves with a ghostly iridescence. Off in the distance, he could see a lifeguard chair sitting halfway across the beach, and, beyond it, the frothy white foam of massive waves cresting and breaking along the shoreline. The unnaturally loud roar emanating from the churning surf led him to question the source of the ungodly sound. Was it the crashing of the waves he heard or the collapsing of his soul? Feeling like he was losing his mind, wishing only to finish his job and escape this horrid nightmare, he grabbed both the shovel and the girl and charged down the beach, running manically along the barrier dunes until he collapsed to the ground and dropped his repulsive burden onto a sand mound under which was buried the Wreck of the *Laura Barnes*.

The *Laura Barnes* was a wooden schooner that had succumbed to the Graveyard of the Atlantic when, on June 1, 1921, it had run aground in a dense fog after venturing too close to the shoreline. First relocated to Coquina Beach, it was subsequently transferred it to the Graveyard of the Atlantic Museum in Hatteras; however, vestiges of it remained buried beneath the palisade dune where Dave had deposited the girl's body. He knew that the park service endeavored to keep people off the dunes to prevent beach erosion and to protect the buried artifact, and he hoped it would provide a peaceful resting place for the unfortunate girl. Of course, he could not trust the wind and weather to adhere to the park restrictions, so he knew he must dig deep.

Rising to his knees, he grabbed the shovel and began digging in the sand like an obsessed child burrowing to China. He dug wildly and feverishly until he thought his arms would fall off, and then he dug some more. The rising full moon, no longer obscured by clouds, was illuminating everything with its radiant glow, and it surprised Dave when he noticed raindrops appearing on the ground beneath him. Although the eastern horizon remained slightly overcast, the rest of the firmament was clear and bright, so he questioned the source of the rain, coming to the sad conclusion that the moisture on the sand was not caused by raindrops falling from the sky but, rather, by tears pouring from his eyes.

Gushing forth in torrents, the tears ran down the sides of his face and fell softly onto the ground to wash and sanctify the sand, transforming the beach into a hallowed cemetery accepting of the young victim's remains. As he dug and wept, Dave apologized to the soul of the deceased girl for what she had endured, especially the indecency of this final outrage. Although he had been only an unwitting witness to her murder, he still regretted his involvement in the tragedy, and his soul bled as if pierced by the additional insult he inflicted on her memory by his own disrespectful actions. He found the guilt crushing and almost intolerable, but he continued digging nonetheless.

When satisfied that the hole was deep enough, he respectfully lifted and cradled the girl in his arms, gently moving her body closer to the makeshift grave. Gone was the violent brutality he had exhibited in transporting her remains to the beach. He now treated her with the utmost respect, ever so tenderly lowering her petite form into its resting place while whispering, "I'm sorry." Unable to arrange her in a more restful position because of her hardened limbs, he simply covered her body with a light dusting of sand before filling in the grave, stamping on it a few times to pack it down before sprinkling more loose sand across the top of it. Knowing that the stiff wind would quickly dry out the top layer of moist sand and sweep away all traces of disturbance, he counted on new growths of sea oats and American beachgrass springing up to stabilize the ground around the grave, making it indiscernible from the rest of the palisade dune.

Upon finishing his work, he stood and gazed down at the grave, his eyes still awash in tears. Near the burial site, some exposed planks of the *Laura Barnes* protruded from the sand, and he felt better knowing that young girl was not alone down there. He knew and accepted that he had become her final caretaker, and yet he did not know her name; therefore, he decided to call her Laura. By naming her, he established a bond that promoted a feeling of kinship, an act that also dispelled some of the guilt and shame he felt. Glancing up, he noticed the top of the Bodie Island Lighthouse projecting above the Loblolly pines on the other side of the road, and its presence provided much-needed solace to his troubled mind. He saw it wink once and then again before going dark, and he interpreted the signal as a personal message to him, telling him not to worry, that it would always be there to watch over Laura and guard her resting place so he could return to Nikki and address the many challenges still facing them.

CHAPTER 12

Dave awoke before dawn despite not having returned home until well after midnight. By the time the first rays of sunlight were brightening the sky, he was already standing beside the open door of the hearse, watching the blazing disc inch above the waves, its crimson aura tinting the wispy clouds marching steadily from the southeast. The sight of the approaching clouds—unwelcome harbingers of things to come—only added to his despair. Burdened by flashbacks from the previous night and unable to sleep, he had abandoned his bed to begin cleaning the inside of the hearse, hoping to remove all traces of Laura's body from the seat and floor of the vehicle.

Having already swept out most of the sand, he sprayed a bleach-based cleaning solution on the seat, trying to eliminate the scent of death still permeating the interior of the hearse. Unsure if he would ever be able to eradicate the pungent odor, he began wondering if the persistent smell might be nothing more than a haunting memory from last night, a traumatic sensory retention that would plague him for the rest of his life. He had no idea what the rest of his life would look like, only that it would be radically different from what he had envisioned, especially if the police ever became involved. Their crime lab investigators and cadaver dogs were very efficient, and he knew they would invariably find something he had missed no matter how hard he scrubbed the leather interior of the old Cadillac.

Things were not looking good for him, and the more he washed the upholstery, the more dismal his future appeared. Not normally one for introspection, he found himself taking stock of his life, assessing what he had achieved during his time on earth and reaching the conclusion that he had little to show for it; therefore, not much to lose. However, there was one item in his pathetic, miserable existence that held some value, and it was something he had only recently discovered, a sparkling jewel having the power to give new purpose and meaning to his life. She was the shining beacon of his deliverance, the singular possession he was unwilling to sacrifice or forfeit.

Nikki was the only thing keeping him from running away; however, the urge to flee was always there, lying just beneath the surface. He suspected that it would reemerge to cloud his judgment again, but he also knew that running would only make him look guilty if Mark decided to involve the authorities, something he had threatened to do. When and how he planned to carry out that threat were questions Dave could not answer, but he expected to find out very soon. Equally worrisome was the issue of the murdered girl's head. Where might it turn up? That thought troubled him greatly, but he did not know what to do about it.

Since it was Saturday, one of the two days each week when Dave was required to work, he decided to go ahead and perform his home inspection duties. Perhaps—he thought—the dull routine of the job would calm his mind and allow him time to devise a plan for dealing with Mark. Nikki would be out of town and safe most of the day. She would not be in jeopardy until later that evening when she returned home to have dinner with her friends at Kelly's; however, he would be there to watch over her, joining her after dark when Mark posed the greatest threat. No matter what—he told himself—he would be there to protect her although he had no battle strategy or even a clue how to combat the unspeakable evil that was Mark Allen.

Arriving extra early at the realty office that morning, Dave picked up the list of homes requiring inspections along with the master keys to unlock the properties. He usually had seven or eight houses assigned to him, but that day it was ten because another inspector had decided to evacuate the area due to the impending hurricane even though there was no sign of it yet. The renters were not required to checkout until ten o'clock, but several families had already departed to get ahead of the storm. That meant that Dave could begin his inspections immediately because many of the homes were already vacant.

Besides conducting property damage assessments and checking the houses for the theft of furnishings, he also evaluated the performance of the housekeeping staff to ensure that the homes were properly cleaned. To avoid tripping over the cleaning crews, he would begin early in the morning by inventorying and inspecting a few of the properties before the arrival of the housekeeping staff, returning later in the day to do a quick cleaning review after they had completed their work. By late afternoon, however, he could inspect the houses in a single visit because the cleaning crews would already be gone. He typically completed his assignments by five o'clock in the afternoon—the time the new tenants took possession of their rentals—but he expected to finish earlier that day due to the exodus of vacationers fleeing the approaching hurricane.

The first house on the list was located in The Village at Nags Head—Mark's development—and he found himself struggling to contain his unease and trepidation as he approached the residential community along the highway. Instead of turning into the development by the Outer Banks Mall, he avoided driving by Mark's house by entered at the other end of West Seachase Drive farther south on the bypass, a route that took him past the clubhouse of the Nags Head Golf Links. Pulling into the driveway of the rental property, he saw that the tenants had already departed, so he climbed the stairs and went straight inside.

His regular routine was to enter through the front door and systematically walk through the house, making consecutive right turns while traveling in the same direction, always completing the first floor before moving to the upper levels. It represented a disciplined approach to his job that ensured he would visit and inspect every room. Carrying with him a checklist as he walked from room to room, he rarely overlooked anything, examining and inventorying all the furniture as well as the appliances and electronics. Additionally, he checked to ensure that the departing guests had closed and locked all the doors and windows, and he searched for any items left behind, looking inside the closets and dresser drawers as well as peering under the beds. The monotony of the job as well as his disciplined approach to it had a palliative effect on him, distracting and calming his mind, which he knew would only be short-lived because of the uncertainty and apprehension bubbling up whenever he paused for even a second. To counter the emotional instability, he endeavored to concentrate on every aspect of his job as if he were performing it for the first time.

The distraction strategy worked reasonably well while he inspected the home's living area, but it proved less effective once he entered the kitchen. Testing the garbage disposal while running water in the sink, he relished the harsh sound of the motor with its robust timbre drowning out the internal voices warning him about his future and what he and Nikki faced if he did not develop a coherent battle strategy. Listening to the gurgling of the water in concert with the mechanical grinding of the disposal motor, he reached up and pushed against the window over the sink, checking the surety of its lock. In doing so, his eyes passed through the glass pane to rest on the rooftop and upper deck of a house off in the distance—Mark's house. The sight of it caused an instant surge of adrenaline, reigniting many of the fears he had temporarily suppressed. Although he did not lower his hand to touch it, he could feel the murderer's house key weighing heavily in the side pocket of his shorts, burning like a blazing coal against the side of his leg.

Suspending all thought, he stood stiff and motionless with his hands braced against the countertop, his eyes fixed on the house in the distance. Despite the vibrating racket of the garbage disposal, he heard and felt nothing but other than the surging of blood through his temples and the thunderous pounding of his heart. Raw emotion supplanted any conscious understanding with fear and anger intertwining so completely that he could no longer differentiate between them. The blinds of Mark's house were tightly drawn, but Dave knew he was in there, a prisoner of his tastefully decorated walls, thin sheets of plasterboard that shielded him and his wicked deeds from the light of day. Thinking about the evil that would be unleashed after sunset, Dave felt an overpowering urge to rush over there and tear down those walls, perhaps even burn the house to the ground. That would teach him!—he thought. Unaware that he was even speaking, he growled under his breath, "Let him come out in the sunlight, and we'll see how tough he is."

Ultimately, the grating sounds of the motor snapped him out of his wrathful trance, and he switched off the garbage disposal and closed the spigot before redirecting his eyes back toward the house. He knew that he must come up with a plan to combat Mark, a real plan that offered some kind of defense against so formidable an adversary. His prior encounter had taught him that the big man was extremely sensitive to light, a weakness suggesting that the brute was not entirely invincible. If he had one vulnerability, Dave surmised, then he must surely have more. Instead of thinking defensively, Dave began attacking the problem proactively with an aggressive attitude that restored some of his diminished confidence. He even went so far as to speculate that Mark might be as fragile and helpless as everyone else in this world, just a breath away from total annihilation. But how would he know for sure?

That critical question had him stymied. How would he know for sure? The only way to find out would be to test his supposition. But what if he guessed wrong? Well, then—he thought—he would be no worse off than he was now, sitting around waiting to be killed by Mark or picked up by the police. One of those scenarios was bound to play out if he did nothing to change the circumstances, so he knew he must act and act quickly.

Once again, he calmed his mind and entered a trance-like state to ponder his next move. Standing relaxed and motionless, he appeared to suppress all bodily functions while focusing his strength and energy on the mental process of devising a plan. As the seconds ticked away on the kitchen clock, he seemed on the verge of collapse when he suddenly jerked back his head and expanded his chest, resuscitating himself with a massive gulp of air that revived him both physically and mentally, leaving him entirely conscious and acutely aware of what he needed to do.

Wasting no time, he grabbed his cell phone from his pocket and traced a familiar number pattern over the virtual keypad. He then pressed the phone tightly to his ear as he returned to work, completing the few tasks left to be performed in the kitchen. When a voice finally came on the line, he was already walking into the dining room.

It was just before noon when Dave passed Sam & Omie's Restaurant and turned onto the beach road extension at Whalebone Junction to cross into the district of South Nags Head. His destination was Garry Oliver's Outer Banks Fishing Pier around the eighteenth milepost, but he had decided to make a quick stop at Ace's house before going there. Up ahead, off to the right, he saw the weathered planks of the small, one-story structure, easily identified by the flags in the yard and a large sign that read *Home of a U.S. Marine.*

He recalled the first time he had visited the place shortly after arriving in the Outer Banks. It had been one evening while he was out driving around after dark trying to get a lay of the land. That was when he came upon what he mistook for an open-air bar. Noticing a string of twinkle lights around a large open doorway and several chairs arranged inside the place, he pulled into the driveway and parked alongside a classic red and white motorcycle. To his great surprise, he had not discovered a quaint little bar but, rather, the home of a former United States Marine, someone who had turned his garage and driveway into a place for drinking and socializing with his friends. Sitting inside the garage were two men engaged in conversation: an older gentleman with a long white beard reminiscent of Santa Claus and another man in his early fifties with a Marine Corps tattoo on his upper arm.

Dave immediately apologized for the intrusion and turned to leave when Ace, the owner of the property, invited him to stay. With his bleached whiskers resting comfortably on his chest, the veteran introduced himself and proudly showed off his home after handing Dave a can of Budweiser and telling him to grab a folding chair from beside the propane grill. Placing his beer can on a fish-cleaning table, Dave unfolded one of the chairs and sat down, barely able to constrain his smile as he admired the collection of unique objects and artifacts comprising Ace's world.

Between the porch and the garage was an old wooden bench inscribed with a written endorsement suggesting that people enjoy Budweiser at Fish Heads Bar & Grill, Mulligan's, Applebee's, and Sam & Omie's. Above it was a sign that read *Home of a U.S. Marine, Budweiser drinking, Earnhardt Jr. fan.* The interior walls of the garage were stacked and lined almost to the ceiling with empty Budweiser beer cans, the contents of which Ace proudly claimed to have consumed. Hanging from the rafters were American flags and Marine posters as well as a sling hammock on which Ace preferred to sit while drinking and conversing with his friends. A refrigerator stood in the corner of the garage filled with ice cold cans of Budweiser waiting to be consumed and added to the interior motif of the garage.

Dave immediately bonded with the older gentleman, and the two became fast friends from that day forward. He also developed a close relationship with the other service veteran sitting in Ace's garage that night, someone who turned out to be the Mayor.

Approaching the ramshackle hideaway, Dave slowed down when he saw his friend sitting inside the garage. Instead of pulling into the driveway, he stopped by the side of the road and prepared to call out to Ace when the bearded veteran surprised him by speaking up first.

"Buddy, aren't you going to come in and have a Bud?" the old-timer yelled to him from across the lawn. Despite his impaired vision, Ace had detected Dave's presence along the road.

Shaking his head in amazement, Dave answered him, "How did you know it was me from that distance?"

"I know the sound of that old bucket you drive," he said with a laugh. "Have you got that dog with you?"

"No, he's at home, Ace. I'm working today—on my lunch hour right now. I'm heading to the pier and thought you might like a ride." He knew that Ace often walked down the road to visit Fish Heads Bar & Grill on the pier, and he thought he would offer him a lift.

The old Marine waved his hand. "Nah, Buddy. I'll go down later this afternoon during happy hour when the band starts playing. Jonny Waters & Company are performing there today. You go ahead without me. Stop back later for a Budweiser, and bring that dog with you."

After saying goodbye to his bearded friend, Dave continued the short distance down the road to the Outer Banks Fishing Pier. As usual, the parking lot was filled with cars, but it was not so crowded that people had begun parking along the road. That would not occur until four o'clock with the start of happy hour and the fifteen-cent shrimp special, so Dave pulled straight into the parking lot and found an empty space beside a red and white 1950 Indian Chief Blackhawk motorcycle complete with attached sidecar. Exiting the hearse, he glanced over at the bike and smiled just before the wing of a swooping gull struck him on the ear. Someone had spilled French fries in the parking lot, and seabirds were swarming overhead, fighting and jockeying for position as they cried out noisily and swept in for an easy meal.

Dave strolled to the end of the parking lot and entered the pier house where he saw the owner, Garry Oliver, standing behind a glass counter in the tackle shop. The owner spoke up as soon as he saw him. "Just head out onto the pier, Buddy," he said with a wave of his hand. "He's already out there waiting for you."

"Thanks," Dave answered with a grin as he walked past the counter and stepped through the screen door without purchasing a dock pass.

Just outside the door of the pier house was Fish Heads Bar & Grill, a favorite eating and drinking establishment for locals and tourists alike. It had a sheltered bar area on one side of the deck with outside seating arranged directly across from it. Brightly colored umbrellas shaded the outside tables and chairs, their decorative colors complementing the flapping flags attached to the railings. Members of the Jonny Waters' road crew were busy setting up for their happy hour performance later that day, but Dave paid them little heed as he walked past them, continuing out onto the pier while glancing toward the beach filled with sunbathers and swimmers.

Puffy cumulus clouds dotted the sky with higher cirrus clouds approaching from the south, their scaly patterns similar to those of the fish being caught on the pier that day. Overhead, the sun burned brightly in the heavens, scornful and defiant of the approaching storm system, while a robust wind swept the entire coastline, driving ashore large, powerful waves that attracted many local surfers eager to take advantage of the optimal surf conditions. Their presence in the water caused Dave to stop and gaze longingly at them as they rode perfectly formed rollers all the way to the beach.

Resuming his trek across the wooden pier that extended out about six hundred and fifty feet from the shoreline, he stepped lightly across the planked surface, careful to follow the twisting, wave-like course of the old structure. Up ahead, he saw many fishermen standing along the railing with several more sitting on wooden benches. A few were busy gutting their catches on fish-cleaning stations, but most were actively engaged in fishing, their long poles sticking out from both sides of the pier.

Dave was somewhat familiar with fishing, but his knowledge was limited to the gear used by the sportsmen. The bait favored by fishermen was a total mystery to him but not to the gulls and other seabirds crying out overhead, occasionally swooping down to steal a morsel from an unsuspecting angler. He understood the passion exhibited by those dedicated to the sport, but he realized that his interests lay elsewhere, in activities above the sea rather than beneath it. He was more in tune with the pelicans he saw flying in close formation above the waves, soaring just inches above the surface of the water, much like a windsurfer or a kiteboarder. Feeling a little envious of their ability to harness the wind while admiring their grace and majesty, he watched them glide effortlessly over the sea as he continued his journey down the pier, pushing harder against the stiff breeze while listening to the snippets of conversations blowing past his ears.

Before reaching the end of the pier, he saw a fisherman in jeans and a beat-up University of North Carolina ballcap hauling in a small sand shark that he pinned to the floorboards with his foot while reaching into his gear box for a pair of needle-nose pliers to unhook it. Dave paused a moment to watch the fisherman as did another man and his young son. The angler noticed the little boy eyeing the shark, so he asked in a thick southern drawl if the boy wanted to touch it. Holding out the fish in both hands, he laughed when the timid child grasped his father's leg, uncertain if he wanted to touch the slippery sea creature despite the prodding of his dad. In the end, the fisherman winked at Dave and said to the boy, "Okay, then, we'll just put him back where we found him." Turning toward the water, he then tossed the shark over the rail where it fell a considerable distance before plunging into the sea and swimming away. Looking down at the youth, the fisherman said with a chuckle, "Just watch your toes when you're in the ocean. He might remember you." Shaking his head, the boy's father moaned, "Oh, don't tell him that."

Grinning at the father's reaction, Dave continued down the pier until he spotted another colorful character, this one wearing a Confederate flag bandana stretched tightly over his bald head, a necessary piece of protective headwear that day given the intensity of the sun. Leaning against the wooden rail of the pier, the guy wore a black Harley-Davidson tee shirt, camouflage shorts, and biker boots; however, he seemed entirely at home in the salty environment with a fishing pole gripped tightly in one hand. On the bench beside him was a bait container and tackle box along with another pole not currently in use. Dave detected smoke coming from the man's graying goatee, creating the impression that it was on fire, but then he noticed the short stub of a lit cigarette protruding from the laid-back fisherman's mouth as the guy stared thoughtfully down the shoreline at the crashing waves tumbling onto the beach.

"And I thought I had the life," Dave said when he was just a few feet behind the man.

The Mayor turned around and laughed. "When I grow up, Buddy, I want to be just like you. Ya' know what I mean?" He then leaned his fishing pole against the railing and extended his hand, which Dave grasped in a hearty handshake.

"I'm not sure you'd want to be me today," Dave said to his friend as he peeked over the rail, looking down toward the end of the Mayor's line submerged in the water. "Catch anything?"

Taking a final drag on his cigarette, the Mayor started to flick the butt over the side but then stopped and quickly looked around, his eyes entirely obscured by his wraparound shades. Despite the dark lenses, Dave could detect a sparkle in Mayor's eyes based on the way he grinned before crushing the spent cigarette on the railing and placing it in his tackle box. "What was it you wanted to know?" he asked his young friend.

"Have you caught anything?"

"Ah, no. Not yet. Just got here, though." He used two fingers to jiggle the line and then looked at Dave. "You know what amazes me, Buddy?"

"What?"

"With all the time you've spend on the water, I can't believe that you never learned to fish. Ya' know what I mean?"

Dave simply shrugged his shoulders.

"I guess you're just a beach boy," the Mayor quipped while watching a tourist attempt to surf fish from the beach. "See that guy out there?" he said pointing to the surf fisherman. "I'll take you out and teach you how to do that. The secret is to find a break in the sand where the water is going out. Ya' know what I mean? That guy doesn't know what the hell he's doing. Like most others, he's trying to cast all the way to England, but it's not necessary. The fish are sitting just beyond the surf. You only have to get your line out that far.

"When I take you fishin', we'll use a six-ounce weight. That's a little heavy, but it won't break the line. Ya' know what I mean? We'll catch us some bluefish." He then began thinking and talking to himself, almost as if Dave were not present. "Yeah, we'll use some finger mullet for bait, better bait than shrimp. We could—" Stopping mid-sentence, he thought quietly for a moment and then turned to Dave. "Bluefish make excellent fish cakes; better than crab cakes. Just follow the recipe on the Old Bay container, add some grated cheese, and grill'em outside. Nothing better. Ya' know what I mean?"

"Okay," Dave said with a grin. "You just let me know when."

Growing silent, they both gazed off into the distance at the ocean, watching the water undulate like an immense blue flag fluttering in the wind. With a stiff sea breeze sweeping away the voices of the fishermen around them, the only sound they heard was the piercing bark of a golden retriever frolicking on the beach, imploring its owner to throw a tennis ball so it could retrieve it by plunging into the briny sea.

The Mayor nodded at the southern horizon. "It's a beautiful day, but there's trouble just beyond those puffy clouds."

"What did you hear today?"

"The hurricane weakened over Florida, but it's out over the Atlantic again and back to full force, maybe even stronger. That means it's coming this way, probably by tomorrow night. Old Kim's been pretty erratic so far, so it's anyone's guess if she'll hit us directly or shoot up the sound. Either way, lots of tourists will be hightailing it out of here tomorrow. The bypass is going to be a complete bottleneck further north. Ya' know what I mean?"

"You leaving?"

The Mayor cupped his hands around his face to light another cigarette. Taking a deep drag, he shoved his lighter back into the pocket of his shorts. "Probably not. I'll put the bike in the truck bed and strap it down tight. Then, I'll wait and see what happens. That monster truck of mine with those huge tires can get through anything. Ya' know what I mean?" He chuckled and took another puff of his cigarette. "But you didn't call me this morning and come all the way out here just to talk about the weather."

Dave's expression changed. "Yeah, I know."

The Mayor stuck the cigarette in his mouth and picked up his fishing pole. Winding in the line, he leaned the pole against the railing and picked up his tackle box. "C'mon with me. Where'd you park?"

"Right next to you."

"Good," he said, and they both proceeded down the pier, walking toward the door of the pier house.

Passing through the building, they both continued outside and headed down the ramp into the parking lot. Reaching the hearse, Dave climbed in on the driver's side, but the Mayor first looked around and flicked away his cigarette butt before plopping himself down on the passenger seat.

"Did you just do your laundry? Smells like Clorox in here," the Mayor asked while crinkling his nose and sniffing the air.

"Yeah, something like that," Dave replied. "So what have you got for me?"

The Mayor started opening his tackle box but then stopped. Looking across the seat at Dave, he said, "I know you're a good kid, Buddy, and that's the only reason I'm doing this for you. But if you get in any trouble, I'm telling you right now; you didn't get this from me. Ya' know what I mean?"

Dave nodded. "Yeah, I understand."

"Okay then."

The Mayor flipped open the lid of the tackle box and moved around a few items before dipping his hand into the clutter of fishing gear to withdraw a compact handgun. It was a semiautomatic pistol housed in a small holster made of rubberized fabric. Pulling the lusterless gun from the holster, he presented it to Dave stock first with the barrel angled downward while he carefully observed his young friend's reaction upon accepting the gun.

Dave had never before handled a firearm, and he took it from the Mayor rather timidly. As he did so, the Mayor called out, "Stop right there!" causing him to freeze with the gun resting on the open palm of his hand.

Reaching over, the Mayor took back the gun from him and displayed it openly in his own hand. "Let me show you how this works," he said. "This is a Ruger LCP semi-automatic pistol. I selected it for you because it is small, light, and concealable. Ya' know what I mean? It takes .380 caliber rounds—that's .380 *AUTO* rounds. Because it is so small and light, it has a slight kick, one that might surprise you. The first time you fire it, be careful that it doesn't fly out of your hand or hit you in the head." He chuckled at his last comment and added, "Ya' know what I mean?" Pointing the gun toward the dashboard, he projected a red dot on the glovebox compartment. "There's also a Crimson Trace laser sight on this gun that activates when you depress the button just below the trigger guard on the grip. Grip it tightly and the laser beam engages. After that, just put the red dot on the target and *pow*."

"I've never fired a gun before," Dave said.

"I know. That's why I took it back from you. I'm going to give you a crash course right now. Number one: never point it in any direction you're not comfortable firing it; namely, at yourself or other people. Number two: always assume that it's loaded even when you *know* it's not."

He dropped the magazine out of the stock and inserted two .380 caliber cartridges. "Here is the button that releases the magazine, and here is how you load it." Pushing in the latch button, he reinserted the magazine. "Although there are bullets in the clip, the gun won't fire because there's nothing in the chamber. As you can see, there is no resistance to the trigger right now. You first have to pull the slide back to chamber the bullet." As he said that, he grabbed the top of the pistol with his left hand and rocked the slide back and forth with a single jerk. "Now there is a bullet in the chamber, and the internal hammer is in a semi-cocked position. Pull the trigger now and the gun goes off. Once you do, the recoil from the discharging bullet re-engages the slide to chamber the next round and re-cock the hammer so you don't have to do it again manually. Also, if you drop the gun now, it could discharge. That's because this gun doesn't have a safety. I never like to walk around with a bullet in the firing chamber and the gun half-cocked, that is, of course, unless I'm in a situation where I'm about to use it. Ya' know what I mean?"

Dave nodded his understanding, attentively watching the Mayor while trying to remember everything he was told.

"Look here, Buddy," the Mayor said, pointing to a small opening near the cartridge extraction slot. "Right here is a port that allows you to view a loaded cartridge. It's just a tiny space, but it's large enough for you to see the brass shell of a bullet when there's one in there like there is now. Do you see the glint of the brass catching the light? If there were no bullet in there, it would be a dark, empty hole. I know it's small and tough to see, but it at least gives you a visual check on whether or not you've got a bullet in there waiting to be fired. And once a round is chambered, it can be fired even if you remove the clip, so don't think you're unloading the gun just by removing the magazine. You've also got to get that bullet out of there like this."

The Mayor then grabbed the top slide of the gun and aggressively snapped it backward, an action that expelled the chambered cartridge, which Dave instinctively snatched from the air with his right hand. The Mayor smiled at him and said, "Good reflexes, Grasshopper!"

Appearing a little confused, Dave asked, "Huh?"

"Never mind," the Mayor said with a grin as he dropped the magazine from the stock of the pistol. Narrowing his eyes behind his shades, he turned slightly in Dave's direction and asked, "Is the gun unloaded now?"

Dave did not immediately respond but thought for a moment before answering. "No," he said, "the second bullet you put in the magazine is still in the gun. It automatically chambered when you ejected the first round. Now it's in there waiting to be fired even though you removed the magazine."

"Good boy," the Mayor said while ejecting the second round, which Dave also caught in the air, this time using his left hand.

The Mayor looked at him quizzically. "You're even quicker with your left hand," he said. "You a lefty?"

Dave grinned. "Actually, I'm ambidextrous. I don't favor one side over the other. I can even write with my left hand, and I swing a baseball bat left-handed too."

"Impressive," the Mayor said before explaining the proper way to hold a gun using a grip no tighter than a firm handshake and how he should *press* the trigger to eliminate movement and flinching whenever firing it. He recommended a two-handed grip that he demonstrated, and he told Dave to forget about trying to hit anything beyond ten yards. "The closer, the better," he said,"especially with such a small, lightweight gun."

"Keep in mind," the Mayor warned, "that the slightest flinch can move the barrel one degree left or right, causing you to miss your target by six inches at a distance of ten yards, and you'll be lucky if the gun moves just one degree. You need to be smooth, solid, and steady if you want to hit your target. Ya' know what I mean?" He then handed the gun back to Dave and patted him on the shoulder. "Buddy, you're probably one of the smoothest, steadiest guys I know, and that's why I'm doing this for you. Ya' know what I mean?"

Dave smiled. "Yeah, I know what you mean. Thanks, and thanks for not asking too many questions. This is my problem, and I'm trying not to drag anyone else into it."

"No worries," the Mayor said with a reassuring smile as he handed him the holster and a small box of shells. "This is an Elite pocket holster that hides the shape of the gun in your pocket. These shells are for target shooting, but you should get yourself some hollow points. Unfortunately, you'll need to drive down to Avon or up to Elizabeth City to get them. Just tell them you want something for self-defense, and they'll take care of you." He grinned at Dave and turned slightly as if he were about to leave but then hesitated. "Oh, one other thing," he said. "That gun might be small, but it's loud. If you shoot it indoors, it's going to have your ears ringing. Ya' know what I mean?"

As Dave nodded, the Mayor climbed out of the hearse, but he did not immediately walk away. Instead, he closed the door and leaned in through the open window, gazing intently at his young friend for several seconds without uttering a word. Dave found the silence disturbing, but he did not know what to say, so he averted his eyes from the Mayor's piercing stare and redirected his gaze to the weathered tattoo on his friend's upper arm, an inscription that spelled out *U-S-M-C*.

"You know, Buddy," the Mayor said eventually, "I've been through a lot of battles in my life, some easy and some—well—some not so easy. I'll share with you something I learned along the way. When faced with overwhelming odds, you sometimes have to retreat for a moment, if only to get your bearings. That's the mark of a warrior. It's usually during those moments of solitude and reflection that the survival instinct really kicks in—along with the fight-or-flight response." He stopped speaking and took a step back from the hearse while continuing to rest his hands on the doorframe. The etched lines of his face deepened and hardened as he said, "Sometimes there's nothing wrong with running away. In fact, it's often prudent to do so. Live to fight another day and all

289

that. Ya' know what I mean?"

With a doleful expression, Dave asked, "But what if there's nowhere to run to? What if all you have is here and now?"

"Then you fight," the Mayor said frankly while grabbing his tackle box off the seat and tapping the roof of the hearse. He then began walking toward the pier but stopped after just a few steps. Craning his neck to look over his shoulder, he spoke firmly and deliberately in Dave's direction. "You fight like it's your last battle on earth. There is an overwhelming power in a man making his last stand. Learn to use it, and you just might win."

As Dave watched the receding figure of the Mayor walk the length of the parking lot to the pier house, he reflected on what the older, more seasoned warrior had said. He wondered where he could find that power to which the Mayor had alluded. It was not something he had previously encountered in his life, a simple life of self-preservation sustained wholly by self-serving actions. If anything, his life up until that point had been utterly devoid of power. Perhaps, he thought, he needed to look elsewhere for it—outside of himself—possibly in someone else, in someone he valued more than himself. That, he decided, was where he would search for the elusive quality, but he would first have to return to work and complete his home inspection duties before beginning the quest.

As expected, Dave completed his work by early afternoon, shortly before three o'clock, so he immediately journeyed south to purchase some self-defense ammo. His real quest, however, involved finding that intangible power referenced by the Mayor, something he thought he may already have discovered in the form of a semi-automatic Ruger tucked snugly in the side pocket of his shorts. Feeling the weapon press solidly against his leg, he contemplated the notion the entire way to the sporting goods store in Avon.

Returning up the highway a little before five o'clock, he smiled placidly as he stared down at a small paper bag sitting on the seat beside him, his expression indicating complete satisfaction with having purchased a box of Zombie Max shells, a product of the Hornady Manufacturing Company. Clearly meeting the definition of self-defense ammo, the bullets had special hollow points filled with a green plastic material intended to hasten their expansion upon impact. This accelerated expansion made them far more destructive than regular hollow points, and they caught his eye the minute he spotted the name of the shells along with the macabre pictures of the walking dead featured on the outside of the box. Then, upon reading the tongue-in-cheek instructions for spotting and killing a zombie, he knew he had to have them. If anyone needed ammunition that could kill a zombie, it was he.

With the gun in his pocket and the box of Zombie shells on the seat beside him, a mollifying, almost soothing feeling of security returned, and he told himself that he had indeed found that elusive power. For the first time in two days, he felt his jaw unclench and his neck muscles relax until a tiny sound robbed him of his serenity, reigniting all the doubts and fears of the past few days. In the silence of the hearse, he recognized the chime of his cell phone announcing the receipt of a text message. Without pulling over to the roadside, he awkwardly reached into his pocket for the phone and glanced down at the message. It was from Nikki, and it read: *Back home. On my way to Mass and dinner with friends. See you at Kelly's - 10 pm.*

Without responding to the text message, he dropped the phone onto the seat and continued driving north, quickly approaching the Herbert C. Bonner Bridge over the Oregon Inlet. Nikki's return to Nags Head and her plans to venture out that night both frightened and angered him because he had no way of explaining to her the danger she faced, at least not in a way she would accept or understand. Likewise, he had no way of explaining it to the police. Hell, he could not even explain it to himself, let alone anyone else, and he would not even try. Doing so would only make him sound insane, just as Mark said it would.

Reaching down, he sought reassurance from the lump of cold metal in the side pocket of his shorts, but it seemed to have lost its power—he had lost the power. Once again, he experienced feelings of hopelessness that overwhelmed him as he pondered what awaited him that night, recognizing his vulnerability and weakness in the face of the threat bearing down on him. In that respect, he was very much like the inhabitants of the region, exposed and powerless against the destructive force of Hurricane Kim churning just beyond the horizon.

Wheeling the old hearse onto the bridge, he then spotted the Bodie Island Lighthouse rising solemnly in the distance, the sight of which triggered another emotional response, one he deliberately tried to suppress along with what had sparked it, the memory of Laura resting in the sand across from the lighthouse. To distract himself from the feelings of guilt associated with the buried girl, he, instead, concentrated on two noble towers of light and virtue: one of granite, brick, and iron, providing guidance and direction to desperate men along a treacherous stretch of coastline; and one of flesh and blood, offering love and support to an anxious man drowning in his own self-doubt.

"I wish he'd stop looking at us," Patty moaned, her grimace reflecting her annoyance with the man sitting along the railing by the dance floor.

"He's not looking at us," Maria said. "He's looking at Nikki."

The girls sat at a large table two rows back from the hardwood dance floor listening to a rock band on an elevated stage wail out its opening song to the syncopated flashes of colored strobe lights swirling throughout Kelly's Tavern. Sitting at a small table between the girls and the empty dance floor was a bald man with a goatee wearing camouflage cargo shorts and a black tee shirt. He was alone at the table except for two open bottles of Budweiser. With his back to the band, he sat facing the girls, squinting in their direction with his eyes almost closed and a grotesque grin on his face that was accentuated by the crinkling of his nose and the puckering of his lips as he nodded his head in time to the music, clapping his hands to the driving beat of the bass drum while stomping the sole of his biker boot on the floor.

"He's giving me the creeps," Patty said, elevating her squeaky voice over the music, hoping her words would reach the ears of the annoying man.

Jan raised her hand. "Wait a minute," she said, "I think he's blind."

"Blind?" Maria asked skeptically.

"Yeah, look at his eyes. They're nothing but slits. I don't think he can see. He's not actually staring at us."

Nikki cast a dubious glance at the man and then shook her head. "He's not blind," she said to her friends.

"And how do you know that?" Jan asked defensively.

"Because—" Nikki said with raised eyebrows and a nod of her head toward the man. "Because he's wearing a watch, dummy."

Jan tilted her body and craned her neck to get a better look at the guy's wrist moving back and forth in time with the music. "Maybe it's a disguise," she said with a giggle, her low raspy snicker causing the rest of them to start laughing.

Patty added with a smile, "I liked it better when we thought he was blind."

Before going to dinner that evening, the girls had attended the five-thirty Mass at Holy Trinity by the Sea Chapel so they could stay out late and not have to get up early on Sunday morning. As was always the case, Patty wore her usual beach attire while Jan and Maria were dressed to kill for their big night out sporting high heels, tight slacks, revealing tops, and lots of jewelry and cologne. Nikki, however, was dressed more conservatively, wearing a white cotton top, wedge sandals, and the same lime-green linen pants she had worn at their last get-together at Mulligan's on the night she had met Dave.

Having eaten in Kelly's dining room with Jan's brother and the rest of the band members, the girls and the musicians then moved into the bar where they enjoyed a few rounds of drinks before the band took the stage. Nikki's friends had hoped to involve her with Jan's brother, but they scrapped their plan upon learning that she had invited Dave to join them later that evening. Maria and Patty were excited about meeting Dave, but Jan was a little disappointed because she had hoped Nikki and her brother would hit it off. Her brother also shared his sister's sentiments, continually staring at Nikki from across the table at dinner and then from his spot on the stage. Polite as always, Nikki graciously acknowledged his advances and gently deflected them because she had already set her sights on other game. Positioning herself with a clear view of the bar entrance, she kept a sharp eye on the doorway, impatiently awaiting Dave's arrival.

Despite the threat of the hurricane, the barroom had filled up quickly with people coming out in droves to hear the band fresh in from Norfolk. Having performed at Kelly's before, the musicians had a good reputation in the area, one bolstered by Jan and her public relations blitz, so they knew the type of music the crowd wanted to hear. Mike Kelly, the owner of the restaurant, had given them the opportunity to cancel their contract because of the threatening weather, but they decided to keep the engagement because they needed the money. With so many predictions about when the storm would make landfall, they chose to believe the one forecasting a delay of another day; however, they had wisely left their tour bus idling in the parking lot so it would be ready to jettison them north the minute they finished their gig. As such, they did not waste any time getting on stage, starting ten minutes early, much to the chagrin of Jan's brother who had hoped to spend more time with Nikki. Because it was their first number that evening, no one had yet stepped onto the dance floor, but Nikki expected her friends to drag her out there the minute the band sounded the initial beat of their second song.

Striking the last chord on his guitar, Jan's brother brushed back the locks of his sandy-colored hair in an attempt to catch Nikki's eye, but the only thing she saw was the sudden illumination of her Android smartphone lying on the table beside her wine glass. Picking it up, she spotted the notification of a text message but hesitated before reading it, fearing that it might be Dave telling her would be delayed or unable to make it.

"What is it?" Patty asked. "Is it from *him*?" Giggling as she said it, she peered around the table at the other girls.

Nikki did not respond to her question but instead opened the text communication and began silently reading it without noticing who had sent it. Confused by the very first sentence, she stopped reading and scrolled up to determine the identity of the author, a discovery that greatly upset her. Everyone at the table noticed her reaction but said nothing as they watched her continue reading with a stern, somber expression that gradually softened into a look of puzzlement and concern. By the time she had finished reading the text, there was not a trace of anger left anywhere in her demeanor. Her friends, having observed her every move, noticed the transformation.

"What is it?" Maria demanded to know.

Nikki looked up in astonishment. "It's from Mark."

"No, no," Maria said. "Delete it immediately!"

"That's right," Patty added. "Delete it right now."

But Nikki had no intention of erasing the message. In fact, she was already tapping out a reply with her fingernails.

"For God's sake, don't respond to it," Jan pleaded. At that moment, the band began playing its signature song, a musical arrangement performed much louder than their first number, making conversation considerably more difficult.

Nikki began pushing herself back from the table, but Maria caught her arm. "Where are you going?" she screamed over the blare of the music.

"Mark needs my help," Nikki replied brusquely, clearly annoyed with Maria's efforts to thwart her departure.

"What do you mean?" Maria asked without relinquishing her grip.

Just then, Jan reached over and seized Nikki's other forearm. "You're not going anywhere until you explain yourself."

With a wild look in her eyes, Nikki glared defiantly at her three friends who stared back at her sternly. "Okay," she said in a slightly calmer tone. "Mark sent me a text saying that he's disoriented and confused and that he needs my help."

"What?" Jan was beside herself.

"Yeah, he said he just woke up in the parking lot of the Bodie Island Lighthouse and doesn't remember anything from the past week. His car won't start, he's dizzy, and he has a large bump on his head."

"Bullshit!" cried Maria. "What did you text back to him?"

"I told him I'm on my way."

Patty tried to reason with her. "Nikki, this is crazy. Screw him."

"He needs my help!" she exclaimed loudly while rising to her feet and forcefully breaking free from both Maria and Jan. Jumping up, Maria tried to grab her, but Nikki was too fast and slipped away before anyone else could stop her. Partially blocked by the annoying clapping man, Maria could not follow her around the table and called out in desperation, "Nikki, don't go!" but Nikki had already disappeared into the crowd and was hastily exiting through the doorway. Disturbed and dazed, the girls found themselves paralyzed and unable to act as they stared at each other in disbelief while the squinting, bothersome man at the table next to them continued nodding and clapping in time with the raucous music.

Unbeknownst to Nikki, Dave was not more than fifteen feet away when she rushed through the lobby and out the front door. Running through the parking lot, she failed to notice his hearse sitting beside an antique red and white motorcycle where he had parked it only five minutes earlier before strolling into Kelly's and diverting to the men's room instead of proceeding straight into the bar. With the restroom door propped open, he had an unobstructed view of the lobby as he stood drying his hands while studying an Outer Banks navigational chart hanging on the wall. Had he turned his head even slightly, he would have caught the blur of a blonde girl with a ponytail dashing madly through the lobby toward the front entrance of the restaurant.

Stepping out of the restroom and into the lobby, Dave glanced around the dimly lit room and noticed a young boy sitting on a steamer trunk, his eyes fixed on a large ship model in an elevated display case behind a sofa. The sight of the boy's absorbed expression brought back memories of his own childhood passion for model building, mostly replicas of military ships, and it made him slightly homesick thinking about it. Just then, the boy's parents emerged from the dining room and led the youngster away, but Dave remained near the display case, comparing the workmanship of the large model to what he remembered of his own awkward attempts at shipbuilding. Suddenly, he recalled bumping into the model sailboat while skulking through Mark's house, and the unpleasant memory made him turn and proceed straight toward the double doors of the bar where two bouncers sat with flashlights checking age identifications and collecting money for the cover charge.

Occupying wooden stools on opposite sides of the door, the bouncers wore identical red polo shirts but shared no other similarities. The one on the right was a few inches shorter than Dave, but the man on the left was massive in height and breadth, bald with no neck except for several folds of skin bulging at the base of his skull. His size and scowling expression made it highly unlikely anyone would consider tangling with him. Dave, however, confronted him brazenly with a feigned look of arrogant defiance while the man sat counting loose dollar bills in a cigar box on his lap. Raising his head to see who had approached him, the big man's face widened, causing the corners of his mouth to curl into an enormous grin while his eyes disappeared into the chasm of his swelling cheeks and forehead. "Buddy, good to see you," he said cheerfully, his soft voice a total contradiction of his outward persona. "You-know-who is already inside." While speaking, he nodded his round head in the direction of the bar.

"Yeah, I saw his bike outside," Dave said to the smiling bouncer. He knew the big man well, and he knew him to be as gentle as a kitten with a heart of gold despite his size and intimidating appearance. Reaching into his pocket, Dave grabbed some money for the cover charge until he saw his friend wag his head and motion him through the doorway with a wave of his hand. With that, he returned the bills to his pocket and glanced at the other bouncer, a smaller, leaner man, muscular but not quite as thin as Dave. Of the two bouncers, Dave knew that he was the one to be feared. He had seen him put down two linemen from the University of North Carolina's football team earlier that summer when the players had caused a commotion in the bar. The smaller bouncer said nothing to Dave, returning his friendly gaze with a challenging glare, one that caused his larger colleague to roll his eyes. Not accepting the visual challenge, Dave merely smiled at the aggressive bouncer and gave a subtle wink to his oversized partner before walking into the noisy barroom where a crowd of people stood milling around just inside the doorway.

Advancing only a step or two past the threshold, Dave stopped and looked around the room, but the lighting was too dim for him to recognize anyone in the place. He then slid away from the doorway, moving next to the popcorn machine, where he stood calmly in the shadows for a few seconds, allowing his eyes time to adjust to the darkness while listening to the electrified music that had lured many people onto the dance floor. Standing like a chess piece on the checkerboard flooring, he remained quiet and motionless, searching the faces of the people in the crowd, their features revealed only in flashes of colored strobe lights swirling and bouncing around the room.

Once his vision had fully adjusted to the interior dimness, his eyes caught the sweeping motion of a man's hand waving at him from a table near the dance floor. Moving at once toward the beckoning signal, he stopped abruptly when a dark-haired woman paused directly in front of him, openly studying his face before running her eyes up and down his body. She was an attractive, Latin-looking girl whom he had never seen before. The only thing he knew about her was that she did not attempt to hide any of her physical assets.

"Are you Nikki's Dave?" she asked.

The phrasing of her question amused him, and he responded with a smile. "Yeah, that would be me," he said. "Where is she?"

The girl's expression instantly changed, and he could sense that something was wrong. After a moment's hesitation, she blurted out, "She left to meet her old boyfriend." Allowing no time for a response, she quickly added, "We tried to stop her. Honestly, we did!"

An emotion he had never experienced before seized his mind, body, and soul. He could not even name it—horror, fright, terror. He grabbed Maria by her upper arm and screamed, "When?" His voice was loud and pleading.

"I don't know," she said. "Three, four, maybe five minutes ago."

Letting go of her arm, he bolted for the door but stopped after several steps and called back, "Where?"

"The Bodie Island Lighthouse," Maria yelled to him over the music as he vanished into the crowd while the Mayor continued waving at him from a table near the dance floor.

Dave rushed into the lobby and then bolted from the restaurant, exiting through a door containing a stained-glass depiction of a sailfish leaping high into the air. Mimicking the spring of the sailfish, Dave leaped over the brick steps onto the sidewalk where he charged toward his hearse, sprinting past a taxicab and an idling tour bus, puffing hard as he ran because of the heat and humidity trapped below a thick canopy of clouds. The dense overcast also blocked the light of the full moon, leaving the parking lot lurid and dark despite a scattering of light coming from several tall lampposts. An eerie silence also pervaded the night, adding to Dave's uneasiness as well as his perceived sense of doom.

Before climbing into the old Cadillac, he first opened the rear compartment and began rummaging around in a wooden box filled with small pieces of windsurfing equipment and other loose items. Finding what he wanted, he jumped into the hearse and threw the object onto the seat beside him before motoring through the parking lot and turning onto the bypass where he sped off in a southerly direction. He had a lot of time to make up if he hoped to catch Nikki before she got to the lighthouse. She would make it there in fifteen to twenty minutes driving in her usually cautious fashion, so he knew he would have to drive like a maniac if he wished to catch her.

Weaving from lane to lane while cursing at all the timid drivers on the highway that night, he made excellent time but found it surprising how many others were out driving around, especially with the threat of a hurricane looming. It was not until he saw the number of cars in the Food Lion parking lot that he understood the reason for the traffic congestion; everyone was out stocking up on supplies before the arrival of the storm. It had not yet begun raining, but the wind was gusting forcefully, buffeting the side of his hearse, especially when he crossed Whalebone Junction and sped down North Carolina Route 12 into the Cape Hatteras National Seashore. Fortunately, he managed to catch all the green lights at Whalebone Junction and got onto the southern highway without having to stop even once.

Continuing his high-speed trek down the darkened road, he no longer had to contend with the delays caused by other drivers, most of whom had diverted to Roanoke Island instead of heading south into the national seashore. All that surrounded him now was a veil of darkness that obscured everything in his field of vision except for the lighted pavement before him and brief glimpses of the distant lights coming from the houses along the beach road extension paralleling his southern route. On either side of the highway were growths of maritime thicket composed of American beachgrass, yaupon, and bayberry bushes that blocked his view of almost everything except the painted lines and yellow reflectors in the center of the highway. Fixing his eyes on the leading edge of his headlight beam, he watched in anticipation of the intersection with the beach road extension because he knew the lighthouse to be just beyond that point.

The panic that had seized him upon learning of Nikki's rendezvous with Mark subsided somewhat as he soared down the coastal highway. He then experienced an emotional metamorphosis, one that transformed his debilitating fear into something different, something more focused and useful. Instead of a wild, emotional reaction to circumstances beyond his control, he became more logical and rational in the way he attacked the problem, addressing it in a thoughtful, measured way, an approach that significantly increased his chances of success and survival. He also sensed a spark of anger flaring up inside of him, one he would need to fan into a bonfire if he wished to burn away the remaining vestiges of raw fear still lingering beneath the surface. Struggling to overcome and suppress his doubts, he remembered something the Mayor had told him one night while they sat around drinking together. It had to do with the Mayor's experience in battle as a young Marine. "You have to learn to overcome your fear," he said, "It takes but a split second—quicker than the blink of an eye or a conscious thought—to switch from defense to offense." Recalling those words, Dave finally understood the message the Mayor had tried to convey.

Searching for Nikki's tail lamps in the darkness ahead, he detected only emptiness beyond the leading edge of his high beams. The Bodie Island Lighthouse was not yet visible, still obscured by the terrain and vegetation growing along the highway, but he could see a radio tower in the distance, its flashing red lights piercing the night with unbroken regularity. Synchronizing his breathing with the rhythm of the tower flashes, he jammed his foot harder onto the accelerator, increasing his speed beyond that which was reasonable or safe for the old Cadillac. Surely—he thought to himself—he should have caught up with her by now or, at least, have spotted her taillights in the distance. However, the only thing visible beyond the windshield of the hearse was a small patch of lighted pavement enshrouded by darkness.

Upon seeing the Nags Head water tower up ahead, his heart rate spiked, racing even faster than the engine of the hearse, because he knew he had only three to four more miles to go. That was when he first glimpsed the lighthouse peeking over the top of the dunes, its first order Fresnel lens projecting a penetrating beam that jolted his senses, filling him with hope as well as despair. He was so close to his destination, and yet he had not overtaken Nikki. Having witnessed firsthand the ruthlessness of Mark and the speed at which he could kill, Dave knew he must get there in time to prevent any harm from befalling her. With that in mind, he again depressed the gas pedal, this time slamming it all the way to the floor, evoking a massive roar from under the hood that propelled him past the intersection with the beach road extension. Peering ahead into the darkness, he saw the lighthouse becoming larger and brighter the farther he traveled down the highway, and he sensed that it was calling to him, crying out on a personal level, beckoning him to rescue the other bright light of his life.

The Bodie Island Lighthouse sat about a thousand yards back from the highway down a winding road through a grove of Loblolly pines. Careening off the highway onto an access road, Dave glanced at two wooden structures sitting near the intersection, houses owned by the National Park Service built in the traditional coastal style of architecture. He was aware that one of them housed law enforcement, but he did not know which one it was. Seeing both buildings completely dark and no vehicles anywhere in the parking lots, he sped past them and plunged down the darkened road at breakneck speed, still hoping to get there in time.

The approach to the lighthouse through the pine grove was long and dark, but Dave maintained a constant speed along the serpentine route without flying off the road or crashing into any of the tree trunks. Emerging into a clearing surrounded by other tall pines and reeds of *Phragmites* swaying in the gusty breeze, he slowed down only when he saw the dim outline of the massive beacon rising one hundred and sixty-five feet into the air behind a visitor's center located about one hundred feet in front of it. At the end of the parking lot, he noticed a few outbuildings, but he was unable to distinguish anything else other than the glowing porch lights of the buildings and one exceptionally bright light flashing twice every thirty seconds in the murky sky above him.

Inside the clearing, he followed the wide, sweeping course of the road as curved around the grounds to the visitor's center, a two-story structure that had once served as living quarters for the lighthouse keeper and his family. Straining his eyes to see through the inky blackness of the night, he thought he could detect the outline of a sport utility vehicle sitting in the parking lot, but he was still too far away to know for sure. It was not until he steered the hearse around the bend and flooded the area with his headlights that he conclusively identified a white Jeep Patriot parked near the visitor's center. Additionally, he saw Nikki standing by the rear bumper of the vehicle, preparing to walk across the parking lot to a gray Infiniti backed into a parking space on the opposite side of the lot.

Instinctively, Dave slammed his hand onto the center portion of his steering wheel, triggering a continuous blast of his horn that stopped Nikki dead in her tracks. Aiming the hearse like a missile, he guided it through the parking lot and halted within ten feet of Nikki, using his headlights to cast a protective barrier across her path. He then turned off the motor but not the headlamps as he grabbed something off the seat and stepped onto the asphalt while peering at the scowling face of Mark, who stood beside the driver's side of his car just outside the spray of Dave's headlights. Locking his eyes onto his opponent, Dave never once glanced over at Nikki, leaving him totally unaware of her shocked expression that quickly morphed into a disapproving glare.

Taking note of where Mark stood, Dave surmised that he had been waiting beside his car for Nikki to cross over to him, something Dave's arrival had thwarted in dramatic fashion. Seeing Nikki and Mark face each other across the impenetrable barrier of his headlight beam, Dave offered a silent prayer of thanksgiving that he had arrived in time. The tragedy that would have resulted had he been delayed even a second longer was too disturbing to ponder, so he shoved aside the upsetting thought knowing that he had no time for such ruminations.

Upon observing Dave step onto the pavement behind the open door of the hearse, Mark walked to the front of his own car in a brazen attempt to move closer to his weaker challenger. Sliding past the front bumper of the Infiniti, he continued skulking through the darkness, jockeying for a better position from which to strike. Despite their close proximity, Dave did not appear frightened. If anything, he looked angry, and he could feel the emotion boiling up inside of him, making him wonder if he could even restrain it. Knowing that Nikki was safe, at least for the time being, he allowed his confidence to soar as he freely nurtured the internal fury while attempting to use it to his advantage. Noticing that Mark was not wearing his sunglasses, he permitted a taunt smile to spread slowly across his face as a surge of bravado buoyed his conviction, making him even more confident in his ability to triumph.

Stepping out from behind the door of the hearse, Dave fully exposed himself to his adversary. Alone and unprotected outside of the vehicle, he appeared vulnerable except for something gripped tightly in his left hand, a dull black object he carefully shielded behind his thigh. Mark slowed his advance in response to the provocative move, coming to a complete stop when his keen vision spotted the unidentified object in Dave's hand. The light spilling into the night from the interior of the hearse painted the side of Dave's slender body as he stood firm and silent like a sheriff at sundown. Besides highlighting the hidden object in his left hand, the dim light also revealed a thick bulge in the side pocket of his cargo shorts. The manner in which Dave's right hand hovered near the pocket gave Mark some pause.

"David!" Nikki cried out.

"Yes," he said in a surprisingly calm tone, speaking confidently without taking his eyes off Mark for even a second.

"David, he's hurt."

"No, not yet he isn't."

Dave intended his remark as a taunt to his larger rival, and that is precisely the way Mark took it. With an ego larger than his biceps, the serial killer was wholly intolerant of mockery, seeing it as a challenge to his power and virility, so he reacted instinctively by lunging out with a predatory ferocity, feeling confident that the smaller man was no match for him. Dave, for his part, remained cool and collected—at least on the outside—with a demeanor that did not betray the emotional battle raging within him.

The split-second after Mark initiated his attack, everything in Dave's world slowed down. Calming his emotions, he melded with the environment around him, sensing the inherent quietness of the remote location while becoming conscious of the powerful ocean gusts passing over the trees and swirling in the open space of the lighthouse grounds. His mind then drifted back to his boyhood, to something he had once read in a western book about gunslingers. It involved the story of Wyatt Earp and his advice for surviving a gunfight—about keeping your head, remaining calm, and taking adequate time to aim and shoot. The old gambler and lawman always counted on his opponents being overly anxious and nervous, thereby negating their ability to shoot straight even if they shot first. With that in mind, Dave smoothly and methodically dipped his right hand into the side pocket of his shorts while simultaneously raising his left hand to expose a hand-held rechargeable spotlight that he pointed in the direction of his opponent. Engaging the trigger of the thirty-five-watt Xenon 4300 Kelvin High-Density Discharge Bulb, he emitted four thousand lumens of intense white light in a narrow focused beam straight into the dilated pupils of his attacker's eyes. The pure white light was painfully intense and extremely debilitating to the big man, causing him to raise his arms defensively as he stepped backward and collapsed against the passenger door of his car.

"David, no!" Nikki cried out while Dave continued his unrelenting assault against his stunned assailant.

Resembling an escaped convict caught in a prison search beam, Mark writhed in pain alongside his vehicle, flailing his arms at the debilitating light while Dave took several steps in his direction, hoping to increase the intensity and discomfort of the light by moving even closer. Rather than trying to escape by running around to the other side of the car, Mark jerked opened the passenger door and used his massive arm to sweep everything off the seat, sending loose items flying into the air and tumbling onto the asphalt. Noisily, a folding shovel clamored onto the pavement followed by sheets plastic drop cloth that instantly began flapping in the strong breeze. Mark's cell phone also flew out into the night, skidding across the pavement into the darkness, but he did not seem to care as he dove into the car and squeezed himself over the console where he quickly started the engine and raced out of the parking lot.

Watching the red taillights of the Infiniti disappear into the pine grove, Dave detected some motion out of the corner of his eye and turned to see Nikki getting into her car. "No!" he screamed while running across the parking lot toward her Jeep, arriving just in time to prevent her from closing the door. "Nikki, don't follow him!"

"Leave me alone!" she said. "He's hurt, and he needs my help." Starting the engine, she tried to close the door, but Dave refused to move out of the way.

"No," he said. "Let me explain." He understood her frustration, but he was not about to let her chase Mark down the highway. Staring down at the side of her face, seeing her profile illuminated by the overhead courtesy lights, he struggled with how to begin his explanation but then noticed a sudden change in her demeanor.

Nikki placed her hands on either side of the steering wheel and slowly closed her eyes in an attempt to collect her thoughts, becoming as still and quiet as a summer evening. She then meditated for several seconds before releasing her grip on the wheel and shutting off the motor. In almost a whisper, she said, "Okay," as she pivoted her body and began climbing out of the car.

Thankful that she had acceded to his wishes, Dave breathed a sigh of relief and moved back a few steps, allowing her room to exit the vehicle, only to be shocked when she unexpectedly leaped back into the Jeep and locked the doors. Angry and dismayed at her deception, all he could do was glare silently at her through the closed window until she started the engine and began reversing out of the parking space. Desperate to make her stop, he screamed and pounded on the glass, but she refused to slow down or even look in his direction, purposefully ignoring his pleas and his bizarre explanations. Reaching the middle of the parking lot, she then shifted the Jeep into drive and defiantly sped off into the night.

"Damn!" he screamed at the top of his lungs before running

back to the hearse where he paused a second to shine the spotlight on the items that had fallen out of Mark's Infiniti. The sight of the shovel and the plastic drop cloth increased his level of alarm, bringing into clear focus the ultimate fate of Nikki if he could not stop her from reconnecting with Mark. Turning toward Coquina Beach where the body of Laura lay in a makeshift grave, he realized just how lucky Nikki had been that night—at least so far. Wondering if she might have a guardian angel watching over her, he raised his eyes toward the heavens in search of the celestial being but saw only the luminous prism of the Bodie Island Lighthouse illuminating his soul with its saving light.

With no time to think about much else, Dave jumped into the hearse and turned the key, becoming distressed and panicked when he heard the low, painful moan of the starter motor struggling to complete several revolutions—slow, halting turns that proved insufficient to start the internal combustion engine. "No, not now," he cried as he extinguished the headlights and made a second attempt to start the hearse. With the electrical load reduced, the starter motor began spinning faster, increasing its speed with each revolution until the old Cadillac engine finally roared to life. Greatly relieved but still concerned about the power reserve in the battery, Dave revved the motor several times before switching on the lights and barreling out of the parking lot in hot pursuit of Nikki.

The time interval between the departures of Mark and Nikki had him feeling confident that the two of them would not encounter each other on the highway. He was more concerned with what might happen once Nikki arrived at Mark's house because that is where he expected her to go. No matter what—he told himself—he would be there to protect her from harm. While committing himself to that pledge, he spotted her taillights on the road ahead of him. No more than glowing red specks on the dark fabric of night, they were enough to ease his mind and boost his confidence in the knowledge that she was safely within view. Cutting his speed in half, he then traveled just fast enough to keep her in sight without getting too close.

Proceeding down the road at a moderate pace, Nikki tried to call Mark on his cell phone, but she was only able to reach his voicemail. Leaving him a brief message that said she was heading to his house, she then texted him a similar note, hoping that he might see it while driving in his car. She also called his landline, but his recorded vacation announcement was still active with no option for leaving a message. Upset and frustrated, she put down the phone and continued down the highway in silence, fighting the intermittent wind gusts by tightening her grip on the steering wheel while dodging the debris blowing past her headlights.

Amid the inner stillness of the Jeep, she tried not to think about Dave, but he crept into her thoughts nonetheless. Angrily, she redoubled her efforts to purge him from her mind, but it was all for naught. If anything, her futile attempts to dismiss him made her think about him even more. Why had he acted that way?—she wondered. Moreover, what was he shouting at her through the window, nonsense about bodies or murder or something? He was obviously unhinged, and she had been foolish to involve herself with him. What was she thinking? She wasn't thinking. That was the problem.

Dave's actions that night may have annoyed her, but things related to Mark also bothered her, oddities not easily explained. For starters, she had gone to pick him up at the lighthouse because of his claim that his car was not running, and yet he had no problem driving away after his confrontation with Dave. There was also the matter of his face. She had only glimpsed it briefly when Dave's headlights had swept the parking lot, but there were anomalies in his features, especially the appearance of his eyes and the location of the scar over his eyebrow that seemed to be on the wrong side of his forehead. None of it made any sense, and the more she thought about it, the more confused she became.

While mentally reconstructing the events leading up to her pursuit of Mark down the highway, she heard the musical jingle of her cell phone announcing an incoming call. All doubt and second-guessing vanished the moment the upbeat music sounded in her ears. Expecting the call to be from Mark, she eagerly grabbed the smartphone but then violently tossed it aside when she saw Dave's name displayed on the screen. Less than a minute later, she heard it ring a second time followed by a third, fourth, and fifth time. Then, after the fifth and final unanswered call, she heard nothing but welcomed silence until the phone emitted a different type of tone, this one indicating the receipt of a text message. Extending her arm to the phone, she angrily deleted the unread message and pledged to erase all current and future messages from David Rasputin without reading or listening to any of them.

The whole way to Nags Head, Nikki never caught sight of Mark's Infiniti, but that did not bother her because she was convinced that their destinations were the same, his house in The Village at Nags Head. For over a week, she had awaited this moment, a chance to have all her questions answered, and she was not about to let this opportunity pass her by. With that in mind, she drove up the bypass and entered the residential development where she observed Mark's house looming dark and desolate in the night, his car absent from the driveway and everything appearing abandoned and forsaken, much like an empty tomb. It struck her as odd that he had failed to return home because she could not imagine him going anywhere else, especially after their bizarre encounter at the lighthouse. However, she had no desire to drive around the Outer Banks searching for him, so she decided to remain and await his return, preferably inside the house where she would be much more comfortable. "He has to come back sooner or later," she declared as she pulled into the driveway.

Rotating the key to turn off the engine, she instantly remembered having given Mark's house key to Dave earlier in the week, and the disturbing memory sparked an angry response in her, revealing her deep contempt for Dave at that moment. "Damn that Dave Rasputin," she growled through clenched teeth while dropping her head in disgust.

Frustrated, yet undeterred by her inability to enter the house, she resolved to wait outside because she was not about to miss this chance to learn the truth, whatever that truth might be. Good or bad—she told herself—she needed to hear it directly from Mark because she could not go on living with the questions of the past week gnawing at her insides. Even if it meant waiting there all night, she was going to get the answers—the finality—she sought and desperately needed. Reclining the car seat to a more restful angle, she then grabbed her cell phone and began deleting with a subtle sense of satisfaction all the unheard and unread messages left by Dave within the last half hour.

Dispatching each text and voice message from her cell phone, Nikki may have thought she was digitally eliminating Dave from her life, but that was not the case because, in another part of the residential complex, not more than twenty yards away, a black hearse sat in the driveway of a vacant home with a direct line-of-sight to her Jeep. Her former sleuth, once again in surveillance mode, had assumed the role of a silent guardian, protecting what he found most precious in life. At one point, he realized that Nikki remained in her car because she could not get into Mark's house without a key, something he now carried in his pocket. That realization caused him to chuckle slightly despite the fact that he knew it was no laughing matter.

It had become apparent to him that Mark was not coming home, that he most likely had sought shelter in his boat in Manteo, and that speculation provided some emotional relief, but it also sparked some fear that Nikki might figure it out and go looking for him. She knew about the sailboat, but she did not know the name of the boat or where it was docked along the waterfront. Still, it was conceivable that she could drive over there and begin knocking on the hatches of all the watercraft until she found the right one. In the defiant, agitated state he had last seen her, there was no telling what she would do.

Despite her anxious and troubled mood, Nikki did nothing that extreme only because the idea never occurred to her. In fact, she mellowed out rather quickly, drifting off to sleep shortly after arriving at the house. Dave, however, remained alert and vigilant, resolute in his role as Nikki's guardian angel, attentively standing watch over her while she slumbered peacefully throughout the night.

CHAPTER 13

The sun had already peeked above the eastern horizon that Sunday morning, but no one was aware of it because of the thick cloud cover shrouding the Outer Banks. Windy as well as gloomy, it would not be long before the first bands of rain began striking the region, announcing the arrival of Hurricane Kim and its expected landfall near Hatteras. Nikki continued sleeping on the reclined seat of her Jeep, her knees pulled to her chest and her body wedged between the door and the console in what should have been a most uncomfortable position but which seemed to cause her little distress. In stark contrast to the previous night, she appeared tranquil and serene, almost angelic, in her awkward pose until her cell phone began playing a familiar jingle that roused her from sleep.

Jumping at the sound of the music, she struggled to get her bearings while looking at the smartphone, trying to decide if she wanted to answer it or not. Recognizing the number on the display screen, she took the call from a fellow veterinarian who requested her assistance in Elizabeth City to help in the birthing of a foal. The other vet had visited the mare on a farm the previous day and was expecting problems because of the size and weight of the foal, the largest she had ever encountered. She knew that Nikki had extensive experience in these kinds of deliveries, so she called to ask for her help.

Nikki acceded to her colleague's request without hesitation, telling her that she would get there as quickly as possible, and she immediately began backing out of the driveway, glancing only briefly at Mark's house as she pulled onto the street. Already channeling her energy into fulfilling her professional commitment, she sped out of the development toward the intersection with the bypass while looking at the sky, wondering what she was doing heading to work on such a day when she should be hunkering down to await the approaching storm.

Dave, likewise, had dozed off during the night, although he remained upright in the driver's seat with his head wrenched uncomfortably against the partially open window. Stirred by an internal locution, he opened his eyes just in time to see Nikki's Jeep turning onto West Seachase Drive, a disturbing sight that jolted him into total consciousness. Speculating that she might be heading to Manteo in search of Mark's boat, he started the hearse and began following her, uncertain if he could do so without being seen. Concealment had been easy last night in the darkness, but it was now daylight—or as close to daylight as it was going to get—and she was bound to see him despite the overcast sky.

Creeping slowly down the lane, he delayed his turn until he saw Nikki's Jeep clear the intersection with the bypass. The fact that she had elected to go south toward Roanoke Island was not a good sign, so he spun his tires and lunged onto Seachase Drive, zooming toward the intersection while keeping Nikki's car in sight as it motored down the highway. Completing his turn onto the bypass just as the traffic signal changed from yellow to red, he positioned himself behind a commercial van large enough to conceal him. It was just blind luck that he had found something to hide behind because there were not many cars traveling south that morning. The bulk of the traffic was heading north as people scurried to get ahead of the hurricane. Although no mandatory evacuation order had been issued, authorities still had broadcast an advisory encouraging people to leave the Outer Banks. Despite their well-intentioned advice, Dave knew he would not be going anywhere as long as Nikki chose to stay.

He was able to follow her unnoticed all the way to Whalebone Junction where she turned onto the causeway toward Roanoke Island. Again, not a good sign. Her chosen route reinforced his fear that she was heading to the Manteo Waterfront, so he prayed for a miracle, hoping that Mark had sailed away last night and had not returned. Thinking back to their confrontation in Mulligan's restroom, he remembered Mark mentioning something about abandoning the Outer Banks to explore new hunting grounds.

Perhaps—he hoped—their encounter last night had prompted him to move up his date of departure. As he followed Nikki along the causeway, he wondered if a sincere desire for something to happen was enough to make it come true.

When Nikki's car crossed Roanoke Sound and started up the arch of the Washington Baum Bridge, Dave slowed down to increase his distance behind her, trying to lessen the likelihood that she would see him from the peak of the bridge. He then quickly increased his speed once he saw her start down the other side. Climbing to the top of the arch himself where he had an expansive view of the land and seascape below him, he witnessed something that set his mind at ease; instead of continuing to Manteo, Nikki had turned into Pirate's Cove at the end of the bridge. "Thank God," he said upon realizing that she was heading home rather than going in search of Mark.

At the bottom of the arch, Dave, likewise, pulled into Pirate's Cove, but he veered off into the parking lot behind the marina instead of driving past the guard station that would have taken him back to Nikki's condo. With a gusty wind blowing dirt and sand throughout the parking lot, he closed the windows and sat quietly in the hearse, thinking long and hard about what he should do next. He came up with only one idea—call Nikki. Perhaps, he thought, she had calmed down enough to talk.

Nikki, however, was anything but calm. Having made a commitment to her northern colleague, she knew that she had a job to do and quickly set about fulfilling her pledge. Always taking her occupational obligations seriously, more so than most other things in her life, she rarely allowed anything to interfere with her professional duties as she saw them. Upon entering the condominium, she walked straight into the bathroom where she showered in less than four minutes and dressed in a white collared shirt and a pair of jeans. Pulling her wet hair into a ponytail, she moved swiftly through her bedroom and then into the kitchen where she collected several items that she wanted to take with her. She briefly considered stopping at the Animal Hospital before heading north but then decided against it, concluding that the other vet would have all the necessary medical equipment.

Grabbing her car keys and cell phone from the kitchen counter, she moved toward the door, pausing briefly when she glanced down at the phone and saw that she had missed three calls while showering, all of them from Dave. Staring blankly at the screen of the smartphone as if pondering what to do, she then began quickly typing out a text message to him. It read: *Stop calling me. Going to Eliz*

City for vet emergency. Back this evening. Will call you then. Need time to think. N. Jamming the phone into her pocket, she then bolted out the front door.

"Need time to think?" she said aloud as she started the car. "Yeah, I need a lot more than that."

With everything that had happened, she did not know what to think or feel anymore. So much about the previous night still had her stumped, especially the lies told by Mark. Why had he lied about his car not running? Moreover, why had he lured her to the lighthouse? She would have gone to meet him anywhere on earth if he had just been truthful with her. There was no reason for dishonesty. Dave had never lied to her, at least as far as she knew, even if he had acted like a jerk last night. She then remembered his phone call to her last week in which he had pretended to be someone needing help with a pregnant cow. The thought of it made her smile, especially in light of where she was going and why she was going there. It was the first time in eight hours she had found anything even remotely amusing.

That moment of levity started her thinking in earnest about Dave and Mark, less individually and more in terms of a comparison between the two. They were so different, and yet she was attracted to both of them. How could that be? She also found herself musing over their odd behavior last night. Acts of irrationality seemed to be the hallmark of Dave, but she found Mark's actions utterly inexplicable. She had never known him to fear anything, and yet he responded like a frightened child when Dave shined the spotlight on him. Clearly, there was something wrong with him, which might explain his dishonesty, another thing that was so out of character for him. It was obvious that he needed her help. Shaking her head, she acknowledged that she understood none of it but, at least, she had the whole day to try to figure things out.

Dave was still sitting in the parking lot reading Nikki's text message when he spotted her driving out of Pirate's Cove. Waiting until she had made the turn onto the causeway toward Nags Head, he pulled out behind her and followed her across the Washington Baum Bridge, keeping her in sight all the way up the bypass. Once they reached the traffic light near The Village at Nags Head and he saw her continue northward toward Elizabeth City, he cut short his surveillance and crossed over to the beach road because he needed to get home to let Grave outside before the poor pooch had an accident inside the cottage.

While on the way, he received a phone call from the reality

company asking if he was planning to evacuate the Outer Banks. They had already relieved him of his inspection duties that day because of the approaching storm; however, they now wished him to perform some pre-hurricane checks of the rental properties if he planned to stay. It would only involve shutting off the water valves and unplugging the electronics as well as closing the storm shutters and securing the outside furniture. They estimated that he could finish by noon, which would still give him plenty of time to escape to the mainland if the weather took a turn for the worse.

It proved an easy decision because he knew he was not going anywhere. His anchor had become firmly set in the sands of the Outer Banks, and he had no plans to leave as long as Nikki chose to remain. With her safe and secure in Elizabeth City for the day, he agreed to help, but he first needed to return home and attend to the needs of his dog. While he was at the cottage, he showered and fixed himself some breakfast before heading to work.

Dave was just one of the many people the property management company had enlisted to perform the pre-hurricane checks, so only a few houses required his attention. By eleven o'clock, he had already arrived at his last inspection site, a home in the Whalebone Junction area. The house sat precariously close to the beach, exposing all its vulnerabilities to the approaching storm, and he wondered if the old structure could withstand the assault of the hurricane. He harbored a similar doubt about his own survivability as he stood on the back deck of the house watching the ocean churn under the black bunting of storm clouds while a light, misty rain pricked at his skin. Reaching out for a heavy wooden chair, the last remaining item on the deck, he hesitated a moment and then dropped his hand in a gesture of defeat, wondering why he should even bother taking the chair inside; it would be a miracle if the house or anything in it survived the storm surge. Isolated and alone out there on the edge of the beach, the doomed structure reminded him of his own untenable situation. He wondered if either of them would be there tomorrow and if anyone would even care.

Looking over the railing at the empty shoreline, he found it shocking how desolate it seemed and how little it resembled the beach on an average Sunday morning in August: no swimmers, no sunbathers, no joggers, no dogs chasing Frisbees. Even the seabirds had abandoned the beach ahead of the storm. The only familiar sight was that of four surfers enjoying the radical surf conditions in the ocean behind the house. Well insulated in their wetsuits, they seemed unfazed by the rain, having far too much fun to notice the inclement weather. He recognized them as the same guys who had been at Mulligan's on the night of the surf party when he had taken Nikki there.

One of them spotted him on the deck and motioned for him to join them in the water; however, he just smiled and waved back at him, wishing he could take him up on his invitation. At any other time, he would have been one of those insane surfers tempting fate in the roaring sea, but he had other pressing matters requiring his attention that day. One of those matters involved an appointment he had scheduled only a few minutes earlier on the phone. Having come to terms with his inability to deal with the moral challenges facing him, he had reached out to someone he thought could offer him sound advice. The meeting would not be until three o'clock, leaving him plenty of time to prepare; however, glancing toward the horizon, he wondered if he would be able to keep the appointment.

The rain, propelled by the wind, was still light and misty, but it did not seem to bother him as he sat on the arm of the splintered wooden chair watching the natural drama unfolding before him. Unlike many others, he did not fear the impending hurricane. After the frightening things he had observed recently, Hurricane Kim seemed rather tame by comparison. Staring down the beach, he saw a hurricane-warning signal in the form of two red flags flapping vigorously in the wind, one flag placed directly above the other, each with a large black square in its center. They flew from a flagpole on Jennette's Pier, a mammoth structure jutting out one thousand feet over the water, a much larger and longer pier than either the Nags Head Pier or the Outer Banks Pier. In addition to catering to the needs of the local fishermen, the pier served as a platform for three ten-kilowatt wind turbines set at intervals across its length. Operated by North Carolina Dominion Power, the turbines were perched high on ninety-foot metal towers, their blades slowed by a feathering of their tail sections to protect the rotors from the damaging winds.

Even from that distance, he could perceive the ferocity of the ocean under the pier where giant waves crashed against the concrete pilings, generating plumes of spray reaching nearly to the top of it. He knew the ultimate fate of anyone or anything trapped beneath the structure in the angry waters around those massive supports. His surfer friends behind the house were a safe distance away, but he spotted two more surfers, farther down the beach, who were getting much too close to the pier. Unable to identify them from that distance, he just shook his head in disbelief while watching them engage in their risky, foolhardy behavior.

When the intensity of rain suddenly increased, he got up and went inside the beach house, bringing with him the last chair from the deck. Pausing briefly by the television, he watched an updated report of the hurricane showing it churning in the Atlantic. The announcer reported that the hurricane had strengthened over open water and had diverted from its projected track, saving the Outer Banks from a direct hit but increasing the speed at which the storm was traveling. The updated forecast now called for Nags Head and the surrounding areas to expect the worst of it sometime after dark. After listening to the forecast, Dave spent a few seconds studying the satellite loop before unplugging the television and turning off all the lights. With his chores completed and nothing left to do, he walked out of the beach house and locked the door behind him, immediately jumping into his hearse and driving to Mulligan's to see if they were open.

As luck would have it, his favorite haunt was still in full operation. That discovery helped raise his spirits until he pulled into the parking lot and spotted two Nags Head police cars sitting side by side near the front entrance of the yellow-shingled building. Coming to an abrupt stop, he stared anxiously at the police cruisers, wondering why they were there. It was unusual to see the police at Mulligan's, but that did not mean they were there looking for him. Still, the urge to flee was strong, but so too was his awareness that he had already been seen; there was no missing his long black hearse in the nearly empty parking lot. Despite his apprehension, he dismissed his fears and parked a short distance from the police cars, willingly accepting his fate as he jogged through the blowing rain while glancing up at the deserted second-floor deck where the tables and benches had been stacked and secured in anticipation of the hurricane.

Stopping just inside the entranceway to shake the rain from his clothes, he looked up and saw a young girl standing behind a wooden counter. She smiled at him and said while nodding toward an open doorway, "He's downstairs in the Gazebo Bar today, Buddy." Rather than proceeding immediately through the door, Dave instead glanced through another open doorway where he saw four officers sitting at a table in the dining room enjoying their lunch while talking to Gus, the owner of the restaurant. "Thanks, Brenda," he said while turning and passing through the door leading away from the officers.

Moving along the side of dining room, Dave walked into the Gazebo Bar, a smaller tavern-style bar replete with sports memorabilia that included a signed jersey of former Major League Baseball player and manager Pete Rose along with two signed photographs of Green Bay Packers' running back Paul Hornung, one of which included Coach Vince Lombardi in the picture. Standing by the framed photographs, Dave looked around the polygon-shaped bar but recognized only one of the three patrons sitting there, so he walked over and took a seat next to him, lightly tapping his friend's shoulder as he sat down.

For once, Gary was not engrossed in reading his book but, instead, sat pensively in his chair while staring at one of the television screens above the bar, a long-necked bottle of Budweiser clasped loosely in his hand. Melville's novel lay inverted on the Formica bar top in front of him as the high school teacher gently stroked the short bristles of his graying beard while acknowledging Dave with a nod and a smile. Glancing down at the book, Dave noticed that there were only a few pages left to be read, and he wondered if Captain Ahab was still pursuing his destiny or if he had concluded his battle with the demonic white whale. He also mused over the fear and doubt the old captain may have experienced upon embarking on his final clash with his adversary, and it made him ponder his own whale hunt, wondering if he would perish or survive, still uncertain if he were Ahab or Ishmael. Seeing the thoughtful expression on Dave's face as he stared at the inverted book, the experienced schoolteacher started to say something but then stopped and awaited a question that never came.

"Buddy!" Travis called out in his usual jovial manner. "Glad you stopped by." Spreading his arms, he added, "As you can see, I've been downgraded today."

"I noticed," Dave remarked to his friend before pointing to the beer tap. "Give me a draft today; doesn't matter what."

"Whoa, breaking with tradition. That tall blonde really has you confused. By the way, we're closing at three today. We've already shut down the upstairs. Sally's up there now battening down the hatches while I get to stay down here and play. She's really pissed off about it too. Right, Professor?" Raising his eyebrows, he looked over at Gary, who just rolled his eyes.

"That's okay," Dave said. "I need to be somewhere at three anyway."

"Oh, big date, huh? Are you two cuddling up together during the storm?"

"Not sure. She's working up in Elizabeth City right now, but she'll be back later."

Gary and Travis glanced at each with the same questioning expression before turning in unison to stare at Dave. Travis spoke for both of them when he said, "I hope she makes it. Old Kim is coming in a little faster than expected."

"I know," Dave said with a hint of concern in his voice. "I was watching the forecast on TV before I came here." He then looked up at the television screens, all of them tuned to The Weather Channel, as Travis turned to pour him a beer.

"They're closing the kitchen early," the bartender said while placing a frosted mug on the bar, "but I can probably get you a bowl of chowder if you want."

"That would be great but no problem if you can't."

Travis looked at his watch and said, "Let me see what I can do." He then walked out from behind the bar and disappeared into the dining room.

While waiting for his friend to return, Dave looked around the small octagon-shaped tavern at the two unfamiliar patrons sitting on opposite sides of the bar. One guy was clearly a local resident based on his words and manner of speaking. He had piercing brown eyes and angular features sharp enough to chop wood while the other man was large and hairy, looking very much like a biker, although this was not a day to be traveling by motorcycle. Neither of them spoke much, which was highly unusual in the Gazebo Bar, and Dave chalked it up to the depression caused by the inclement weather along with his own quietness resulting from more than meteorological conditions. Trying not to dwell on his own problems, he sipped his beer and stared at the television screens, quietly watching a video loop of Hurricane Kim tracking toward the coastline.

It was several minutes past three when Dave steered the hearse into a large parking lot off West Kitty Hawk Road near the bypass between the fourth and fifth mileposts. Dodging the deep puddles of water while straining to see through the unrelenting rain, he approached a building at the end of the lot and parked as close as possible to its front entrance before jumping from the hearse and jogging to the shelter of an overhang above the door. Besides the wind and rain, another major impediment to his getting there that afternoon had been the bumper-to-bumper traffic on the bypass caused by the hordes of evacuees trying to outrun the hurricane. The highway had already bottlenecked at the Wright Memorial Bridge over Currituck Sound, and he knew it would only get worse as the day wore on. Standing outside the door of the Holy

Redeemer by the Sea Catholic Church, he questioned his reason for being there, wondering if the guidance and reassurance he sought would be worth the effort he had expended in getting there.

Except for Dave's hearse parked in a reserved handicapped space, the parking lot was deserted, making the church and its grounds appear abandoned and forsaken. Cupping his hands around his eyes to counter the reflection in the glass doors, he peered into the vestibule where everything seemed dark and unwelcoming. His initial reaction was to give up and go home, but he instead grabbed the door handle and gave it a half-hearted tug, fully expecting it to be locked. To his great surprise, it moved easily in his hand.

The church was an odd-shaped building of a contemporary design consisting of three pie-shaped divisions, each section doubling the length of the one adjacent to it. There was a long brick wall forming one side of the church with curved, segmented walls expanding in concentric arcs around the opposite side of the building. Dave had been in a Catholic church on only one other occasion, and that was when he was a boy attending a wedding with his parents. He remembered that church, but it was nothing like this one. That one was an ancient Gothic-style building with spires, arches, buttresses, and colorful stained glass windows. Based on his one-time experience, he had assumed that all Catholic churches looked like that.

It was ghostly quiet when he first walked into the large open vestibule, but the soles of his shoes, squeaking loudly on the tile floor, instantly shattered the solemn silence. Crossing through the vestibule, he opened the door leading into the main hall of the church and paused briefly to look inside before entering the room. In the distance ahead, he observed a white marble altar sitting on a raised platform. Brick steps led to the altar over which hung an enormous crucifix mounted on the wall. Three sections of wooden pews spread out from the altar to fill the great room with an organ and an encasement of pipes occupying the far side of the church. Carved images of the Stations of the Cross adorned the walls of the interior space, and Dave remembered hearing from someone that Glenn Eure, a local Nags Head artist, had designed, carved, and painted them. On many occasions, Dave had driven past the artist's Ghost Fleet Gallery located between the tenth and eleventh mileposts, but he had never visited the gallery nor had he ever met the artist.

Walking down the side aisle toward the altar, he marveled at the eclectic design of the church. It was not what he had expected.

There were several stylized stained glass windows at the far end near the organ, but they were not the ornate depictions of saints and angels he had remembered from his youth. About halfway down the aisle, he stopped by a white marble Baptismal font set in a small alcove near six stained glass windows arranged in two columns of three. The brightly colored windows depicted nature scenes of land, sea, and sky; once again, not the saints and angels he had expected to see.

"They are the Outer Banks," a cheerful voice called out from a short distance away, its bright tone filling the large, empty room.

Dave turned and looked toward another alcove along the opposite wall in which stood an ornate tabernacle made of gold, bronze, or polished brass; he could not conclusively identify the metal from that distance. Facing the burnished coffer were two prayer kneelers along with two chairs positioned directly behind them. Father Andal sat on one of the chairs wearing neatly pressed slacks and a black short-sleeved shirt with a Roman collar. Remaining purposefully quiet, he had been watching Dave closely for several minutes.

"The stained glass windows depict the Outer Banks," the priest explained while remaining seated on the other side of the church. "The sound side is represented by the left windows and the ocean side by those on the right." He beamed a wide grin that Dave could see even from that distance. "You have fish, water, trees, birds, animals—everything you find in the Outer Banks," he declared quite jubilantly.

Dave did not immediately respond but instead turned to reexamine the windows. Yes, he could now see the visual representation of the region in both landscapes and seascapes, all depicting the world he had come to know and appreciate over the past several months. When he looked back, Father Andal had risen and was genuflecting solemnly before the tabernacle, so Dave began walking toward him across the middle of the church. The priest did not move but waited patiently for him to arrive, at which time he extended a welcoming hand toward his new friend. While locked in a handshake with the slender priest, Dave felt his eyes drawn toward the relief-sculpted tabernacle as well as three tiny stained glass windows cut into the wall behind it, two readily visible and one obscured by the tabernacle itself. In one window, he could see a colorful depiction of grapes and in the other a basket of bread. It was not necessary for him to ask the significance of those windows even though Father Andal stood alert and ready to answer any question he might have.

Turning back, Dave saw the African priest staring at him with large open eyes, so he nervously glanced out toward the empty pews and said, "You have a beautiful church here. Not what I had expected."

"No?"

He smiled at the priest. "No, I was expecting flying buttresses and gargoyles."

Andal laughed effortlessly and said with a large grin, "We hide the buttresses and take the gargoyles in during the day." The priest then turned and began ambling toward the back of the church with Dave walking beside him. "So my young friend, you wish to talk to me about something?"

As they strolled down the aisle, they passed a relief sculpture hanging on the wall. No more than a partial figurine, it displayed the ivory head of a woman mounted on a plain dark background encircled by a carved wooden frame. The woman appeared extremely sad with her eyes cast downward and her mantle gathered softly around her face. Her disembodied head seemed to float in space, and it impressed Dave with its power, causing him to stop and study it quietly for a few moments. Father Andal watched him carefully but remained silent until Dave grinned and said, "This is from Michelangelo's *Pietà*, isn't it?"

"Very observant. Yes, it is the head of Mary from the famous sculpture. It leaves you to mentally complete the rest." The priest seemed pleased that Dave had recognized the Virgin Mother. He was about to say something else but then stopped himself, choosing instead to walk quietly beside his young friend. Rather than try to preach or sermonize, he decided to wait and simply provide answers to questions whenever asked.

They then rounded a corner and started past another sacred carving, this one also attached to the wall. The statue was that of a woman wearing a blue star-adorned mantle that covered her head and enveloped her delicate shoulders. Descending in folds to her feet, it was supported by a small cherub-like angel that reached up to grasp it along with the hem of her robe while she stood upon a crescent moon, using her body to obstruct the sun. With her hands folded in prayer, she cast her eyes downward, her face bearing the same sad expression as the sculpted head of the *Pietà*. Immediately upon seeing it, Dave came to a halt and began studying it with more scrutiny than he had the other sculpture, furrowing his brow as he did so.

"She is the Virgin of Guadalupe, the Patroness of the Americas," Father Andal said in response to an unasked question.

Dave looked at him as if he wished him to continue, causing the priest's eye to sparkle as he said, "We have many Hispanics in the congregation, and the Virgin is very precious to them because she made her appearance on a hill outside of Mexico City back in the 1500s.

"It was at a time when the New World was being colonized. Before then, the Aztecs had ruled that region of Mexico, their empire dating back to the fourteenth century. They were a society rich in culture, but also a brutal people who regularly engaged in human sacrifices to their gods. They ritually killed their victims by cutting out their hearts and tossing the bodies down the temple steps. Often, the priests would eat the limbs of the unfortunate victims, many of whom were children, prized for being pure and innocent. It is estimated that the Aztecs sacrificed between twenty thousand and fifty thousand victims yearly, and I have heard it reported to be as high as two hundred and fifty thousand per year!

"But that came to an end in 1521 when the Spaniards, led by Cortés, conquered Montezuma and the Aztec Empire. The Spanish then forbade human sacrifice and cannibalism, and they attempted to convert the Indians to Christianity. Because the Aztec rulers had been so effective in indoctrinating the people in the superstitions of their culture, the transition to the teachings of Christ proved difficult for the native Indians, especially when advanced by their conquerors. It was during that period when Christianity was getting a foothold in the post-conquest era that the Blessed Virgin appeared to an Aztec Indian convert named Juan Diego on the Feast of the Immaculate Conception. He was an authentic Indian native, but he had assumed a Christian name at his Baptism. We now know him as Saint Juan Diego!"

Andal lifted his eyes and gazed lovingly at the sculpture on the wall. "What you see here is a recreation of an image that was miraculously imprinted on Juan Diego's cloak or tilma, as it was called back then—a burlap-like material made from cactus." He then turned to face Dave. "It was a gift from Our Lady to Juan Diego—and to us—offered as proof to the local bishop and to the Indians that her visitation on earth was authentic and real. She used images and words to reveal the true nature of God to the Indians, to put an end to their worship of false gods and their practice of human sacrifice. Imagery was something the Indians understood, something to which they would respond.

"If you look at her features, you can see that she is not exactly Indian and not entirely European but a mixture of the two races. Her clothing, however, is in the style of a Middle Eastern woman.

She is very humble in her pose and pregnant! She bears a vibrant life within her, the promised child of the Old Testament who is the Son of God! The Aztecs worshiped the sun and moon, yet she subjugates both of them, blocking the sun with her body while standing on a crescent moon. The stars on her mantle, the Aztec flower designs on her robe, the cross on her brooch are all symbols that had profound and relevant meaning to the Indians then and to us now. In recent times, enlargements were made of her eyes, revealing the reflection Juan Diego kneeling at her feet while staring up at her." The priest paused a moment to watch Dave as he studied the statue. "The tilma with Our Lady's image, still miraculously preserved in all its exquisite beauty, is on display in Mexico City if you ever wish to see it," he informed his young friend.

When Dave did not respond, Father Andal continued, "Because of her effort to make the Indians appreciate the value of human life, the Virgin of Guadalupe is also the patroness of the pro-life movement in this country." He then became somber and said, "We condemn with outrage the savagery and barbarism of human sacrifice committed by many in the past, and yet we allow human sacrifice to continue on a much grander scale today without any remorse or the least amount of regret. Since 1973, we have killed over fifty-seven million children through abortions! That is a number that would make Montezuma take notice. I ask you, who are savages now? Who are the barbarians?"

On that solemn note, Dave dropped his eyes only to raise them again to look at the African priest. He said to him, "I've seen an image very much like this one before. It had a woman dressed similarly, wearing a veil that fell down across her shoulders. Her likeness was imprinted on an oval-shaped, gold medallion worn by a girl around her neck, but her pose was slightly different. Her hands were down at her sides with her palms exposed, and there seemed to be writing along the sides and top of the medallion."

"Did she have beams of light extending from her fingertips?"

"It was so small; I didn't notice. I only saw it for a few seconds."

The priest nodded his head. "Your description matches that of the Miraculous Medal, also called the Medal of the Immaculate Conception. It was the result of another Marian apparition in 1830, this time in France to Saint Catherine Labouré, a member of the Daughters of Charity of St. Vincent de Paul. Her body remains incorrupt, interred in a glass coffin at the motherhouse in Paris. Perhaps another place you may wish to visit in the future." He again displayed his trademark smile.

"Our Lady asked that the image be struck in the form of a medal and worn around the neck with fidelity and devotion. Those who do so reverently may receive great graces and special protections, especially at the hour of death. The Virgin stands upon a globe representing the earth, and she crushes a serpent beneath her feet. From the rings on her fingers, she emits beams of light signifying graces bestowed upon those who seek her intercession. The words you saw surrounding the medal are a prayer that encircled her during the apparition: *O Mary, conceived without sin, pray for us who have recourse to thee.*" Andal saw Dave's lips moving slightly as if he were mentally repeated the words to memorize them.

"Yes," the priest said before reciting it again. "*O Mary, conceived without sin, pray for us who have recourse to thee.* It is an excellent prayer to say anytime, but especially in times of danger. There is also a reverse side to the medal on which appears a circle of twelve stars, the letter M entwined with a cross, and two hearts—the Sacred Heart of Jesus crowned with thorns and the Immaculate Heart of Mary pierced with a sword. We typically say the Perpetual Novena of Our Lady of the Miraculous Medal on Mondays. There is a line in the novena prayer that I especially like. It goes *O Lord, Jesus Christ, who for the accomplishment of Your greatest works, have chosen the weak things of the world.* That is what happened in France with Sister Catherine Labouré and also in Mexico when our Lord sent his mother to Juan Diego, a simple, powerless Indian peasant." He stopped and awaited a reaction from his young friend, thinking he might have a question.

Dave thought for a moment and then queried the priest about his description of the Miraculous Medal. "She's crushing a serpent with her feet? That's not something I'd expect to see in a vision from heaven."

"Yes," the priest responded with a grin, "a serpent—Satan. Recall the story of Adam and Eve where the serpent tricks the woman, and sin enters the world. Mary is the *New Eve*, who brings Christ into the world to defeat the evil that is consuming it. In the image on the Miraculous Medal, the serpent is wrapped around the world, but it is having its head crushed by the woman, the mother of the Christ—religious symbolism directed at us much in the same way it was used to influence the Aztec Indians."

The mention of evil seemed to stir something in Dave, making him less guarded in how he spoke to his newly acquired confessor. "You had talked of evil and Satan before when we were sitting at the bar the other day."

"Yes."

"When Travis brought up the subject of demonic possession, you said that it happened mostly in the past."

"No, I said that Satan is more devious today than in the past; he is not as flashy. He moves through the world unnoticed, creating havoc without receiving any of the blame. The people of today refuse to believe that he exists, so their unbelief becomes one of his greatest strengths. He achieves his goals using stealth tactics, and one such tactic is perpetuating the notion that evil does not exist. What is good? What is evil? People portray them as being the same. It just depends upon your point of view and how you interpret the situation—moral relativism, the scourge of our age!"

Dave turned and asked the priest sincerely, "But evil does exist, right?"

"Most assuredly, but do not get me wrong. Just because evil can accomplish its goals covertly does not mean it will not revert to its old ways." He paused and looked Dave square in the face. "Even though it is not necessary for Satan to personify himself in a fiendish or diabolical manner, one that is designed to terrorize, he still does it from time to time just because he likes it."

The priest displayed no emotion while making his remarks about the cruel nature of evil, unlike Dave, who reacted expressively through the widening of his pupils and the tightening of his facial muscles. Nervously blinking, Dave looked away for a second but then glanced back to find the African priest still staring at him, so he asked him, "Why is there evil in the world?"

Father Andal broke the tension with a smile. "That my friend is a question many have asked over the centuries. The answer is relatively straightforward but difficult for anyone unwilling to accept it ... or for those unprepared for the truth of it. Would you like to know the answer to that question?"

"Yes." There was no hesitation in his voice.

"Very well," the priest said assuredly, "then let me tell you. We are creatures endowed with free will, but freedom requires that we have the capacity to make a choice—to choose to do wrong. Without evil to offer us an alternative, there would be no free will. It is as simple as that. We have the ability—and I would say the obligation—to choose that which is good, but you can only have that choice if there is something else to choose, the opposite of good—evil. At its very essence, evil springs from the refusal of man to conform to the will of his Creator with its primary causes being pride, covetousness, lust, anger, gluttony, envy, and sloth. Here is something else you need to understand: good must always confront evil, even in the face of its own inevitable destruction. To do anything else would be to succumb to evil or to work in league with it." He then smiled a fatherly smile. "Is that what you came to hear, young David?"

Dave graciously returned his smile. "Yes," he said, the tone of his voice conveying a message of gratitude.

Andal laughed in his usual boisterous manner that echoed throughout the empty church. Grabbing Dave by the upper arm, he said, "Since you seem interested in our statuary, let me show you something else."

Tugging him a short distance down the aisle to a set of glass doors, he led Dave into a vestibule different from the one through which he had entered the church. Just beyond the doorway, they stopped at a large glass encasement displaying a four-foot crucifix composed of a polished material resembling black onyx. Segmented in nature, the pitch-black crucifix appeared to be an assemblage of interlocking pieces joined in a mosaic-like fashion.

"What do you think about my black brother here?" Andal asked with a broad grin.

Dave's eyes widened as he studied it. "It is beautiful. How was it made?"

"By the hand of God," the priest said proudly.

Dave had come to understand that his new friend enjoyed making vague statements and then waiting for him to respond. Instead of taking the bait, he turned back to the case and examined it again, this time with a more attuned eye. "I like his handiwork," he said after a few moments. "Tell that to your boss the next time you're talking to him."

Andal let fly another great laugh as he slapped Dave on the back. He then pointed his finger higher on the wall to a small framed photograph of a crucifix. In the picture, the pale—almost white—crucifix hung from the rafters of what appeared to be an old wooden building. "Look familiar?" he asked.

Staring up at the wall, Dave recognized the photographed crucifix as the same one in the display case before it had undergone its astonishing transformation. With a perplexed look, he started to ask, "How—"

The priest did not give him a chance to finish his question before offering an explanation. "This black crucifix is the one that hung above the altar of the old church." He again pointed to the small framed photograph on the wall. "There it is above the altar before the church was destroyed by arson in 1998. As you can see, the old crucifix possessed its own inherent beauty, but the transformed one—the one that arose from the ashes—is by far the more exquisite and precious one of the two. And so it is with us. God often uses terrible situations to create magnificent works of beauty, burning away our impurities in a transformative fire, one that remakes us into something new—someone we never thought we could be—someone we never would be if left to our own designs."

Dave studied the crucifix more intently than before, realizing the error of his prior observation. Its irregular, segmented surface was not an assemblage of black mosaic pieces but, rather, the charred fragmentation of the wood due to the tremendous heat of the fire that destroyed the former church. Father Andal was right; no sculpture or artisan could have produced something this lovely using so volatile a creative process. Only the hand of God could have accomplished what he saw displayed inside the case. With his attention focused entirely on the blackened body of the condemned man hanging on the cross, rejected and abandoned but still willing to sacrifice himself for those he loved, Dave tuned out everything and gazed attentively at the enigmatic image of the sacrificed savior until the sound of the priest's voice nudged him from his quiet contemplation.

"So, my young friend, you drove a long distance in dreadfully bad weather. How can I help you?"

Dave straightened his back and extended his hand to the priest who accepted it willingly in a hearty handshake. Graciously, he said to his friend and advisor, "I think you already have."

Father Andal nodded his head in agreement. "Well, then, you are welcome," he said as they both turned and began walking toward the doors leading to the parking lot. Passing through the vestibule, Dave glanced at a table containing religious literature, and he noticed a card lying off by itself near a stack of brochures. The card was about the size and shape of a playing card, it contained the image of an angel unlike any he had ever seen before. Rather than a friendly, good-natured spirit with soft features and gentle disposition, this angel appeared intimidating and mighty with enormous spreading wings and a flowing blue cloak. Shielded in armor, the powerful angel stood tall and proud over a serpent-like dragon into which it had thrust a sword, leaving the impaled serpent to writhe in pain and hiss defiantly at the warrior angel, signaling its refusal to surrender to the conquering spirit. Finding the depiction a little shocking, Dave picked up the card to examine it closer.

"That is Saint Michael the Archangel," the priest said.

Flipping over the card, Dave noticed a prayer to Saint Michael written on the back along with some personal data about a man named Michael Ortiz, information that included his date of birth as well as the date he died.

Father Andal took the card from Dave and looked at it. "Yes," he said. "This is a prayer card from a funeral this past week." As he spoke, he fluttered the card lightly in his hand. "It is common to have these printed and distributed as memorials at the funeral of the deceased. Michael Ortiz was a good man and a good parishioner who lived a long life. Saint Michael was his patron saint. If you recall, Saint Michael was the angel enlisted by God to drive Satan from heaven. He was—and is—a great warrior. His feast day is the twenty-ninth of September."

Dave smiled and said, "Funny, that's my birthday."

Father Andal's eyes seemed to sparkle as he again displayed his incredibly white teeth in a broad grin. "It is unfortunate that your parents did not name you Michael to gain the protection of the great archangel."

"Well, if you must know," Dave said a little sheepishly, "Michael is my middle name."

"There you have it!" Andal exclaimed. "That is probably why they gave you that name."

Looking sideways at the priest, Dave said with a chuckle, "I really doubt it."

Father Andal ignored his denial and handed the card back to him saying, "We all have patron saints who watch over us, even you. Like my deceased friend, Michael Ortiz, you too have a patron saint, a very powerful one who was also a legendary warrior: David, the great king of Israel. Even Christ himself was called *Son of David*."

While listening to the priest, Dave stared intently at the prayer card, focusing on the sword wielded by Saint Michael and the way he had used it to slay the dragon. The priest watched him silently for a few seconds and then patted him softly on the shoulder saying, "You have a *good* day, my friend, and be careful on your journey through the storm." He then turned and began walking through the vestibule toward the interior doors of the church, stepping briskly and evenly before calling back over his shoulder, "Remember, my friend, David prevailed over Goliath even when no one believed he could." Passing through the doors, he then walked gaily up the side aisle, quietly singing to himself as he went.

Dave did not say anything as he watched the receding figure of the priest step lightly across the tile floor. Turning toward the parking lot, he then stared at the wind and rain for several seconds before jamming the prayer card into his pocket and charging through the doors of the church, fully prepared to face the perils of the oncoming storm.

By six o'clock that evening, the leading edge of the hurricane had breached the coastline, thrashing and pounding the coastal communities with damaging winds and unrelenting rain, an assault that seemed to increase by the minute. Trying her best to see through the windshield, Nikki wondered what she was doing driving back into all of this. It had occurred to her that she should be heading north like everyone else on the highway, possibly to her sister's place in Norfolk where she could wait out the storm in safety; however, she was unwilling to turn around, stubbornly continuing south on her journey toward Nags Head. The foaling in Elizabeth City had gone smoothly, but it had taken longer than she had anticipated, forcing her to drive home just as the hurricane was making landfall farther south.

She had never before experienced rainfall of this severity. Tremendous downpours would fall for ten minutes or more and then ease up, only to resume a few seconds later with even greater ferocity. The wind hammering the side of her Jeep was just as bad, forcing her to use a death grip on the steering wheel just to maintain control. She was thankful that she owned a four-wheel-drive vehicle and even more thankful that she had followed her father's advice about replacing her worn tires; however, despite the roadworthiness of her Jeep, she still drove slowly and carefully, undisturbed by the amount of time it was taking her to get home. With no one else foolish enough to be heading into the storm, she did not have to worry about other drivers pressuring her to go faster.

Fortunately, the rain subsided somewhat once she approached the Wright Memorial Bridge over Currituck Sound, but the winds were still formidable, driving white capped waves directly into the bridge supports, generating plumes of water that spilled over the guardrails and onto the road surface. Passing onto the southbound span of the bridge, she noticed a slight easing the wind due to the shielding effect of the northbound highway, but it was not enough to lessen her anxiety due to what she observed in the sound, an ungodly tempest just beyond the guardrail that sent a flash of terror through her body. With white knuckles, she gripped the steering wheel even tighter, locking her eyes on the road while plowing straight ahead, afraid to glance at the dangerous waters on either side of her.

Approaching the arch of the bridge, she felt a little more secure as she rose above the raging water, but the higher altitude made her more vulnerable to the crosscurrents of the wind. The powerful gusts then began battering the side of the Jeep with such force that they threatened to shove the car into the guardrail or toss it over the side. It was only by slowing down and over-steering that she was able to counter the effect of the wind and stay within her proper lane. Ascending higher into the air, she remembered how much she hated Ferris wheels, mainly because of her aversion to heights. Whenever she yielded to someone's insistence that she ride one, it never failed that the car would stop directly at the top, causing her to freak out until it started moving again. Her phobia had been especially severe back in her childhood, which she blamed on her sister's cruel habit of rocking the car to scare her. That is exactly how she felt upon reaching the crest of the bridge at the precise moment a new surge of wind and rain struck with a vengeance. At that point, she abandoned all caution and made a mad dash for land, hitting the accelerator with a heavy foot in the hope of escaping the lethal wind and hostile waters.

The highway at the end of the bridge may have offered Nikki refuge from the waters of the sound, but her situation was far from safe. The Outer Banks had not yet experienced the worst of the hurricane, and she hoped to make it home long before that happened. Although it was just a little past six o'clock, the gray landscape appeared as dark as night due to the thick cloud cover and the blowing sheets of rain obscuring her vision. With her headlights barely able to illuminate the road and her windshield wipers slapping at their highest setting, she strained to see more than a few yards ahead of her as she made the seventeen-mile journey along the bypass from the Wright Memorial Bridge to Whalebone Junction.

At Whalebone Junction, she turned onto the causeway toward Roanoke Island where she faced the challenge of crossing another disturbed body of water. Clenching her teeth, she barreled straight ahead while eyeing the rising seas on either side of her, recognizing that both ends of the causeway would soon be under water. Fortunately, she was able to cross Roanoke Sound without all of the drama of her Currituck Sound crossing, and she soon found herself breathing a sigh of relief while sitting in her parking space at the condominiums of Pirate's Cove. The only positive thing about the stressful drive down from Elizabeth City was that it had kept her from thinking about either Dave or Mark; however, thoughts of the two men came flooding back the moment she stepped from the Jeep.

Trying her best to banish the unwanted thoughts, she climbed the stairwell and let herself into her condo where she planned to lie down and sleep for several hours after first keeping her promise to phone Dave. She really did not want to talk to him, but she knew she must do so; otherwise, he would begin bothering her again, disturbing whatever rest she hoped to get. With that in mind, she tossed her car keys onto the kitchen counter and walked into the living room. Pulling her cell phone from her pocket, she plopped herself down on the couch where she sat quietly for several seconds while mentally grappling with what she planned to say to him. Several scripts played out in her mind, but none of them expressed what she was feeling or relayed the message she wished to convey. Suddenly, she remembered having silenced her phone while in Elizabeth City, so she checked it for missed calls and discovered one along with an accompanying voice message. Bristling at the thought that Dave had begun calling her again despite her admonition, she was shocked to learn that the call had not come from him but, rather, from Mark, who had phoned her using his landline. Cheered by this surprising turn of events, she happily accessed her voicemail account.

Mark's voice on the recorded message was composed and sincere: "Nikki, I'm sorry about last night. I'm home now, and I think you should come over. It is safer for us to be together during the hurricane. I also have some disturbing news about the guy in the hearse. It has to do with the police. I'll tell you more when you get here."

Lowering the phone from her ear, she checked the timestamp of the call—shortly after six o'clock. No thought or plan was necessary as she raced into the kitchen and grabbed her car keys off the counter. With only one objective in mind, she then charged back into the storm, hoping to revive her relationship with the man she had once considered her soulmate.

It was already past seven o'clock, and the storm had not abated for even a second since his return from Holy Redeemer Church. In fact, it had cranked up another notch within the last half-hour, and Dave knew it would only get worse as the night wore on. The beach road was already underwater, but that was mostly due to the rain;

the destructive flooding of the storm surge had yet to be unleashed. At this point, he still felt he could plow through the standing water to get out, but that window of opportunity was rapidly closing. Travis had called to offer safe harbor at his place, telling Dave that he needed to leave immediately because the waters of the sound were rising rapidly. Before long, the flooding would cut off Colington Island, and he would be unable to get there. Well aware of the vulnerability of his small cottage on the beach, Dave had declined Travis' offer of shelter because he still hoped to hear from Nikki.

Although his tiny beach house stood elevated off the ground, its support stilts were very short, nothing like the tall, thick pilings supporting the other homes along Cottage Row. The low construction of his house almost guaranteed that it would be flooded once the storm surge hit with full force. Within the last few minutes, Dave had noticed the wind gusts increasing in strength, their amplified pressure causing the windows and walls to bow like rawhide drum heads, producing pulse-like vibrations oddly reminiscent of Afro-Caribbean rhythms that scared Grave, making him pace aimlessly around the room looking for a place to hide. Dave could see how anxious the dog had become, and he was beginning to share his anxiety, not so much about the weather but because he had not yet heard from Nikki. The cloud-induced darkness also added to his apprehension because he knew that Mark could already be on the prowl. Sunset was not for another thirty minutes or so, but it was already as black as night outside, a circumstance that did not bode well for Nikki—or for him either.

Running his hand through his thick hair as he was prone to do whenever nervous, he joined Grave in pacing back and forth across the floor of the tiny cottage. Each time they passed one another, Grave would look at him searchingly, hoping his master would give the nod so they could abandon ship and get out of there before it was too late. Dave, however, was too distracted to read the signals coming from his canine friend. Instead, he used his cell phone to call Nikki, once again getting no answer, his fifth unanswered call in the last fifteen minutes. Unlike his previous attempts in which he had left long, pleading voicemail requests for her to call back, he hung up without recording a message, realizing that he had wasted too much time already and that he needed to do something other than sitting around waiting for her to call.

Completing his fifteenth lap through the house, he glanced down at the prayer card lying on the kitchen table where he had dropped it upon returning home a few hours earlier. Once again, the imposing image of the warrior angel with its projection of power and confidence touched something in his soul. If only he could be that valiant and self-assured, he thought to himself. Reaching down, he picked up the card and flipped it over, reading aloud the prayer on the back: "*Saint Michael the Archangel, defend us in battle, be our safeguard against the wickedness and snares of the devil. May God rebuke him we humbly pray; and do thou, O Prince of the Heavenly Host, by the Divine Power of God, cast into hell Satan and all evil spirits that prowl about the world seeking the ruin of souls.*" After a brief pause, he spoke the last word, "*Amen.*"

Placing the prayer card in his pocket, he grabbed the keys to the hearse and looked over at Grave, who was by then lying on the couch beneath a large pillow that entirely covered him except for his head. Without a word spoken, he communicated to his furry friend what was about to happen, and the dog, relieved that this moment had finally arrived, perked up his ears and jumped off the couch, running straight toward the door where Dave met him with an understanding smile. Glancing back at the interior of the cottage, he wondered if he would ever see it again, and he briefly considered gathering some belongings to take with him. After a few seconds, though, he decided against it, concluding that whatever he owned of value was already outside in the hearse or in the pockets of his shorts; so, with that in mind, he and Grave charged out into the darkness, running swiftly and determinedly through the punishing wind and rain.

The distance from the porch to the hearse was just a few yards, but the short jaunt left them both thoroughly drenched. Although sopping wet, Dave did not feel cold or particularly uncomfortable due to the tropical air keeping things relatively warm across the region. Noticing the lights shimmering off the flooded roadway, he realized how difficult it was going to be navigating anywhere that night, let alone traversing the sandy moat at the end of the driveway. Unsure about the best way to cross the soupy mixture of water and sand, he relied solely on instinct and depressed the accelerator of the old hearse, using its mass and momentum to power through the watery barrier, lunging and bouncing onto the flooded pavement where he plowed slowly through the standing water to the first cross street leading to the bypass.

With few drivers on the highway that night, the only real obstacle he encountered on his way to Nikki's condo was the weather. It was the pelting rain more than anything else that slowed him down, mainly due to his worn out wiper blades failing to keep up with the deluge of water obscuring his vision, making him feel as if he were driving through an automatic carwash.

Despite the ferocity of the storm, which seemed to be getting worse with each passing minute, he now felt less vulnerable and more in control because he was acting with a sense of purpose rather than passively waiting for Nikki to call. Even Grave appeared less anxious now that they were on the road. Although the hurricane raged all around them, the tired-looking basset hound sat serenely on the front seat, projecting an air of contentment, unfazed by the storm and indifferent to the water dripping from his nose and ears. Dave speculated that his canine friend had sensed the imminent danger facing them back in the cottage and now felt relieved at having escaped the threat. Dave had to admit that he felt better about it himself.

Upon reaching Whalebone Junction, they turned onto the causeway where Dave's newfound feelings of safety quickly vanished. Roanoke Sound was a nightmarish mixture of waves, foam, and sea spray, its waters rising rapidly along the banks near the edge of the road. From what he could see of it through the rain-streaked windows, it looked ominous and evil. Driven by powerful winds and storm surge, the ocean was pouring into Roanoke Sound in fulfillment of an earlier prediction that the hurricane might track up through the sound. If that were the case, he surmised, his cottage would survive, but poor Travis would find himself hammered out there on Colington Island. It would also put the causeway underwater and might even take out the Washington Baum Bridge that lay directly ahead of him on his way to Nikki's condominium.

His hearse was the only car on the bridge as he slipped up and over the raised section closest to Roanoke Island. Descending the arch, he looked over at the Pirate's Cove and saw several lights burning in the windows of the condominiums, indicating that not everyone had evacuated, and he prayed that he would find Nikki behind one of those glowing rectangles. Wishing to get there even faster, he jettisoned all safety concerns and increased his speed dramatically, only to pay the price when he began hydroplaning near the end of the bridge. It launched him straight into the oncoming lane, but he managed to regain control just in time to make a careening turn into Pirate's Cove where he steered the hearse toward the guardhouse at the entrance of the residential complex. Expecting to find no one at the guard station, he intended to drive straight through until he made the astonishing discovery that someone was on duty that night.

Outside the small wooden security structure on which hung

three sets of bright floodlights, there stood a large, muscular man totally exposed to the weather. Dressed like a fisherman in yellow foul weather gear that included a rain slicker, bibs, and a Sou'wester fisherman's hat, he appeared to be waiting for someone. The brim of his vintage hat concealed his face while the loose hat ties flew freely around his head, one flailing out to the side and the other one fluttering under his chin. Despite not having secured the hat to his head, he seemed in no danger of losing it to the stiff wind; in fact, nothing in his appearance suggested the slightest hint of turmoil except for the flapping hat ties. If anything, he looked unruffled and relaxed.

Notwithstanding the peaceful demeanor of the yellow-clad figure, Dave could not help feeling some trepidation as he approached the guardhouse. Based on the sheer size of the man, he quickly concluded that it was not Gene, the elderly night watchman he had met before while visiting Nikki's condo, and he worried that the man might be Mark in disguise. The stranger was big—incredibly big—and the rain suit made him look even larger and more intimidating. Uncertain if he should approach the guardhouse or veer into the parking lot behind the Blue Water Raw Bar & Grill, Dave decided to proceed cautiously ahead, driving at only a snail's pace with his left foot on the brake to slow his approach and his right shoe on the accelerator to facilitate a speedy departure if necessary. His fears, however, proved unfounded when the man raise his head in a non-threatening manner, smiling joyously as he exposed his face to the light.

The guard was young—about the same age as Dave—with a sublime countenance not easily categorized or described. Dave recognized it as soon as he laid eyes on him, and he found it odd that he would be so intrigued by the appearance of another man. Based on the hard, chiseled features of the young man, combined with his dark piercing eyes and smooth ruddy complexion, Dave concluded that he must be Hispanic. No, he thought, not Hispanic, something more—something different—Aztec perhaps or possibly Mayan. The young man appeared incredibly happy, beaming a broad smile that trumpeted an enormous joy welling up from within him. Despite the havoc and mayhem of the unsettled night, he seemed totally at peace. Moreover, he seemed capable of conferring that sense of tranquility onto others. Dave felt it the moment he looked into the young man's eyes.

"You've got to be crazy standing out in this weather," Dave said to the guard with a slight shake of his head. "I knew Gene wouldn't be here. And, to tell you the truth, I didn't expect anyone to be working tonight."

Closing his eyes, the young man tilted back his head, allowing the rain to strike his face and flow down the sides of his cheeks. "Actually, it's not that bad," he said, still exposing his skin to the elements. "Just a late-summer shower." Lowering his head, he again displayed his engaging smile. "It could be worse—a lot worse. I'm Miguel. I'm new."

"I see how they treat the new guys around here," Dave said with a grin. He was about to say something else when Miguel interrupted him.

"She's already gone."

"What ... who?"

"She drove through here a short time ago, maybe an hour or so. I waved at her, and she waved back to me."

Dave felt his heart climb into the back of his throat, making it difficult for him to form a sentence. "She evacuated?" was all he could utter.

Miguel thought for a moment and said, "No ... no, she wasn't evacuating. When she passed by, I could see into her car, and it was totally empty, no clothes or suitcases or anything. Besides, we asked all the residents to notify us if they planned to leave so we could keep an eye on their properties. Her name's not on the list of evacuees." Miguel's face remained expressionless as he spoke.

Both fear and confusion flooded Dave's brain, each one fighting for control over his mind as he stared blankly at the guard's face. Finally, he asked in desperation, "Are you sure it was her?"

The large yellow man chuckled. "Beautiful blonde? White Jeep Patriot?"

In the battle for cognitive control over Dave's mind, fear triumphed over confusion with anxiety providing the necessary reinforcements. He dropped his head and sat motionless on the front seat, stunned and unsure of what he should do. Entering a state of zero consciousness, one Zen masters spend lifetimes striving to achieve, he found himself urgently in need of a thought or, rather, a nudge toward a thought. Breathing slowly and evenly, he remained still and quiet, much like a saturated seed crystal in a petri dish awaiting the right catalyst to trigger an explosive growth of awareness, one capable of transforming thoughts into ideas, ideas into actions, and actions into results. Although his mind had shut down, his senses stayed highly attuned, enabling him to hear and feel everything: the staccato of rain striking the metal roof of the hearse, the mechanical whine of the slapping windshield wipers, the wet smell of Grave panting on the seat beside him, the coolness of his waterlogged shirt pressing against his skin—sensations and stimuli simultaneously experienced and cataloged deep within the confines of his dormant consciousness.

Miguel was the one who provided the required nudge when he issued an ominous warning, uttered in a tone so severe that it commanded Dave's full attention. "The water is cresting on the other side of the Washington Baum Bridge," he said with absolute certitude.

Dave's reaction to the guard's portentous statement was instantaneous. He raised his head and looked searchingly into Miguel's hardened face, shocked by the dramatic change in the young man's countenance, a transformation in which Miguel now appeared far older than his years. There was no mistaking the urgency in the guard's expression, one that mirrored Dave's own internal alarm, so he punched the accelerator of the old hearse and executed a U-turn around a small island that sent him racing back toward the causeway. Glancing into the mirror on this way out, he no longer saw the yellow-clad figure standing outside in the rain, and he assumed that Miguel had taken shelter inside the guardhouse. It then occurred to him that he should have asked the brawny security guard to come along for backup and support, but by then it was too late.

Pulling out of Pirate's Cove, he charged onto the bridge over Roanoke Sound without hesitation. The wind and rain battered his vehicle the entire way, but he paid little heed to the storm, never once slowing down. His total focus was on where he was going and what he would do when he got there. However, he became more conscious of the dangerous conditions once he reached the other side of the bridge and learned that Miguel had been right about the causeway flooding on the Nags Head side. It then became unnervingly evident that a delay of even an additional thirty seconds would have prevented him from reaching his intended destination. Plodding through the deep water, he struggled to get to higher ground while Grave found the whole ordeal quite enjoyable, once even whining because he wished to stick his head out the window.

It was not until he reached Whalebone Junction and turned onto the bypass that Dave had time to think about Nikki's untimely departure from Pirate's Cove. It then dawned on him that Miguel had volunteered the information about Nikki without being asked. Dave found it odd that the guard would have known his reason for being there, especially since the two of them had never met. There was also the matter of Miguel foreseeing the flooding beyond the Washington Baum Bridge. Three bridges serviced Roanoke Island, but only the Washington Baum Bridge led to Nags Head; the other ones connected the island to the mainland. For some odd reason, Miguel had chosen to address only the Washington Baum Bridge in his warning, almost as if he were steering Dave in that direction. Of course—Dave reasoned—it was the nearest and quickest route off Roanoke Island from Pirate's Cove.

Driving north at a rapid pace despite the reduced visibility, Dave was practically alone on the bypass. The few cars he encountered all had drivers looking extremely anxious to find shelter from the storm. As of yet, there had been no power disruptions, and the retail business signs were still glowing brightly throughout the region; however, the whole landscape appeared ghostly and desolate, much like the film set of a movie about the end of the world. It was hard for him to see anything through the rain-drenched windows, but a quick glance in the direction of the ocean confirmed that the beach road was now completely underwater. The sight of the flooding sparked some concerns about his abandoned cottage, but he quickly banished those thoughts upon arriving at the southernmost intersection of West Seachase Drive. Making the turn into The Village at Nags Head, he then snaked through the development toward Mark's house using the longer, more clandestine route past the Nags Head Golf Links clubhouse. Although the residential community sat near the rising waters of Roanoke Sound, the streets were not flooded due to the higher elevation of the development.

Shedding much of the urgency that had propelled him up the bypass, he became like a stalking leopard, alert and focused, as he drove slowly and warily along the empty streets. Most of the houses in the development were dark and empty with only a few of them displaying lights in their windows, but even those homes looked abandoned that night. Upon reaching the turn leading onto Mark's street, he switched off his headlights and began maneuvering solely by memory, mentally recalling of how the lane curved and twisted through the neighborhood. He moved carefully and stealthily along the street until he reached his ultimate destination where he saw Nikki's Jeep parked in the driveway next to Mark's Infiniti. Emotionally distressed by the sight of the two vehicles sitting side by side, he tore his eyes from them and directed his vision toward the house, focusing instead on the absence of light coming from anywhere inside the darkened structure. Mark's home appeared exactly as it had on previous occasions—dark and foreboding— much the same as every other house on the street that night. In fact, the only light in the entire neighborhood came from the neighbor's two floodlights.

Pulling into the driveway of a vacant home, the same one he had used to hide the hearse two nights earlier while searching Mark's house, he again hid his vehicle under the raised deck of the rental property, using its overhang to shelter the hearse from the wind and rain. Because the house sat on an elevated lot at the highest point of the street, he did not worry about flooding, feeling confident that it would provide a safe place for Grave to wait while he went in search of Nikki.

At that point, he began operating on instinct more than conscious thought as he switched on the dome light and started examining the small semi-automatic Ruger given to him by the Mayor. Grave also seemed curious about the gun and began sniffing it while Dave dropped the clip from the stock and inserted six Zombie bullets into the spring-loaded magazine before sliding it back into the handle with a resounding click. The dexterity he demonstrated in loading the magazine and the manner in which he handled the weapon made it appear as if he had been wielding guns all his life. It then occurred to him that he should take additional ammo with him, but he quickly dismissed the idea, guessing that there would be no time to reload. He would literally get one shot at this, and he would have to make it count.

His previous encounters with Mark had led him to develop a theory, one based solely on an unproven premise. Mark was definitely not from this world, but it seemed as if physical aspects of this world greatly affected him. In the restroom at Mulligan's, he had confessed his need for blood to survive. He had also demonstrated an unusual sensitivity to light while not wearing his sunglasses. Knowing that blood and light were fundamentals of our existence, blood being an organic compound and light a form of electromagnetic energy, both shown to impact Mark on a primitive level, it followed—at least in Dave's mind—that Mark should then be vulnerable to other aspects of our existence as well and, thereby, subject to all the natural laws governing our world.

Dave surmised that as long as Mark stayed on this side of the glass, he was required to play by the same set of rules as everyone else, strictly adhering to the physical laws of our reality, especially the ones dealing with life and death. After witnessing Mark's surprised reaction to a four-thousand-lumen spotlight shined directly into his eyes, Dave wondered how he would respond to a .380 caliber Zombie slug shot straight through his heart. Betting all his chips on this one hand, he hoped to discover the answer to that question. For Nikki's sake as well as his own, he prayed he was right.

Grave could sense that something was up, but he remained stone-faced as he watched his master tuck the gun into the pocket of his shorts. He did not move or react until Dave reached over and began scratching his ears. "You smell like a wet dog," Dave said to his canine friend, who licked his face and started panting softly. Grabbing the folds of skin around the dog's neck, Dave looked deeply into Grave's eyes and told him, "You stay here. I promise I'll be back." With that said, he turned off the dome light and slipped out of the hearse, moving quickly down the road while listening to the bellowing howls of the basset hound echoing in the darkness behind him.

The gusts were blowing harder and with more force than before, making it difficult for him to maintain his footing. Instead of a direct frontal assault on the house, he approached it from behind, reversing the escape route he had used two nights earlier. This night, however, things were quite different, and he found the going slower and much more challenging because of the wind, rain, and mushy ground. Crouching low to reduce his windage, he steadied himself by grasping the beach grass lining the dunes along the fairway as he crept over a small sand mound into Mark's backyard. Although the neighbor's floodlights illuminated much of the grounds, he successfully dodged their exposing beams to remain hidden in the shadows.

Rising before him in the darkness, only partially exposed by the floodlighting, was the back of the house with its intersecting staircases adjoining the three tiers of decking. From his position on the ground, Dave could see all the way to the upper deck and the sliding glass doors of the living room where the vertical blinds were now wide open, not drawn tight as they had been during his previous flight from the house. On that night, he had not used the stairways, opting instead to drop straight to the ground rather than risk walking past the glass doors of the bedroom on the second level. Standing there now, his clothing completely drenched and the rain blowing in vertical sheets, he knew he could not climb the support posts all the way to the top, not without falling or creating a racket.

Mark's failure to secure his outside furniture on the upper level had resulted in the wind blowing everything down onto the deck below where several chairs had become wedged between the glass doors and the Jacuzzi. This was something Dave immediately noticed and thought he could use to his advantage. If Mark were waiting in his bedroom to attack from behind the sliding doors, the chairs might present enough of a barrier to keep him from getting through or, at least, slow him down a bit. With that in mind, Dave swiftly and stealthily raced up the staircases to the top deck, being especially cautious and alert as he crept past the Jacuzzi and the fallen chairs on the second level.

Because the neighbor had attached his floodlights at the midpoint between their houses, they did not shine directly onto Mark's rear decks, illuminating only a portion of them in addition to the side of his house. Stepping onto the upper deck, Dave remained hidden in the shadows as he moved closer to the edge of the glass doors. Despite the heaviness of his rain-soaked clothing, he moved with the grace of a cat, pausing only a second to catch his breath while tightly pressing his back against the house next to the sliding doors. Slowly and cautiously, he twisted his head to peek around the edge of the glass, straining his eyes to see through the murky darkness at an appalling scene that shocked his sensibilities and practically stopped his heart.

The only source of lighting in the living room came from the outside floodlights penetrating the slats of the window blinds to shoot through the air like laser beams, striking and highlighting various objects in the room, the most prominent one being Nikki sitting on the loveseat facing the deck. The whole scene had an artificial, almost staged appearance to it, and Dave suspected that Mark had arranged it just for him. Looking at Nikki through the glass, he struggled both emotionally and mentally to maintain his composure while suppressing his rage at seeing her so physically and emotionally distraught.

Nikki sat perfectly still in the center of the loveseat, a gag pulled tightly around her mouth and her hands tied behind her back, although her feet appeared to be unrestrained. She looked stiff and frozen, almost lifeless, projecting a sense of helplessness and vulnerability that was totally out of character for her. The sight of her blank expression triggered an emotional collapse in Dave that rendered him nearly inoperative until he regained control by focusing his attention on a narrow beam of light spreading across Nikki's cheekbone to expose her eyes. Moving closer to the glass to confirm something he thought he had seen, he studied her face, straining his vision like a mariner at sea searching the darkened horizon for a reassuring flash from a distant lighthouse. He received his proof-of-life through the movement of her eyelids when she blinked once and then twice more in quick succession, almost as if she were delivering a message—or perhaps a warning.

Wholly absorbed in his struggle to get to the house and climb the stairs to the upper deck, Dave had ignored the muffled barking of Grave left behind in the hearse, but Nikki had not. Attuned to the sounds of injured animals, she was conscious of the distant baying of a hound, which she heard despite the roaring of the storm, mainly in the lulls between the erratic wind gusts. Hoping that the barking meant that Dave was nearby, she silently prayed for deliverance, becoming quietly elated upon seeing his shaded figure out on the deck. At that point, she ceased praying and focused her mind on what she could do to help him.

Dave's presence outside may have provided Nikki some emotional relief, but it could not entirely erase the terror in her soul, an intense fear gripping her tighter than the cords binding her hands. Recognizing the need for alertness and mental acuity in this dire situation, she used the discomfort of the bindings to keep her mind sharp by slowly twisting her wrists back and forth, increasing her level of pain while watching Dave make several unsuccessful attempts at opening the sliding glass doors. More agonizing than the cords cutting into her skin was the emotional anguish she felt upon seeing the tortured look of defeat on Dave's face when he failed in his efforts to breach the glass barrier. She already knew that Mark had locked the doors, but she had no way of conveying that information to Dave.

It had been awhile since she had seen Mark, so she did not know his exact whereabouts in the house, only his general location based on random noises she heard coming from behind her. Adjusting the angle of her head to ensure that the light cut directly across her face, she used her eyes to motion to her left, the side of the house from where she heard sounds of movement. There was no guarantee that Dave could see her eyes through the rain-doused window or if he would even understand what she was trying to communicate, but she continued nonetheless, darting her eyes back and forth in a leftward direction while holding her head perfectly still, hoping to avoid attracting the attention of Mark. Continuing to broadcast her message as long as she could, she eventually stopped when the aching around her eyelids became too much to bear.

Fortunately, Dave had taken notice of her efforts to communicate despite the streaks of rain distorting his vision. Drawn to the bluish cast of her eyes, he saw their erratic movements, although he was unsure how to interpret what he saw. Rather than see it as a clue to Mark's presence somewhere on the left-side of the house, he took it as something more ominous, a warning sign that Mark was standing to her immediate left, lurking just out of sight on the other side of the glass, ready to pounce if the doors should be breached.

Dave briefly considered breaking the glass panel to reach Nikki, but he abandoned the idea because of his suspicion that Mark lay hidden beside the sliding doors. He also knew that escape would not be possible with Nikki bound the way she was. The only way to save her—he told himself—was to slip into the house undetected and get the drop on Mark. Frustrated by the fragile glass barrier keeping him from the woman he loved, he stared blankly at the locked panel while his mind struggled to devise a plan. It was then that a memory exploded across his consciousness like a flash grenade, causing him to turn away from the glass doors and quickly descend the stairs. Creeping stealthily down the steps toward the ground, he patted the side pocket of his shorts to confirm that he had with him the key to the front door.

Upon seeing Dave's figure vanish from sight, Nikki's heart sank to its lowest point yet. She knew that he must have a plan, or he would not have left; however, she wished he had been able to communicate his intentions before leaving. Still, losing sight of him on the deck deflated her emotionally, robbing her of the hope and confidence his physical presence had inspired. Once again, feeling lost and alone, she closed her eyes and resumed praying as a weapon against despair, pleading for aid and intercession by internally reciting the prayer etched into the golden Miraculous Medal she wore around her neck: *O Mary, conceived without sin, pray for us who have recourse to thee.*

Unaffected by the disturbing aspects of the weather, Dave descended the stairs with relative ease. Like Miguel standing outside the guard station at Pirate's Cove, he now seemed immune to the scourging blasts of wind and rain as he raced around the side of the house and up onto the porch. Using his right hand to retrieve the loaded Ruger from his cargo shorts, he passed it off to his left hand and then began rummaging around in another pocket for the house key. Finding it, he quietly inserted it into the slot after first confirming that the door was indeed locked.

Still operating on the assumption that Mark had placed Nikki on the loveseat in full view of the rear deck to precipitate a rescue attempt from that side of the house, Dave prayed that his interpretation of Nikki's signal had been correct, that Mark lay in wait beside the sliding glass doors. If that were the case—he surmised—and if he could slip into the house undetected through the front door, he might have a chance to fire off a few quick shots before Mark saw him. Aware that he was basing his entire battle plan on two questionable assumptions, he decided to proceed anyway because he had no other strategy. Moreover, he had no backup plan.

As he silently turned the key with his right hand, it struck him that the mere act of opening the door amounted to the most significant undertaking of his life, one that would ultimately determine his future or if he would even have a future for that matter. Whatever his fate—he told himself—he must be prepared to accept the consequences. Grasping the gun in his left hand with a grip no tighter than a firm handshake as instructed by the Mayor, he then took a deep breath and gently turned the doorknob.

Having become acclimated to the sound of the storm outside, he had not considered the mayhem he would be ushering into the house once he opened the door, but the shattered silence of the home's interior jolted his senses the moment he stepped across the threshold. Thrown into a panic by the noise and chaos surging in through the open doorway, he quickly closed the door and raced up the stairs to the living area where he fully expected to find Mark charging at him from the back of the house. If he could get just one clear shot—he told himself—perhaps he could stop the brute dead in his tracks before being overrun by him. Crouching in the darkness at the top of the stairs, he pointed the Ruger toward the rear of the house while maintaining a loose grip on the gunstock to prevent the laser sight from revealing his location. He wished to keep his whereabouts unknown until he had a visual target in sight, at which time he would engage the laser beam and project it onto the heart of his enemy.

Several seconds passed, but nothing happened. Still, he waited in the darkness, sucking in massive amounts of air while straining to hear over the sound of the blood pulsing through the sides of his head. It was inconceivable to him that Mark had not heard him enter the house, and yet there had been no counteroffensive launched in his direction. Everything appeared quiet and calm except for the howling of the wind and the clattering of rain against the vinyl siding of the house. Uncertain and agitated, he rose slowly from his crouched position and took a step forward, startled by the squeaking of his shoes on the hardwood floor. The water dripping from his hair and clothing also disturbed him due to the sound of the water droplets hitting the ground like cannonballs, increasing his level of paranoia due to the amount of noise he was making. However, when nothing happened, he wondered if he was overreacting, being far too sensitive to the sounds around him. Perhaps, he thought, fear and anxiety were over-stimulating his senses, most notably his sense of hearing.

Turning to look over his shoulder, he spotted the framed mirror hanging on the wall and the closed bathroom door directly behind him. To his right was the dining area along with the entranceway to the kitchen, and to his left, down the stairs, was the foyer leading to the lower level rooms that included Mark's bedroom and office. From his perch high at the top of the stairs, Dave could see through the darkened room all the way to the back of the house where leaked ribbons of light sliced the living room in thin divisions, casting zebra stripes of illumination across the back of the loveseat on which Nikki sat bound and gagged. Against the brighter backdrop of the glass doors, he could see the outline of her head as she faced away from him, staring out at the deck where he had been only a few minutes earlier. He then directed his line of sight to the side of the glass doors where he expected to see Mark lurking in the shadows, only to have his plans upended when the only thing visible in that corner of the room was a menacingly dark void. Flummoxed and frightened at finding no one standing there, he swallowed hard on the massive lump in his throat.

Panic immediately set in, clouding his judgment and robbing his muscles of all fluidity. Fearing that Mark might be stalking him from below, Dave jerked his head to the left and peered down into the darkened foyer where everything appeared quiet and still. Satisfied that his left flank was clear but still feeling vulnerable, he swung his body erratically to the right, frantically searching for his deadly adversary but not finding him anywhere. That was when it happened.

Concentrating so much on an attack from one side or the other, Dave had neglected to secure his rear flank, leaving him unaware that the bathroom door had opened to reveal a large shadowy figure standing behind him in the darkened doorway. Still glancing to his right, Dave detected a brief flash from the corner of his eye the moment an enormous hand reached out to grab him, clutching his neck and practically crushing his trachea in its mighty grip. When he tried to point the weapon in the direction of his assailant, another huge hand clasped the gun, completely encasing both his hand and small Ruger in its large spreading fingers. The pressure binding his hand to the gun was so powerful that Dave could not have released the pistol even if he had wanted to, and he quickly realized that he was no match for the strength of the man now in control of his body.

Still grasping Dave by his neck, Mark lifted him off his feet and positioned him so that he could view him face-to-face while he carefully pointed the gun off to the side. Their pose suggested two macabre waltzing partners with Mark playing the role of an overbearing dance instructor forcing his reluctant partner to succumb to his lead. Holding Dave slightly at arm's length to keep water from dripping on his neatly pressed shorts and unsoiled deck shoes, Mark said triumphantly when he heard the smaller man gasping for air, "Calm down. You're getting water all over my new shoes. If you relax, I'll put you down." He then smiled while pulling Dave closer to his face, glaring at him through his ghostly, unshaded eyes. "By the way," he added, "what took you so long to get here? I don't like to be kept waiting." His tone and physical demeanor gave no indication that suspending Dave in the air like that required any exertion on his part nor did it seem to cause him any discomfort.

Dave tried to calm himself as he had been instructed to do, but the lack of oxygen made it impossible, causing him to kick and squirm like a thief at the end of hangman's noose. Struggling to remain conscious, he felt himself losing the battle when Mark suddenly stayed the execution by lowering him a few inches, allowing the toes of his shoes to touch the hardwood floor. Additionally, Mark softened his death grip so that air could reach Dave's lungs. He laughed and said, "There, now isn't that better? Not quite as cocky today, are we?"

Barely able to breathe, Dave could not respond, so he remained quiet and offered no resistance as Mark dragged him across the floor to the other side of the room where they stopped directly in front of Nikki, whose eyes immediately filled with tears upon seeing the strained, pitiful look on Dave's face.

"Don't look so glum, little one," Mark said. "We both knew your boyfriend would show up sooner or later. I told you he couldn't stay away."

Dave tried to glance down at Nikki but was unable to see her because of the way Mark was holding him, an awkward position that required Dave to tilt back his head to facilitate breathing. He knew that Mark could crush his throat with a flick of a finger, so he did his best not to provoke the brute while trying to come up with a way to reverse this disastrous turn of events. Only his right hand was free, so he used it to grab the wrist of his captor, not in any attempt to overpower the larger man but merely to take the weight off his neck and make it easier to breathe. Mark looked disapprovingly at the hand clutching his wrist, so Dave let it drop to his side and instead concentrated on struggling to remain on his toes, keeping his balance as best he could on the floor that was becoming increasingly slippery due to the amount of water dripping from his clothing.

Mark then pushed Dave slightly away from his body and began examining him as he would a newly purchased item, using his grotesquely dilated pupils to study him in the darkness. "You know," he said in a casual manner, "this is going to work out just fine. Nikki and I had a nice long conversation before you got here." Smiling down at her, he pulled Dave a little closer to him and said caustically, "She told me a lot of interesting things about you, and, I must say, I couldn't have found a bigger fool if I had advertised for one in the Outer Banks Sentinel." Pausing a moment, he added in Nikki's direction, "Don't you think so, my dear?"

Nikki was on the verge of tears, and it took all her strength to maintain her composure. The part she found most disturbing was the tortured look on Dave's face, an expression she had seen only on the faces of dying and infirmed animals scheduled for euthanasia. How could Mark do this?—she wondered. And why was he acting this way?

"What's wrong? Mark asked sarcastically. "Am I the only one here interested in talking? Well, I guess that's okay because I really don't care what either of you have to say. So, let's get right to the point. Here's what's going to happen." As he said that, he eased the strain on his arm by lowering Dave to the ground while maintaining a firm grip on his neck. It was the first sign of fatigue exhibited by Mark, and it offered Dave a glimmer of hope, the only one he had experienced since becoming a human marionette. With his feet planted firmly on the ground, he could now breathe normally plus he could see Nikki for the first time, her face clearly exposed in a crossbeam of light. Beneath the few golden strands of hair falling softly across her forehead, he noticed bruising and redness on her cheekbone as well as some swelling around her eye, newly sustained injuries that made his blood boil.

"So, here's the plan," Mark continued. "My girlfriend, Nikki, comes over to my house to ride out the hurricane, and I run out to get some food and supplies. While I'm at the store, something terrible happens." He stopped and looked at Dave. "This is where you come in." He made the remark with a chuckle before continuing, "It turns out that, while I'm gone, a low-life drifter breaks into my house and finds my girlfriend here all alone. He ties her up, gags her, and then kills her, shooting her with this gun, which conveniently has your fingerprints all over it."

At the sound of Mark's words, Nikki's eyes widened with alarm. She could not believe what she was hearing. Additionally, she could not understand how Mark could be speaking or acting this way.

Looking searchingly at Dave for answers, she was shocked to see no sign of awareness in his eyes, his face appearing blank and unaffected, almost as if he were distracted by something else.

With a broad smile, Mark resumed his morbid tale, "I arrive home and walk into the house just minutes after the murder has occurred; however, I get the jump on the murderer before he has the chance to kill me too. We fight, and I almost strangled him, but then I wrestle the gun from his hand and shoot him with it ... or maybe I just strangled him. I haven't decided yet. Anyway, that's how it ends for both of you." He then snickered and asked, "Any questions? ... No? ... Well, then, I guess there's nothing to discuss."

Mark paused to look at his two captives, trying to assess their reaction to his proposed scenario before adding, "Of course, I'll be incredibly heartbroken and distraught over all of this. I'll berate myself for not having returned home sooner. 'If only I had arrived two minutes earlier,' I'll tell myself, 'I could have saved poor Nikki.' Of course, after that, I won't be able to live in this house any longer ... or even in this area. I'll have to move away and start over again." He stopped and grinned. "Yes, that's it. I'll start over. Plenty more towns to visit. Plenty more people to sample." He looked down at Dave and added, "And plenty more surfer dudes to take the fall."

Dave did not react or even appear to be listening.

"You understand, don't you, that the police will find residue of human remains inside your vehicle and conclude that you're a serial murderer, especially when they receive word of a body buried on the beach in a shallow grave. By the way, I know where you dumped the girl I put in your hearse. You're not the only one who likes to follow people around in the dark."

Again, he looked directly at Dave but got no reaction. As before, Dave seemed distant and unaffected.

"Well, anyway," he said, "let's get to our first order of business. Don't worry; everyone in the neighborhood has gone away, so no one will hear the gunshots. Even if they were still around, I doubt they'd be able to hear anything over the noise of the hurricane. My only regret is that I'll be forced to waste all this tasty blood, but I guess it's incumbent on all of us to make sacrifices. Wouldn't you agree?" Just then, a powerful blast of wind hit the house, causing the windows and walls to bulge slightly and the whole structure to shudder on its supports. "Wow!" he said breathlessly. "That was a big one."

Knowing what the "first order of business" entailed, Nikki squirmed and tried to stand, but Mark raised his foot and kicked her solidly on the thigh, sending her falling back onto the loveseat with a whimper and moan that was barely audible through the fabric of her gag. Dave's reaction to the assault was an angry jerk, prompting Mark to tighten his grip and again lift him into the air by his neck, holding him there until he calmed down. The promptness with which Mark then lowered him to the ground provided Dave additional confirmation that the big man's arm was becoming fatigued.

Mark then spoke coldly and purposefully to both Dave and Nikki. "Like I said, time to get to business." Turning his head toward Dave, he announced, "Last chance to say goodbye to your sweetie—ah hell, forget it. No time for such things." With that said, he used his superior strength to direct Dave's hand and pistol toward the loveseat, aiming the lethal weapon directly at Nikki's head.

The position of the gun was such that Dave could stare directly down the sight into Nikki's despairing eyes, fully exposed by a piercing beam of white light cutting across her face. Awash in tears, they appeared unanimated and somber, a stark contrast to the joyful confidence they typically projected, and they mirrored the despondency of her body revealed by another shaft of light illuminating her drooping shoulders.

Dave could read the silent plea in her eyes, a desperate appeal for him to do something, but he knew and accepted that he was out of time and out of options. He had failed her as he had failed himself and everyone else in his life, and he now found himself forced to witness, yet again, the death of someone he loved. His only consolation was that it would be the last time he would ever have to endure something so tragic and heartbreaking. This was indeed the end, and he could conceive of no power on earth capable of changing that outcome. Nikki saw the capitulation in his eyes, and it robbed her of all remaining hope, ultimately forcing her to give up as well.

Despite his own apparent surrender, he found the look of finality on her face unbearable, so he lowered his eyes to hide his shame. In doing so, he caught sight of something unusual when Nikki inhaled deeply to stop herself from crying. Appearing as a sparkle in a stray beam of light, it shimmered for a brief second before settling into a warm glow against the smooth skin of her bosom, visible only because of a torn button off her shirt that had opened her collar to reveal the golden Miraculous Medal she wore on a chain around her neck. He instantly recognized the Virgin on the face of the medal, appearing precisely as Father Andal had described her with her hands issuing forth protective, intercessory rays as she stood atop a globe while crushing a serpent's head with her feet. As he stared intently at the iconic image, he detected a subtle change in the medallion's appearance the moment its brilliance faded and its color became somewhat duller, appearing more like brass than gold. The sight of it stopped his emotional plunge and stirred within him a vital memory.

He quickly recalled his firearm training with the Mayor in the parking lot of the Outer Banks Fishing Pier, and it made him redirect his gaze toward the gun, zeroing in on the viewing port of the Ruger's cartridge extraction slot. Either by fate or chance—or through some intercessory power—Mark had positioned the gun so that it was fully exposed in a horizontal shaft of light leaking through the side window; however, unlike the open neck of Nikki's blouse, Dave saw no glint of metal inside the small viewing portal. Rather than the luster of burnished brass, he saw only a deep, black hole—dark as an unfilled grave—providing immediate confirmation that the firing chamber was empty. In the rush and struggle of getting into the house to save Nikki, he had forgotten to chamber a bullet by sliding back the cocking mechanism.

This, he realized, was his lifeline—the extra time he needed—and it breathed new life into him as he jettisoned all despair and directed his gaze back toward Nikki. Seeing him look down at her, she noticed a change in his demeanor, but she did not know what to make of it. Not only was there an energetic twinkle in his eye, but she also observed something in his expression that seemed slightly mischievous, a facial tic that he would exhibit whenever he was playing a trick on her. Confused but now somewhat hopeful, she watched intently with a look of bafflement on her face until she noticed Mark forcing back Dave's trigger finger, at which time her expression changed from one of confusion to blind fear.

The pivotal moment had arrived—Dave told himself—the one described by the Mayor in which a warrior momentarily retreats with the intention of returning to the battlefield stronger and more lethal than before. For that reason, he let his body go entirely limp as he channeled all his energy into the trigger finger of his left hand. With the firing mechanism un-cocked, he knew that the trigger would lack resistance, so he struggled to create a false sense of trigger pressure, hoping to fool his captor. Mark easily overcame the simulated resistance by vigorously tugging on Dave's protruding index finger while increasing his overall grip on Dave's hand that engaged the laser sight to project a tiny red dot on Nikki's forehead. Nikki did her best to control her fear by gazing trustingly at the look of confidence and determination on Dave's face. As inexplicable as it seemed, he appeared to be smiling.

Ever so slowly, the trigger inched back while Dave struggled to prolong the outcome as long as possible, making good use of each addition second yielded by the charade. Unaware that the war already had begun and misled by the limpness of Dave's body, Mark erroneously assumed that his small captive had surrendered, leading him to unconsciously ease his chokehold while focusing his attention on aiming the pistol. Sensing the decreased pressure around his neck, Dave turned his head just enough to stare directly into the face of his deadly assailant. Only about a foot separated them, and he wished to observe Mark's facial expression when the gun failed to discharge.

Within two seconds, Dave received his wish with the scenario playing out exactly as he had anticipated. The smug look on Mark's face vanished the minute the trigger struck the gunstock with a tiny click rather than a loud explosion, and his expression changed into one of confusion as he struggled to comprehend what had just happened. It was then that he noticed Dave looking at him instead of Nikki, so he turned to meet his captive's gaze, stunned by the sight of Dave grinning at him in open defiance.

As Mark's bewilderment morphed into blind rage, Dave seized the moment—perhaps the last one of his life—to return to the battlefield with renewed strength and vigor. It was then that everything slowed and time began progressing gradually as it always did whenever he found himself in intense or dire situations. He immediately sensed a stiffening of Mark's body along with the tightening of the big man's thumb and fingers around his throat; however, the sluggish contraction of Mark's fatigued muscles were no match for the speed and nimbleness of Dave's lean body exploding from a state of lethal contraction to strike a blow at the heart of his enemy. Nikki had marveled at Dave's physical prowess while watching him windsurf on Roanoke Sound a few days earlier, and she observed it again there in the confines of Mark's living room where his actions bore considerably more consequence.

With the athletic symmetry and balance of a surfer shooting the curl, coupled with the speed and proficiency of a gunslinger drawing his revolver, Dave pulled from his pocket an unfolded pocketknife gripped tightly in the fingers of his dangling right hand. Always an invaluable survival tool, he had transformed the old Cub Scout knife into a lethal weapon by opening it covertly in the side pocket of his cargo shorts using just one hand, an amazing feat requiring total concentration as well as incredible dexterity. Having achieved his goal of opening the knife in time for the feigned discharge of the gun, he then demonstrated the power and accuracy of a warrior fighting his last battle on earth by driving the blade into the solar plexus of the would-be assassin, slicing through the skin, tendons, and muscle of his adversary like surgeon wielding a scalpel. A final shove of the deadly instrument then sealed Mark's fate when, using the heel of his hand, Dave drove the knife—handle and all— directly into the heart of the beast without flinching, blinking, or taking his eyes off his opponent's face for even a second.

Mark's expression went from anger to confusion to fear, all in quick succession. With a flick of his arm, he tossed Dave aside like a piece of unwanted debris, flinging him toward the wall by the television cabinet and fireplace. He then reached down for the gun that had fallen onto the floor, but Nikki extended her foot and gave it a quick kick, sending it sliding beneath the leather couch several feet away. The large wounded man seemed bewildered and uncertain of what to do next, so Dave used that moment of hesitation to regain his footing and begin searching for a new weapon. Finding a fireplace poker in the stand next to him, he moved back toward Mark with the iron rod gripped tightly in both hands while Nikki jumped to her feet and sought refuge behind him.

Offensively opposing the injured giant with the poker raised for striking, Dave looked like a batter awaiting a pitch in some deadly game of baseball; however, Mark seemed uninterested in playing or accepting the challenge, ignoring the provocation and looking straight through Dave as if he were not even there. Rotating the weapon in his hand, Dave then pointed the sharpened tip at the dazed monster, holding it like a harpoon or a lance, assuming the pose of a whaler or a warrior archangel. His intention was to drive it into the beast and finish him off, but he never got the chance to strike.

The blood oozing from the wound on Mark's chest saturated the fabric of his polo shirt, turning it from brilliant white to a fatal shade of ruby red. Despite the darkness of the room, both Nikki and Dave could see the spot increasing in size like a blossoming red rose, confirming for Dave that his theory regarding Mark's mortality had been a correct one. Observing the confusion and disorientation of the injured man, Dave hoped he was witnessing the last of the murderous fiend. Mark no longer cared about Dave or Nikki, and he looked past them while searching the interior space like a wounded animal seeking an avenue of escape, the instinct to survive supplanting his desire to fight.

As Mark's eyes panned the room, they stopped and focused attentively on something near the top of the stairs at the far end of the house. Reaching to the neck of his polo shirt, he ripped it open with single a tug of his mighty arms, tearing it from his body like a flamboyant professional wrestler entering the ring. He then cast aside the remnants of the shredded fabric while trudging bare-chested toward the location where he had first assaulted Dave. Stumbling slightly, he caught himself on the arm of the loveseat but struggled onward, intentionally stepping out of his deck shoes to proceed barefoot across the wooden floor.

It was not until Mark reached down and began loosening the belt of his shorts that Dave realized where he was heading. Gripping the poker tightly in one hand, Dave attempted to stop Mark's retreat by hurdling the loveseat, only to have the former All-American swat him away with his massive forearm, sending him flying through the air like so many others who had challenged the gifted running back. Even wounded, Mark remained a powerful and dangerous adversary.

Regaining his footing, Dave again lunged forward but slipped on the wet floor made slick by his rain-soaked clothing. That allowed Mark sufficient time to remove his shorts and underwear as he continued his death march toward the wall. Faltering, but then catching himself, he paused naked in front of the full-length mirror where he stared blankly at the glassy surface projecting a reflection of the room behind him and nothing more. No longer appearing neat and manicured but disheveled and bleeding, he seemed on the verge of collapse as he extended one hand toward the wall, supporting himself with his arm while gasping for air. With each strained breath, more blood bubbled from the open wound on his chest to roll down the front of his body and drip onto the floor in thick strands of red liquid. The life source he had stolen from so many others now ran freely onto the ground, pooling in puddles around his feet.

For a brief second or two, he seemed to recover his strength as he pulled himself together and turned to observe his pursuer still scrambling to get to his feet. Dave was unaware that the killer was watching him until he spotted Mark's bleached face—white as Ahab's whale—hovering in the darkness, the black dots of his eyes peering morbidly at him from across the room. Realizing that he could not get to the mirror in time to thwart Mark's escape, Dave ceased his frantic efforts and stared back at the harpooned giant with a sense of curiosity. Despite the whistling of the wind and the thunderous pounding of the rain against the house, Dave could hear the labored breathing of Mark's death rattle, indicating what awaited the expiring giant if he remained much longer on this side of the glass. From that distance, he could not clearly discern Mark's expression, whether it was smugness or scorn, but he knew there was a message in it only because it was delivered with such intensity and purpose. It lasted only a second before the dying predator turned and passed unimpeded through the surface of the mirror while Nikki watched in shocked disbelief from the other side of the room.

Dave rushed forward without hesitation, but he could not follow his wounded prey into the mirror because the glass hardened immediately after Mark passed through it. Uncertain of what to do next but unwilling to take any chances, he surrendered to his basic instincts and began violently smashing the mirror with the wrought-iron poker, striking it with the same force he would have used against the giant had he been standing there. Refusing to stop even after demolishing the mirror, he swung wildly at the jagged pieces falling through the air, shattering them into even smaller shards before they hit the wooden floor with a resounding clatter. During all of this, Nikki stood motionless by the loveseat, paralyzed by what she had just witnessed while Dave completely ignored her, focusing all his attention on destroying the mirror and its pieces.

Reaching for the switch on the wall, Dave turned on the recessed lightening and then charged into the kitchen where Nikki heard him opening and closing cabinet doors. He then returned with a heavy-duty trash bag along with an empty cardboard box into which he put the broken pieces of the mirror before running downstairs, taking with him both the box and the fireplace poker. As Nikki walked toward the stairs, she could hear him dashing from room to room smashing every the mirror in the place until the interior of the house finally grew quiet again. That was when Dave raced back into the foyer and suddenly stopped when he saw Nikki standing at the top of the stairs still bound and gagged.

"I'm sorry," he said while charging up the steps to kiss her softly on the cheek. Gently placing his hand on the swelling beneath her eye, he asked, "Are you okay?" In response to her nod, he turned her around and started loosening the restraints of her wrists by prying at the knots with his fingertips. Not waiting for him to remove the gag, Nikki reached up and pulled the cloth from of her mouth as soon as her hands were free, immediately spinning around to embrace him by locking her arms tightly around his neck. He said jokingly after a few moments, "My throat is never going to be the same after tonight."

Releasing him suddenly, she said, "I'm sorry; I forgot." She then glanced over and peered questioningly at the empty frame still hanging on the wall. "But how—"

"Not now," he said with a sense of urgency. "I'll explain later." His tone implied that he had more work to do. Putting the cardboard box into the plastic trash bag, he tied it securely and tucked the whole thing under one arm. He said, "You stay here until I get back. I don't want these mirror fragments anywhere near us." Without waiting for a response, he turned and started down the stairs while adding, "I'm getting rid of them for good."

"Where?" she asked.

Her words reached his ears just as his hand touched the doorknob, and he paused briefly before looking back at her. "The sea," he said with a feigned tone of assurance as he opened the door, an action that released into the foyer an unexpected blast of wind and rain that nearly knocked him off his feet.

"Will that work?" she asked skeptically.

He did not respond to her question, choosing instead to lower his head and charge into the stormy night, unwilling to acknowledge his own misgivings about the practicality of his intended actions.

Nikki walked over to the empty frame next to the bathroom door, and she reached through it to touch the wall with her fingertips, trying to determine if the wall behind the mirror was indeed solid. Hammering it a few times with her fist, she looked for a trap door or a passageway into the bathroom but found none. Further inspection from inside the bathroom also turned up nothing, so she walked out and began probing the blood on the floor beneath the frame, poking it a few times with the toe of her shoe to confirm that it was not a figment of her imagination. Nikki did not like questions without answers or problems without solutions—she never had—but this whole thing had her flummoxed. Everything she had witnessed was impossible by any set of standards; however, she knew in her heart that it was not a magician's trick. The violence, the pain, the blood—it was all too real.

Lingering near the top of the stairs, Nikki stared blankly at the floor and began mentally reviewing the events of the past week, hoping to gain a better understanding of what had happened. It was then that the front door unexpectedly opened, releasing into the house all the chaos and violence of the storm. Clutching her chest, she instinctively shrieked at the torrent of water and rain surging into the foyer until she saw Dave standing there drenched to the bone with Grave tethered to him on a leash. Seeing Nikki at the top of the stairs, the drowned basset hound issued an excited bark and then twirled its body like an airplane propeller, sending droplets of water flying in all directions.

Smiling down at the dog, Dave said, "I wish I could do that." He then looked up at Nikki and asked, "Where's your car keys? I need something with four-wheel-drive to get around out there." Without hesitation, Nikki raced to the dining room to get her keys off the table. Tossing them down to Dave while Grave charged up the stairs to greet her, she was about to say something when Dave cut her off. "Wait here," he said to both Nikki and the dog. "You'll be safe until I get back." With that, he turned and vanished through the door, once again plunging into the storm with the box tucked securely under his arm.

In the brief time it had taken Dave to retrieve Grave and leave him with Nikki, the weather conditions had grown much worse. Walking against the wind was now practically impossible, especially while carrying a cumbersome box enclosed in a plastic trash bag. He needed the covering to keep the cardboard from becoming saturated, but the plastic had become wet and slippery, making it hard to grip and control in the driving wind. At least three times on his short trek from the porch to Nikki's Jeep, he nearly lost it to the night.

The rain was blowing sideways when he turned off Mark's street and steered onto Seachase Drive. He was still quite anxious, not yet having calmed down after his deadly confrontation with Mark, and he found himself driving a little too fast for conditions until reduced visibility made him slow down. Straining to see the road ahead of him, he failed to notice a dark object moving erratically off to his right, a large projectile that plowed into the passenger door of the car before flipping over the roof to tumble off into the darkness. Although startled by his close encounter with a plastic garbage can, he remained committed to reaching his destination, vowing not to let flying debris deter him from his mission. Just then, a yellow steel highway sign soared past his headlights, and he began seriously considering the dangers posed by airborne hazards that night. Reaching the intersection by the Outer Banks Mall, he turned slowly and carefully onto the rain-soaked pavement before proceeding south along the bypass.

The traffic signals suspended over the highway were still functioning properly, although they swayed and rocked excessively on their long metal booms. He paid them little heed as he increased his speed and raced recklessly toward his destination, hydroplaning over the deeper pockets of water. At one point, while skimming across a flooded section of pavement, a blast of wind nearly shoved him off the road, but he regained traction just in time to veer back into his lane and continue down the bypass.

Occasionally, he would glance uncomfortably at the box of broken mirror pieces sitting next to him on the passenger's seat, wondering if it were possible for Mark to materialize right there inside the car. After what he had observed over the past week, nothing seemed impossible. He knew that he was in uncharted territory in which there was no way of knowing what could or could not occur. With reality no longer evident or certain, all he could do was suspend judgment and lumber along in a state of anticipation, nervously awaiting the next surprise with an open willingness to accept whatever happened.

His destination was only three miles away along a route leading down the bypass to East Gray Eagle Street, a cross street connecting the bypass to the beach road in the vicinity of Whalebone Junction. The intersection had no traffic signal, so he had to slow down to keep from missing it, straining his eyes to see through the blowing rain and roadside debris tumbling across the highway. Whalebone Seafood Market sat on the corner of the intersection, so Dave searched the darkness for the *Fresh Seafood* signs displayed on the sides of the building. Despite the distraction of the highway signs flapping wildly in the wind, he spotted the lighted signs of the seafood market and determined where he needed to turn.

Reducing his speed even more, he quickly engaged the four-wheel-drive while turning onto the cross street and plowing straight into the standing water covering the road. He hoped to travel as far as possible before becoming mired in water and sand, but he knew he was close enough to his destination to finish the journey on foot if necessary, although it would not be easy given the circumstances. As it turned out, he did not encounter excessively deep water on the street, but he could see it up ahead near the Dare Building at the corner of East Gray Eagle Street and the beach road. Unable to predict the water's depth but unwilling to halt his forward progress, he threw caution to the wind and plunged directly into the swollen lake while turning south on the beach road.

His discovery that the water was not as deep as he had feared both surprised and delighted him. The depth of the flooding was only about two-thirds the height of his wheels, so he plowed through it with relative ease, proceeding just a little slower than normal due to the extreme weather conditions. His biggest challenge was visibility as he strained to see through the rain while endeavoring to keep himself centered on the pavement. He could not afford to veer into the sandy soup along the berm, not even in a four-wheel-drive Jeep, but he could not see the edges of the road, forcing him to align himself using only the lighted business signs that were hard to distinguish in the blinding rain. Passing Cahoon's Market on the left, he searched ahead for the Sam & Omie's sign on the right, a lighted landmark that told him he was traveling safely in the middle of the road. A quick glance to his left then confirmed that he had arrived at his intended destination, Jennette's Pier.

Despite the glowing light from the numerous tall lampposts rising high above the ground, it was still dark and gloomy in the pier's parking lot due to the blowing sheets of rain obscuring the powerful overhead floodlights. Using Sam & Omie's Restaurant as a guide, he approximated the location of the pier's entrance ramp and plowed straight into the parking lot, fighting his way onto the flooded asphalt by spinning his tires over the buildup of sand along the berm of the road. With the parking lot completely empty, he encountered no obstacles as soared across the wet pavement and parked near the pedestrian ramps leading to a large pier house on which hung the logo of Jennette's Pier, a stylized fish silhouetted by blue fluorescent lighting glowing eerily in the blustery night.

Of the two ramps providing access to the shingled pier house, Dave chose the ramp on the right, the one leading directly to the main entrance. Laboring hard against the wind, he used the squat lampstands in the center of the incline to pull himself up the ramp while he clutched the box tightly to his chest, its plastic covering shielding his body from the pelting rain but leaving his face and legs totally exposed. With wet, blowing sand filling his eyes and nostrils, he could neither see nor breathe, but he trudged on nonetheless, struggling hard to hang onto his load while trying to maintain his footing on the slippery wooden planks of the ramp.

Upon reaching the covered walkway leading to the fishing pier at the back of the building, he picked up his gait and began hustling across the floorboards with the box tucked securely under one arm. Passing the locked doors of the education center and gift shop, he approached a five-foot high stainless steel gate, closed and bolted shut for the night. Without slowing down, he reached out with one hand and attempted to vault the barrier in a single bound but lost his grip and dropped to the ground on the other side of the gate. Unwilling to acknowledge the pain of the fall, he jumped to his feet and plunged back into the severe weather, running straight onto the fishing pier with the hurricane raging all around him.

The twenty-two-foot wide pier extended one thousand feet out over the ocean. It usually stood twenty-five feet above the surface of the water, but the sea had breached the slatted railings at the top of the structure due to the waves crashing around the pilings, shooting plumes of seawater into the air like water cannons. When Dave saw the spray of the waves and the horizontal torrents of rain rushing past the lighted lampposts along the center of the walkway, he began questioning if he could traverse the pier without being blown away or washed into the sea. The told himself that if he could just get to the end of it and dump the mirror pieces into the water, then the colossal forces of the ocean, especially in a tempest such as this, would pulverize them into sand against the two hundred and fifty-seven concrete pilings of the giant structure.

Unwilling to risk walking upright, he dropped down and began crawling across the wooden planks on his elbows and knees, hoping to lessen the likelihood that the wind would blow him into the sea or rip box from his arms before he reached the end of the pier. Although he could not see them high above him in the darkness, he could hear the moaning of the three ten-kilowatt turbines spinning on their ninety-foot towers. Despite the feathering of the turbine blades, they still turned quickly in the hurricane winds, and their creaks and groans reverberated inside the metal towers, simulating the sound of humpback whales singing a melancholy hymn. Hearing the unholy dirge, Dave reflected on Captain Ahab and the White Whale, relieved that he had escaped the captain's fate in his contest with Mark but fearful that he might not survive this final chapter.

Creeping along at a snail's pace amid the nightmarish conditions of the storm, Dave mentally disassociated himself from the dangers he faced until he finally reached the end of the pier where he sat with his back against the security railing, only then becoming truly conscious of the perilous situation in which he found himself. Assaulted from every side by rain, spray, and wind—separated from the frothy, unforgiving sea by only a few thin boards—he grew increasingly uneasy as he clutched the box to his chest while pondering his next move. The violence and brutality he had experienced at the hands of Mark earlier that evening now seemed tame compared to what Mother Nature was unleashing on him, and it made him question his chances of survival. Feeling the concrete structure sway and shudder with each pounding wave, he feared that the whole thing might fold and collapse into the ocean at any moment, ultimately condemning him to Ahab's fate.

Not wishing to dwell on negative outcomes, he restrained his alarm and set about completing the task-at-hand. Removing the trash bag from around the cardboard box, he released it to the wind

where it soared off into the blackness of the night with a quick snap
and flutter. He then shielded the box from the rain by holding it
close to his body while awaiting the right moment, counting the
seconds between wind gusts to discern a predictable pattern that
would allow him to act with a modicum of safety. Upon
encountering an extended lull, one slightly longer than the rest, he
popped to his feet and spun around toward the savage ocean with
the box lifted high above his head. With all the strength he could
muster, he hurled the box over the railing toward the sea, exposing
it to the unbridled fury of the wind that slammed it into one of the
concrete pilings, obliterating the box and spilling its contents into
the air where the mirror fragments collided with other pilings before
plunging into the raging sea to face even greater destruction. Then
and only then did Dave experience a feeling of relief and closure, a
sense that Mark was truly gone, that his evil, menacing presence had
finally departed this world.

Conscious of the danger he still faced and the foolishness of
remaining there any longer than necessary, he began making his way
back to the pier house amid the low, mournful dirge of the turbine
whales droning in the night. Feeling the shifting and shuddering
beneath him, he began fretting over the structure's ability to
withstand the onslaught of the storm. Several years before,
Hurricane Isabel had swept away the entire fishing pier, but the
North Carolina Aquarium Society had spearheaded an effort to
replace it with this new one, a stronger, sturdier structure with
pilings made of concrete rather than wood. He prayed that it would
fare better against the current tempest, at least for a few more
minutes.

Arriving at the end of his nightmare and wishing to avoid killing
himself now that it was almost over, he snaked the whole way back
on his stomach, unwilling to risk even crawling on his hands and
knees for fear of being blown into the sea. It was not until he
reached the pier house and the shelter of the covered walkway that
he began feeling a sense of confidence returning, although he
understood the challenges still facing him in getting back to Nikki.
Standing sopping wet at the edge of the building, he readied himself
to charge down the ramp into the parking lot when he saw a
brilliant blue flash light up the sky near the bypass. The fiery light
came from an electrical transformer that blazed brightly for a
second or two before plunging the entire region into darkness.
Aware of the difficulty he had experienced in getting to Jennette's
Pier with the aid of lighted signs and street lamps to guide the way,
he moaned despairingly at the thought of making the return trip in

total darkness. "Great," he said. "That's all I need."

Dave was not the only one to witness the explosive flare that left the Outer Banks squatting beneath a pall of darkness. Nikki also had seen the flash in the sky while watching for him through the rain-streaked glass of the sliding doors at the back of the house. Her familiarity with Mark's home then helped her find several candles that she placed throughout the house, mainly in the living room but also on a table in the foyer near the front door. Afterward, she anxiously resumed her watchful vigil, returning to the glass doors where she had a clear view of the bypass. Grave, who had not left her side the entire time, sat calmly on the floor next to her, leaning heavily against her leg while she scratched the wet fur on the top of his head. With her other hand, she lightly stroked her swollen cheekbone, wondering what story she would tell to explain the injury.

She watched for a long time but saw nothing in the sea of darkness extending out from the deck. At one point, she spotted the flashing strobe of an emergency vehicle speeding down the bypass toward the damaged transformer, but that was the only light she saw anywhere in the outside world. The weather seemed to be getting worse, and the house had begun quivering and quaking even more than before under the relentless pounding of the wind, sparking safety concerns that only added to her anxiety over Dave's extended absence. Having already proven himself to be resilient and incredibly resourceful when placed in dangerous situations, she was confident that he would survive; however, she was still burdened by an overwhelming sense of doom.

Dropping to her knees, she began gently stroking Grave's head while looking into his large, soulful eyes, pretending to console him but knowing that he was the one consoling her. Grave was her only link to his master at that moment, and touching his soft, moist fur provided her an emotional connection to Dave in his struggle against the darkness. Tugging gently on the long, brown ears of the basset hound, she nervously smiled as Grave put his nose into her face and curiously sniffed the wound below her eye.

While kneeling on the floor beside the dog, Nikki noticed a flash of light dance across the ceiling of the room, and it caused her to jump to her feet and peer through the glass doors where she spotted the trademark round headlamps of a Jeep driving cautiously up West Seachase Drive. Unable to contain her emotion, she raced across the room and down into the foyer where she waited impatiently for Dave's arrival, surprising him the moment he stepped through the doorway by falling into his arms and burying her head in his neck, hugging him tighter than anyone she had ever embraced in her life. This time, however, Dave made no complaint about the bruising around his throat. Instead, he stood quietly in the flickering candlelight of the foyer, holding Nikki firmly and tenderly in his arms while Grave feverishly wagged his tail and lapped at the water dripping from his master's clothing.

Outside the house, the rain continued pummeling the earth in wind-driven torrents as the hurricane roared across the Outer Banks with unbridled fury while the three occupants of the house nestled together in peace and love, safe within the confines of their private sanctuary and happy in each other's company, especially Dave who felt real joy and contentment for the first time in his life.

Chapter 14

The day had a luminous quality to it, much like that of a highly polished mirror, with the sun burning brightly in the sky and the seagulls soaring effortlessly on the heat thermals rising above Coquina Beach. Not far away, Dave and Nikki stood atop a palisade dune dressed appropriately in tee shirts and shorts while Grave zigzagged erratically through a patch of sea oats, the white tip of his tail the only visible part of his squat, muscular body.

Standing barefoot in the sand, Dave held in his hand a small bunch of the flowers, blossoms Nikki had picked on their way to the beach that day. He had always called them as Firewheel, but she had referred to them as Indian Blanket upon spotting them growing wild along the side of the road. Knowing where they were going and why they were going there, she had insisted that they pull over and pick some. The blooms were about two inches in diameter, and they contained brilliant red petals with yellow rims. Arranging them in his hand, Dave bent down and placed the small bouquet respectfully on the dune amid some shoots of American beachgrass sprouting from the sand.

Nikki could see the sadness in his eyes as he stared down at the unmarked grave of the girl he had laid to rest in the sand. On their drive to Coquina Beach that day, he had told her the gruesome story after hearing a news report on Beach 104 updating the names of the people missing and presumed dead in the aftermath of the hurricane. Of those identified, only one was male—Mark Allen—with the rest being women whose names were unfamiliar to either Dave or Nikki. According to the radio report, the authorities believed that they all had perished in the hurricane, most likely swept out to sea in the storm surge. Gazing down at the sand, Dave wondered which one of those names lay buried at his feet alongside the Wreck of the *Laura Barnes*.

"It's not right," he said somberly. "She deserved a proper burial in a cemetery."

"But this is a cemetery," Nikki said to comfort him, "or, at least, a burial ground—and a legitimate one at that." Slipping her hand around his arm, she moved closer to his side. "This is the Graveyard of the Atlantic, and she is resting in hallowed ground. She is also not alone or forgotten because we know where she is, even if we don't know who she is ... and we're here to pay our respects." They both looked down at the flowers lying on the sand as Nikki continued, "Like the Lost Colony, her true fate will always remain a mystery to the outside world, which puts her in good historical company. Besides, no one would ever believe us if we tried to explain what actually happened. It's better for everyone involved if they think she was lost in the hurricane."

He knew she was right, even if he found the whole thing disturbing. Lifting his eyes, he glanced across the highway at the Bodie Island Lighthouse hovering just above the tops of the pines. It had been his sympathetic witness on that dreadful night when he had buried the girl, and it remained his silent sentry, vigilantly protecting that stretch of coastline, acting as a guide to the living and a testament to the lost. Turning his head, he looked upon the other bright beacon in his life, and he felt the soothing comfort of her eyes smiling back at him, helping to dispel the pain and remorse he felt over the fate of the poor girl in the sand. Overcome by the beauty of Nikki's face, he could not help but gaze longingly at her soft yet firm features, wondering how he deserved such a prize.

The way he looked at her made Nikki blush, tinting her face with a pink glow that blended with the redness of her injured cheekbone. Nervously breaking eye contact with him, she likewise looked across the highway at the lighthouse, becoming slightly melancholy the longer she stared at it. Dave spoke to her consolingly, almost as if he could read her mind. "You know," he said. "He wasn't really Mark—not your Mark—just a cheap imitation of the man you once knew, no more than an obscene reflection."

She glanced back at him, her eyes watering slightly. "But what happened to the real Mark?" she asked, her voice trembling slightly as she made the sobbing plea.

Dave did not respond immediately but stared quietly at her instead, allowing his silence to convey the answer, something he reinforced with a downward cast of his eyes toward the unmarked grave in the sand. Wishing to avoid acknowledging what she already knew to be true, Nikki distracted herself by reaching down and stroking the tops of the sea oats, picking one of the sprigs and kneading it between her fingers. Allowing the scientist in her to take over, she said in an attempt to change the subject, "Lots of invasive species moving into the Outer Banks. It's no longer just our native sea oats, cordgrass, and such." She then glanced across the highway and nodded in its direction. "Over there near the lighthouse, as well throughout the entire sound area, there's such an invasion of *Phragmites australis* that it—" Stopping abruptly, she threw the sprig to the ground in frustration and turned toward Dave. "What was he ... really?" she asked in an angry tone.

Dave thought for a moment and responded with a tortured smile, "You just said it yourself. He was an invasive species, one we managed to eradicate."

"Did we really?"

Pausing a moment, he remembered what Mark had said about the many opportunities for passing between worlds. Unfortunately, the marauding invader had not elaborated on how often those opportunities arose. Brigadoon materialized once every one hundred years, but Mark had given no indication how often he and others like him could make the leap into our world. He had revealed only that it had been occurring for centuries.

"I don't know," Dave said in response to her question. "I think so, at least for a while." He again paused to gauge her reaction and then continued, "He may have looked like Mark, but we both know he wasn't Mark. One thing we do know for sure is that he embodied evil, and evil will always be with us, as I'm sure your priest friend would say if he were here. Our only recourse in dealing with evil is to stand our ground and hopefully defeat it now and then."

Nikki cocked her head, eyeing him with a quirky smile because she found it odd and somewhat refreshing to hear him speak in moral and spiritual terms. Just then, a robin landed on the sand near them, and its appearance surprised Dave because it seemed so out of place. Nikki noticed his reaction and answered before he could ask the question. "Yes, we do have robins here," she said. "They're more common on the mainland and near the sound. It's unusual to have one come over to the beach."

He smiled as he watched the bird stand tall and alert on the sand, seeming to ponder the immensity of the ocean stretching out before it. "Stupid robin," he said. "Up north, they're a big deal, at least toward the end of winter. During the cold months, people watch for them, seeing them as a sign of the coming spring. When you spot one, there's this feeling of renewed hope; however, at the end of summer, no one pays them any attention. You just wake up one morning and realize that they're gone. You have no idea when they left; you just know that they're not around anymore."

"Are we still talking about robins here?" she asked quietly, wondering if he heard or understood her insinuation.

When I was a kid," he continued, "I'd record the date of my first robin sighting each year. I'd write it on a calendar that my dad kept on his desk. Whenever he'd get a new calendar, I'd immediately transfer the dates from the prior years to compare with the new sighting that spring. A few times, the dates were identical, making me wonder if I was seeing the same robin year after year."

"That's a possibility. They can live up to fourteen years, although most only survive about two."

"You know," he said, "I once spotted a robin on New Year's Day, and I immediately diagnosed it as an insane robin because it had forgotten to leave at the end of summer."

"Maybe it found something—or someone—to make it stay."

"Not much to eat in the snows of Michigan in the month of January."

"It could have found a job, earned some money, made enough to buy its own food. There are worse things in life than that, you know."

He glanced away without commenting, attempting to hide his awareness of the point she was trying to make. When he looked back and saw the playful twinkle in her eyes, he grinned and said, "Yeah, I know."

After a few moments of awkward silence, Nikki asked, "So, do I have to go home and write on my calendar the day I first spotted you at Mulligan's?"

He did not answer but remained quiet for a few seconds while watching the robin fly over to another dune. Taking Nikki's hand, he turned and led her toward the water where the surf was advancing in short, evenly spaced rollers. With a shrill whistle, he called back to Grave who came stampeding across the beach, his short, stumpy legs struggling in the soft sand until he reached the shoreline where he charged after some sandpipers scurrying before the waves.

There were just a few families on the beach that day enjoying the gorgeous post-hurricane weather, so Dave allowed Grave to run without a leash, hoping that no one would object to his being unrestrained. Generally, that stretch of shoreline did not attract many beachgoers due to its remote location along the national seashore; however, it was a favorite spot for those staying at a nearby campground. As Dave and Nikki walked through the sand, they approached an oversized lifeguard chair on which sat a young blonde girl in a red two-piece bathing suit. A male lifeguard, also wearing a red bathing suit, stood beside the chair talking to her. Dave remembered meeting both of them in the bar at Tortuga's Lie, although he could not recall their names, so he acknowledged them with just a nod of his head as he strolled past the chair with Nikki by his side.

When they were away from everyone, Nikki said slyly, "I have something for you."

"Sorry ... what?" Dave had been watching the gulls circling overhead and had not been paying attention.

"I said, 'I have a present for you,'" she answered with a grin.

They both stopped walking and turned toward each other. "Okay," he said. "I'll bite."

"Actually, I have two things," she said excitedly while reaching into her pocket to pull out a small rectangular box that she handed to him. "Here's the first one."

He took the box into his hand while eyeing her suspiciously, wincing slightly as he peeked playfully under the lid, acting as if he expected something to jump out of it; however, his expression softened the moment he saw its contents. He then raised his head to gaze at Nikki, communicating his genuine, heartfelt appreciation by the look in his eyes.

"It's to replace the one you lost because of me," she said in a soft, loving tone.

Reaching into the box with his fingers, he lifted out an expensive scrimshaw knife, one slightly larger than his old Cub Scout knife. He then examined it in the palm of his hand, instantly recognizing the familiar carvings on the bone handle, images that included a lighthouse, compass rose, whale flukes, and a sailor wearing a vintage Sou'wester fisherman's hat. Unfolding the high-grade stainless steel blade, he admired it for its fine edge honed to the sharpness of a razor and its highly polished surface adorned with ornamental engravings. With a bemused look on his face, he seemed lost for words.

Nikki smiled and said, "I saw you looking at it the night we went to the Port O' Call for dinner."

He opened his mouth to express his gratitude, but she cut him off by exclaiming, "Wait, there's something else!" Reaching a second time into her shorts while Dave cautiously folded the blade into the handle of the knife, she said craftily with a sly glance in his direction, "This is an early birthday present ... in case you leave before next month."

Pretending to have missed the implied meaning of her words, he stood quietly on the sand while she pulled from her pocket a second box, smaller and squarer than the first one, which she held in the palm of her hand before revealing its contents. He then patiently waited while she reached into the box and withdrew a stainless steel chain on which hung a sterling silver medallion emblazoned with the image of a warrior angel plunging a sword into the body of a serpent. Leaning slightly forward, he allowed her to slip it over his head where it hung loosely from his neck on the outside of his shirt. Taking the religious medal into his hand, he stared at the familiar image for a few seconds before closing his fingers around it and raising his eyes to meet hers.

"It's St. Michael the Archangel," she said, "the great protector who drove Satan and his followers from heaven."

He grinned slightly and said, "Yeah, I was recently reminded of the story." His voice then became quiet and sorrowful. "But I don't have anything for you."

With the fingers of her right hand, she lightly caressed the bruises on his neck. "You've already given me enough."

Just then, they heard the garbled barking of Grave a short distance away, and they turned to see him chasing crabs into the receding surf. With his ears floating on the surface of the sea, he kept plunging his head into the ocean, frantically trying to catch the fleeing crabs, baying at them in frustration without bothering to lift his head from the water. Focused entirely on his pursuit of the crustaceans, he failed to notice a jogger running past him along the shoreline, a black man of medium build with beads of sweat dotting the top of his shiny bald head. Nikki cried out joyfully when she spotted him, "Father Andal!"

The priest, totally lost in meditation, had not noticed the couple standing nearby until he heard the sound of his name. Breathing rapidly but not totally winded, he stopped directly in front of them and smiled joyfully. "My dear, Nikita, it is so *good* to see you," he said warmly with a broad grin while sliding his eyes in the direction of Dave.

"Oh," Nikki said as if she had forgotten something, "let me introduce you to my friend. This is Dave."

Father Andal extended his hand toward Dave as if meeting him for the first time, and they both shook hands with neither one betraying their shared secret. Returning his attention to Nikki, the priest noticed the discoloration around her eye. "My dear, you are hurt," he said with a wrinkling of his brow while he reached up and lightly touching her cheek. Glancing further down her body, he noticed the rope burns on her wrists and a nasty bruise on her thigh.

"Yes," she said a little hesitantly. "I got myself into some trouble but—" She directed her gaze in Dave's direction. "Fortunately, there was someone there to help me."

The priest followed her eyes and noticed for the first time the bruising around Dave's neck. The sight of it triggered an epiphany of awareness that resulted in an enormous grin spreading across his face, one that indicated his satisfaction at having solved a perplexing riddle. Dave saw the glimmer of understanding in the priest's eyes and concluded that there would be no need for further explanations. It was then that Father Andal spotted the religious medal hanging from Dave's neck. "Ah, Saint Michael casting out the Devil," he said as took the image of the archangel into his hand, allowing it to rest lightly on the underside of his fingers.

Dave looked down at the priest's hand supporting the medal and said, "Yeah, Nikki just gave it to me."

"Is that right?" Andal said with a grin as he glanced back at Nikki. "A protector for the protector. Have you had it blessed?"

"No, I haven't had a chance yet. I just bought it."

"Well then, let me do it right now."

Father Andal closed his eyes and softly spoke some prayer, the words of which Dave could not clearly discern due to the clamor of the gulls crying overhead. Then, while still holding the medal in his left hand, the priest used his other hand to trace a cross over the top of it, after which he let it dangle on its chain while pressing it firmly against Dave's heart. As he did so, he stared deeply into his young friend's eyes, conveying an unspoken message of understanding laced with gratitude.

Turning to Nikki, Father Andal then offered a bit of explanation of why he was on Coquina Beach. "I like to jog here because it is quiet and isolated, and because there are showers and changing rooms. Whenever my duties take me to Holy Trinity, our chapel at Whalebone Junction, I always drive down here to run on the beach. I know that you are a runner too, Nikita. You should join me sometime." Before she could answer, he added, "You too, David."

Nikki and Dave looked at each other and began laughing at the priest's suggestion. Nikki said to Father Andal, "I'm afraid Dave is not much of a runner—at least not until he gets a better pair of running shoes."

Based on their reaction, the priest sensed a private joke between them, so he let the matter drop and did not pursue it further. "Well, then, I must continue," he said. "I will see you later, my dear—at church on Sunday." He took a step as if he were leaving, but then hesitated and turned back toward Nikki. "You should bring your friend, David, with you on Sunday. Yes?"

Instead of responding, she looked searchingly in Dave's direction.

Finding himself in an awkward position with both Father Andal and Nikki staring at him expectantly, Dave answered rather uncomfortably, "I work on Sundays."

"Ah," said the priest with an enormous grin as he pointed toward Nikki. "Perhaps on Saturday night then. Yes? That would be good, would it not?" He laughed cheerfully and began running again, repeating one more time over his shoulder, "Yes, that would be *good.*"

Dave and Nikki stood quietly on the sand while watching the receding figure of the happy priest bounce joyfully down the beach. After a few seconds, they heard singing in the distance and realized that it was coming from him. Slipping the knife into his pocket while taking Nikki by the hand, Dave led her across the beach in the direction of the parking lot. This time, however, it was not necessary for him to whistle for Grave because the dog noticed the couple moving away from the water and came barreling up from behind, charging off toward the dunes once he got out in front of them.

As they crossed the palisade dune near where the hearse was parked, Dave glanced over at several exposed planks marking the resting place of the shipwrecked *Laura Barnes*, and he made a silent pledge to the buried girl that he would return to visit her again. Nikki saw him looking in that direction, so she squeezed his hand reassuringly and pulled him over the dune, stepping lightly around some scattered debris while tugging him down the sand path toward the parking lot. They then approached the hearse from the passenger's side where Dave opened the door for Grave to jump in and then held it open for Nikki, affectionately touching her shoulder as she slipped by him and climbed onto the seat. In response to his light touch, she glanced up and waited for him to say something, but he remained mute and merely smiled at her while closing the door.

Walking around the back of the hearse, he stopped briefly to observe the Bodie Island Lighthouse rising majestically on the other side of the highway. He admired it for its constancy and endurance, seeing it as a newfound symbol of hope for his newfound life. Although not conscious of every change occurring within him, he sensed a dramatic unburdening of his soul, the loss of a debilitating emotion that had haunted him throughout his life, something he knew only as an internal darkness—a specter—from which he had continually run, moving from town to town without reason or purpose other than wishing to avoid facing his past. The urge to run, however, now seemed to have vanished, as had the internal fear and darkness, swept away by a revealing, redemptive light, a dazzling brilliance heralding his renewed confidence in himself as well as his desire to participate in the lives of others. He now found himself drawn toward the light, to the radiance of something new, something worth pursuing, worth treasuring—worth loving—something for which he had been searching all his life.

Buoyed by his renewed love of life and a rising optimism that soared like a bird on the wing, he recalled the robin in the sand, the one whose migratory nature Nikki had likened to his own unfettered lifestyle, and he wondered if it might be an omen of other changes to come. Looking around but unable to find the elusive bird, he lightheartedly concluded that it must have departed for Florida, slipping out of town before some alluring female robin asked it to stay. Amused by that thought, he continued walking around to the driver's side of the hearse where he came to an abrupt stop the moment his eyes locked onto an object protruding from the frame of the door. No more than six feet away, it displayed an altered reality that he found both shocking and challenging, a disturbing vision that caused his jaw to clench and his spine to stiffen as his expression changed from joyful amusement to one of curious bewilderment. Standing by the side of the vehicle, he then peered somberly and intently into the side mirror of the hearse, feeling a slight twinge of anxiety while struggling intellectually to grasp the incongruity of the image he saw staring back at him.

Acknowledgments

Almost any creative endeavor requires the input of many different people, those who contribute consciously or unconsciously to the overall process. The writing of a novel is no different in that respect. Although the author spends a majority of his time in isolation, quietly hammering out characters on a keyboard, the final product is a compilation of information gleaned from multiple sources and numerous people, all interpreted and packaged by the author himself as a product of his creative imagination. The key to the process, however, lies in the external influences and contributions of those who, by simply living out their lives, generate a vast reservoir of inspiration and ideas without which the author would have at his disposal only the limited musings of his own mind.

In that vein, I would like to thank everyone who aided, inspired, and informed me as I set about the task of researching, planning, and writing this novel. There are, however, a few who deserve special thanks, those who contributed something unique or exceptional to the creative process be it nothing more than an intriguing idea, a comical line, or an inspiring glance.

First and foremost, I would like to thank Sister Patricia Maria, my earliest and most trusted literary critic, someone who encouraged my writing despite the fact that I never paid attention in her English class. I would also like to thank my friend Brian for his meteorological advice as well as Steve and "911 Dave" for sharing with me their hurricane survival methods. Jan's fashion sense proved invaluable, as did the ecological information provided by Kate at The Nature Conservancy along with the national park rangers and employees of the Bodie Island Lighthouse. Both Lynn and Phil deserve a special "thank you" for their early proofreading and editorial advice in addition to their offers of encouragement when it was needed the most. Michelle, Richard, and Dave were very helpful in providing Indian Motorcycle information as was Larry for his investment counseling, Tim for his marketing strategies, and Lori for her colorful metaphors. I would also like to thank Wink for allowing me access to his hearse, and Sam, Moira, Sydney, and David for providing the final proofreading and copyediting services. Additionally, I would be remiss if I did not acknowledge Francisco and Eugene for their "contributions" to the creative process by their constant interruptions of my writing schedule.

I especially wish to express my gratitude to the residents and business owners of the Outer Banks, a charming and delightful group of people who enabled my research by patiently answering all my questions and enthusiastically offering a bounty of information about their lifestyle and culture. Additionally, to the many people who have touched my life, especially the ones who inspired the characters in this book through their words, phrases, gestures, and actions; I offer a heartfelt thank you. Lastly, I would like to express my appreciation to Dave (also known as "Buddy"), the consummate windsurfing enthusiast who was last seen one warm summer day in Somers Point, New Jersey, sailing on a broad reach toward the horizon.

Made in the USA
Middletown, DE
16 May 2016